HELLSING 10

ヘルシング

平野耕太
KOHTA HIRANO

translation
DUANE JOHNSON

lettering
WILBERT LACUNA

DARK
HORSE
MANGA

DMP
Digital Manga
Publishing

publishers
MIKE RICHARDSON and HIKARU SASAHARA

editors
TIM ERVIN and FRED LUI

collection designer
DAVID NESTELLE

English-language version produced by
DARK HORSE COMICS and DIGITAL MANGA PUBLISHING.

HELLSING VOLUME 10

published by
Dark Horse Manga
a division of Dark Horse Comics, Inc.
10956 SE Main Street
Milwaukie, OR 97222

DarkHorse.com

Digital Manga Publishing
1487 W. 178th St. Ste. 300
Gardena, CA 90248

DMPBooks.com

To find a comics shop in your area, call the
Comic Shop Locator Service toll-free at 1-888-266-4226

First edition: May 2010
ISBN 978-1-59582-498-1

5 7 9 10 8 6 4

Printed in the United States of America

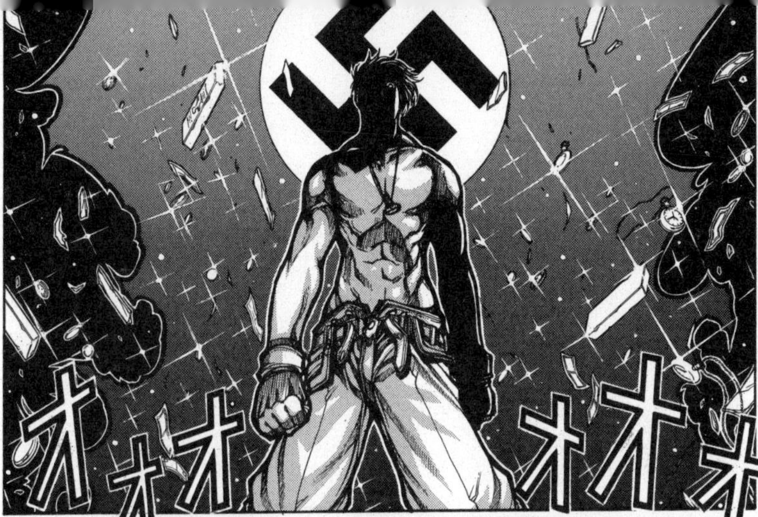
オォオ
オオオ

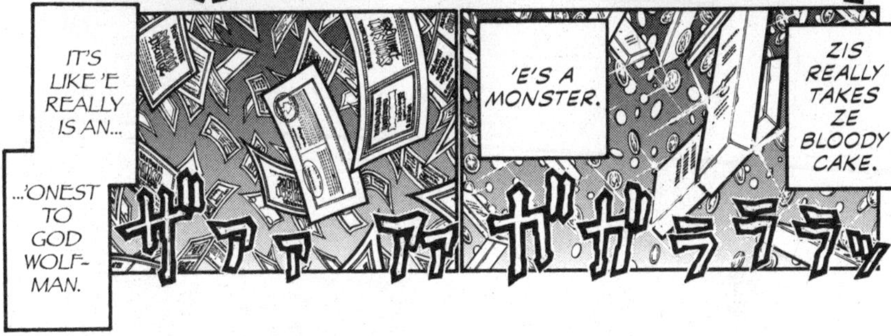
ZIS REALLY TAKES ZE BLOODY CAKE.
'E'S A MONSTER.
ガガララッ
IT'S LIKE 'E REALLY IS AN...
...'ONEST TO GOD WOLF-MAN.
ザァァアァ

⚜ ORDER 1
WOLF FANG ①

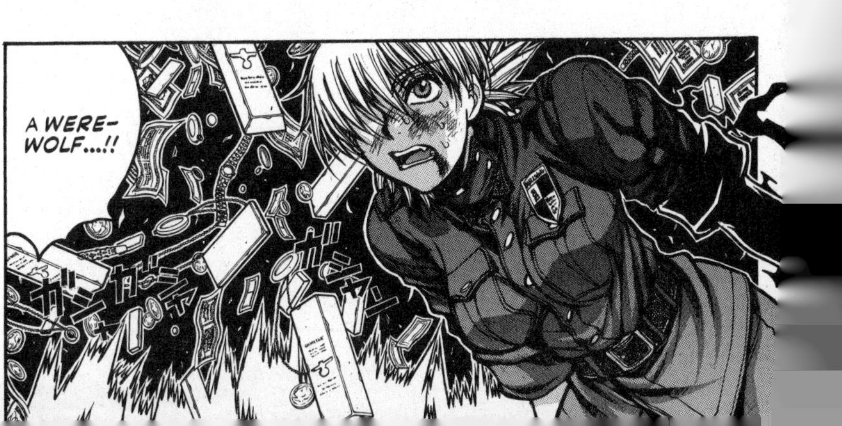
A WERE-WOLF...!!

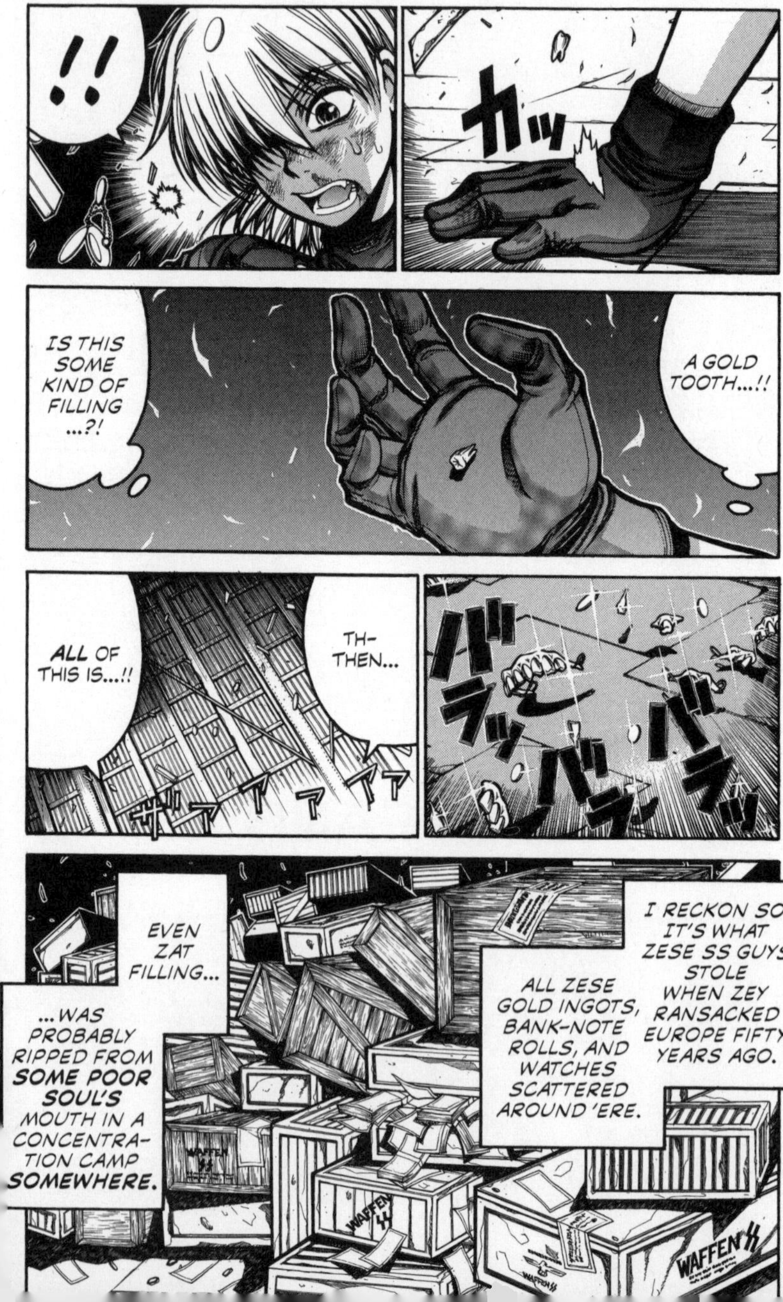

カッ
!!
A GOLD TOOTH...!!
IS THIS SOME KIND OF FILLING ...?!
バラッ
バラッ
バラッ
TH- THEN...
ALL OF THIS IS...!!
I RECKON SO. IT'S WHAT ZESE SS GUYS STOLE WHEN ZEY RANSACKED EUROPE FIFTY YEARS AGO.
ALL ZESE GOLD INGOTS, BANK-NOTE ROLLS, AND WATCHES SCATTERED AROUND 'ERE.
EVEN ZAT FILLING...
...WAS PROBABLY RIPPED FROM SOME POOR SOUL'S MOUTH IN A CONCENTRATION CAMP SOMEWHERE.
WAFFEN SS

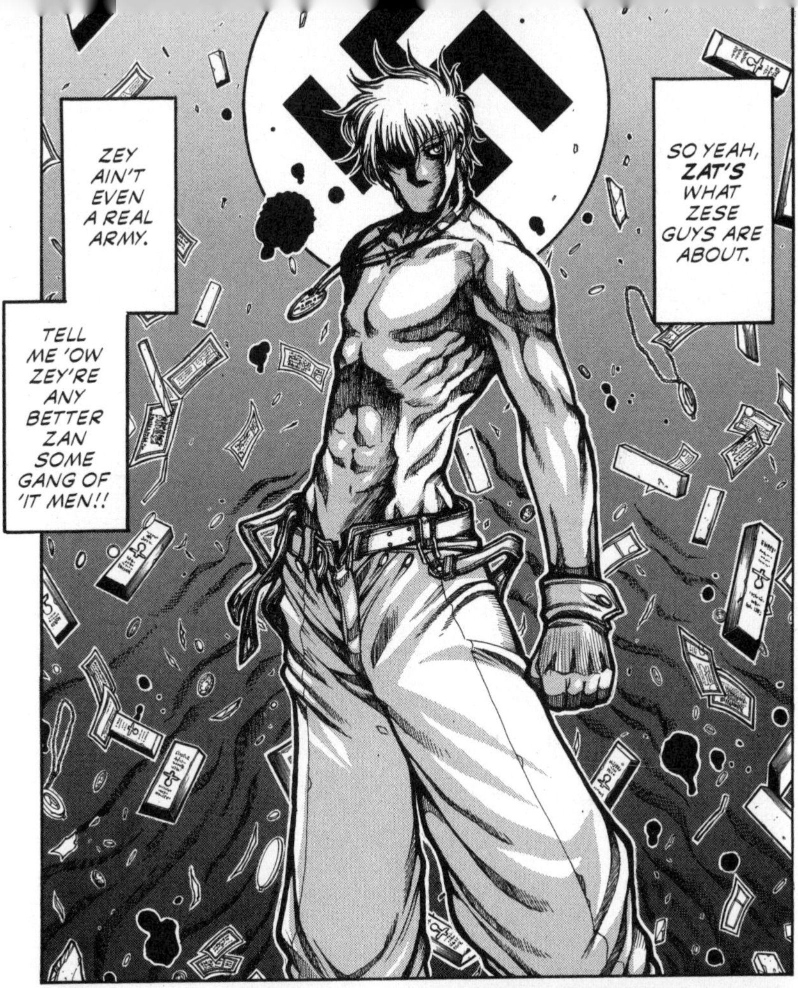
SO YEAH, **ZAT'S** WHAT ZESE GUYS ARE ABOUT.
ZEY AIN'T EVEN A REAL ARMY.
TELL ME 'OW ZEY'RE ANY BETTER ZAN SOME GANG OF 'IT MEN!!
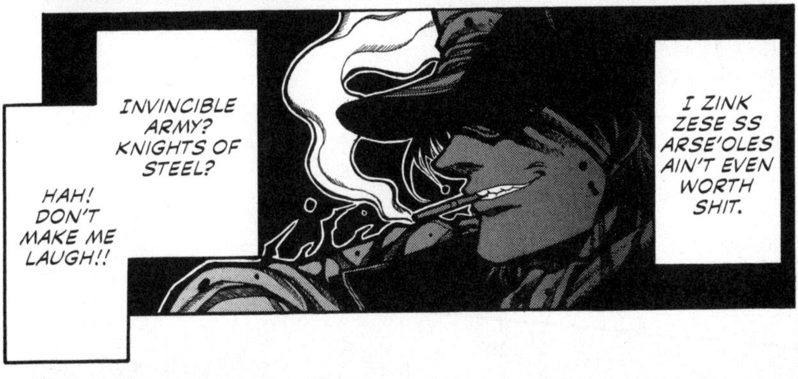
I ZINK ZESE SS ARSE'OLES AIN'T EVEN WORTH SHIT.
INVINCIBLE ARMY? KNIGHTS OF STEEL?
HAH! DON'T MAKE ME LAUGH!!

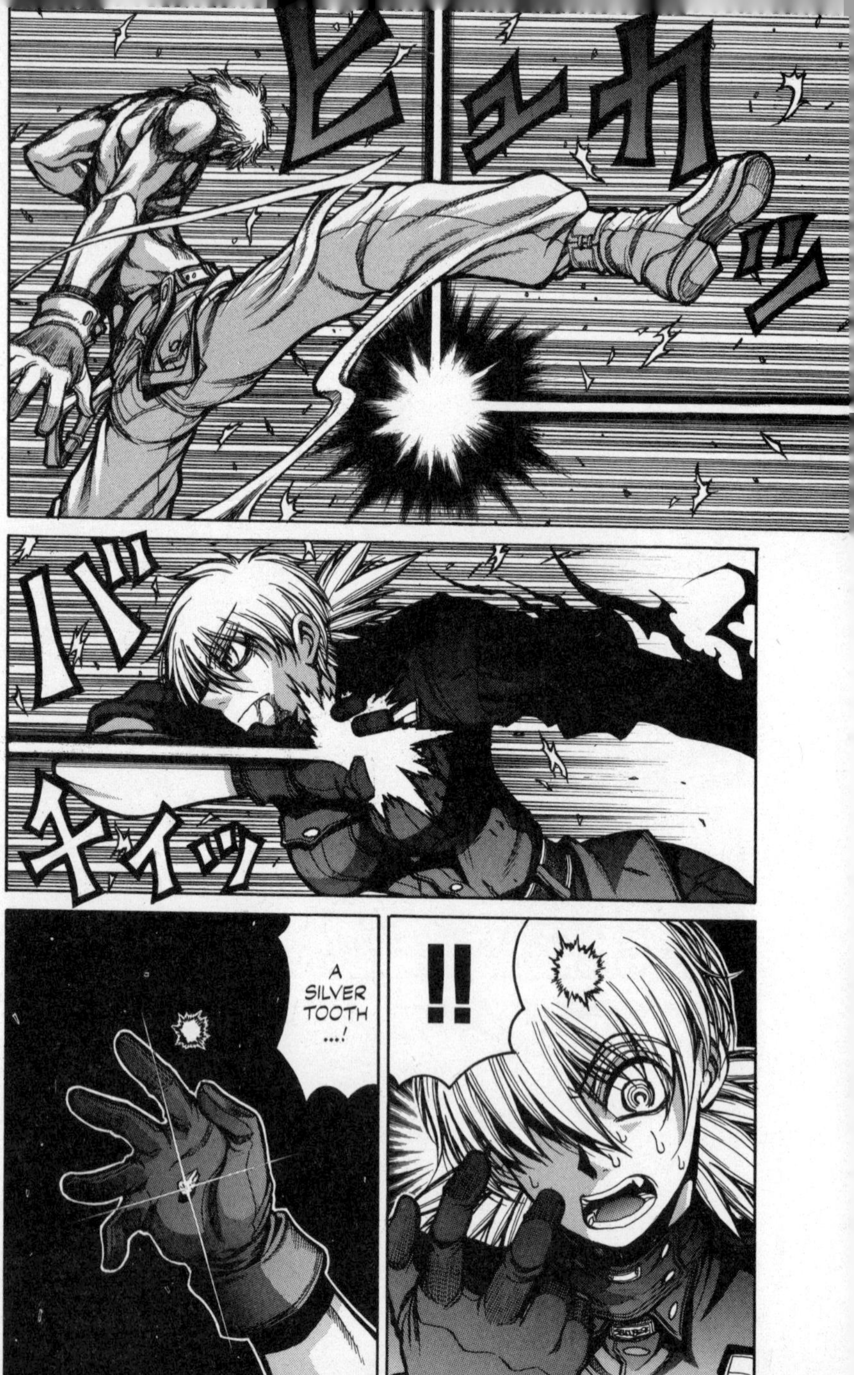
ヒュカッ
!!
A SILVER TOOTH ...!

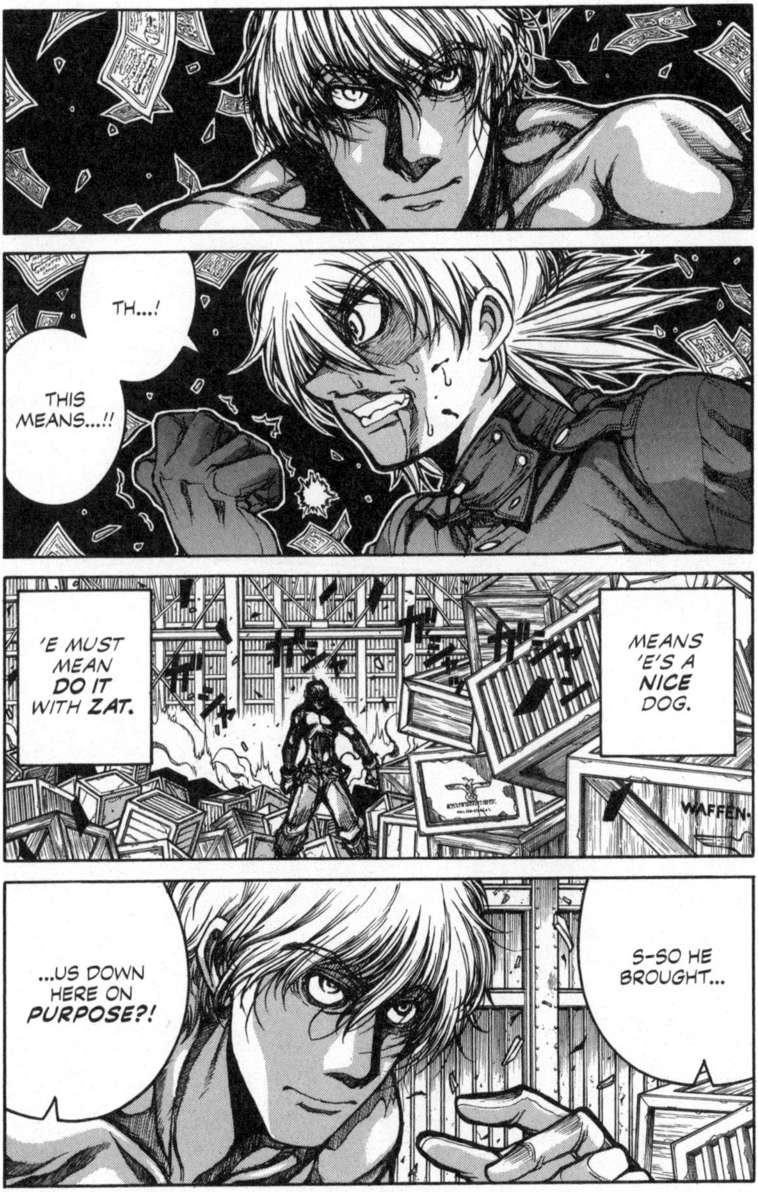
TH...!
THIS MEANS...!!
MEANS 'E'S A NICE DOG.
'E MUST MEAN DO IT WITH ZAT.
WAFFEN.
S-SO HE BROUGHT...
...US DOWN HERE ON PURPOSE?!

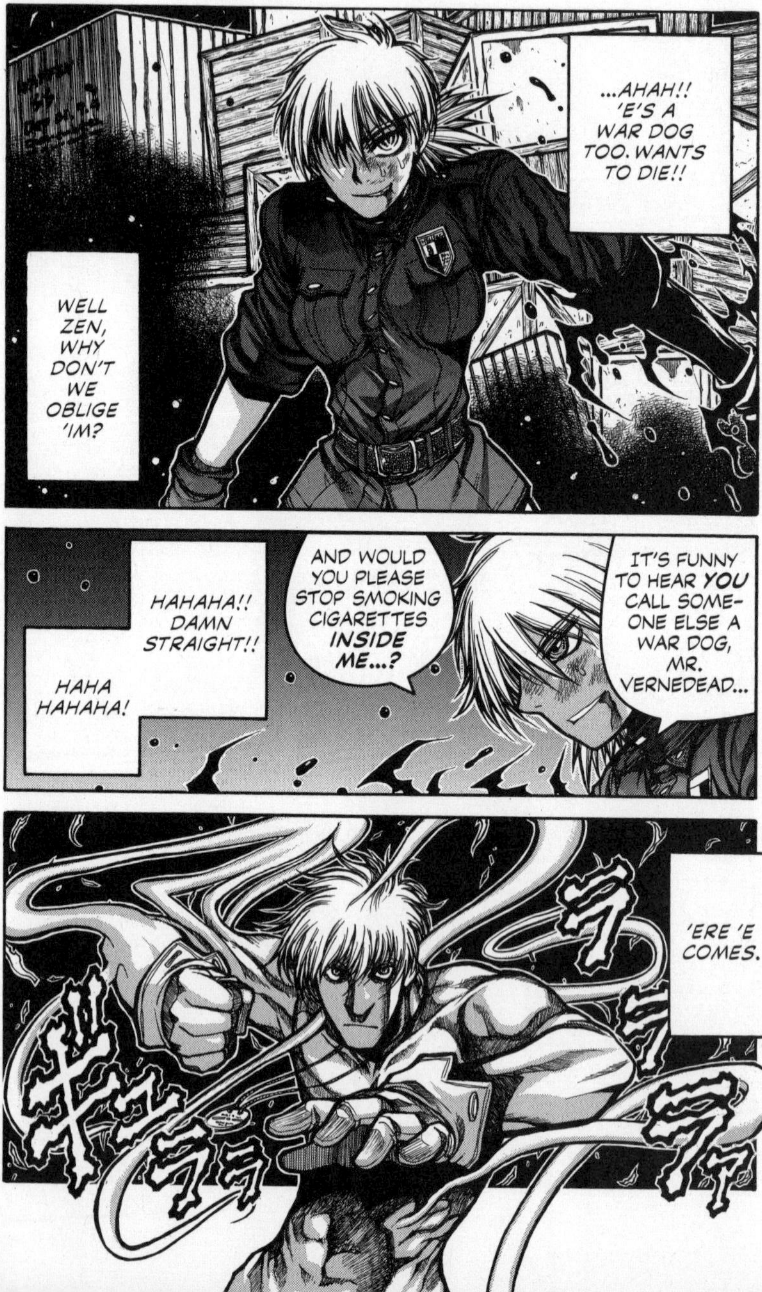
...AHAH!! 'E'S A WAR DOG TOO. WANTS TO DIE!!
WELL ZEN, WHY DON'T WE OBLIGE 'IM?
IT'S FUNNY TO HEAR **YOU** CALL SOME-ONE ELSE A WAR DOG, MR. VERNEDEAD...
AND WOULD YOU PLEASE STOP SMOKING CIGARETTES **INSIDE ME...?**
HAHAHA!! DAMN STRAIGHT!!
HAHA HAHAHA!
'ERE 'E COMES.

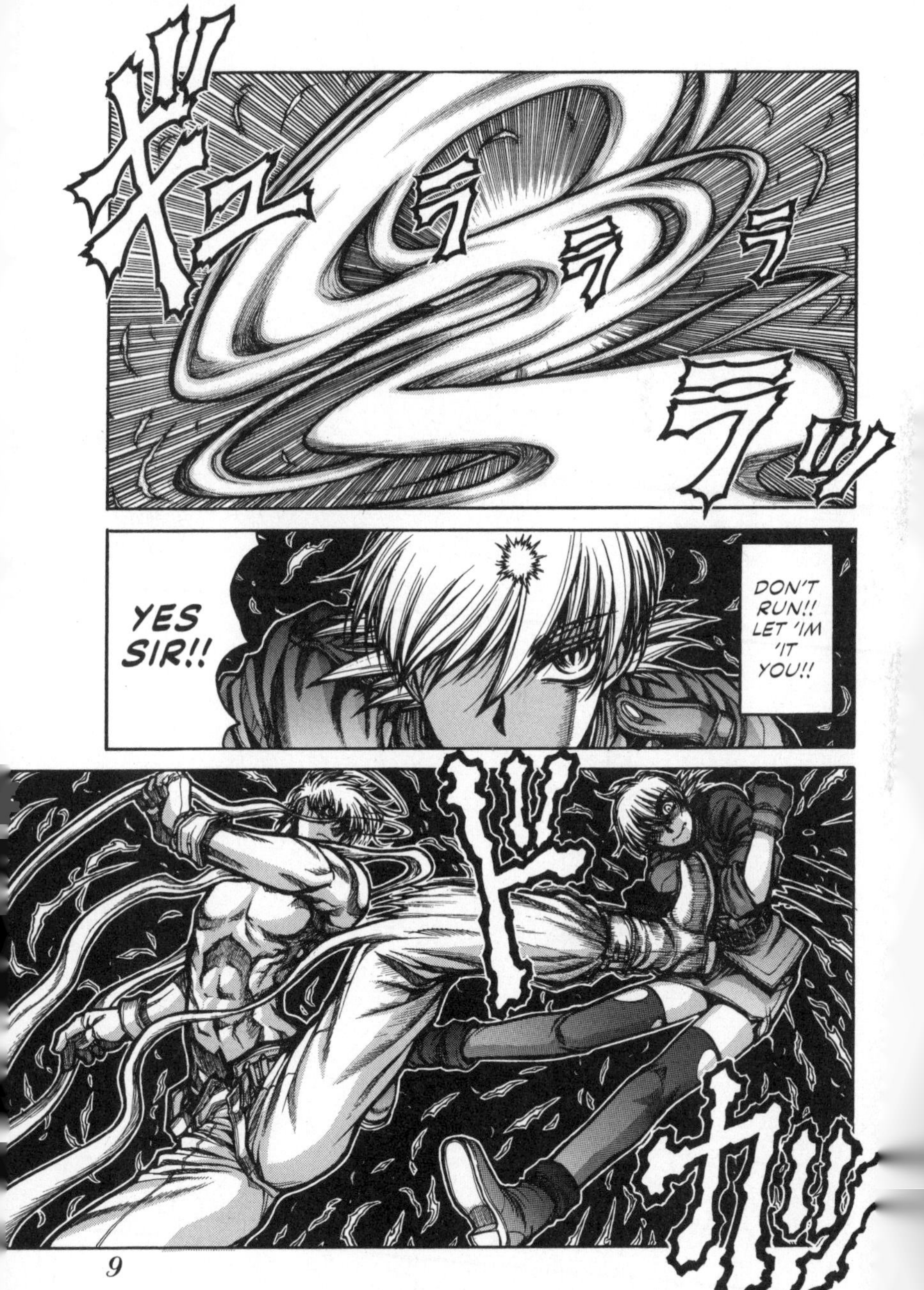
ギュララララッ
DON'T RUN!! LET 'IM 'IT YOU!!
YES SIR!!
ドカッ

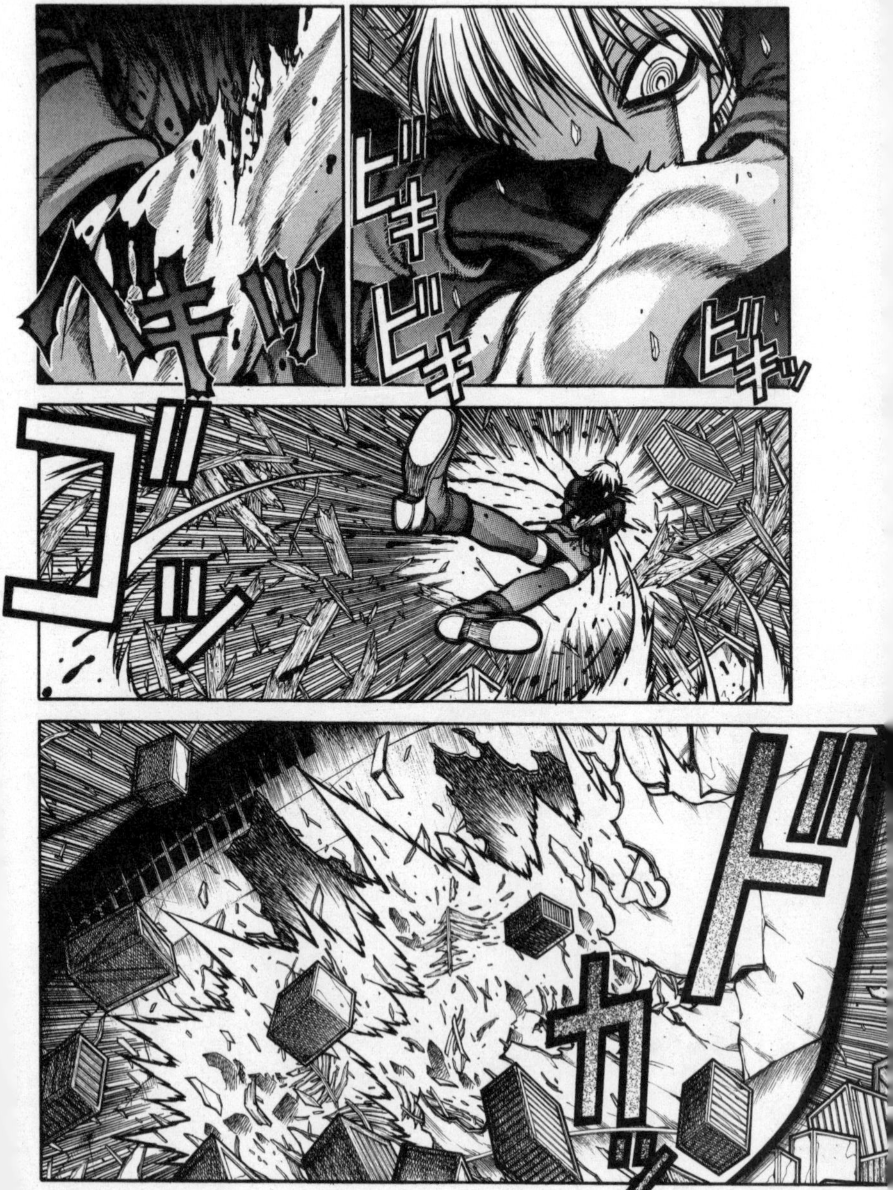
ビキビキ
ビキッ
ベキッ
ゴッ
ドカッ

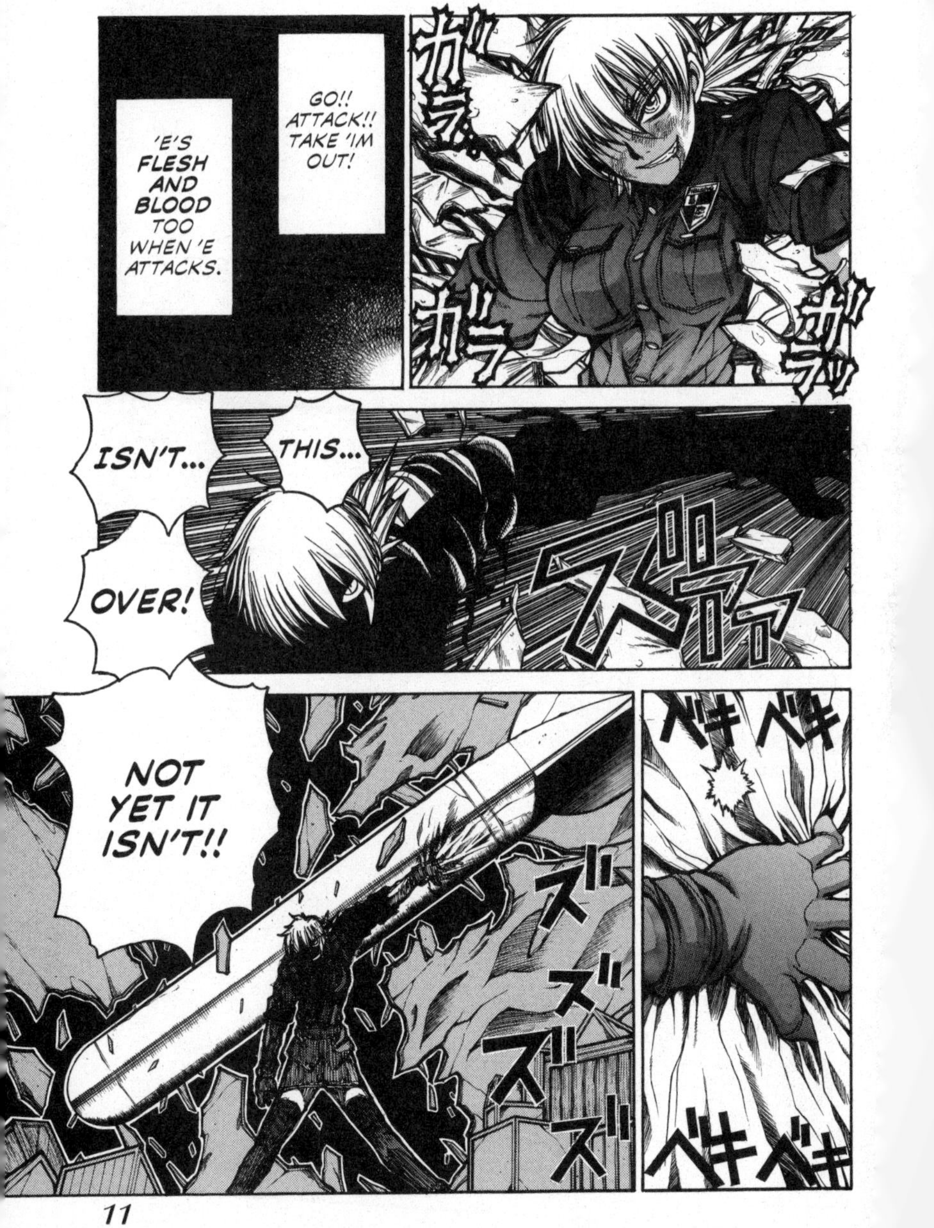
ガラッ
ガラ
ガラ
GO!! ATTACK!! TAKE 'IM OUT!
'E'S FLESH AND BLOOD TOO WHEN 'E ATTACKS.
THIS...
ISN'T...
OVER!
ベキベキ
NOT YET IT ISN'T!!
ズズズ
ベキベキ

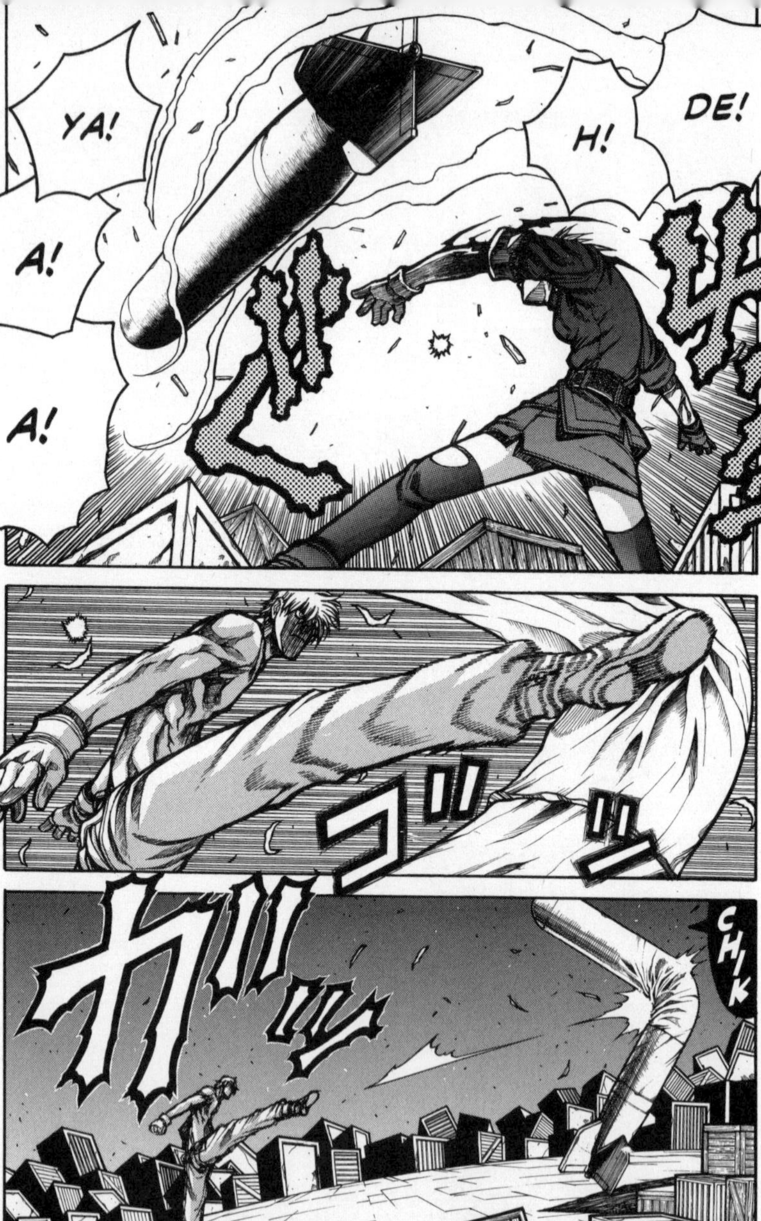
DE!
H!
YA!
A!
A!
CHIK

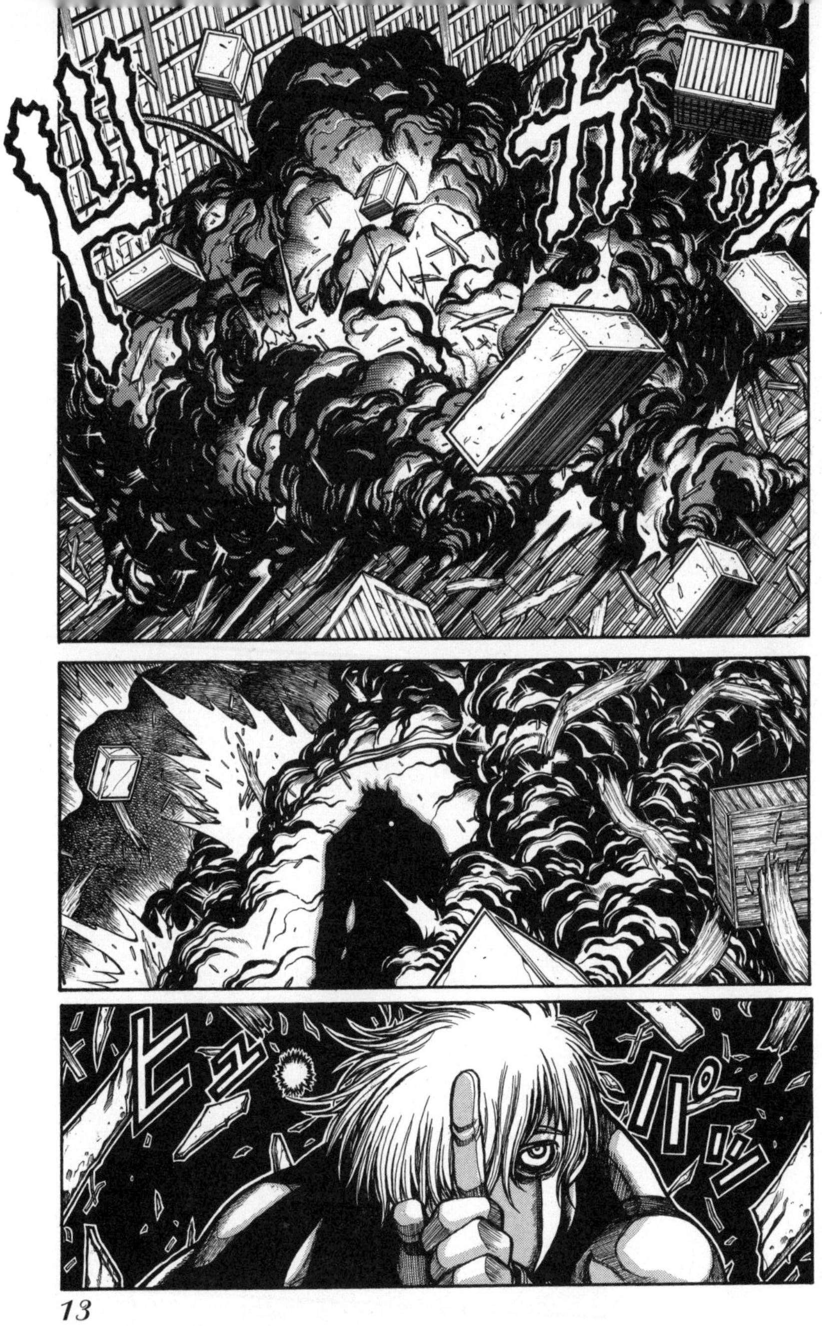
ドカッ
ヒュ
パッ

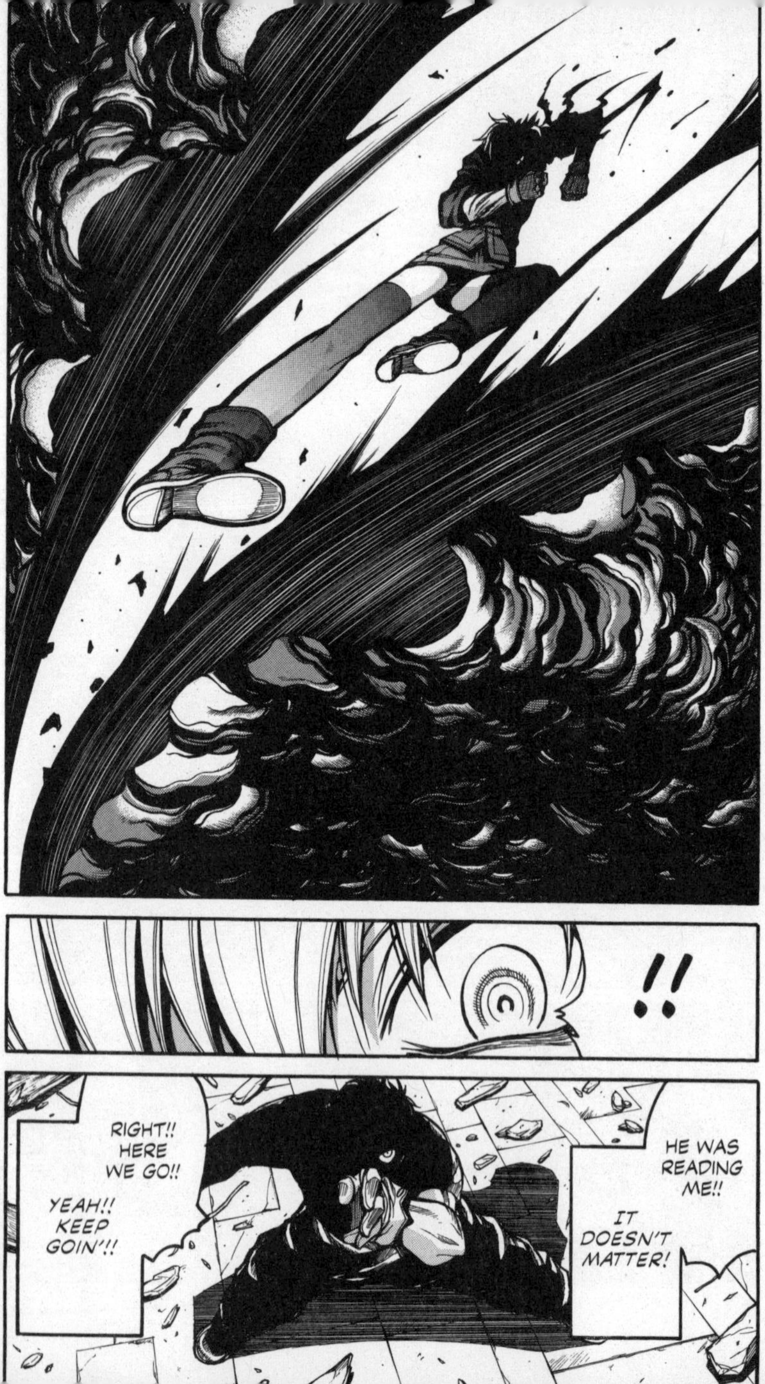
!!
HE WAS READING ME!!
IT DOESN'T MATTER!
RIGHT!! HERE WE GO!!
YEAH!! KEEP GOIN'!!

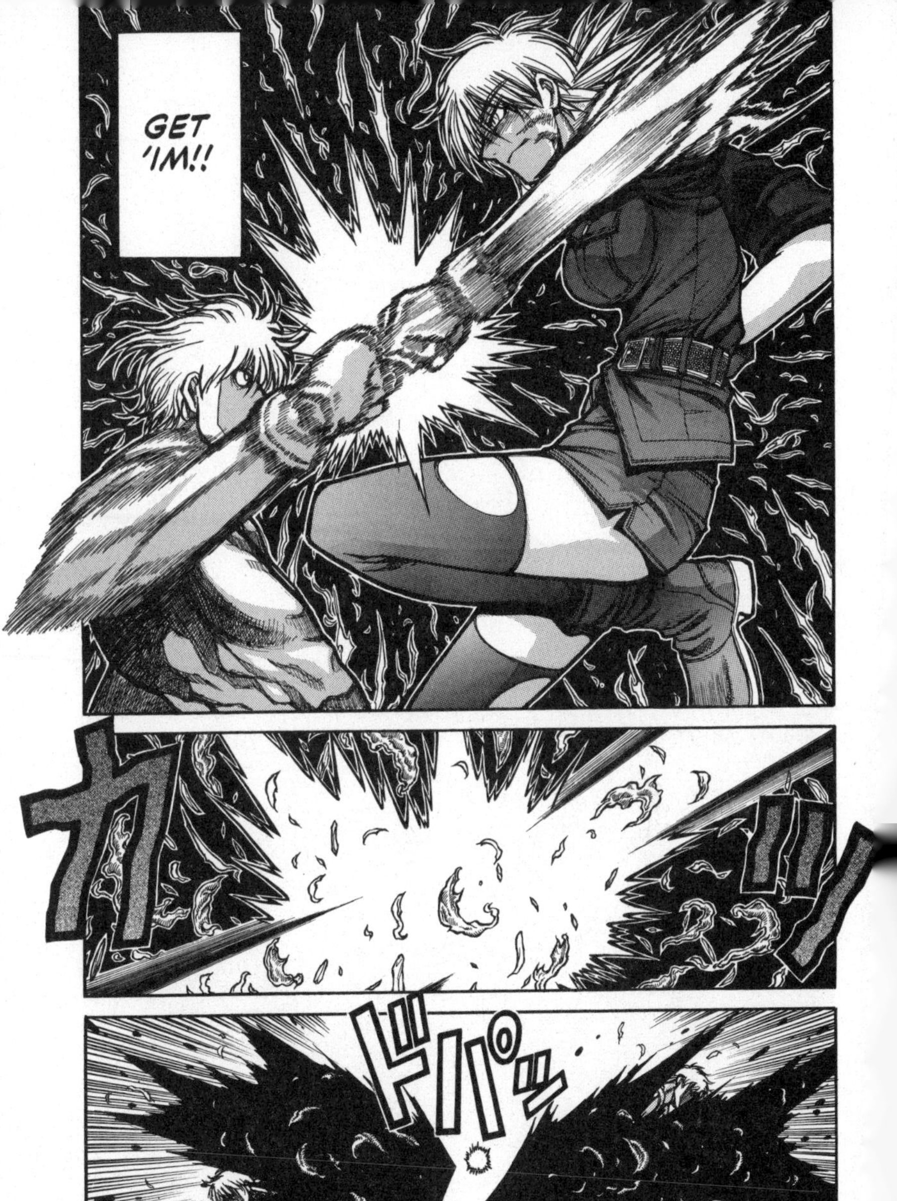
GET 'IM!!
カッ
ドパッ

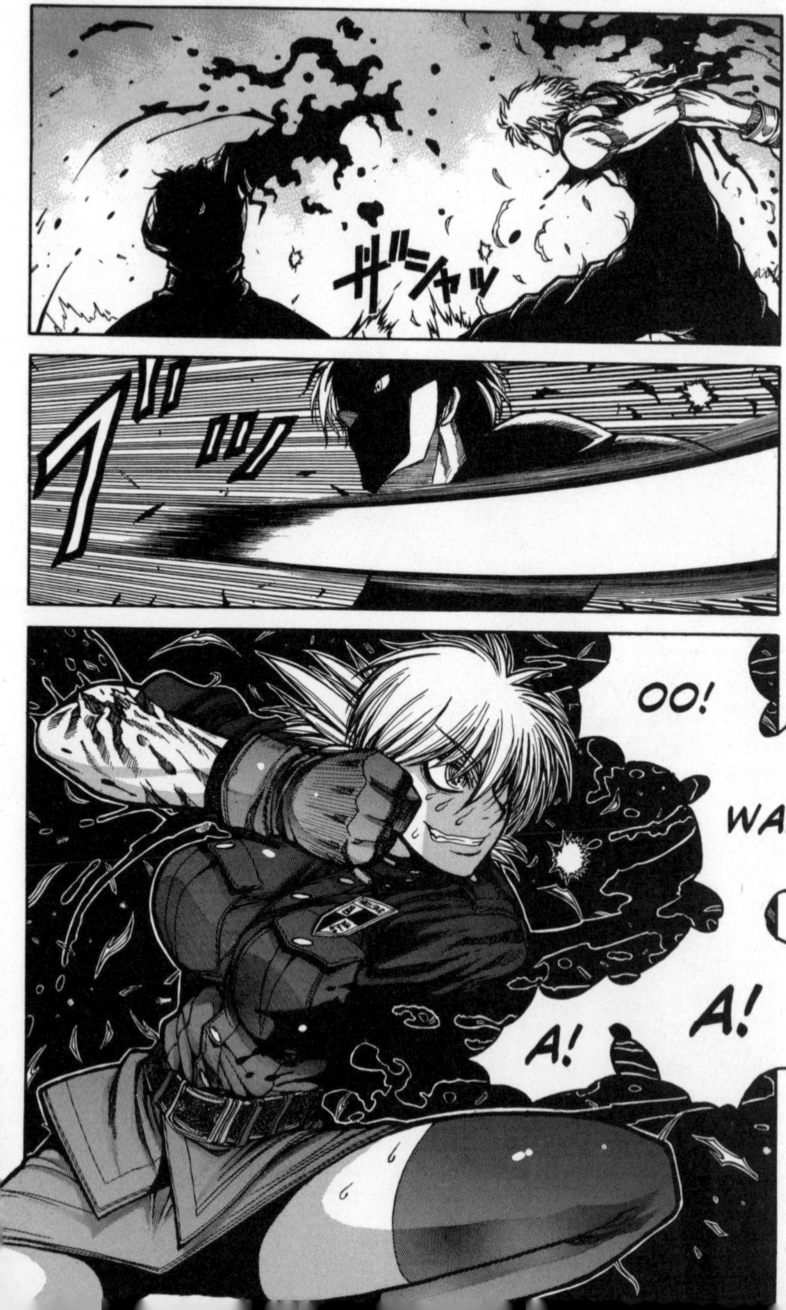
ザシャッ
OO!
WA!
A!
A!

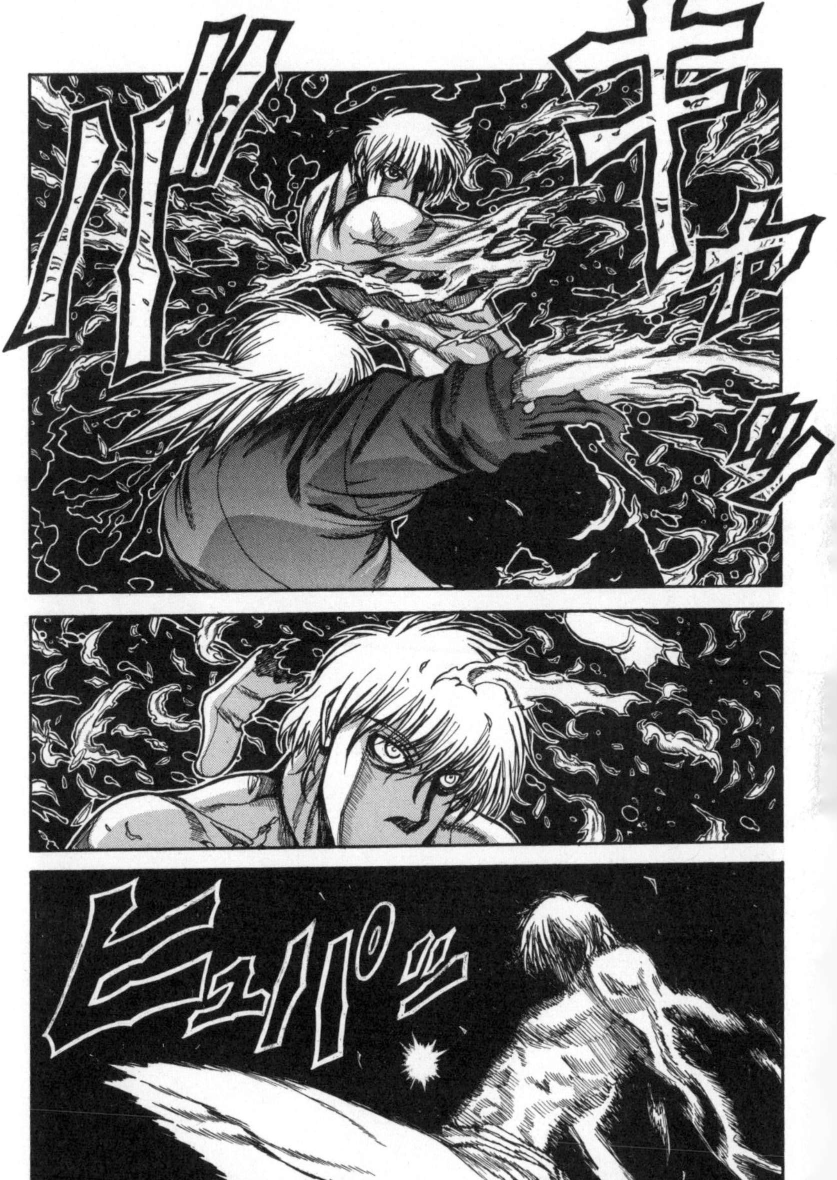
ギャッ
バリ
ヒュパッ

HIS HIME.
HI GOH YOU!!
ミチ
ミチ
ミチッ

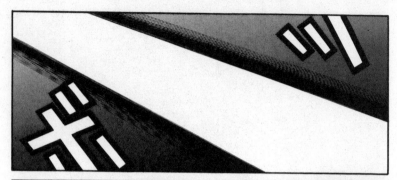

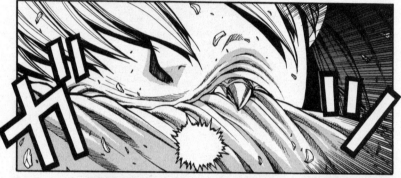

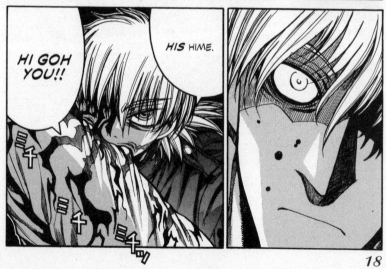

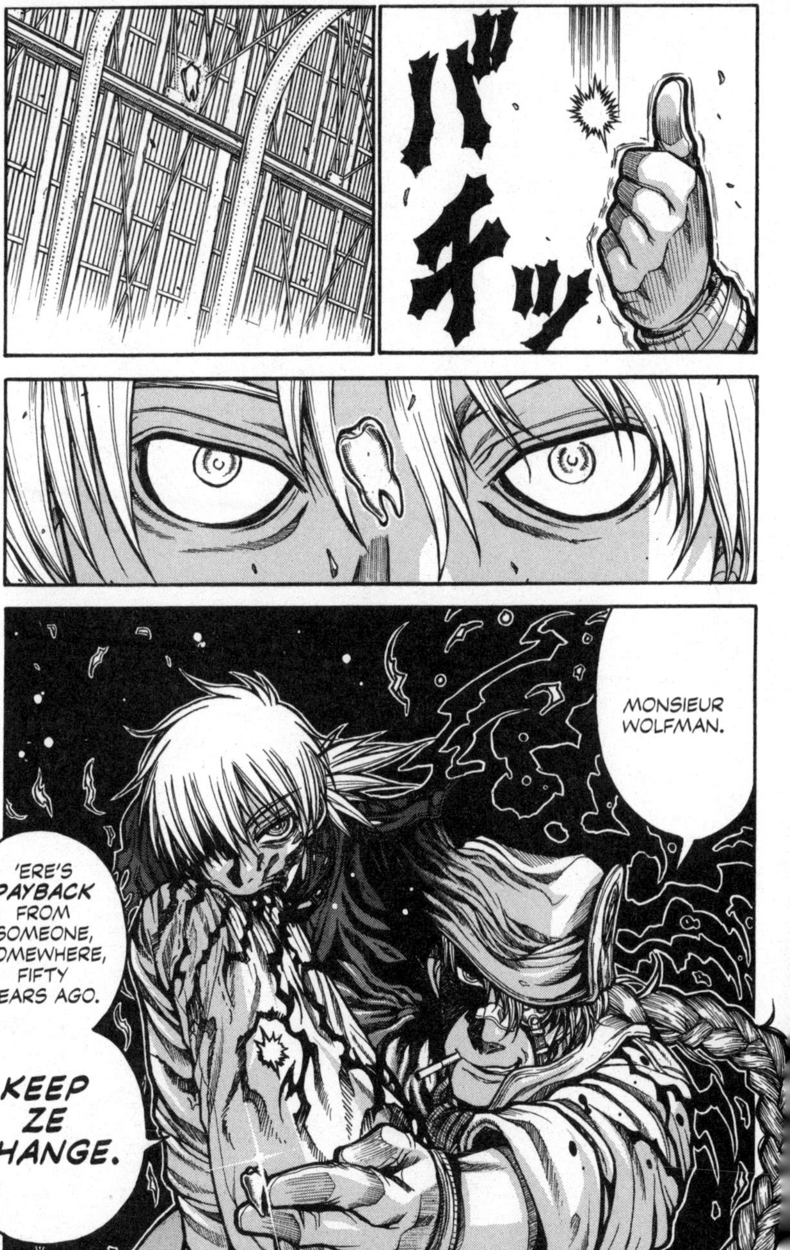

パキッ
MONSIEUR WOLFMAN.
'ERE'S **PAYBACK** FROM SOMEONE, SOMEWHERE, FIFTY YEARS AGO.
KEEP ZE CHANGE.

SNp
カッ

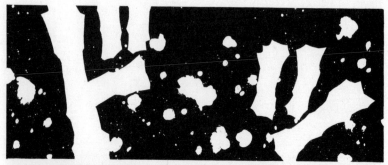

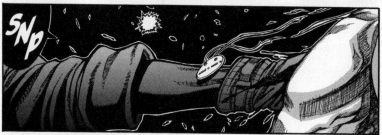

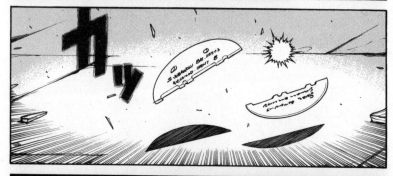

TO BE CONTINUED

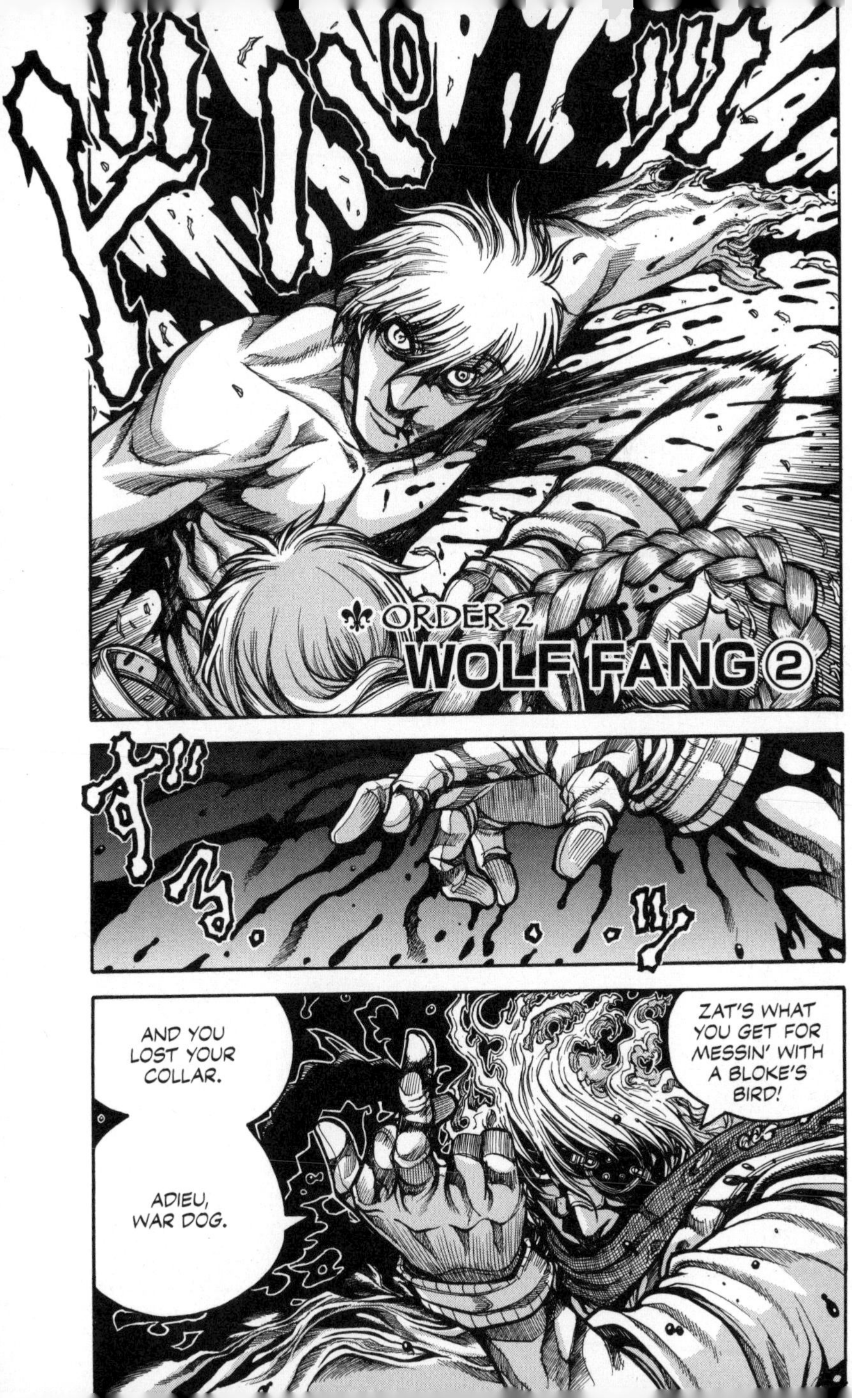
ORDER 2
WOLF FANG ②
ZAT'S WHAT YOU GET FOR MESSIN' WITH A BLOKE'S BIRD!
AND YOU LOST YOUR COLLAR.
ADIEU, WAR DOG.

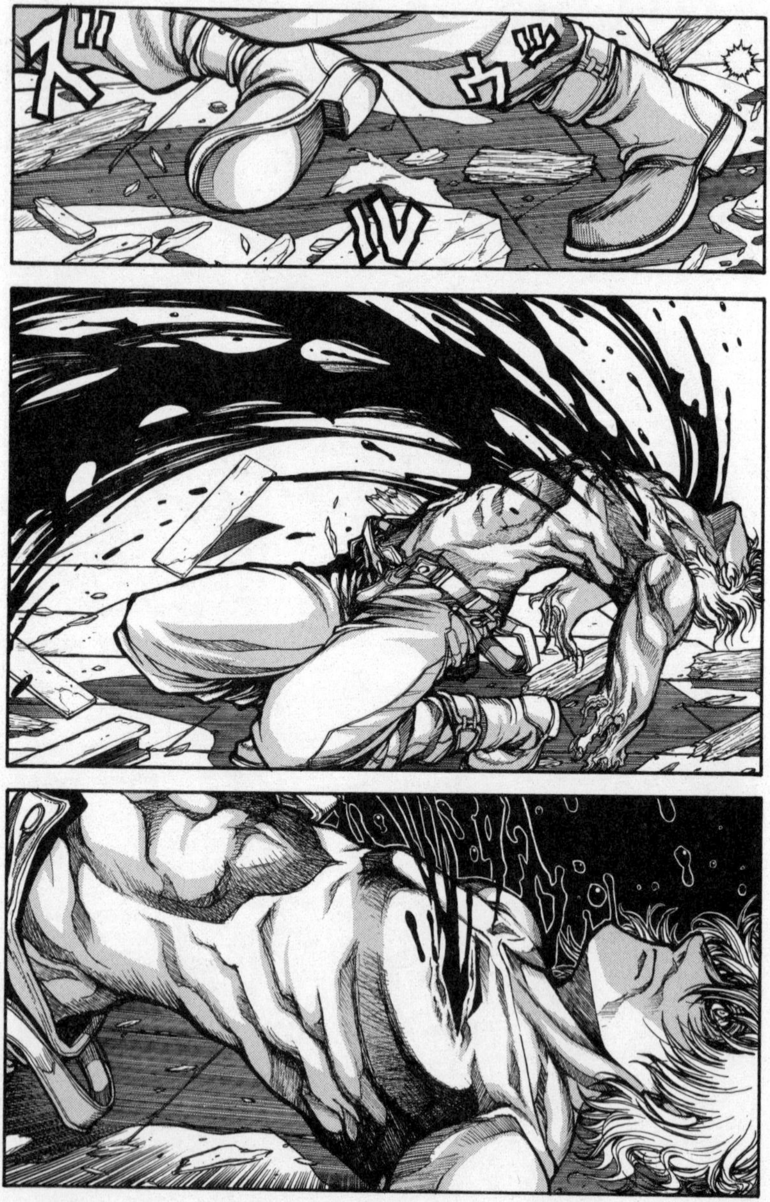
ガ
ズ
ル

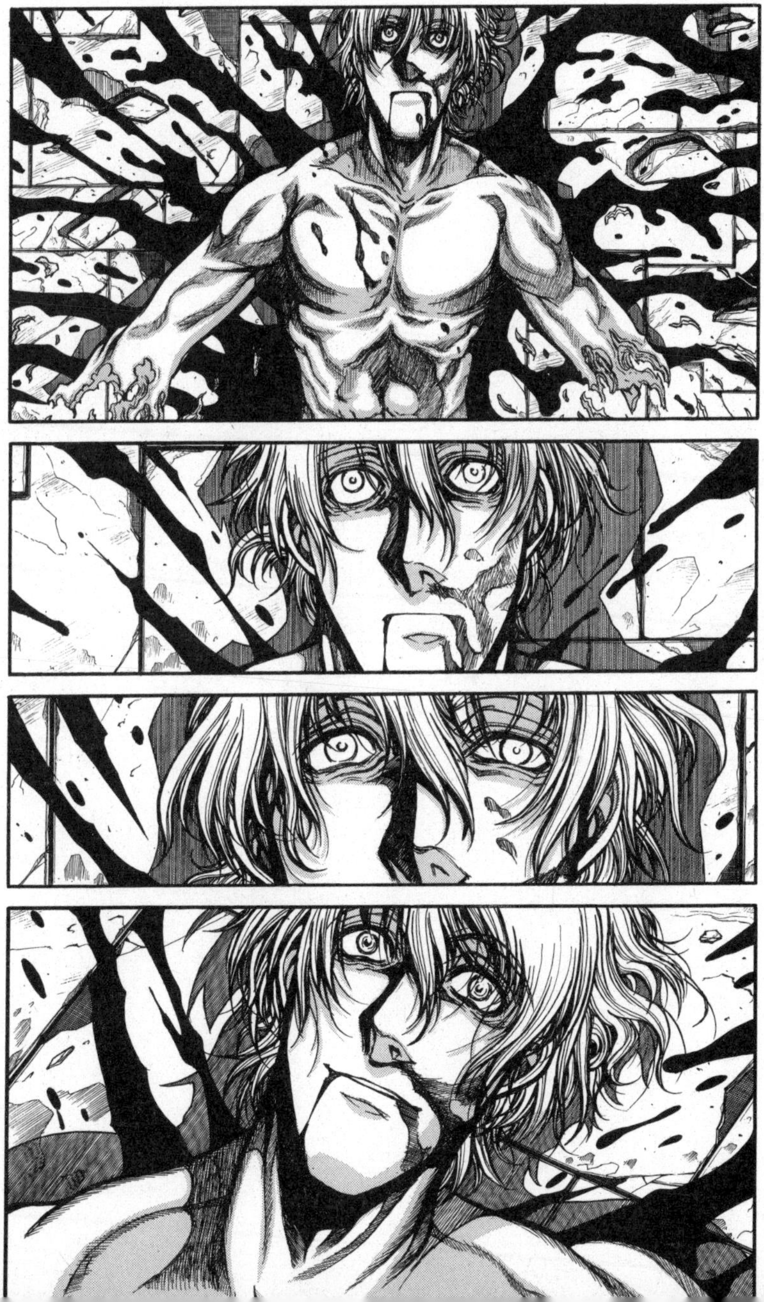

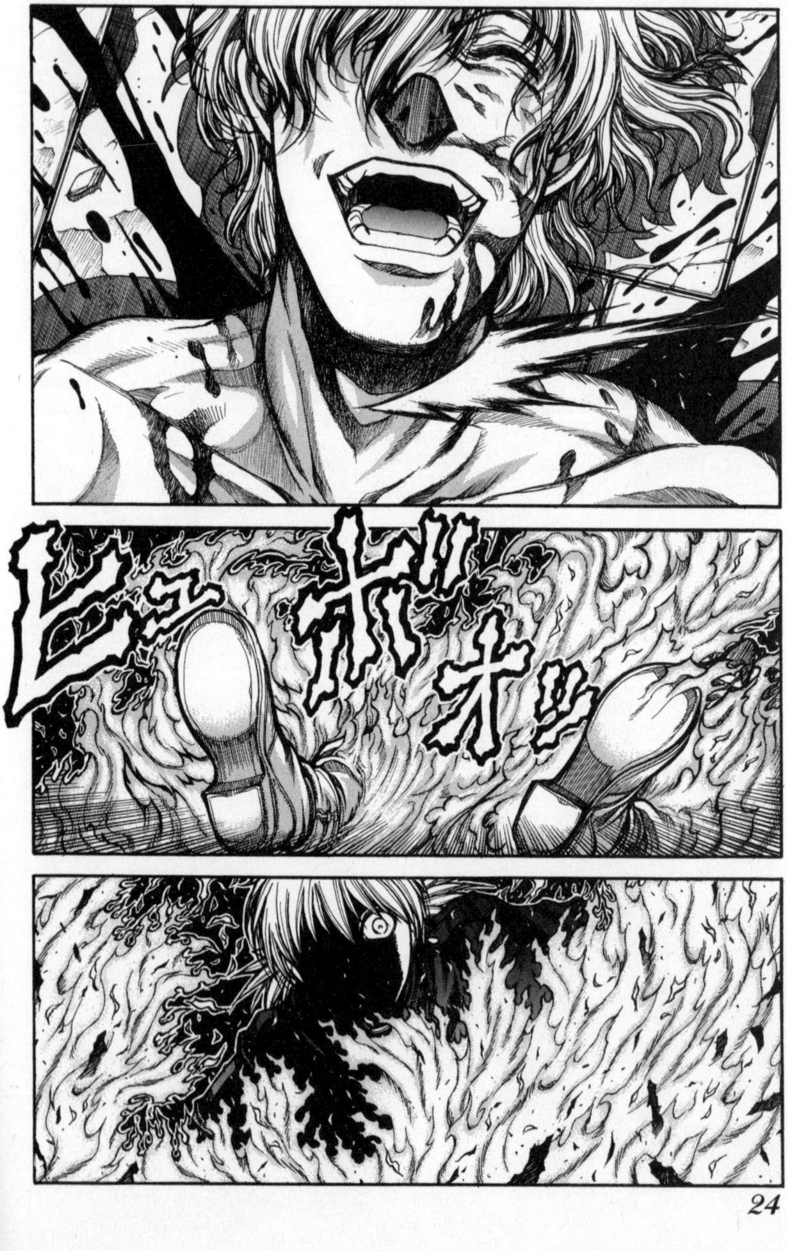
ヒュオ゛オッ

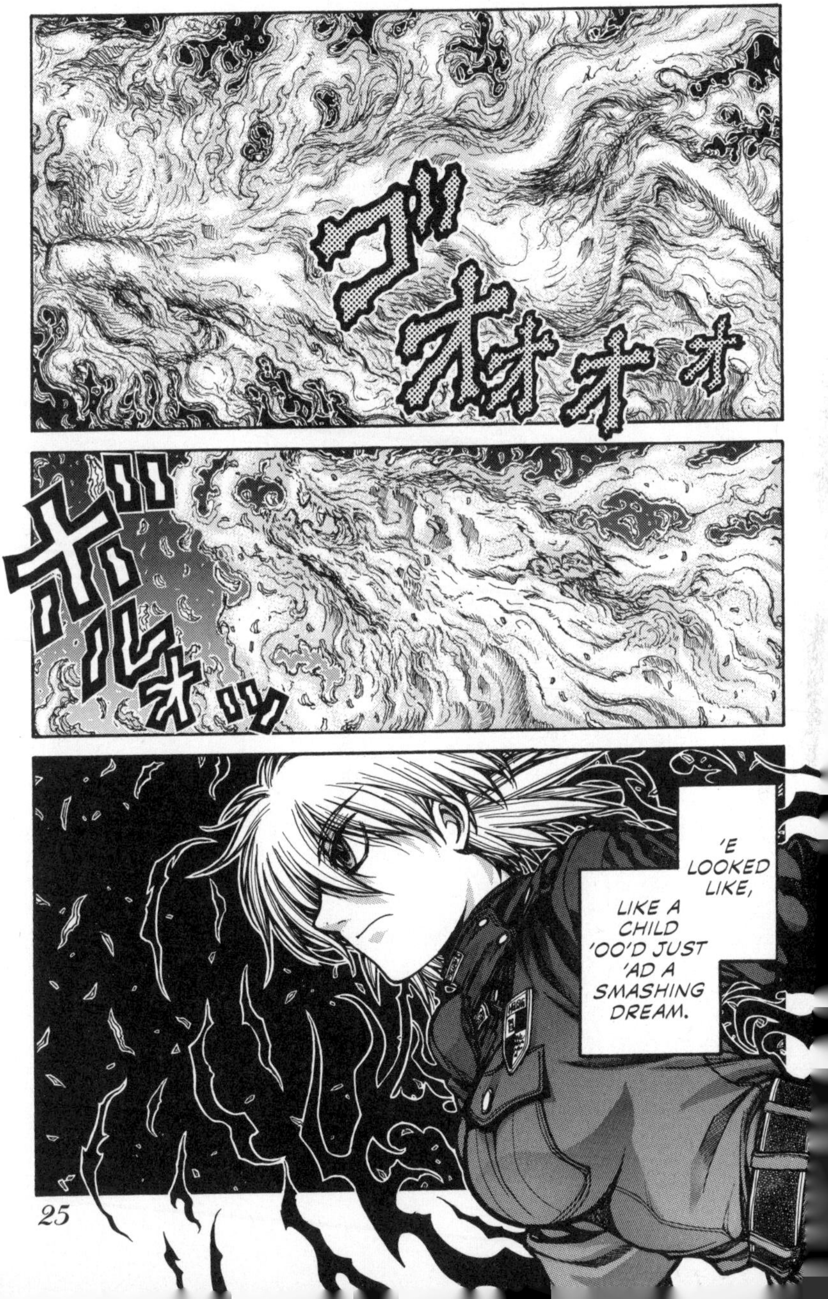
ゴオオオオ
ボルォ
'E LOOKED LIKE, LIKE A CHILD 'OO'D JUST 'AD A SMASHING DREAM.

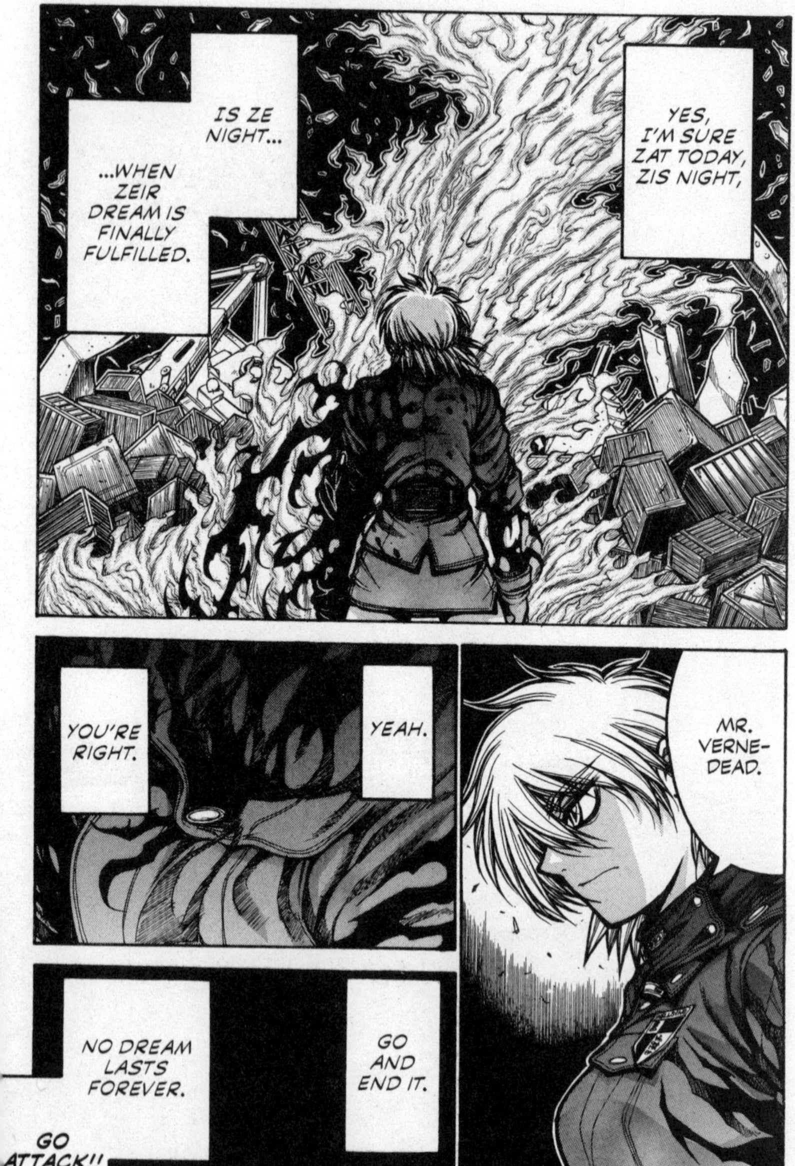
YES, I'M SURE ZAT TODAY, ZIS NIGHT,
IS ZE NIGHT...
...WHEN ZEIR DREAM IS FINALLY FULFILLED.
MR. VERNE-DEAD.
YEAH.
YOU'RE RIGHT.
GO AND END IT.
NO DREAM LASTS FOREVER.
GO ATTACK!!

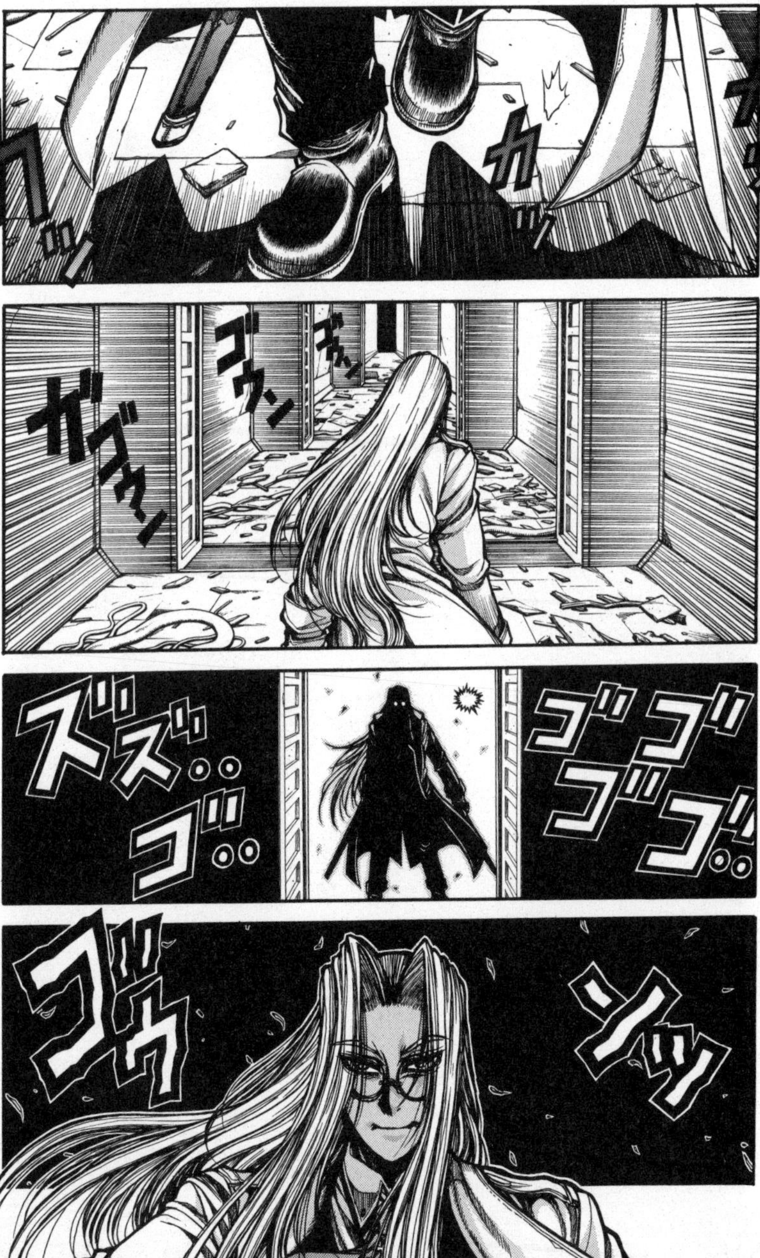
カッ
カッ
カッ
ゴウン
ゴウン
ガゴウン
ゴゴゴゴ..
ズズゴ..
ゴウ
ンッ

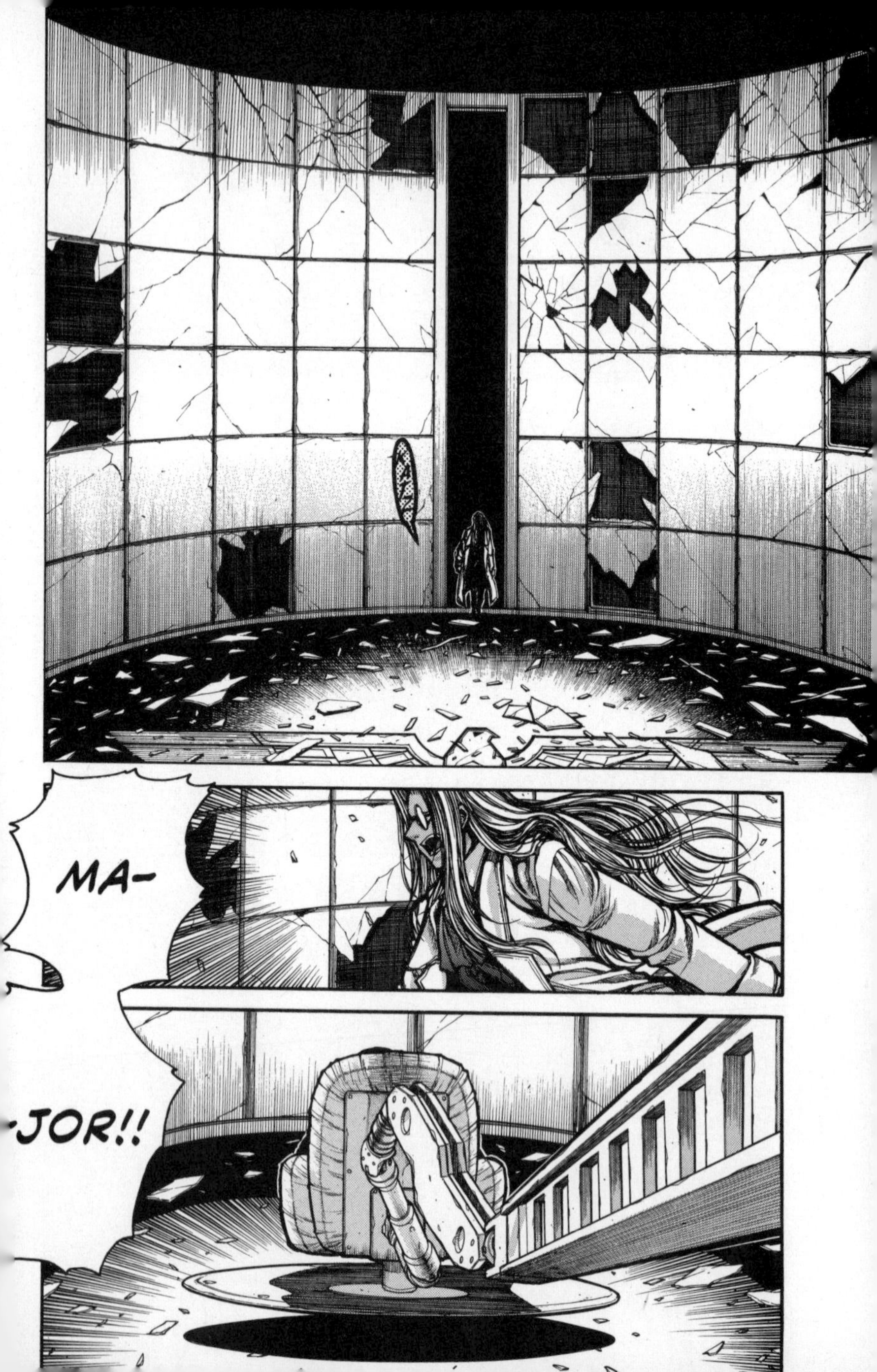
MA- -JOR!!

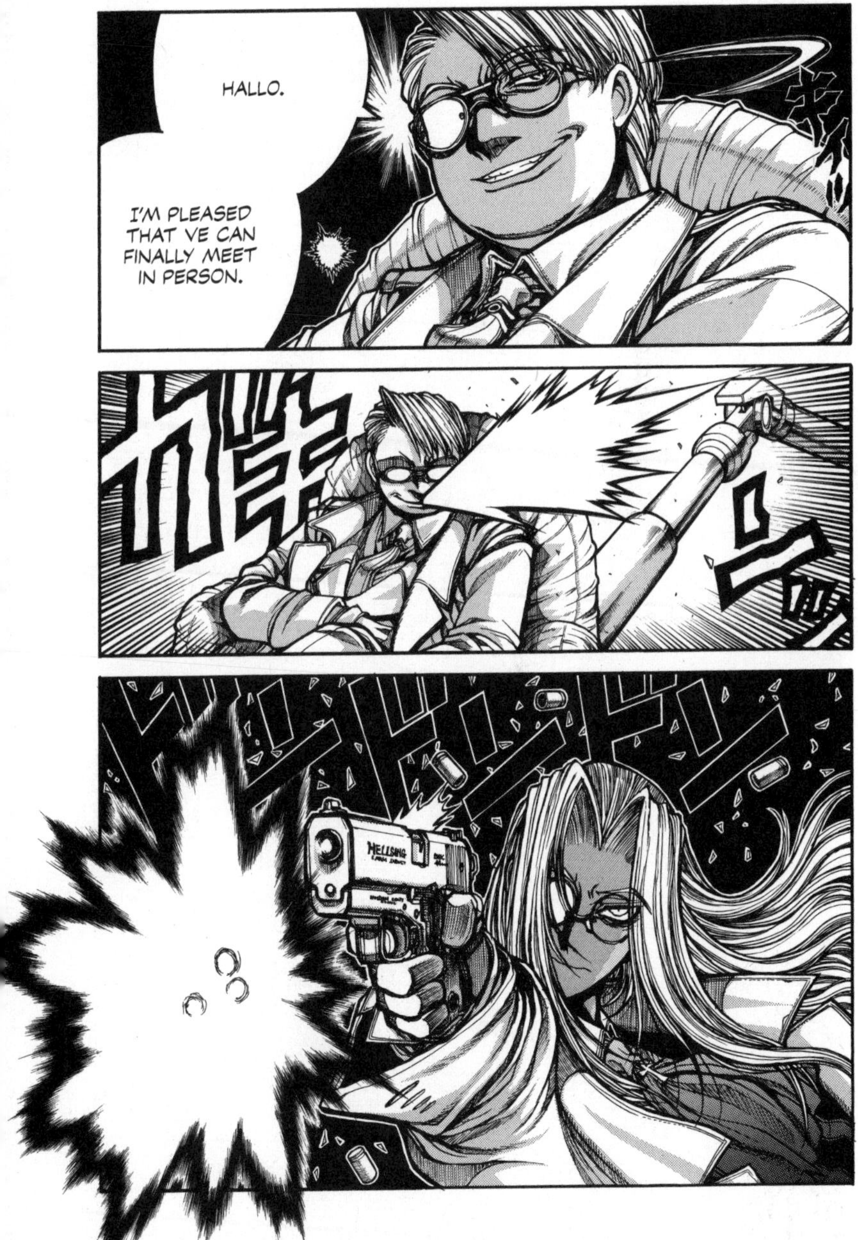
HALLO.
I'M PLEASED THAT VE CAN FINALLY MEET IN PERSON.

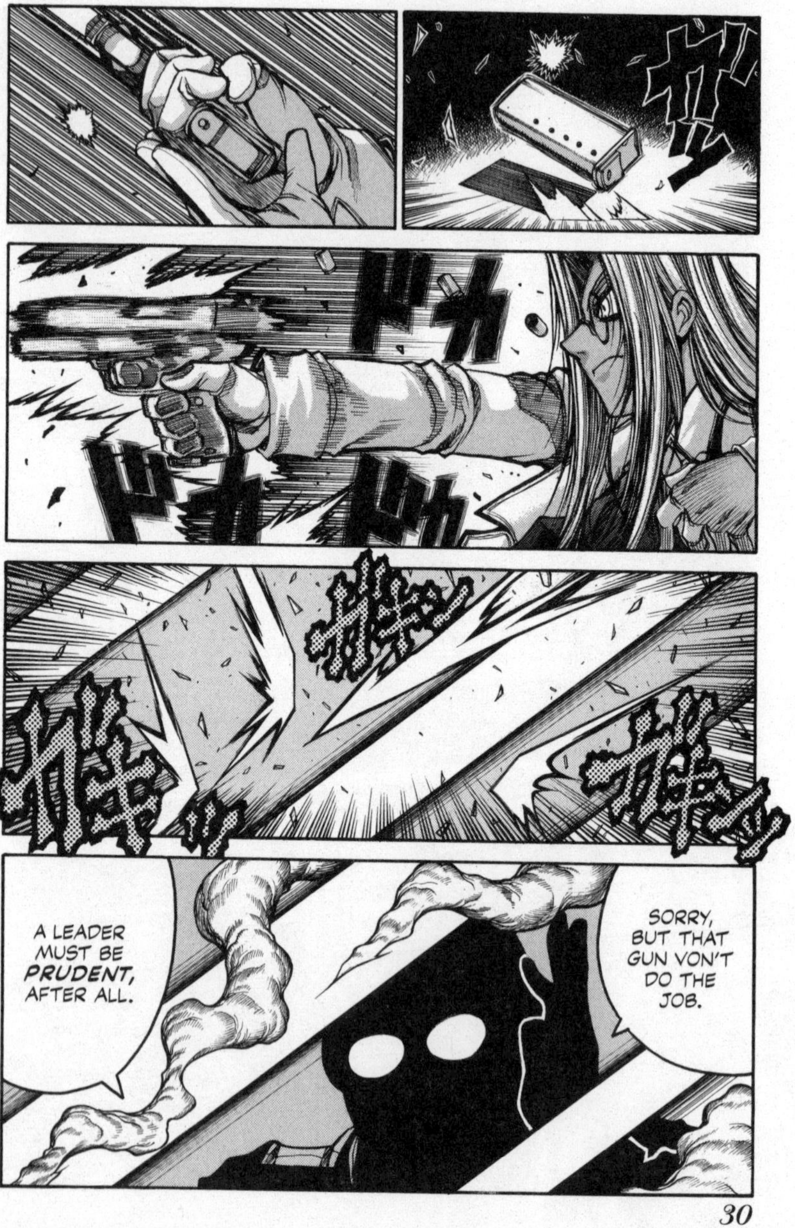
SORRY, BUT THAT GUN VON'T DO THE JOB.
A LEADER MUST BE *PRUDENT*, AFTER ALL.

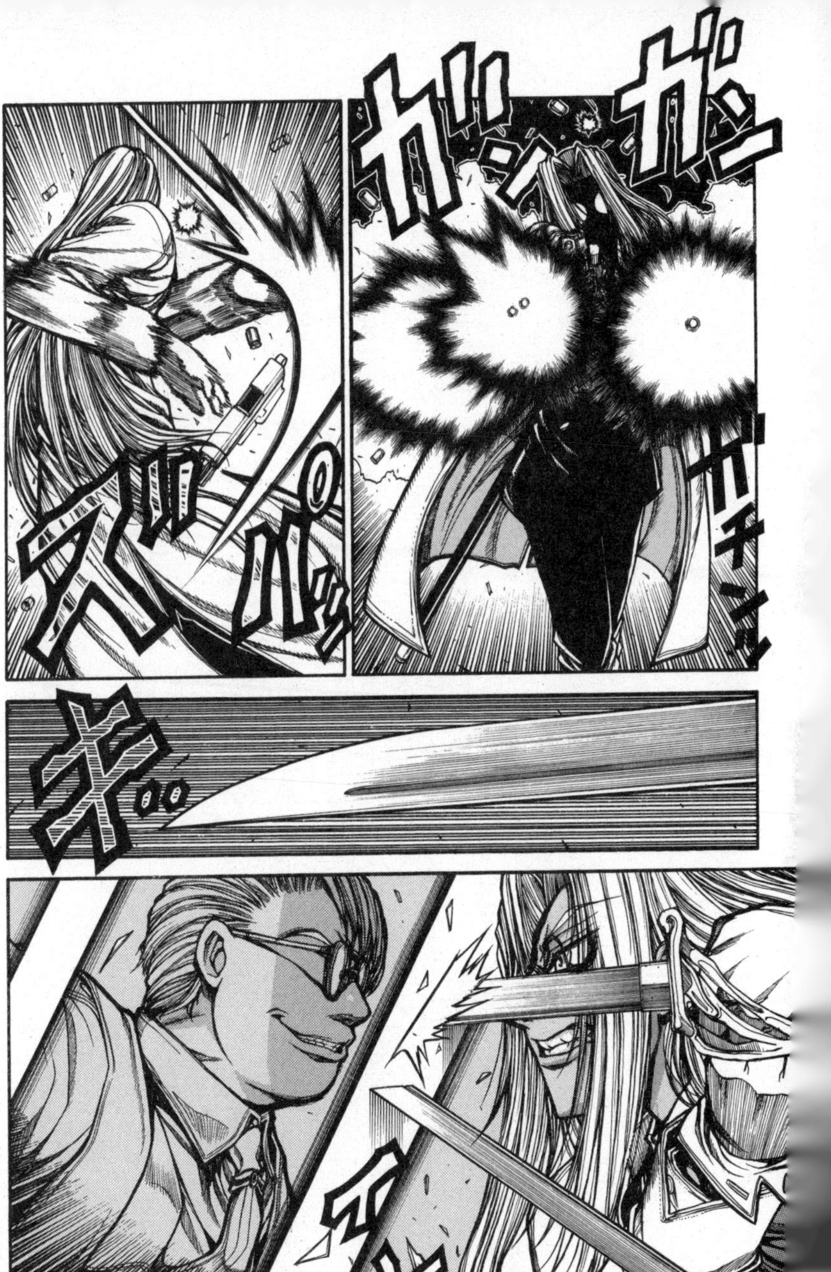
ガッガン
ガチン
ズパッ
ギ‥
ズン

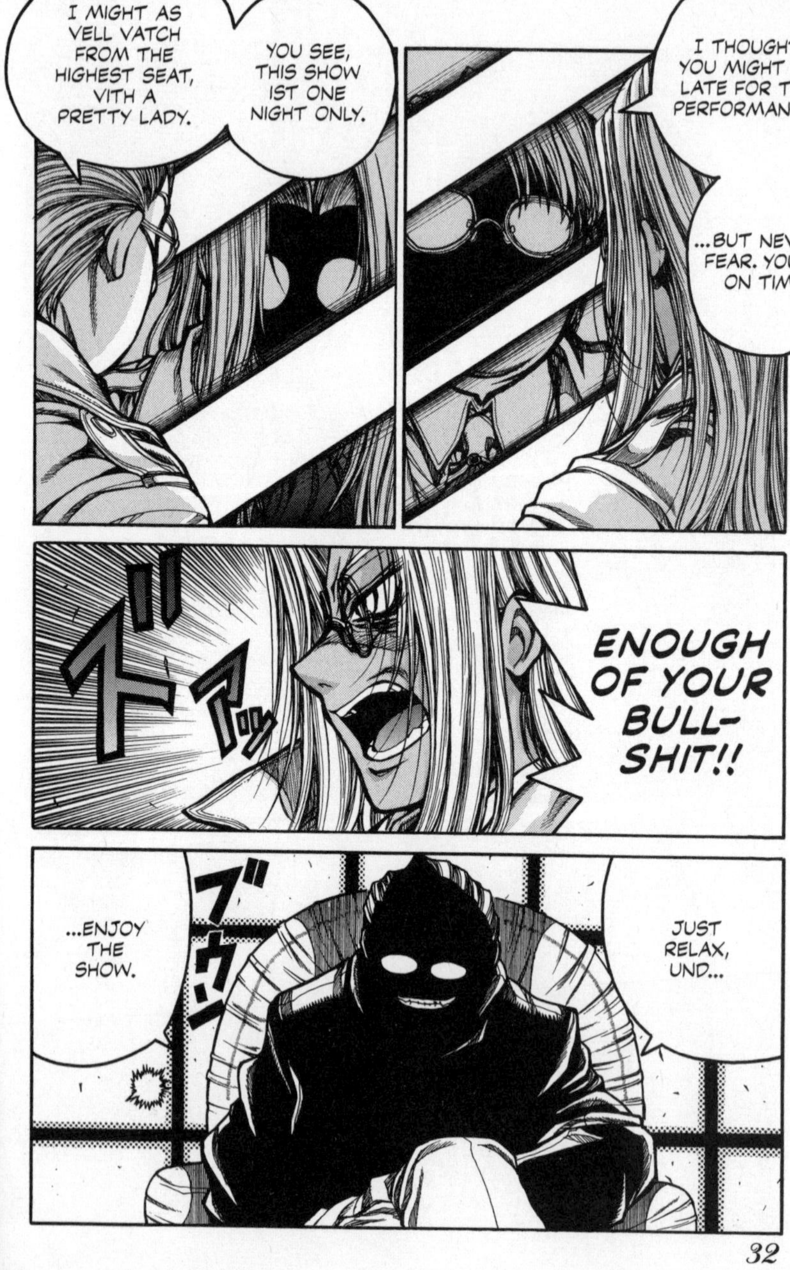
I THOUGHT YOU MIGHT BE LATE FOR THE PERFORMANCE...
...BUT NEVER FEAR. YOU'RE ON TIME.
YOU SEE, THIS SHOW IST ONE NIGHT ONLY.
I MIGHT AS VELL VATCH FROM THE HIGHEST SEAT, VITH A PRETTY LADY.
ENOUGH OF YOUR BULL-SHIT!!
JUST RELAX, UND...
...ENJOY THE SHOW.

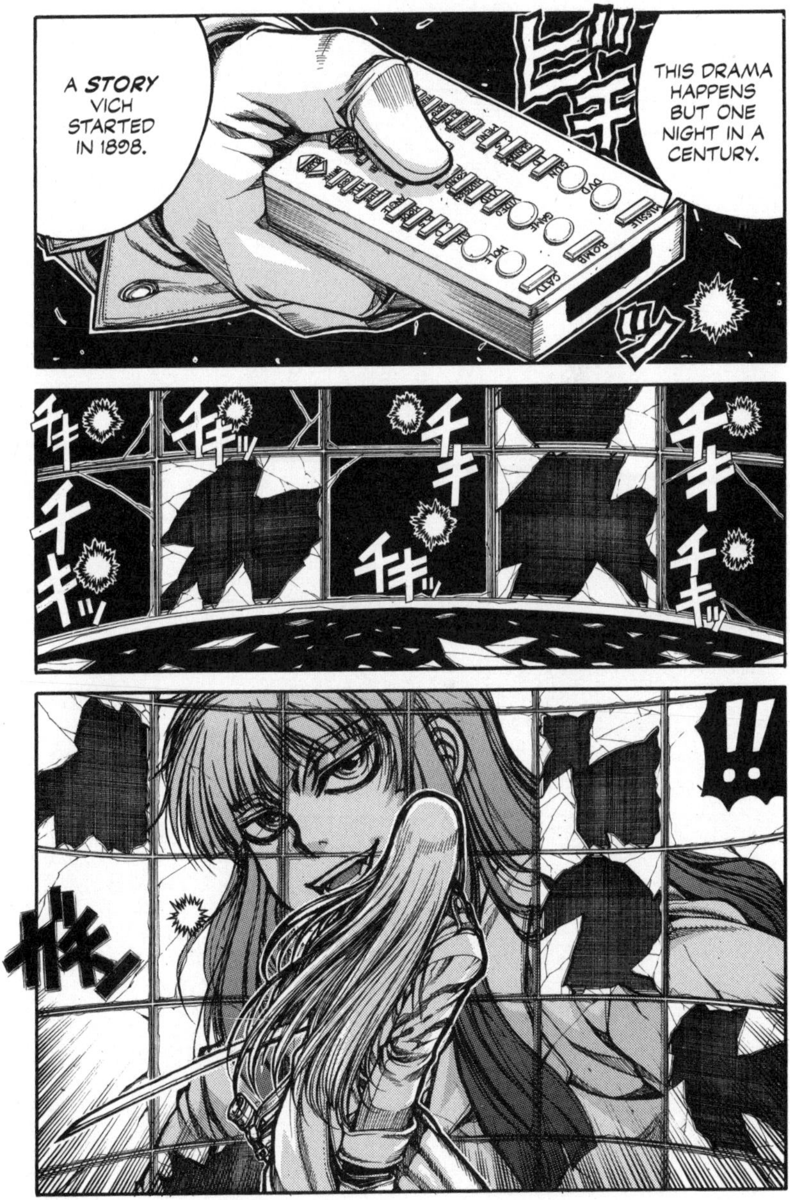
THIS DRAMA HAPPENS BUT ONE NIGHT IN A CENTURY.
A STORY VICH STARTED IN 1898.
!!

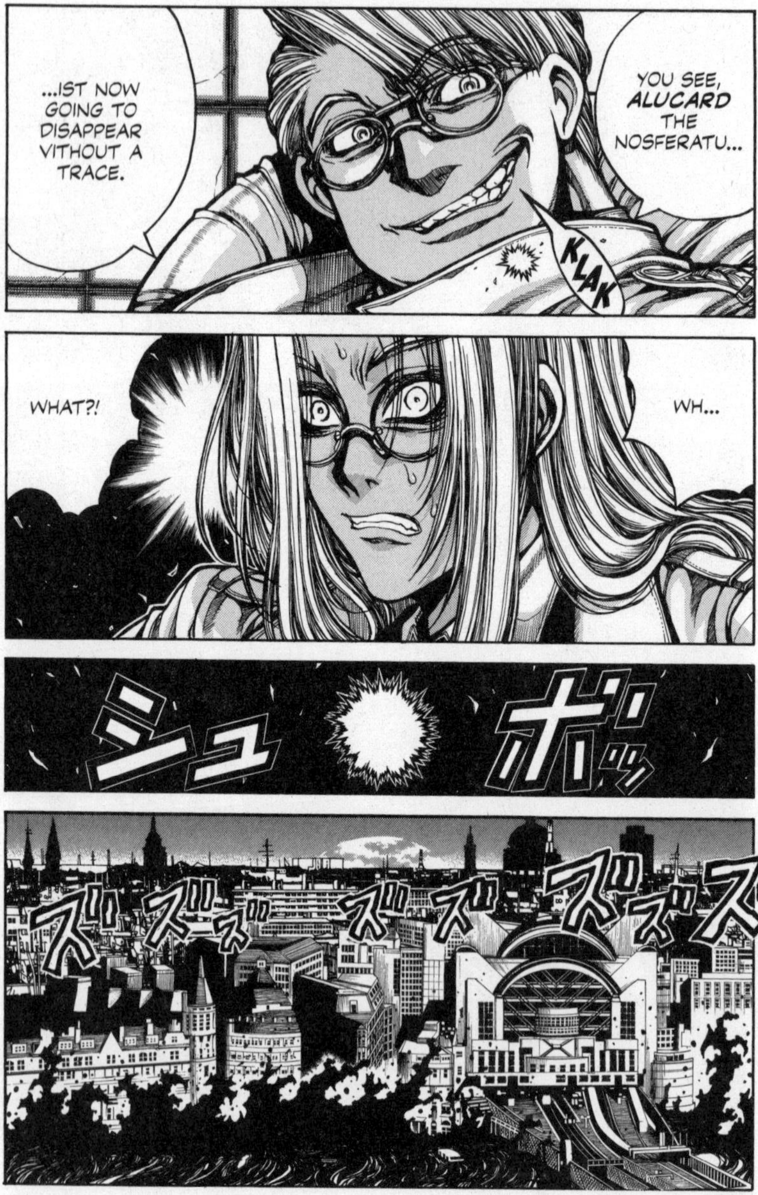
YOU SEE, ALUCARD THE NOSFERATU...
...IST NOW GOING TO DISAPPEAR VITHOUT A TRACE.
KLAK
WH...
WHAT?!
シュ
ボッ
ズズズズズズズズ

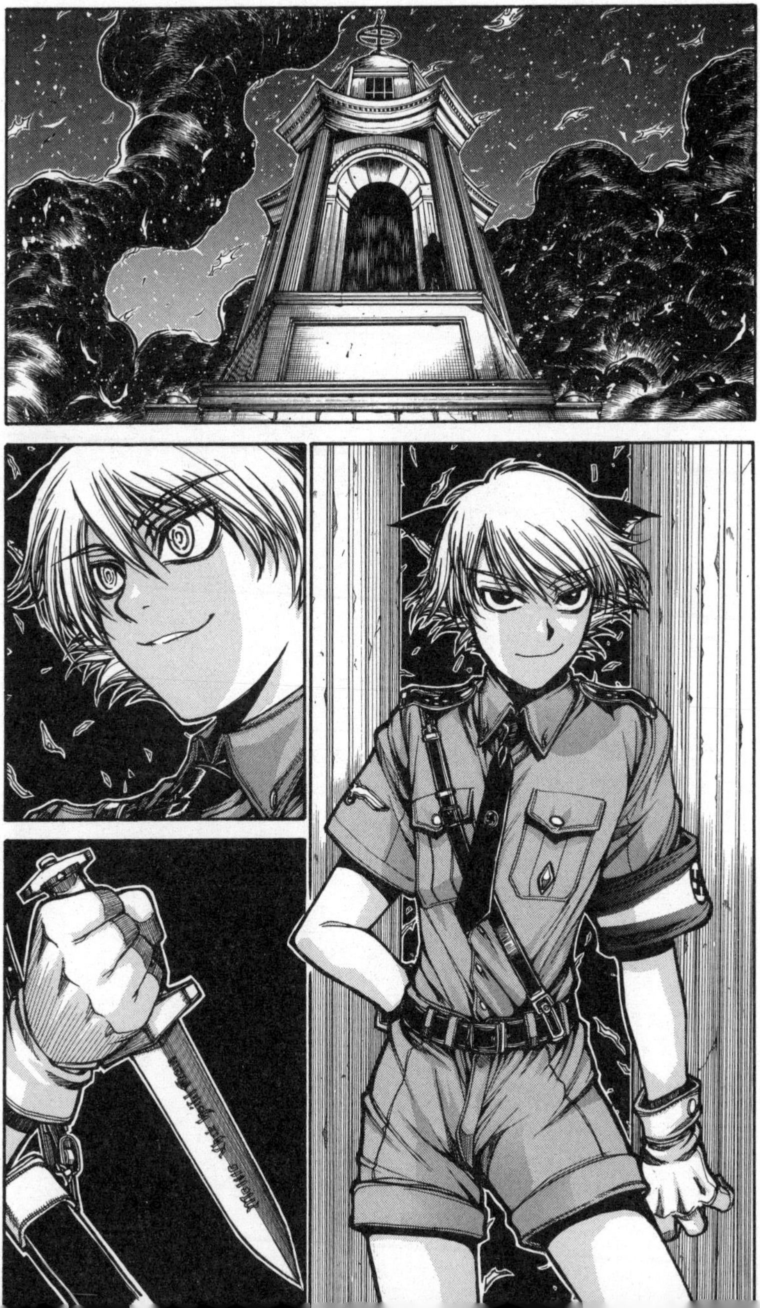

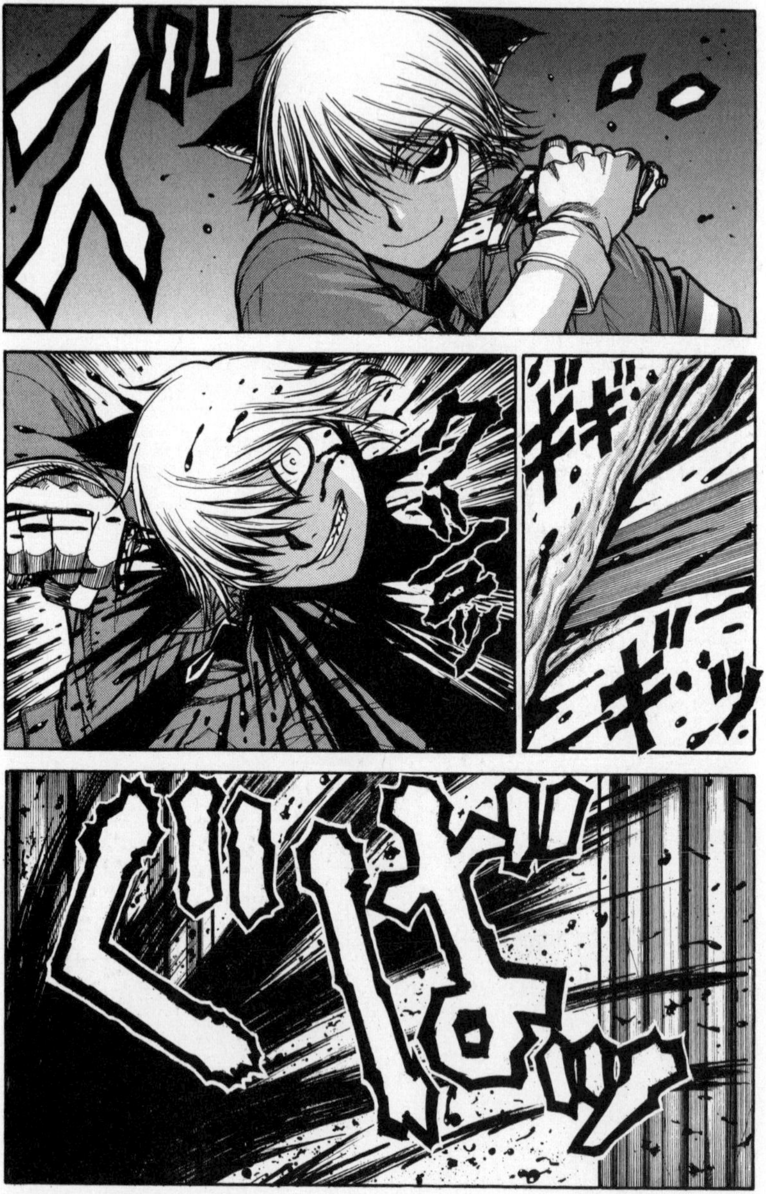
ズ
ギギ
ギッ

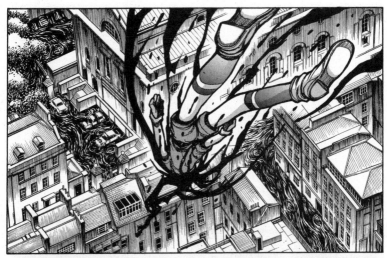

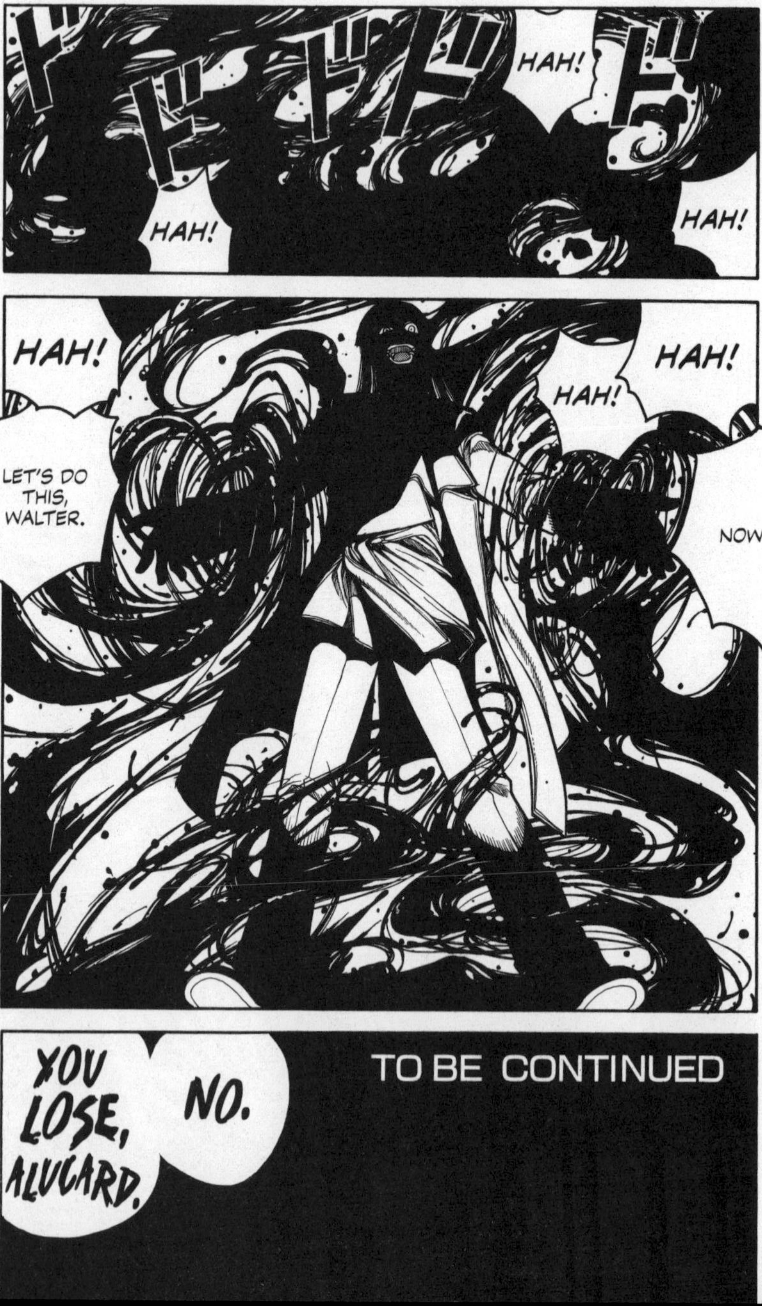
HAH!
HAH!
HAH!
HAH!
HAH!
NOW...
HAH!
LET'S DO THIS, WALTER.
TO BE CONTINUED
NO.
YOU LOSE, ALUCARD.

ORDER 2/ END

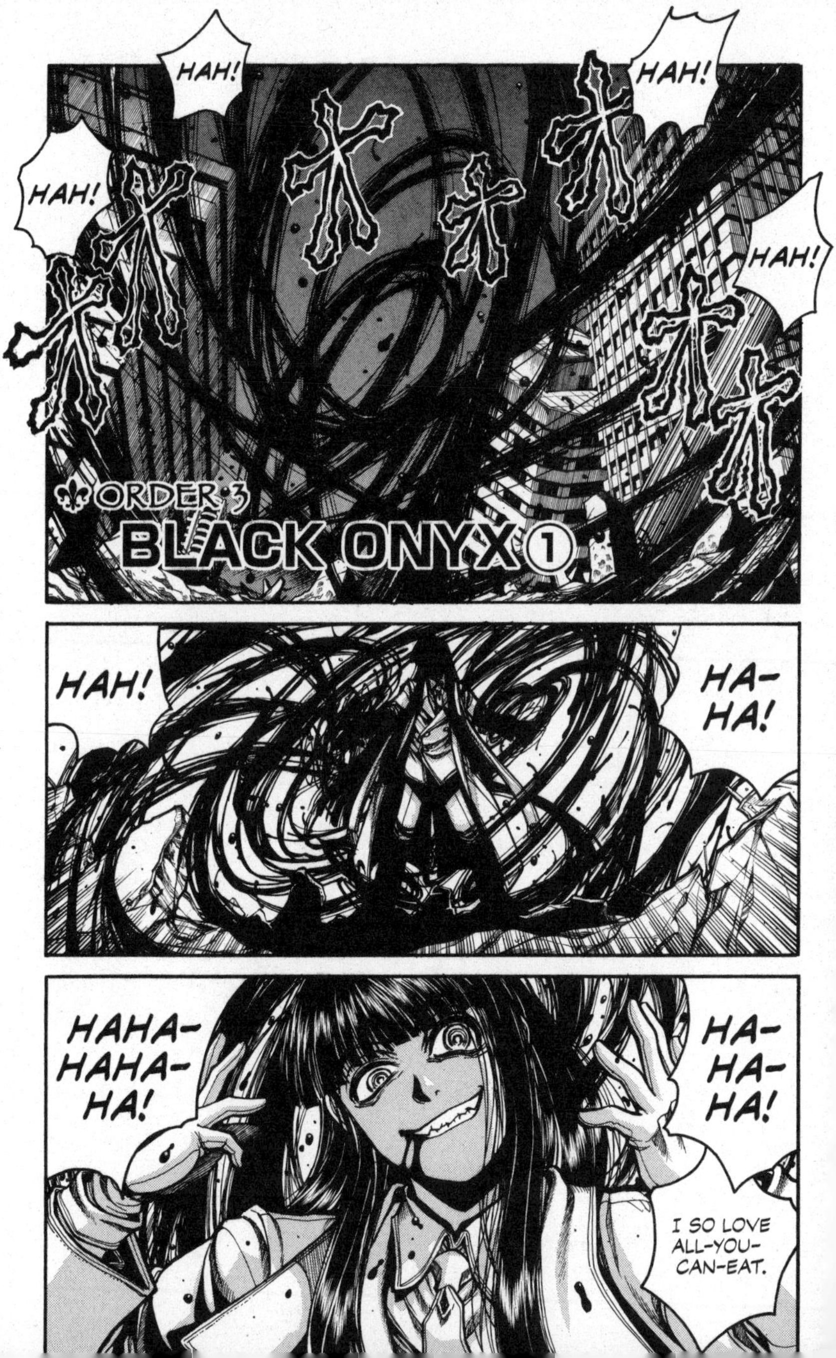
HAH!
HAH!
HAH!
HAH!
ORDER 3
BLACK ONYX 1
HA-HA!
HAH!
HA-HA-HA!
HAHA-HAHA-HA!
I SO LOVE ALL-YOU-CAN-EAT.

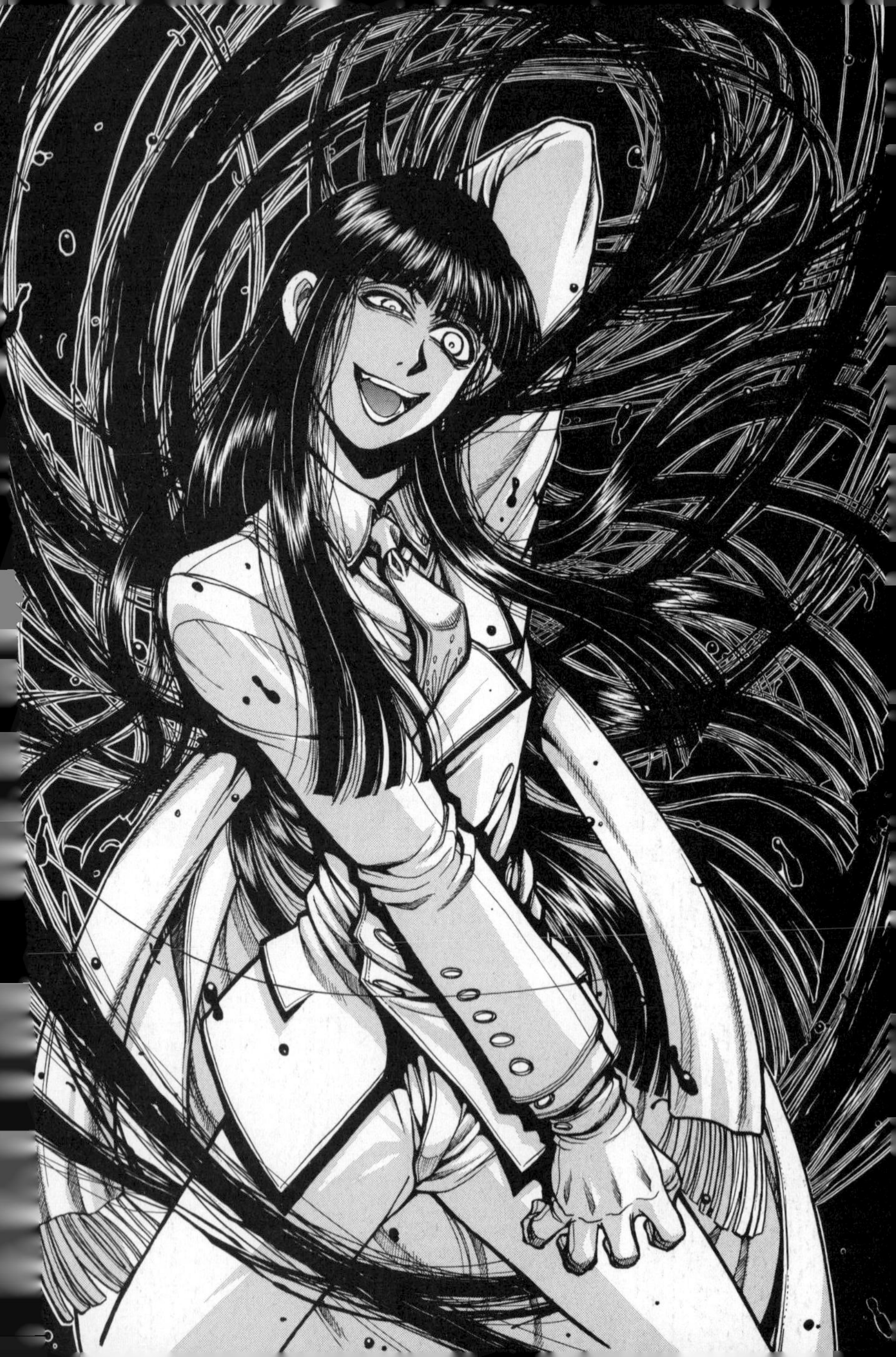

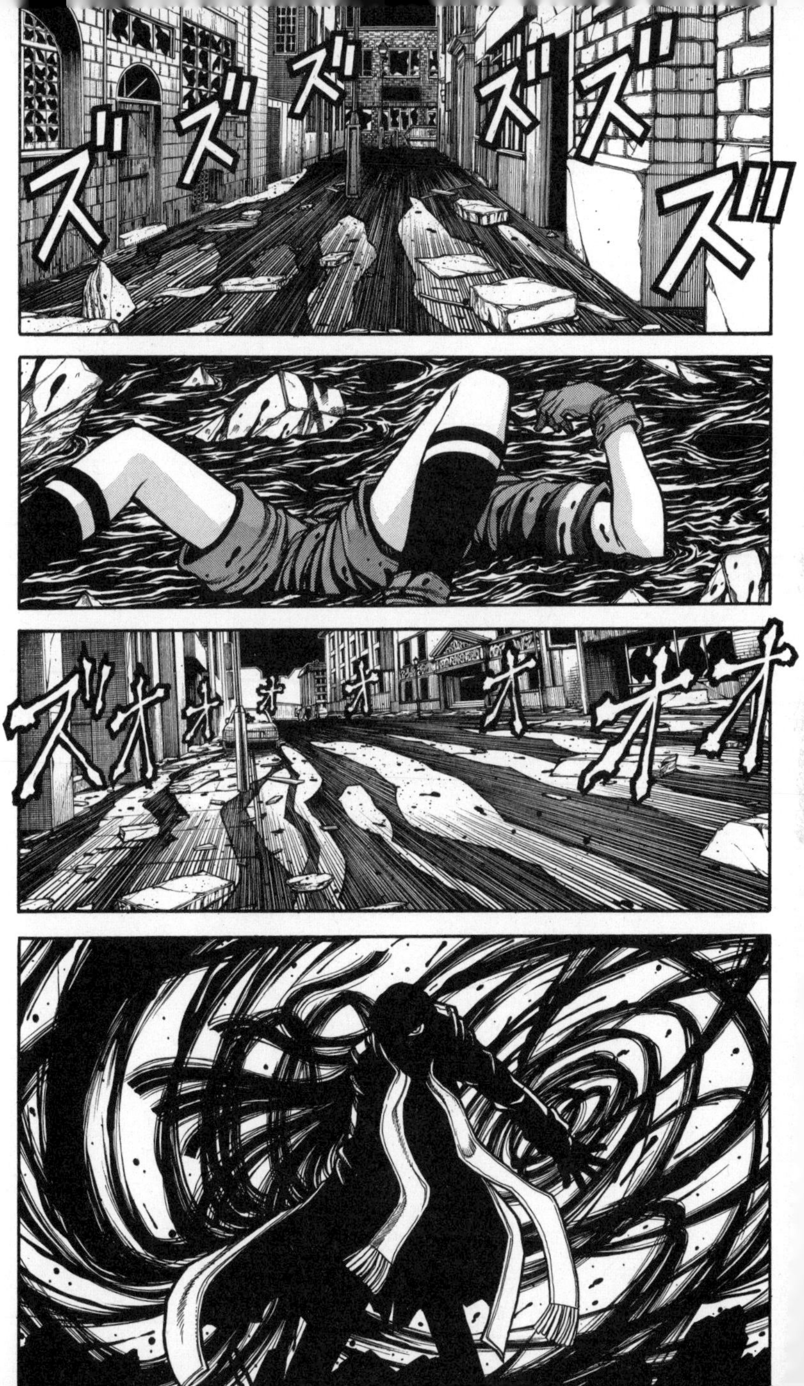
ズズズズズズ
ズオオオオオオオ

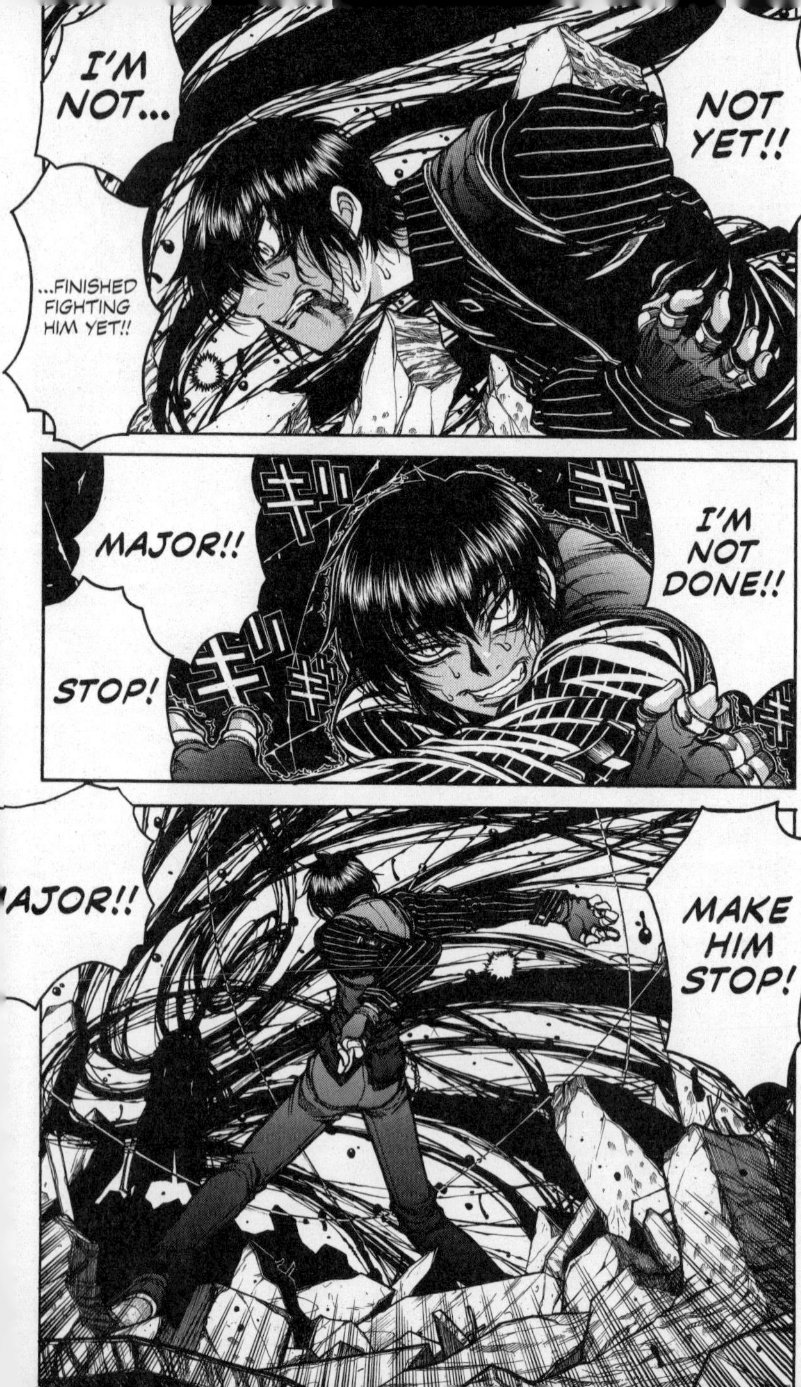
NOT YET!!
I'M NOT...
...FINISHED FIGHTING HIM YET!!
I'M NOT DONE!!
MAJOR!!
STOP!
MAKE HIM STOP!
AJOR!!

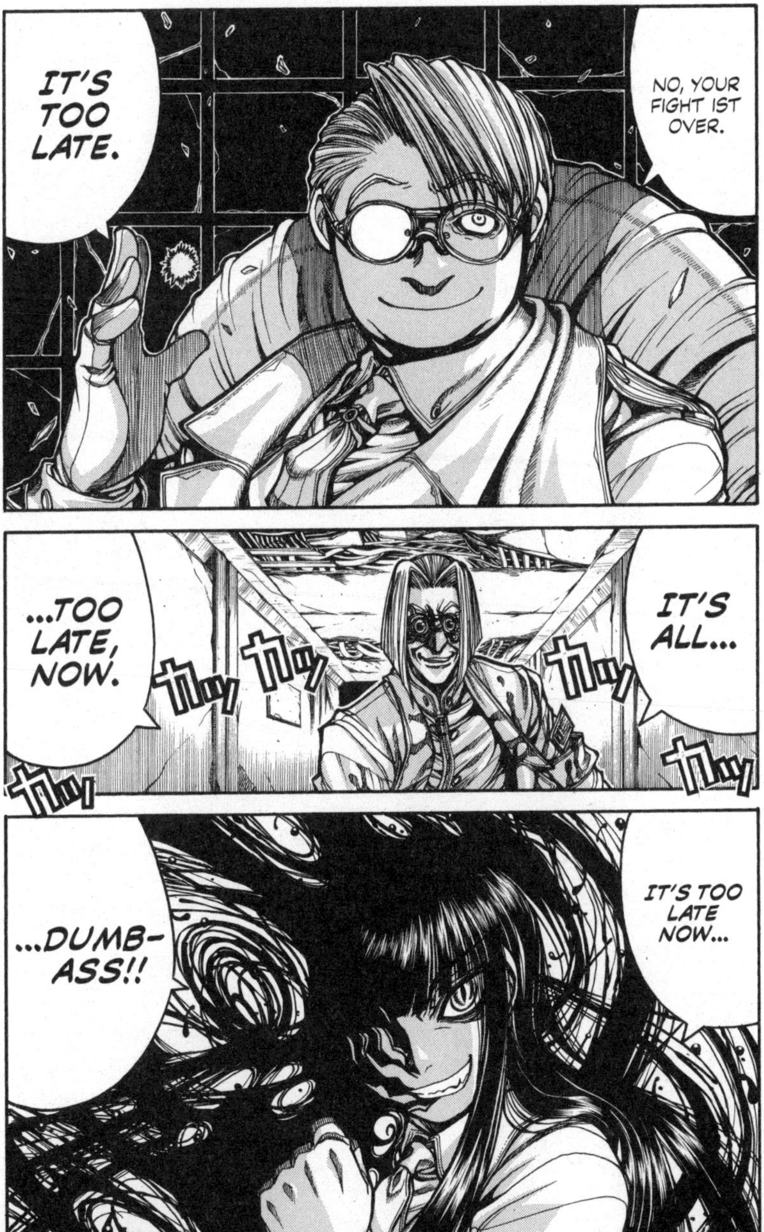
NO, YOUR FIGHT IST OVER.
IT'S TOO LATE.
IT'S ALL...
...TOO LATE, NOW.
IT'S TOO LATE NOW...
...DUMB-ASS!!

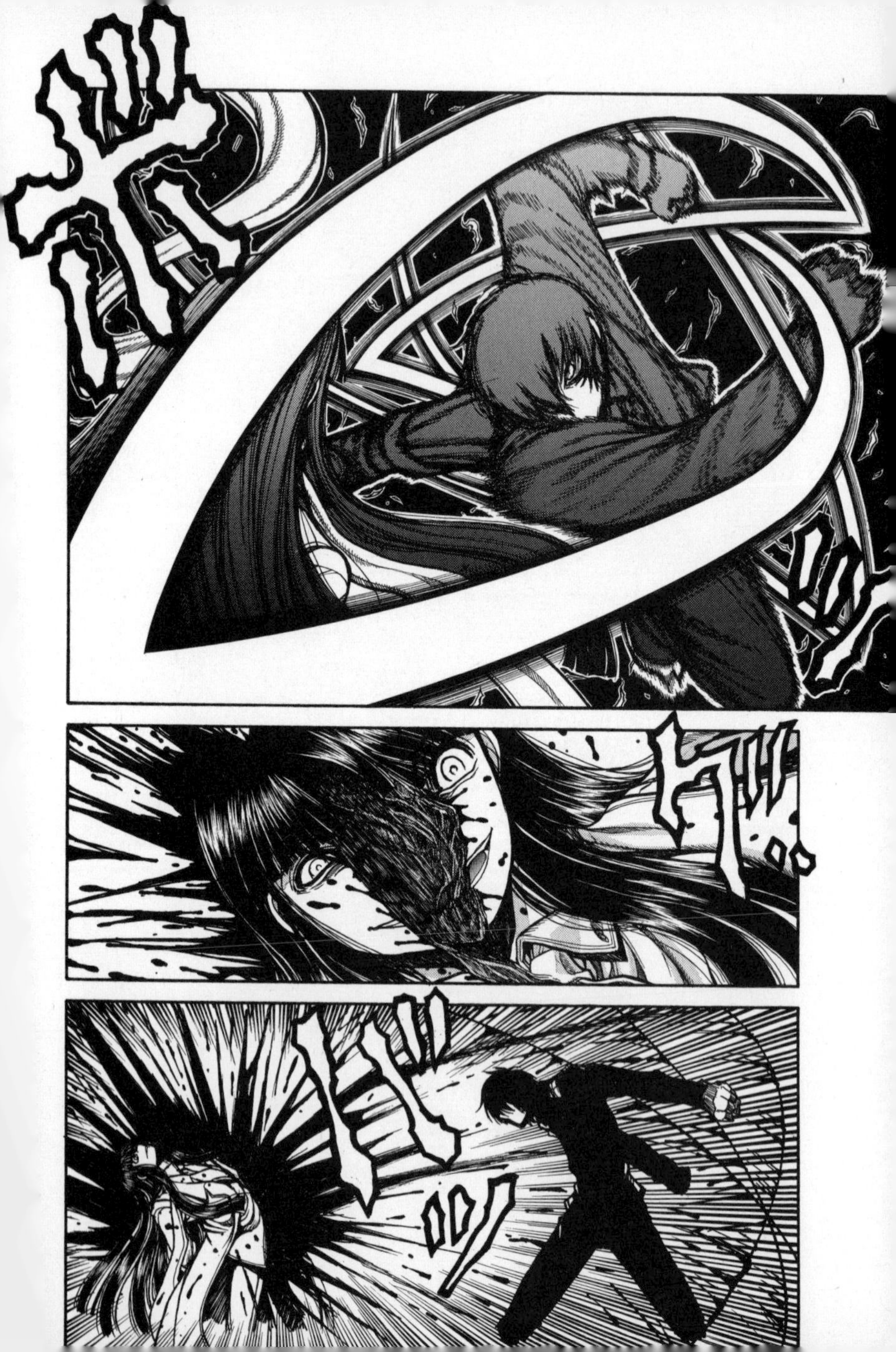

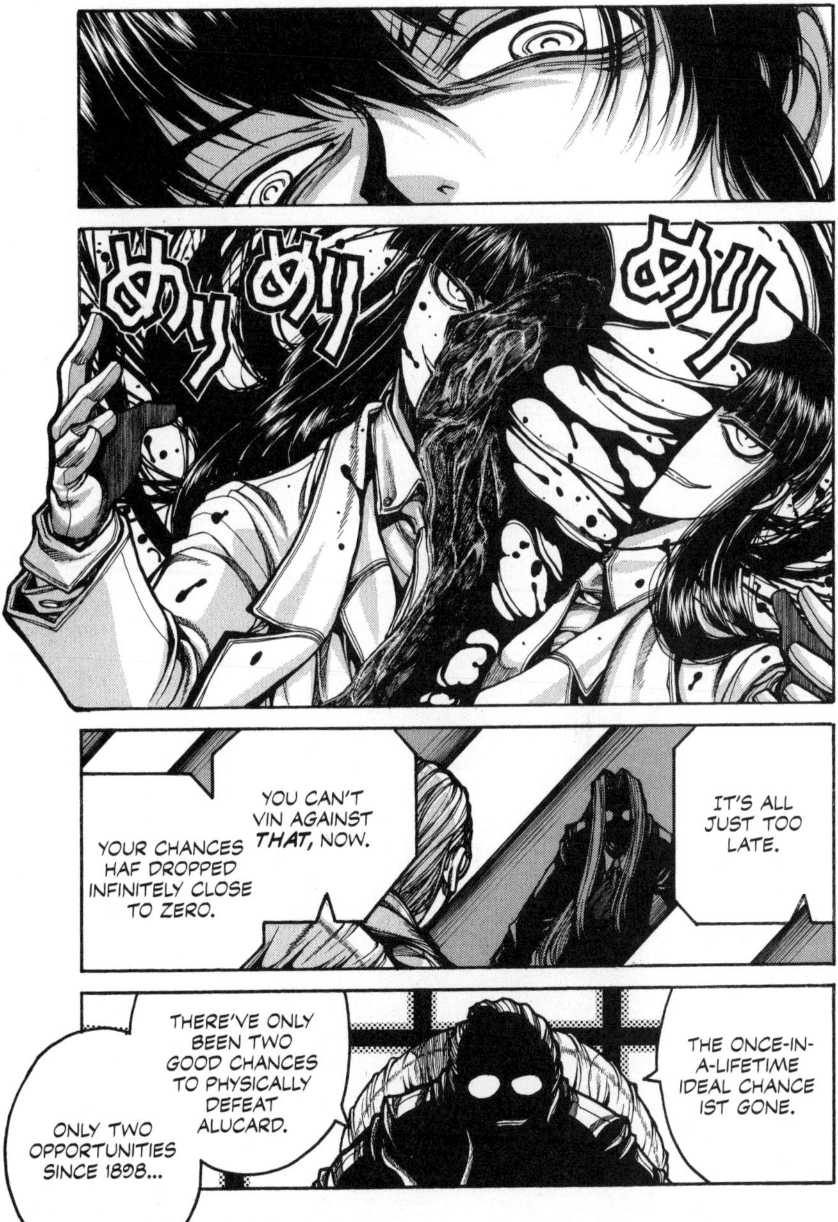
めり
めりめり
IT'S ALL JUST TOO LATE.
YOU CAN'T VIN AGAINST *THAT,* NOW.
YOUR CHANCES HAF DROPPED INFINITELY CLOSE TO ZERO.
THE ONCE-IN-A-LIFETIME IDEAL CHANCE IST GONE.
THERE'VE ONLY BEEN TWO GOOD CHANCES TO PHYSICALLY DEFEAT ALUCARD.
ONLY TWO OPPORTUNITIES SINCE 1898...

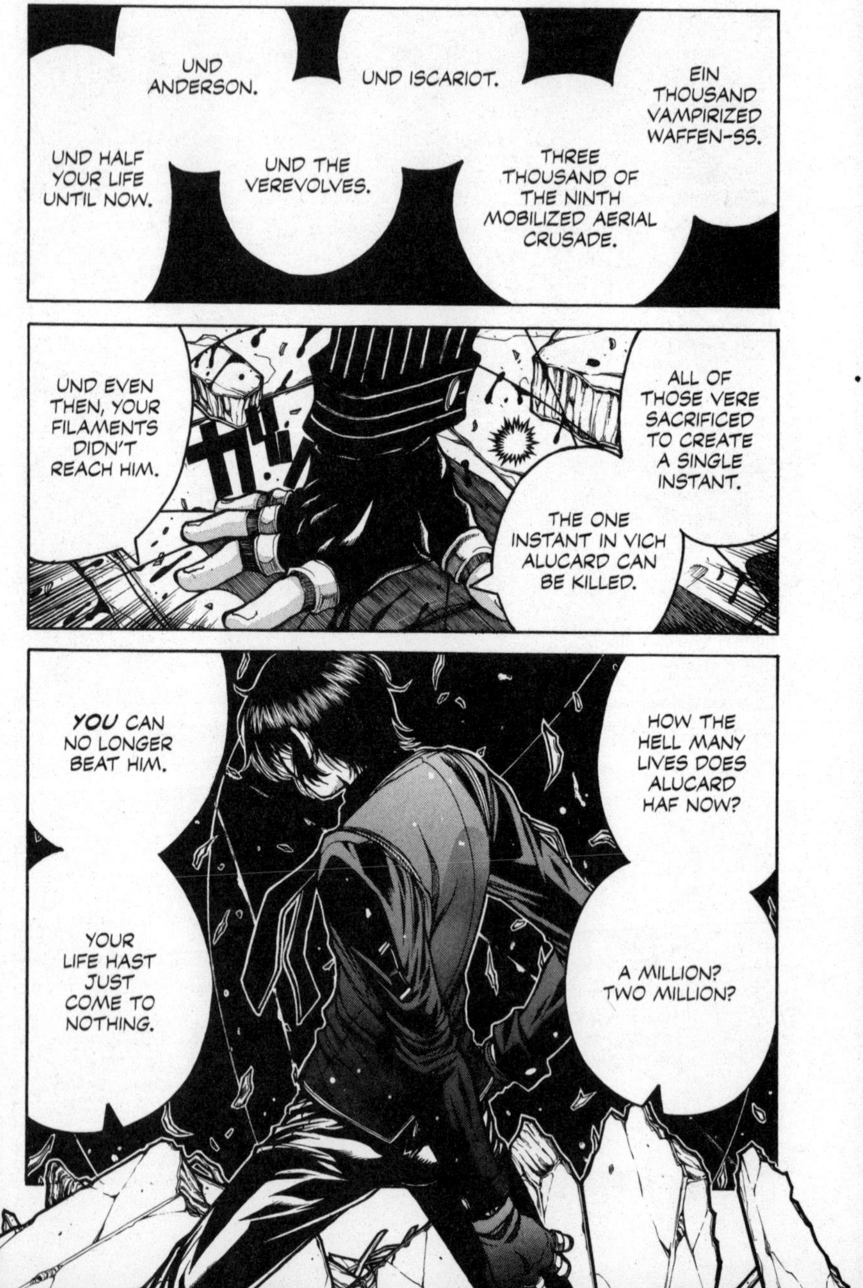
EIN THOUSAND VAMPIRIZED WAFFEN-SS.
THREE THOUSAND OF THE NINTH MOBILIZED AERIAL CRUSADE.
UND ISCARIOT.
UND THE VEREVOLVES.
UND ANDERSON.
UND HALF YOUR LIFE UNTIL NOW.
ALL OF THOSE VERE SACRIFICED TO CREATE A SINGLE INSTANT.
THE ONE INSTANT IN VICH ALUCARD CAN BE KILLED.
UND EVEN THEN, YOUR FILAMENTS DIDN'T REACH HIM.
HOW THE HELL MANY LIVES DOES ALUCARD HAF NOW?
A MILLION? TWO MILLION?
YOU CAN NO LONGER BEAT HIM.
YOUR LIFE HAST JUST COME TO NOTHING.

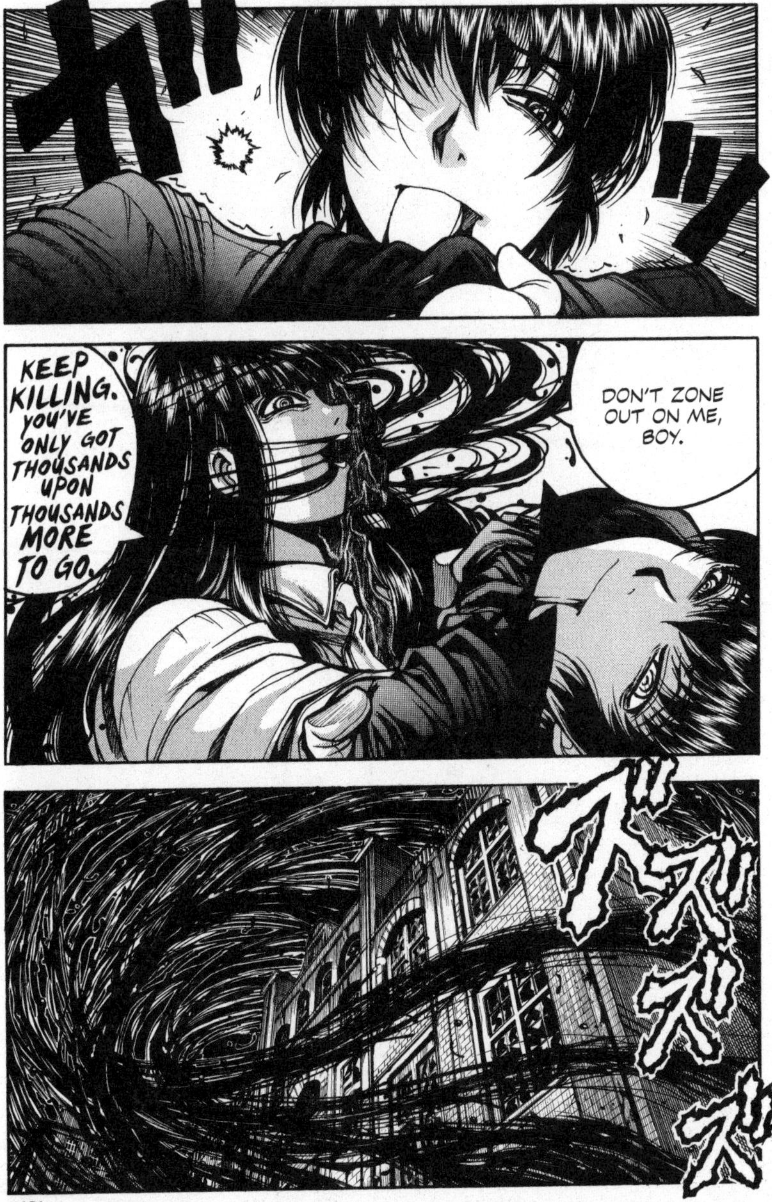
DON'T ZONE OUT ON ME, BOY.
KEEP KILLING. YOU'VE ONLY GOT THOUSANDS UPON THOUSANDS MORE TO GO.

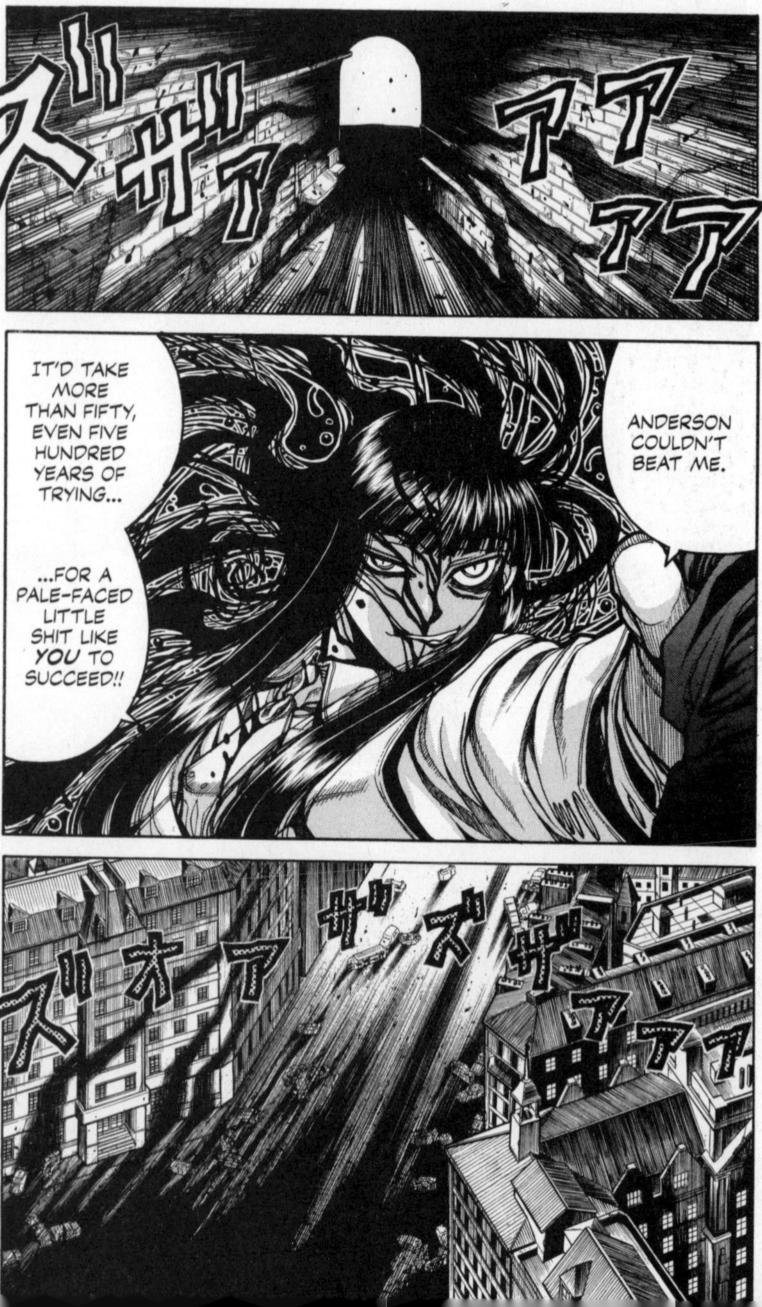
ズザァ
アアアア
ANDERSON COULDN'T BEAT ME.
IT'D TAKE MORE THAN FIFTY, EVEN FIVE HUNDRED YEARS OF TRYING...
...FOR A PALE-FACED LITTLE SHIT LIKE *YOU* TO SUCCEED!!
ズオァ
ザ
ズザァアア

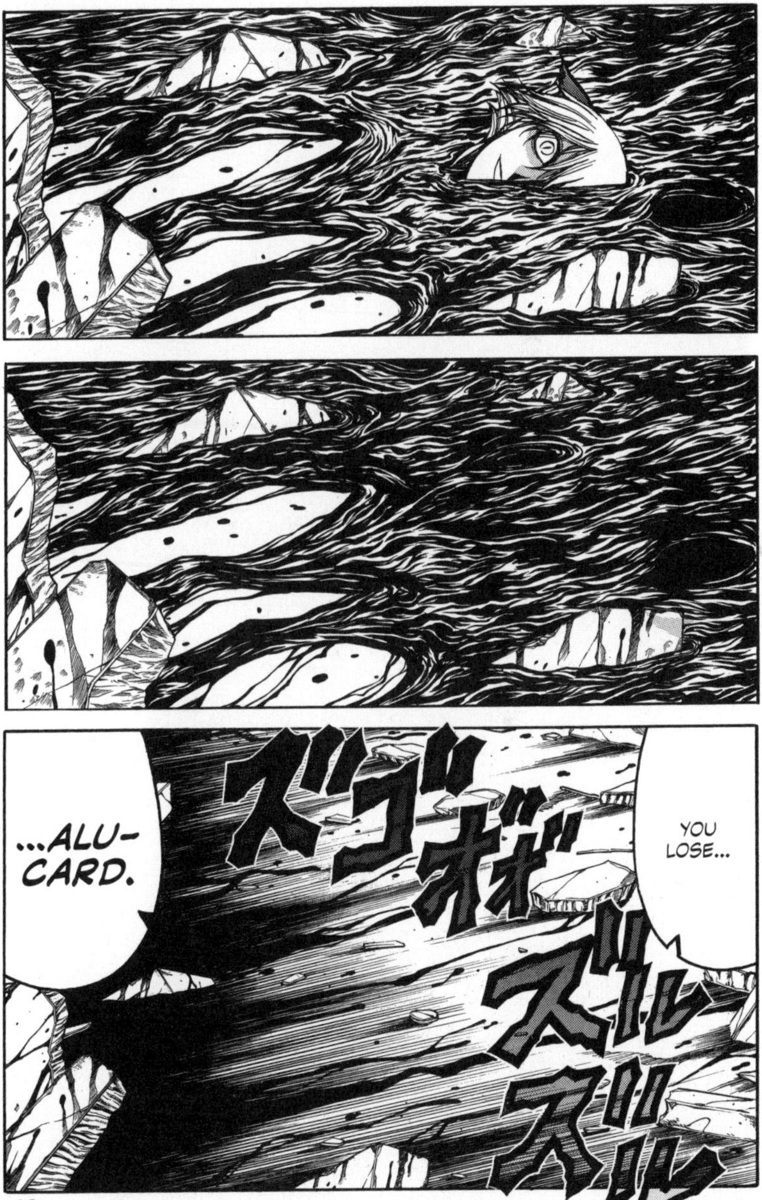
YOU LOSE...
ズゴオオ
ズルズル
...ALU-CARD.

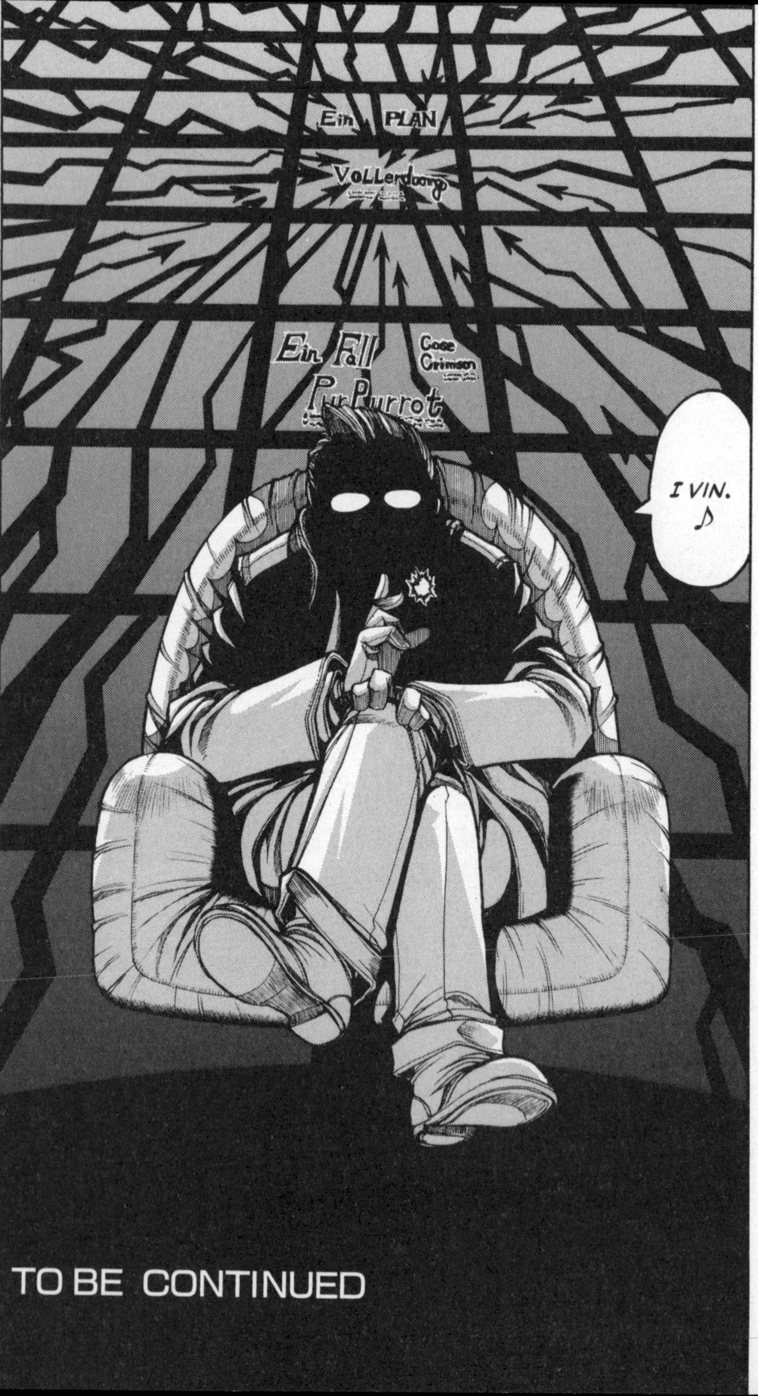
Ein PLAN
VoLLendung
Ein Fall
Case Crimson
PurPurrot
I VIN. ♪
TO BE CONTINUED

ORDER 3/ END

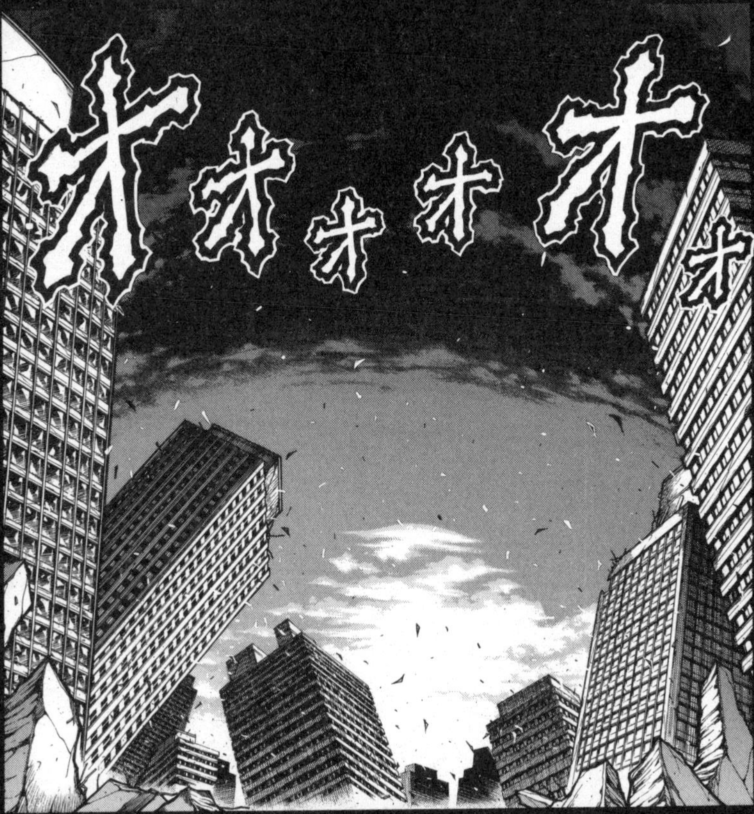
オオォオオォ

⚜ ORDER 4

BLACK ONYX ②

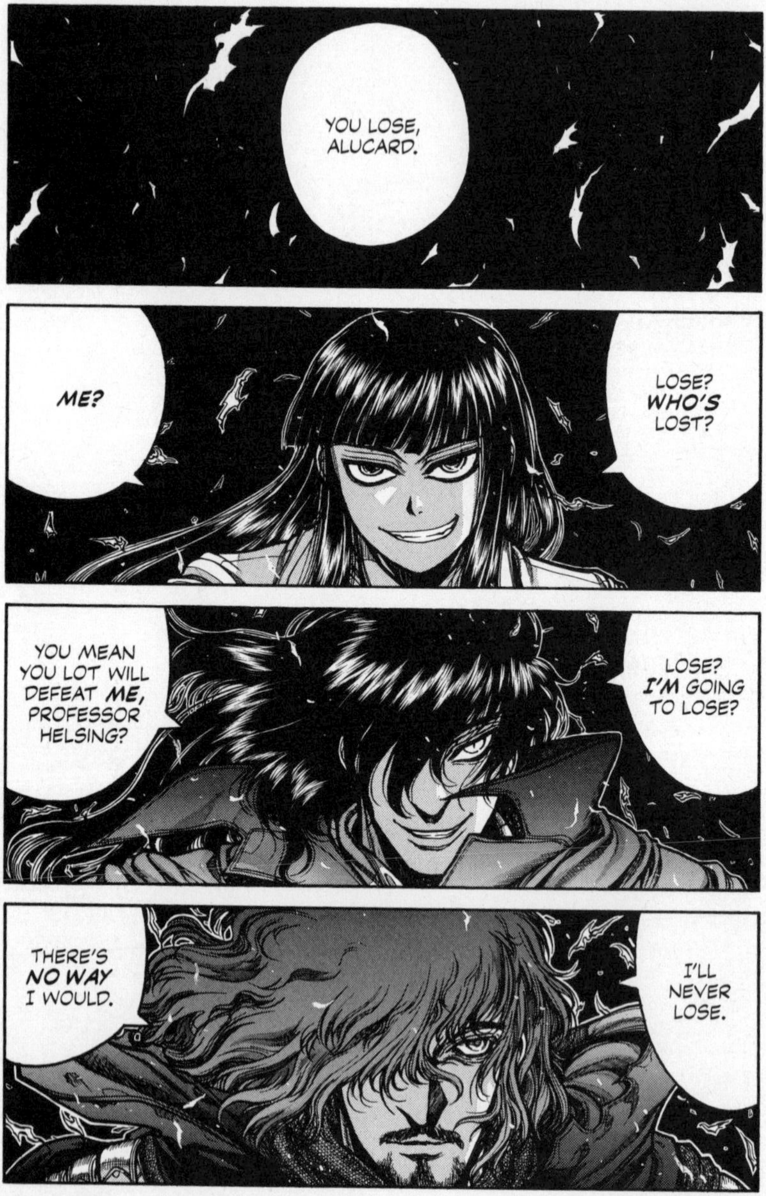
YOU LOSE, ALUCARD.
LOSE? WHO'S LOST?
ME?
LOSE? I'M GOING TO LOSE?
YOU MEAN YOU LOT WILL DEFEAT ME, PROFESSOR HELSING?
I'LL NEVER LOSE.
THERE'S NO WAY I WOULD.

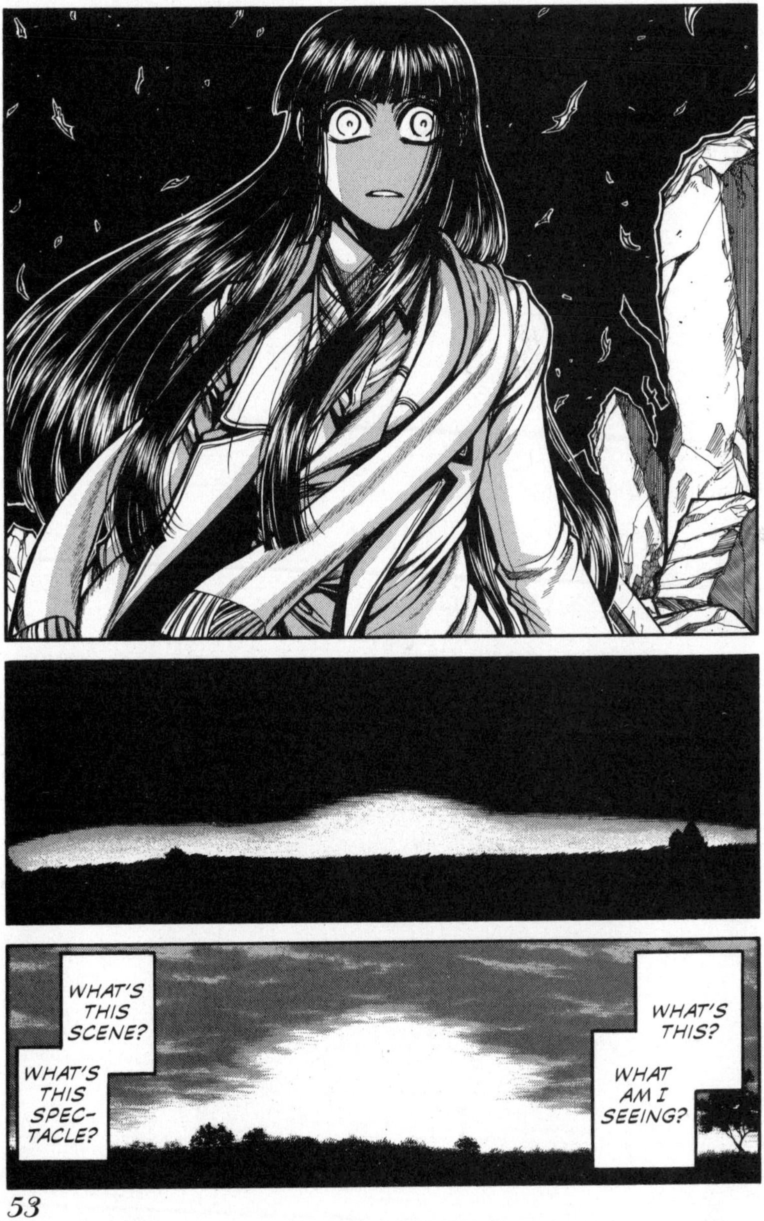
WHAT'S THIS?
WHAT AM I SEEING?
WHAT'S THIS SCENE?
WHAT'S THIS SPEC-TACLE?

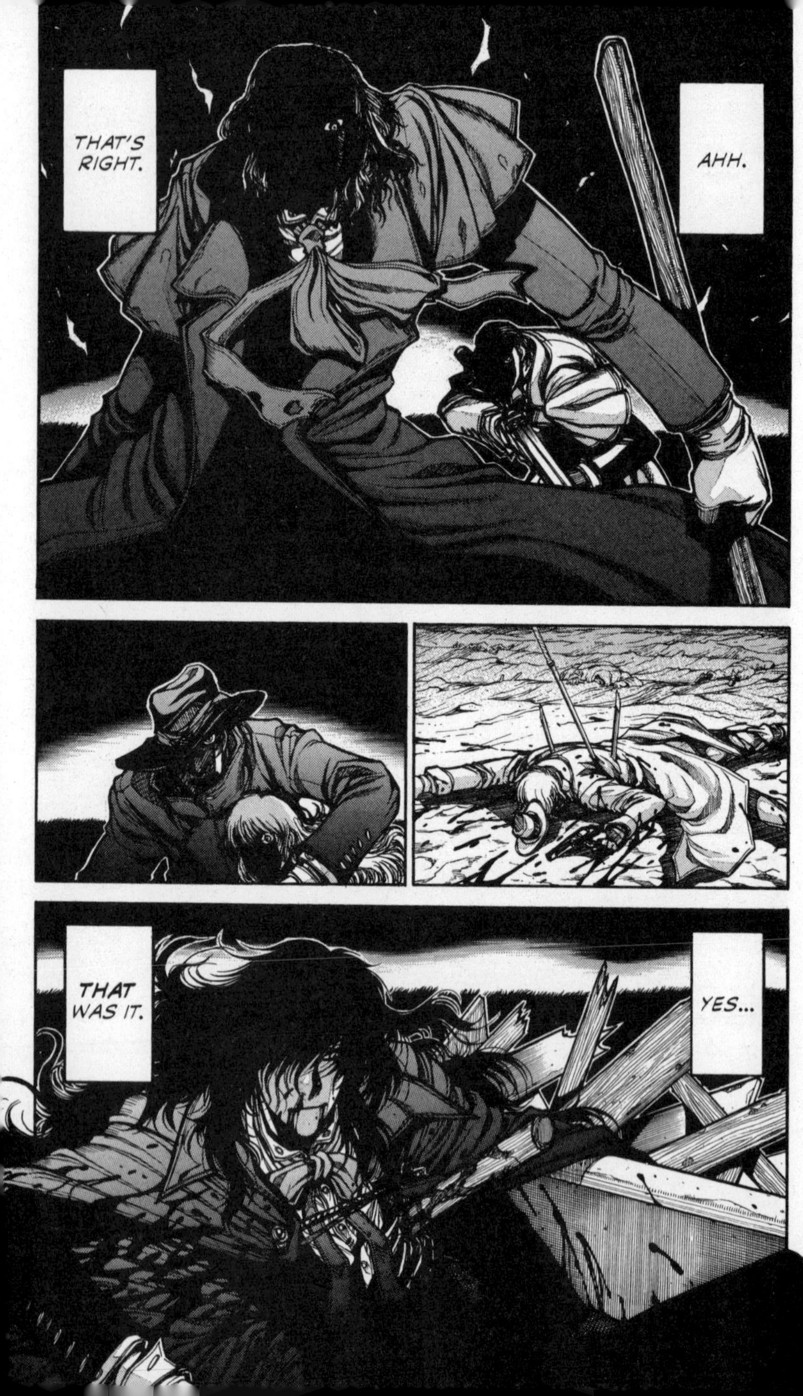
AHH.
THAT'S RIGHT.
YES...
THAT WAS IT.

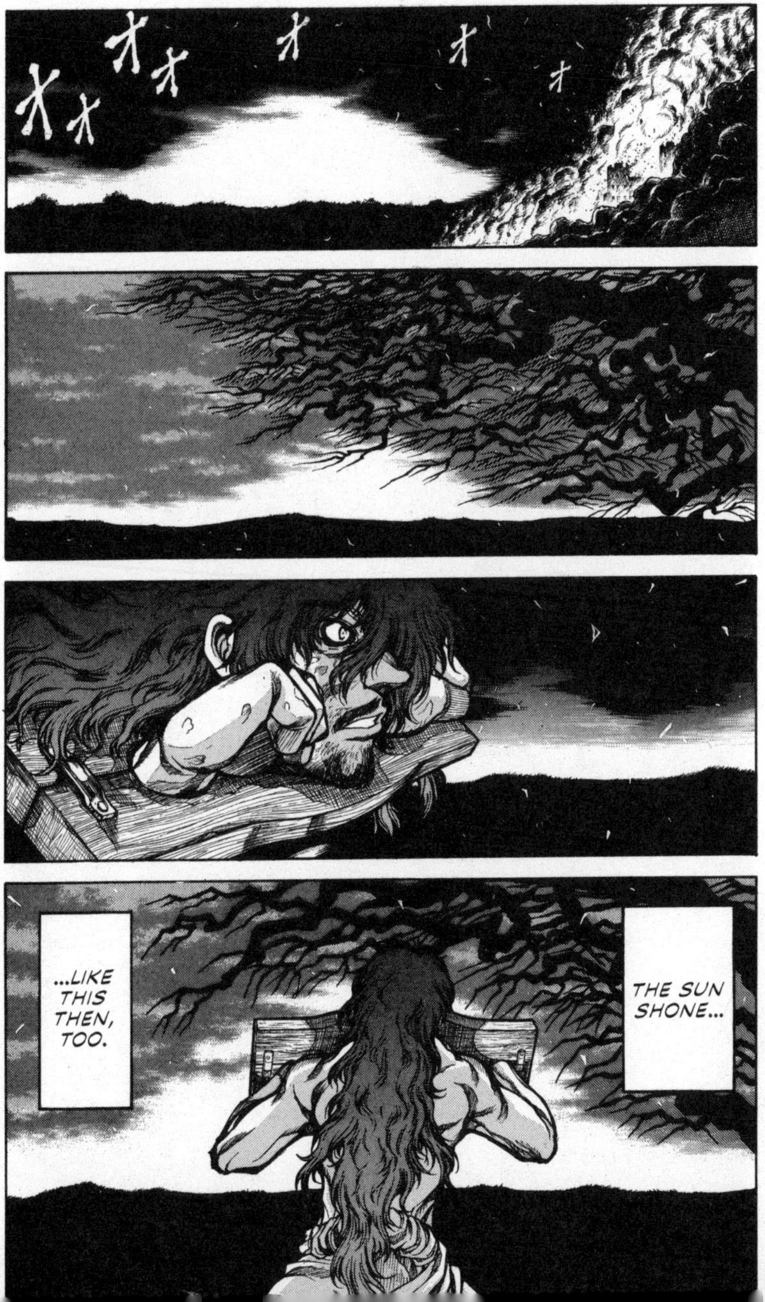
オオオオオオオ
THE SUN SHONE...
...LIKE THIS THEN, TOO.

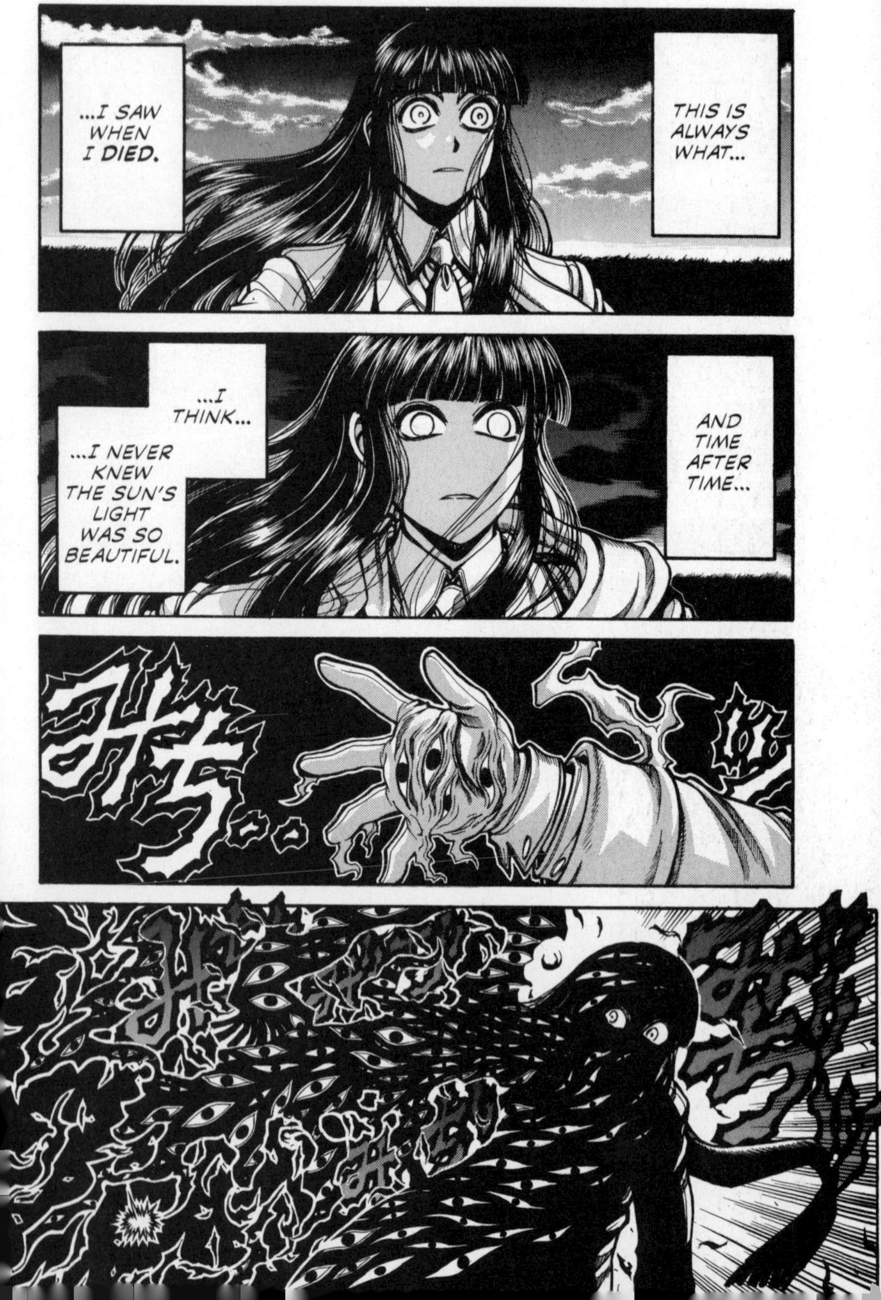
THIS IS ALWAYS WHAT...
...I SAW WHEN I DIED.
AND TIME AFTER TIME...
...I THINK...
...I NEVER KNEW THE SUN'S LIGHT WAS SO BEAUTIFUL.

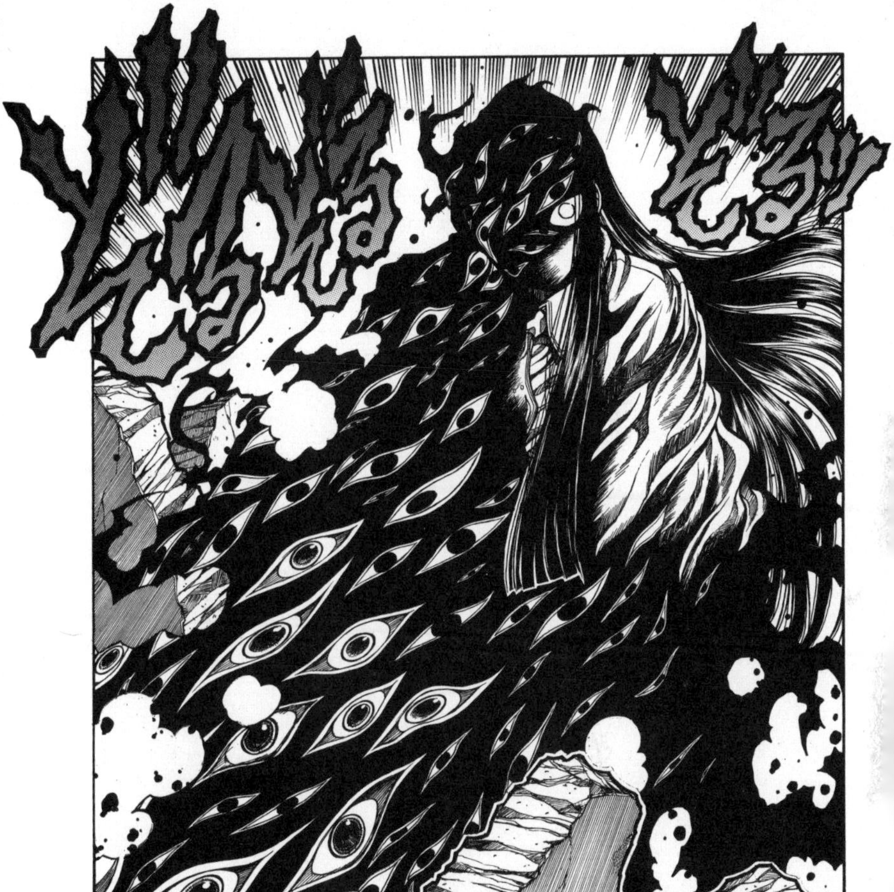

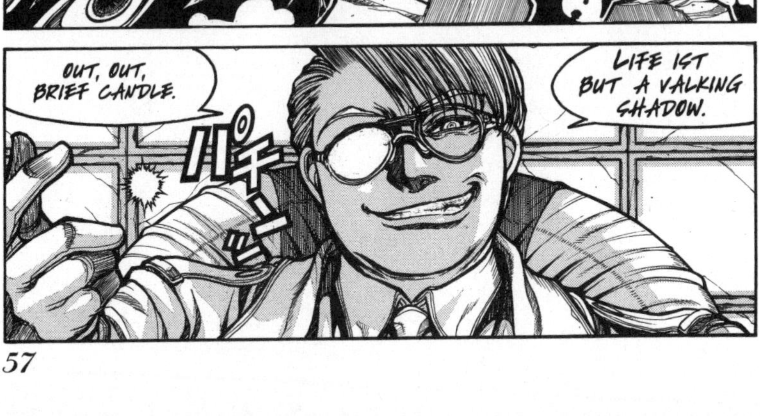
LIFE IST BUT A VALKING SHADOW.
OUT, OUT, BRIEF CANDLE.
パチーン

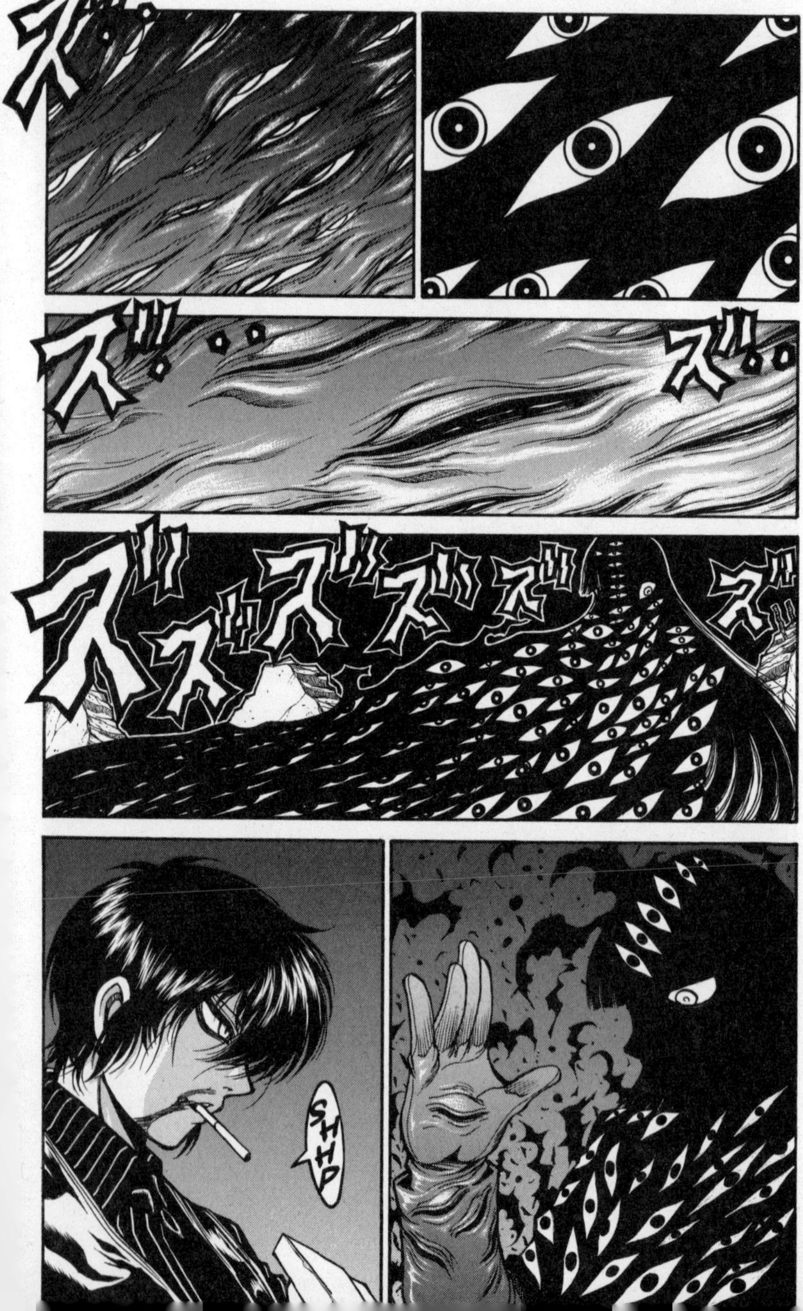
ズ…
ズ…
ズ…
ズズズズズズ
SHHP

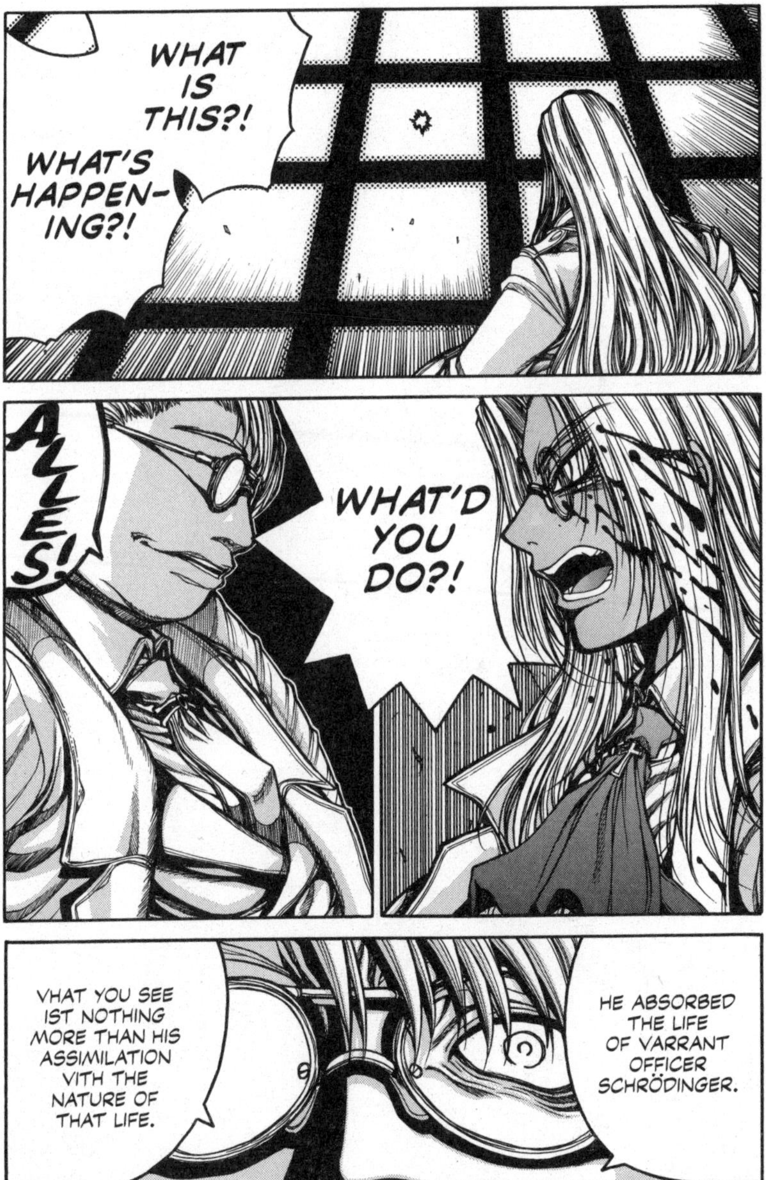
WHAT IS THIS?!
WHAT'S HAPPEN-ING?!
WHAT'D YOU DO?!
ALLES!
HE ABSORBED THE LIFE OF VARRANT OFFICER SCHRÖDINGER.
VHAT YOU SEE IST NOTHING MORE THAN HIS ASSIMILATION VITH THE NATURE OF THAT LIFE.

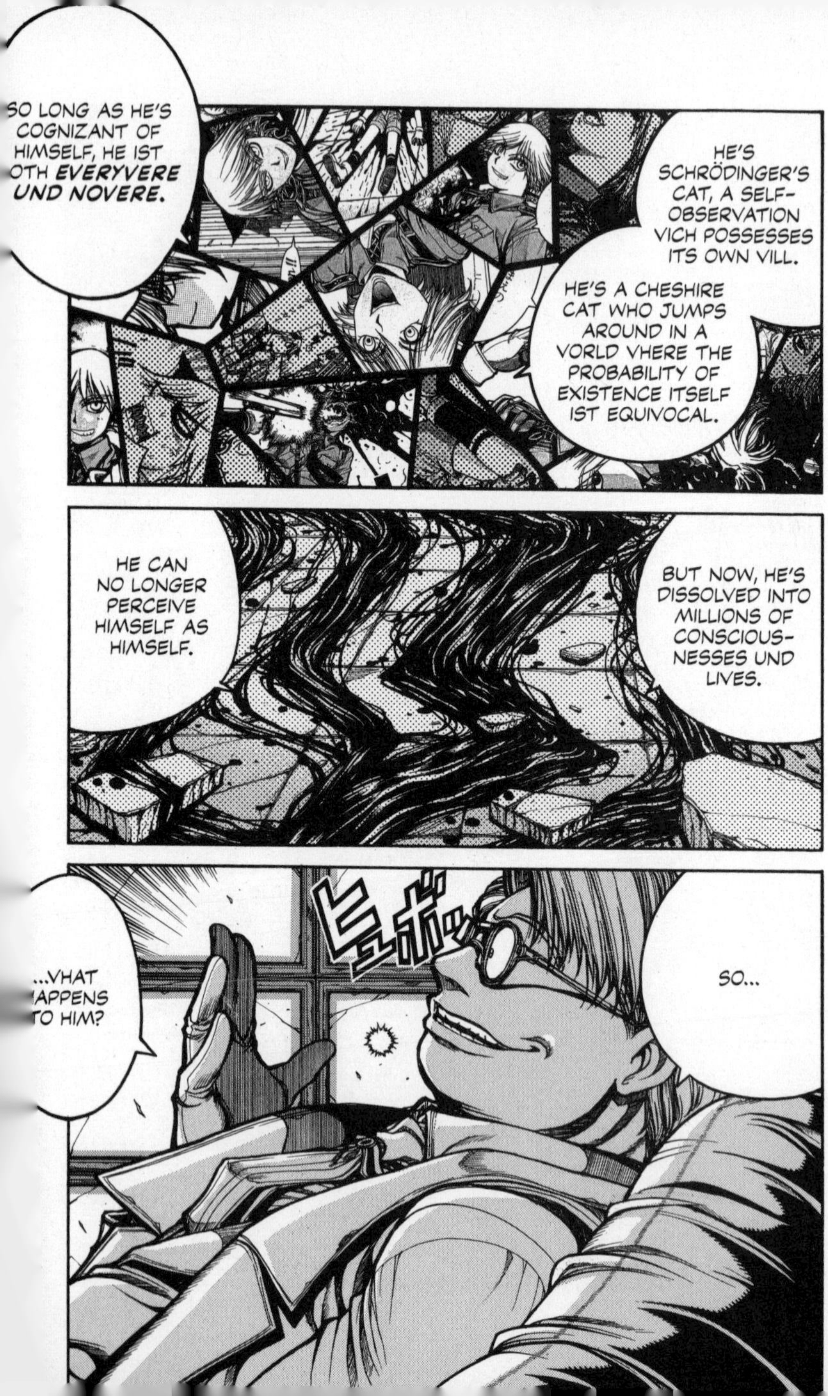
HE'S SCHRÖDINGER'S CAT, A SELF-OBSERVATION VICH POSSESSES ITS OWN VILL.
HE'S A CHESHIRE CAT WHO JUMPS AROUND IN A VORLD VHERE THE PROBABILITY OF EXISTENCE ITSELF IST EQUIVOCAL.
SO LONG AS HE'S COGNIZANT OF HIMSELF, HE IST OTH **EVERYVERE UND NOVERE.**
BUT NOW, HE'S DISSOLVED INTO MILLIONS OF CONSCIOUS-NESSES UND LIVES.
HE CAN NO LONGER PERCEIVE HIMSELF AS HIMSELF.
ヒュボッ
SO...
...VHAT APPENS TO HIM?

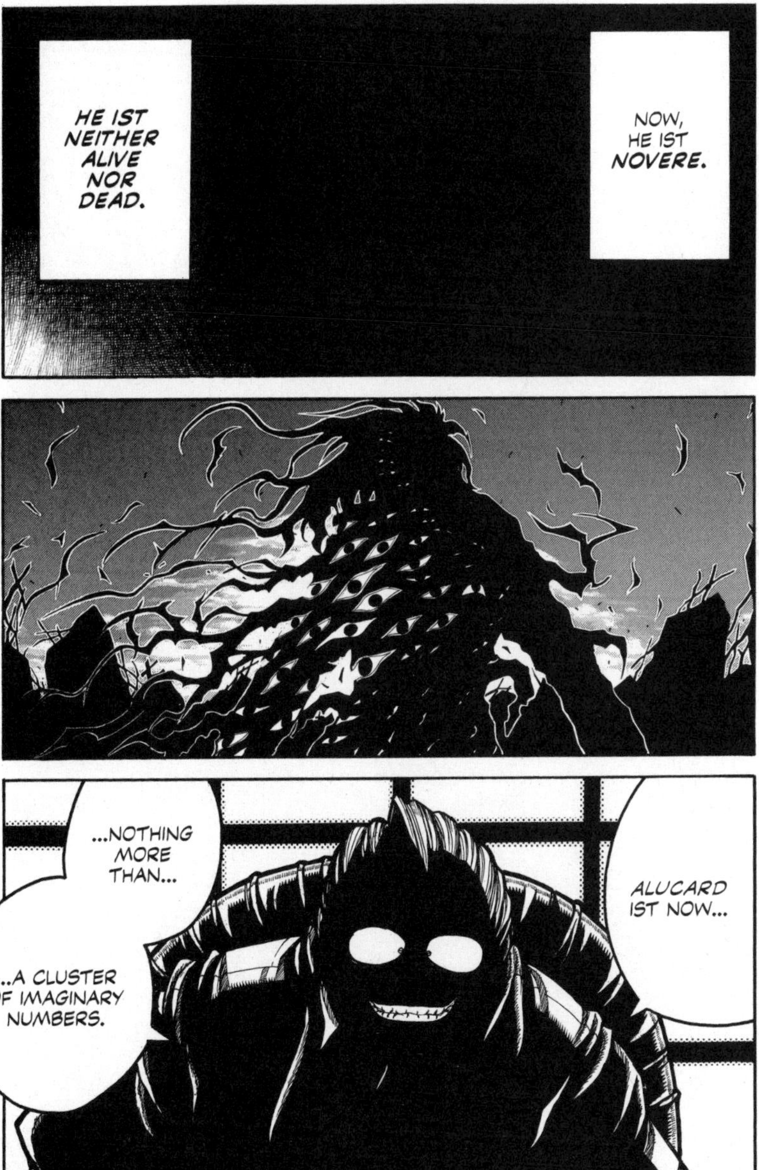
NOW, HE IST NOVERE.
HE IST NEITHER ALIVE NOR DEAD.
ALUCARD IST NOW...
...NOTHING MORE THAN...
...A CLUSTER OF IMAGINARY NUMBERS.

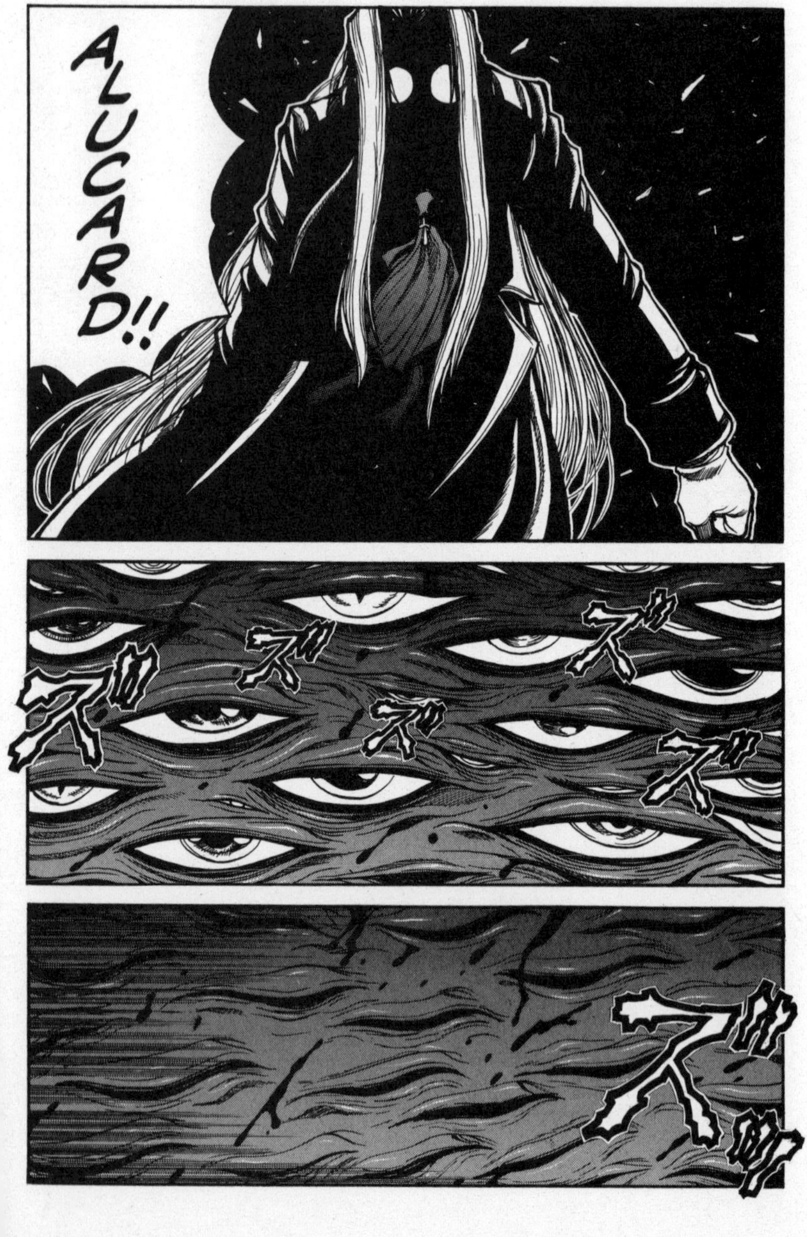
ALUCARD!!

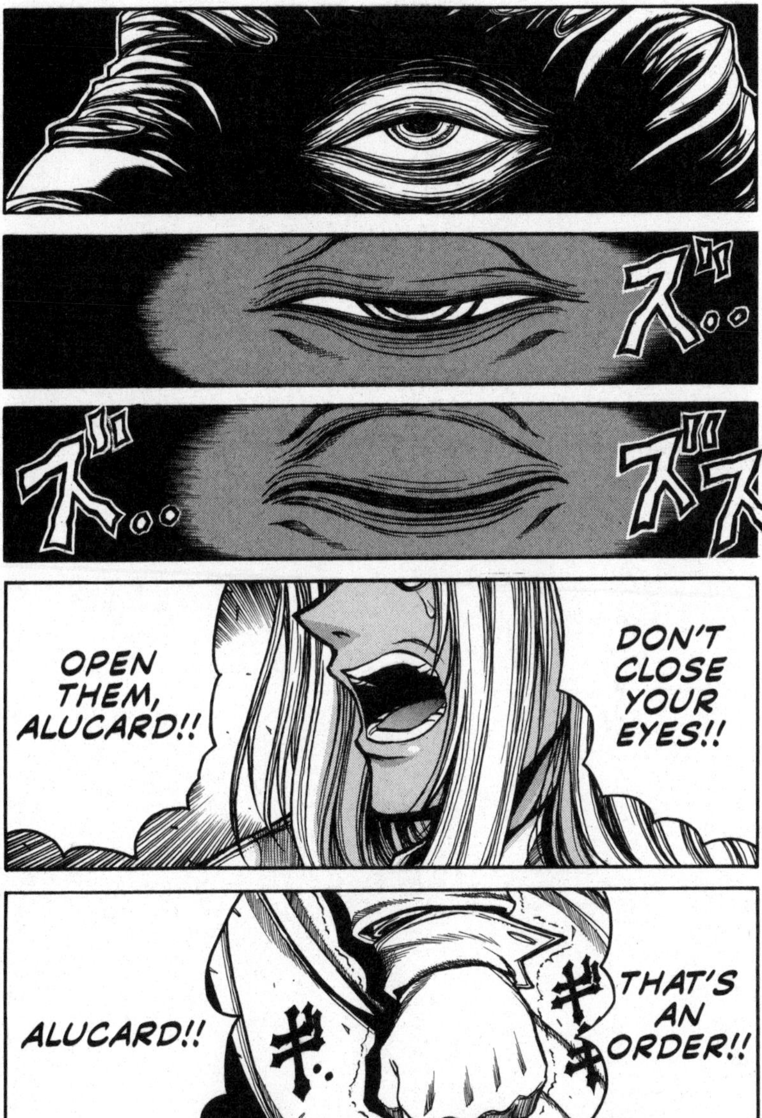
ズ‥
ズズ‥
ズ‥
DON'T CLOSE YOUR EYES!!
OPEN THEM, ALUCARD!!
ギギ
THAT'S AN ORDER!!
ギ‥
ALUCARD!!

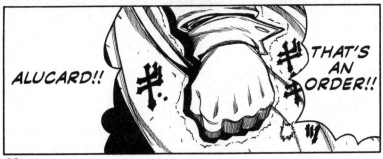

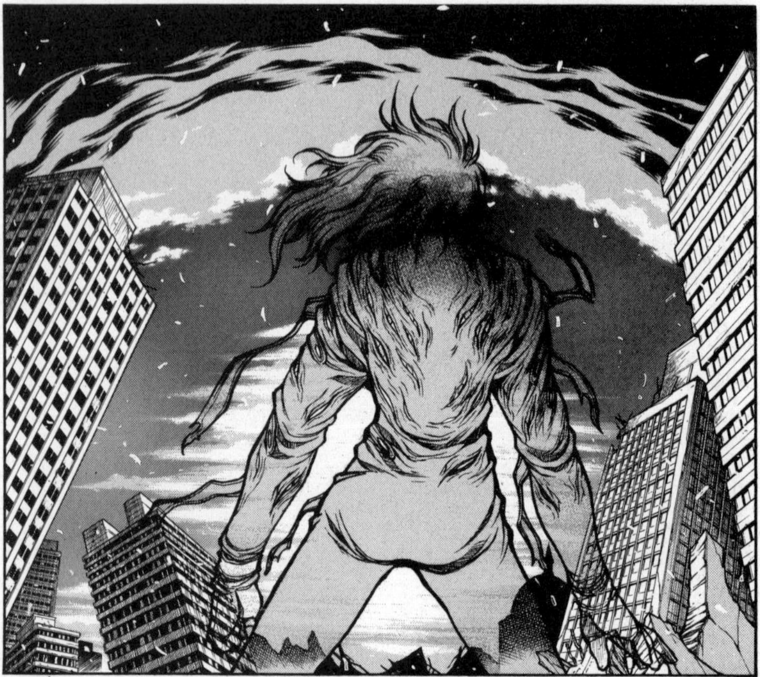
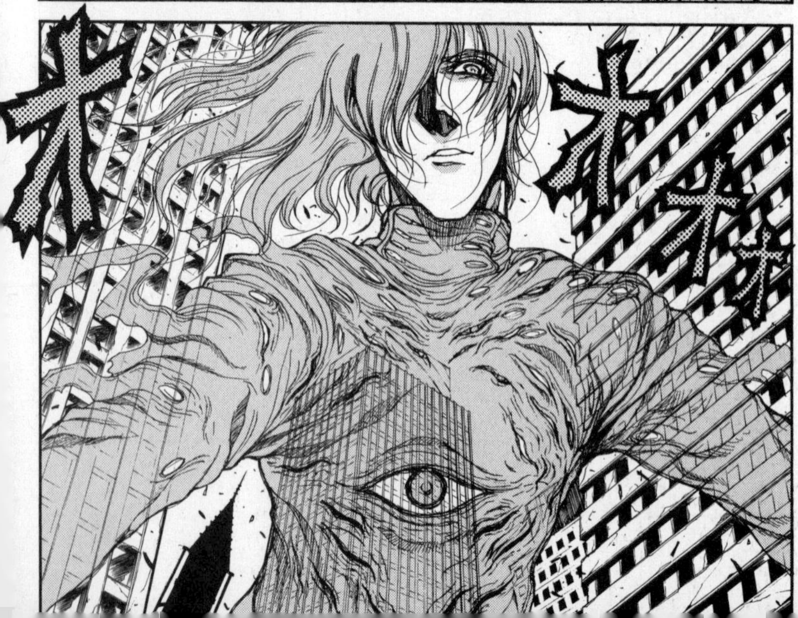
オオオ
オ

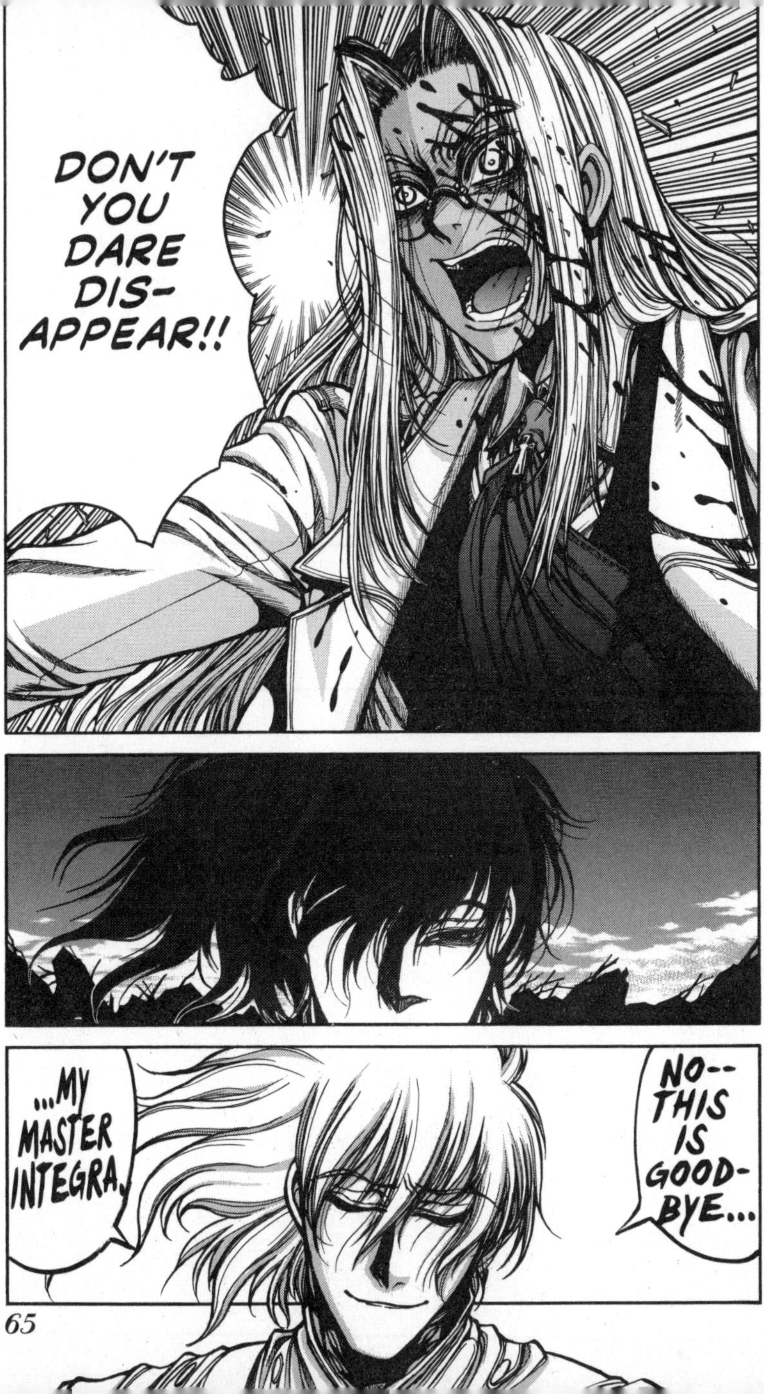
DON'T YOU DARE DIS-APPEAR!!
NO-- THIS IS GOOD-BYE...
...MY MASTER INTEGRA.

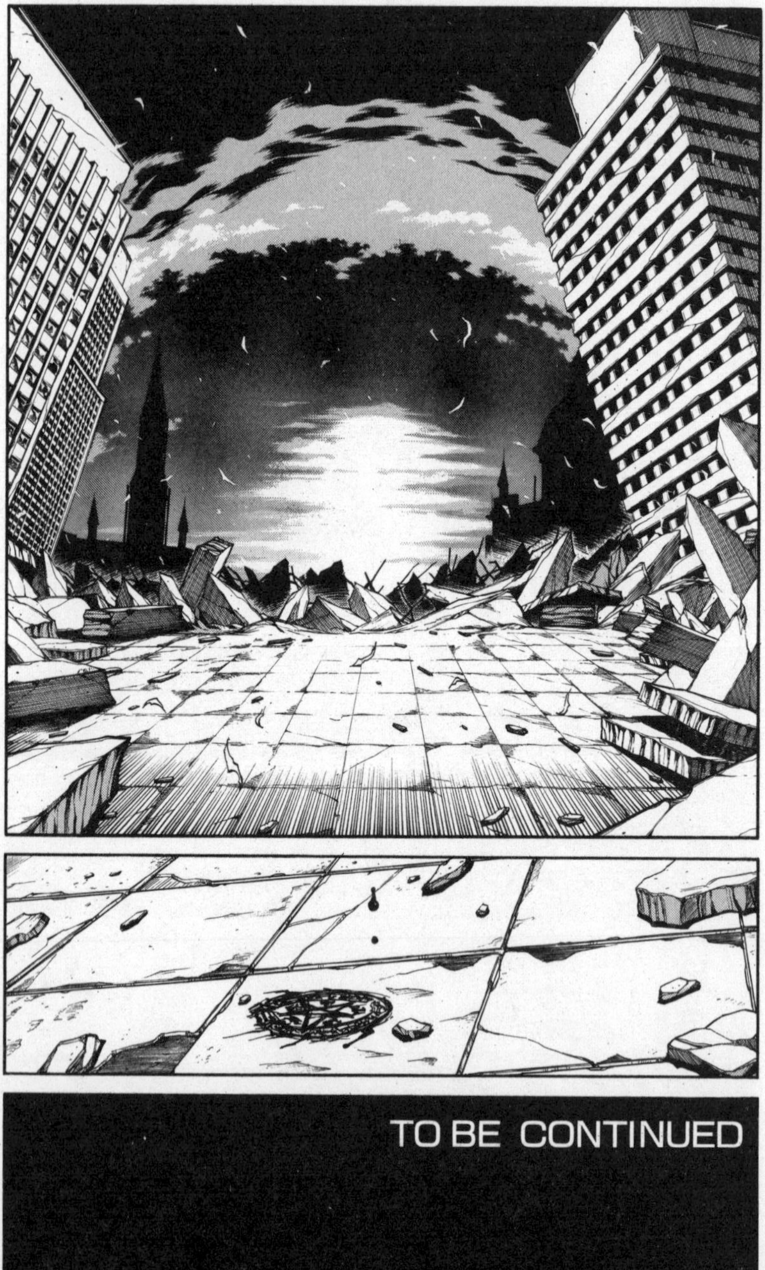
TO BE CONTINUED

ORDER 4/END

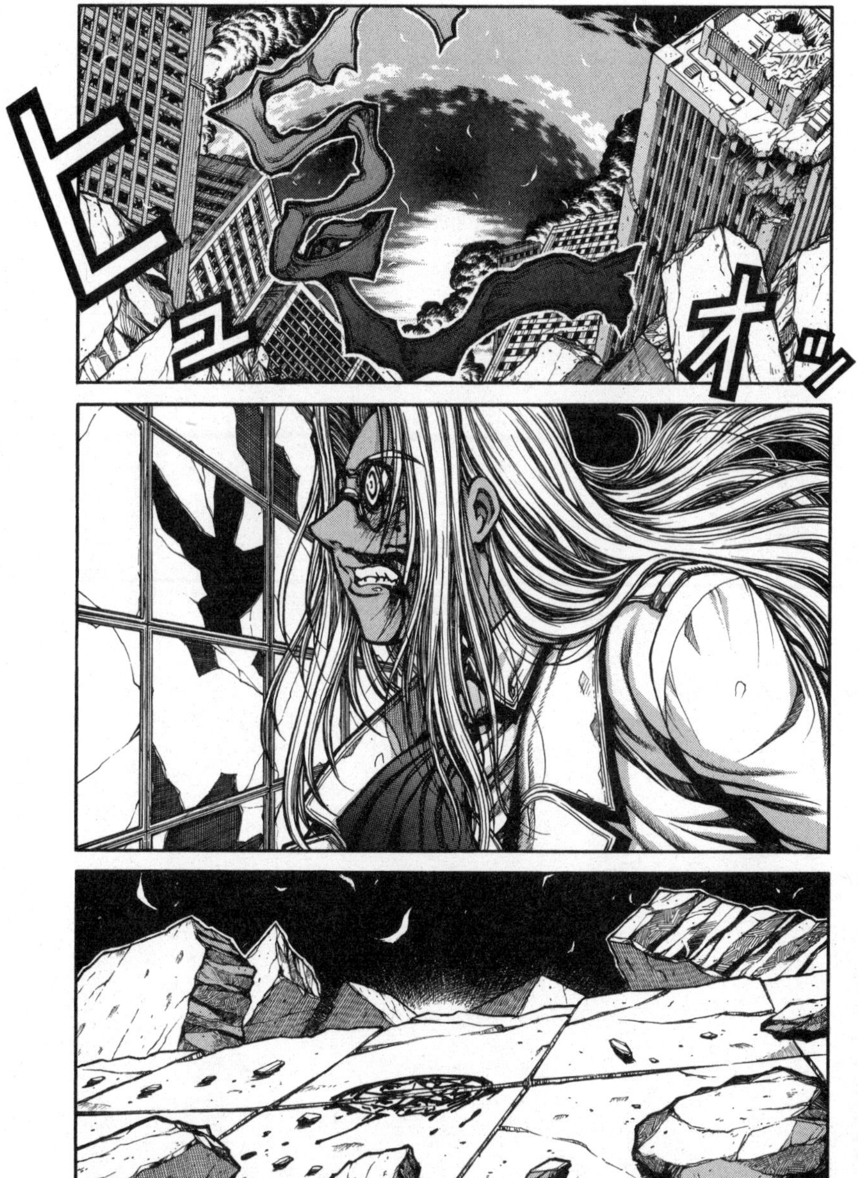
ヒュオッ

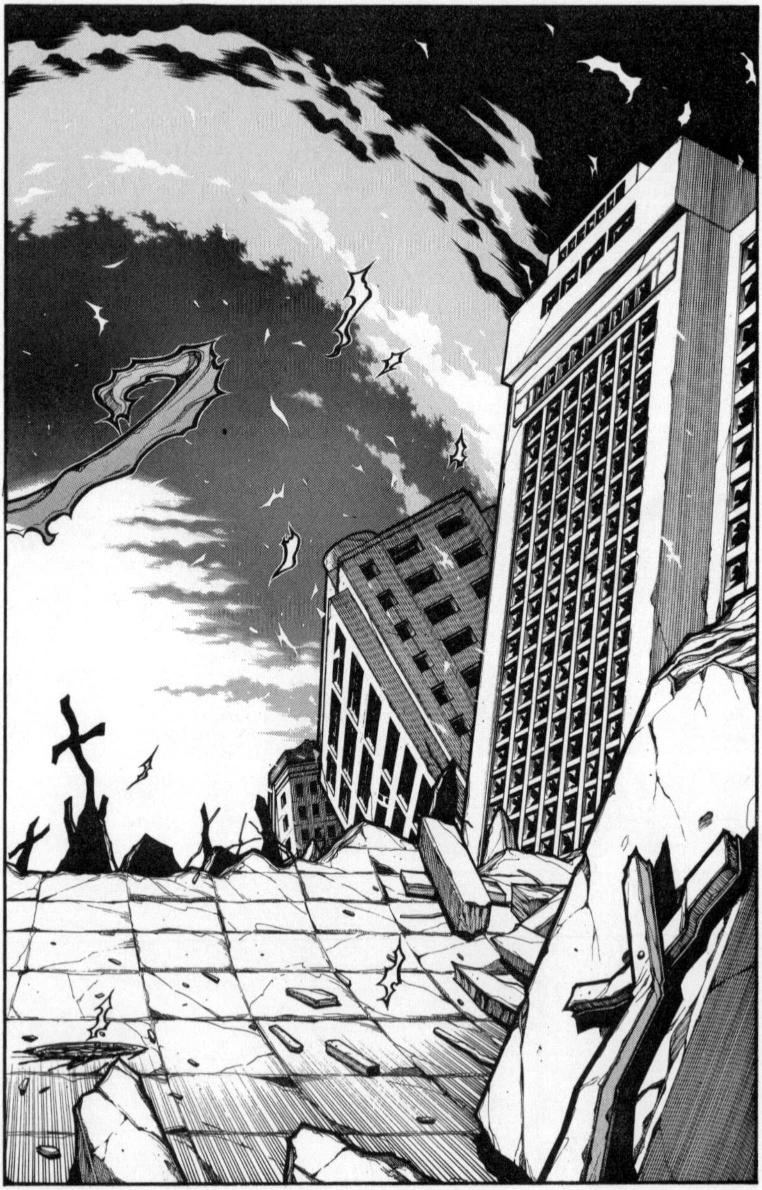

ORDER 5

BLACK ONYX ③

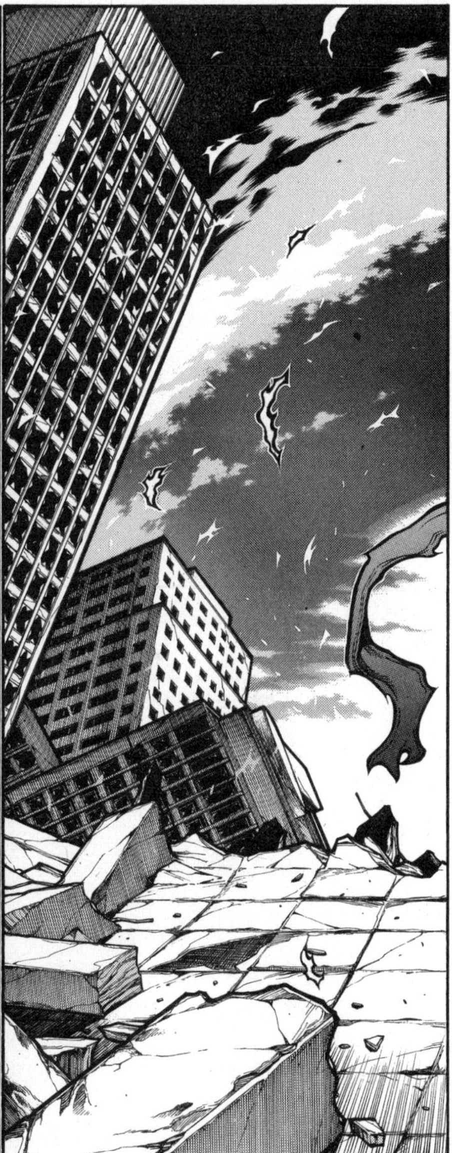

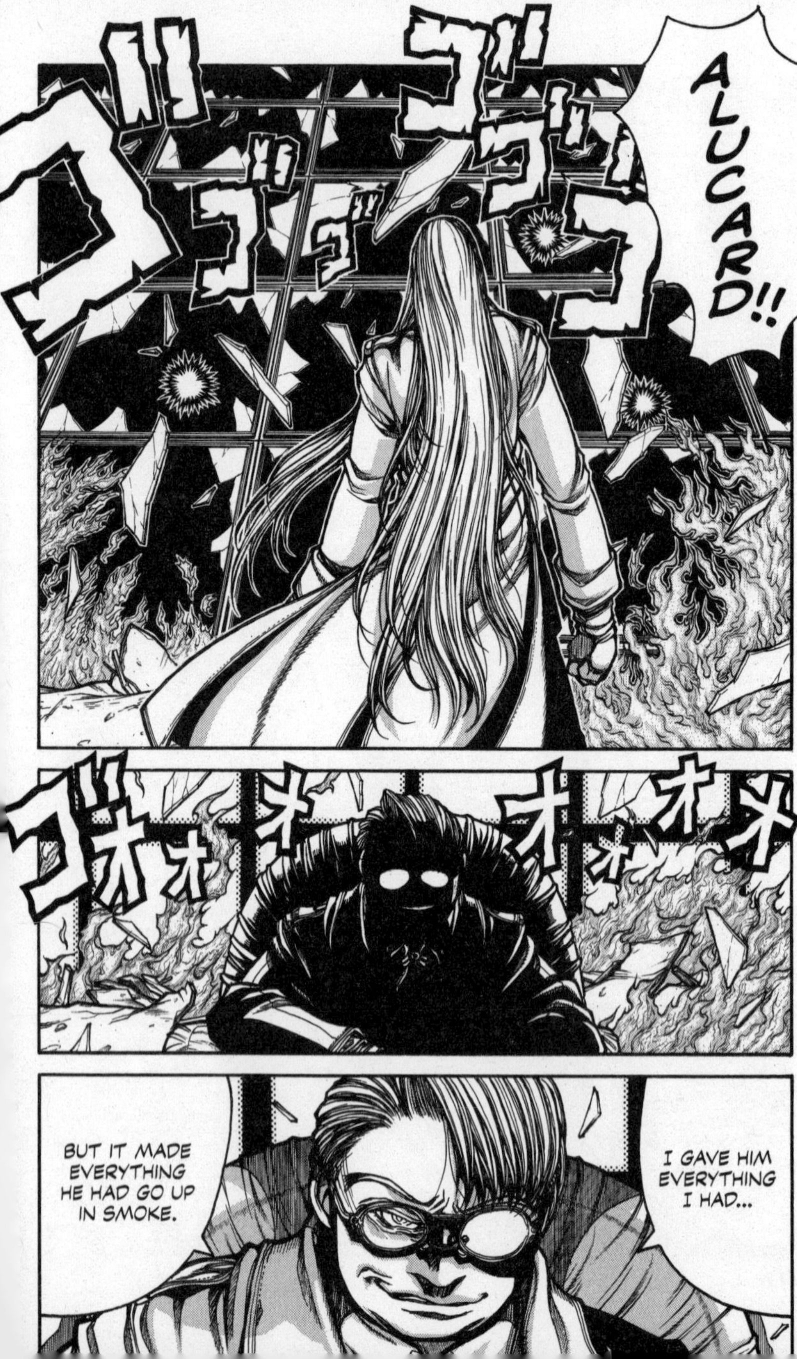
ALUCARD!!
I GAVE HIM EVERYTHING I HAD...
BUT IT MADE EVERYTHING HE HAD GO UP IN SMOKE.

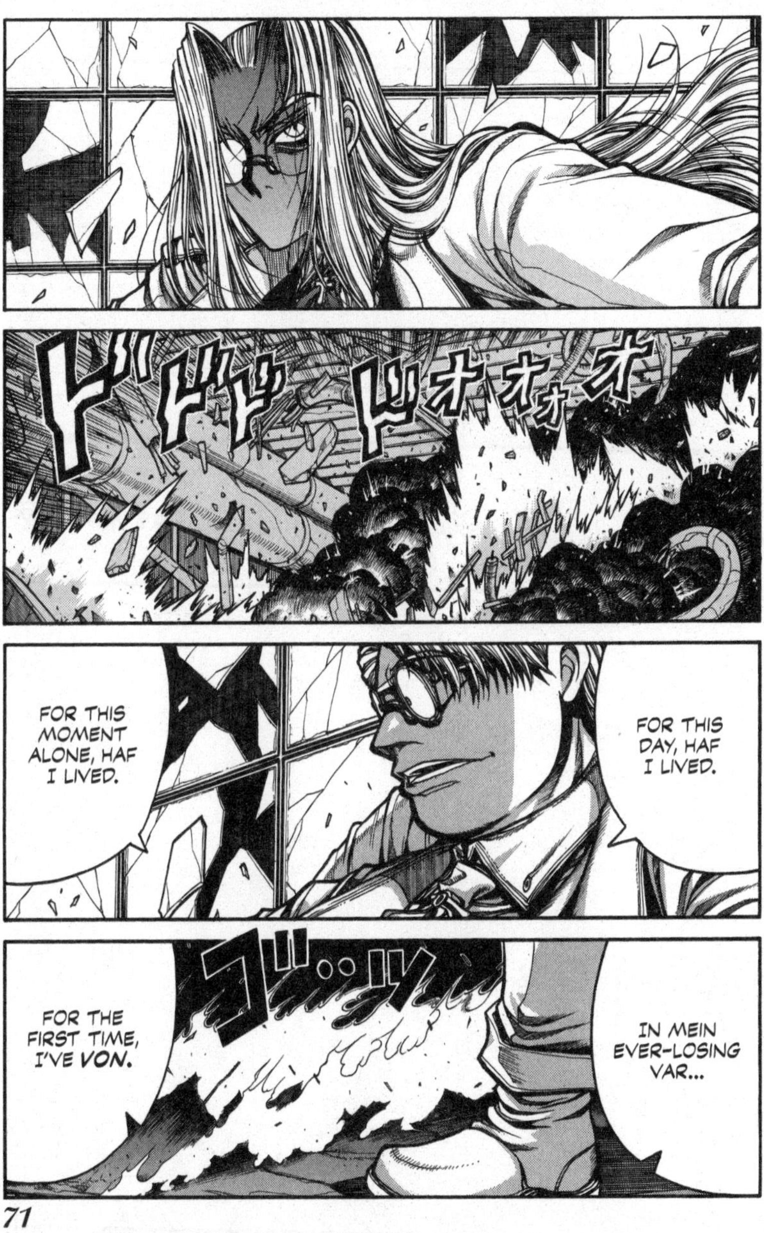
FOR THIS DAY, HAF I LIVED.
FOR THIS MOMENT ALONE, HAF I LIVED.
IN MEIN EVER-LOSING VAR...
FOR THE FIRST TIME, I'VE **VON**.

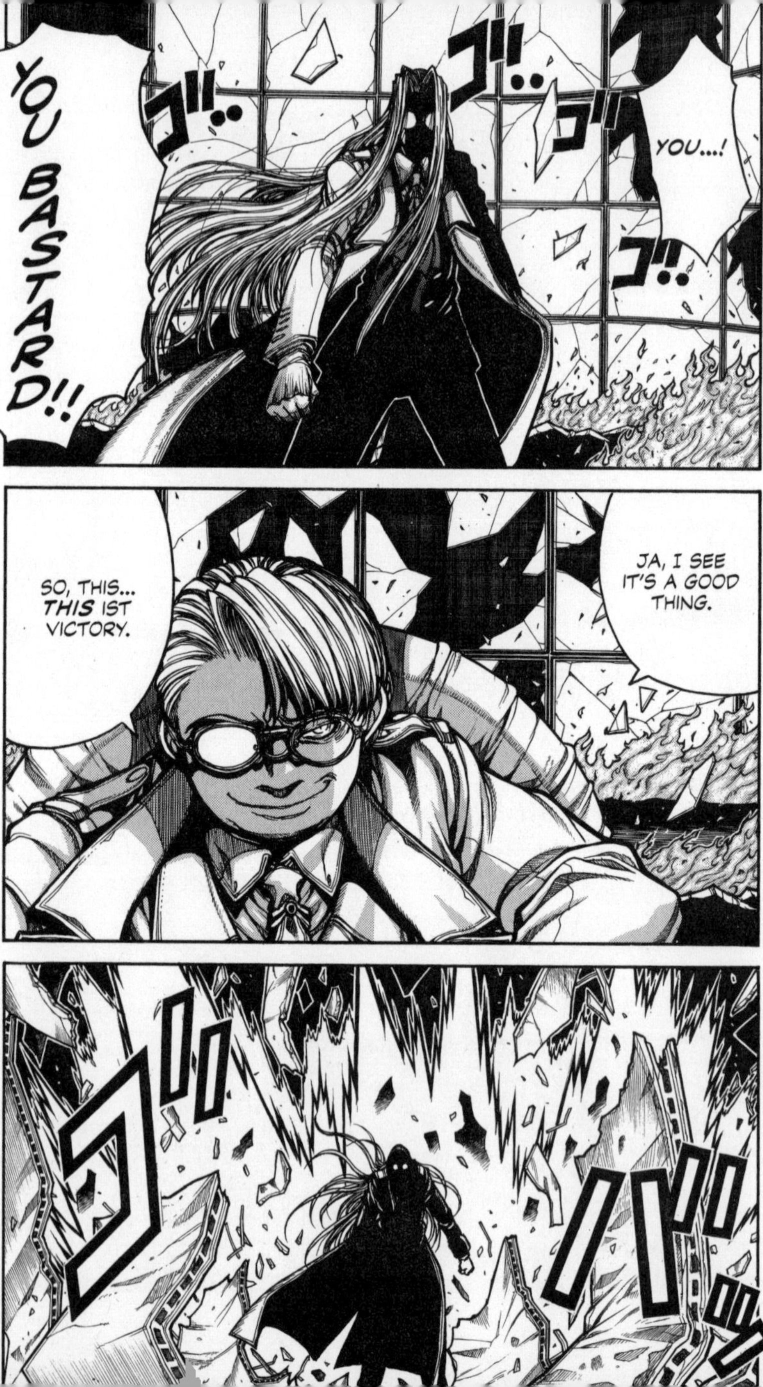
YOU...!
YOU BASTARD!!
JA, I SEE IT'S A GOOD THING.
SO, THIS... *THIS* IST VICTORY.

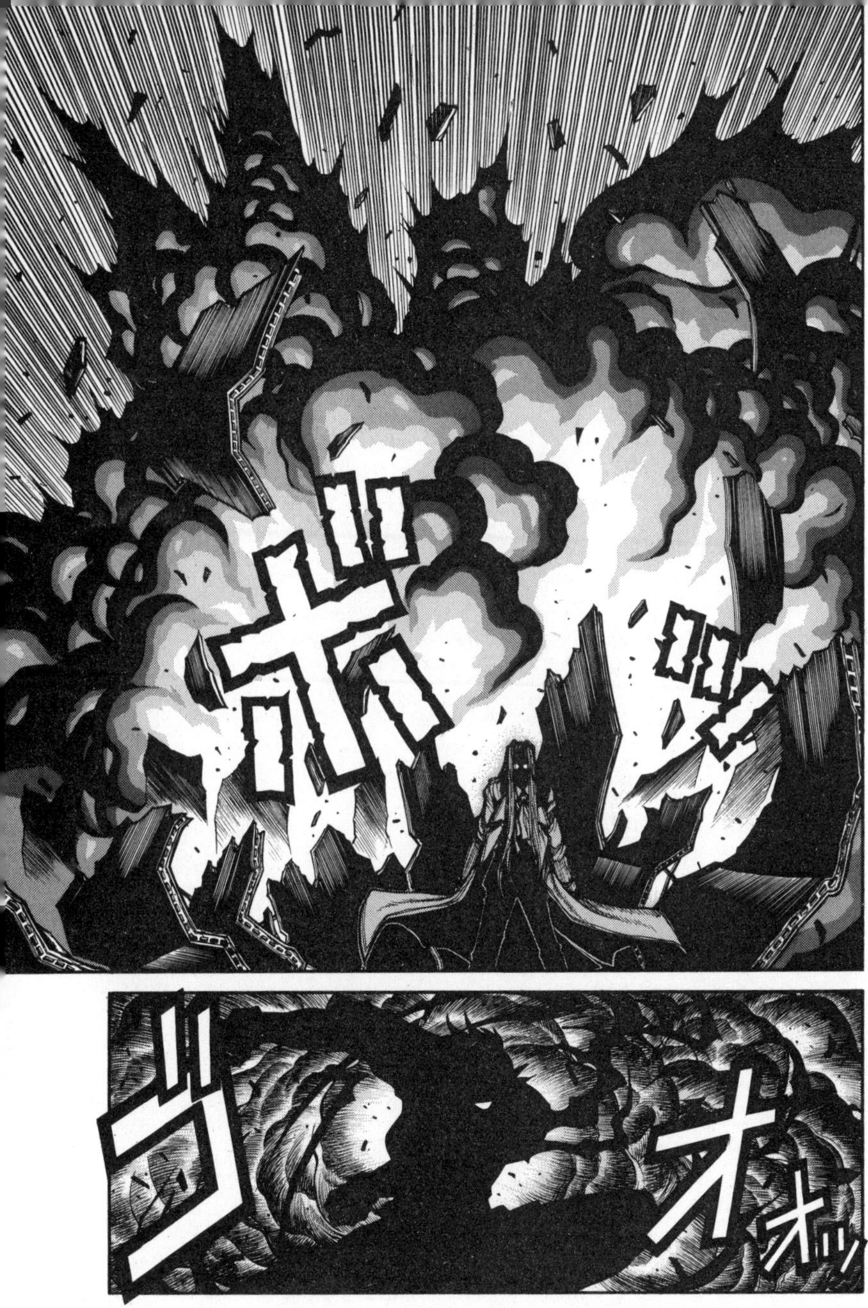
ボ
ゴオオッ

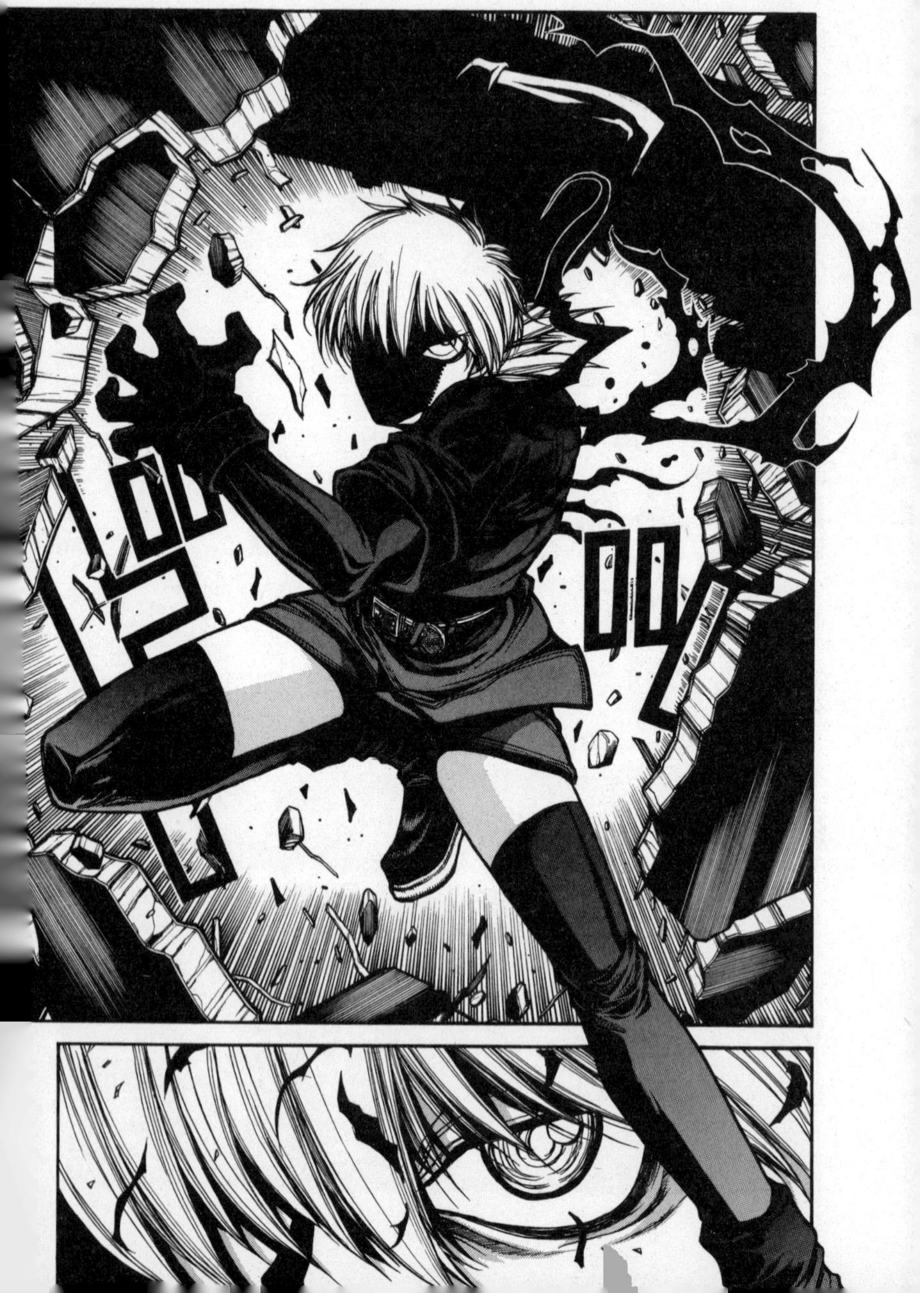

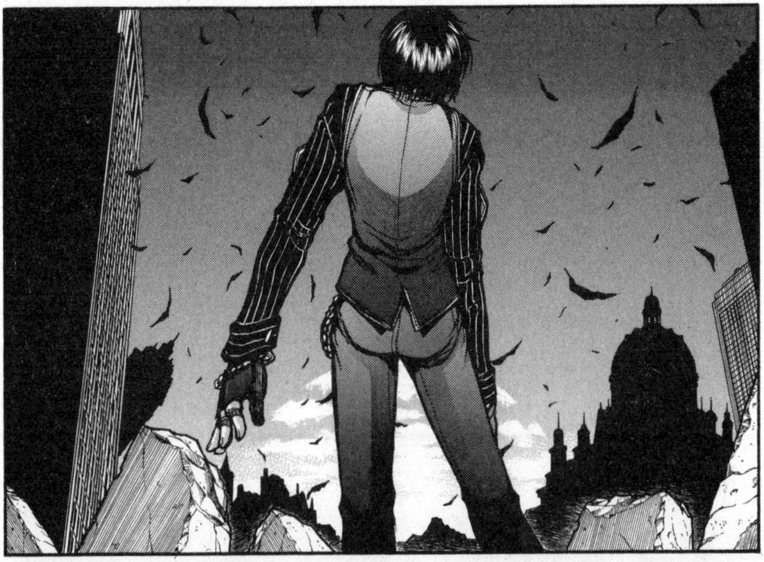

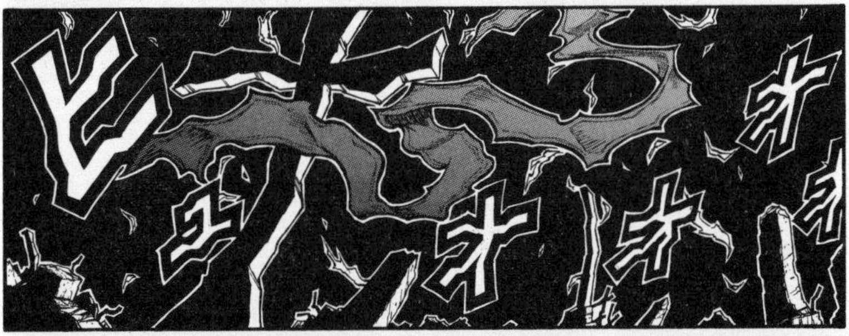
ヒュゥオオオオ

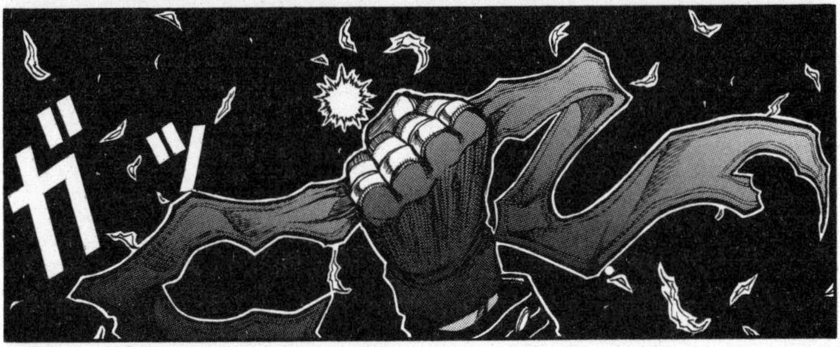
ガッ

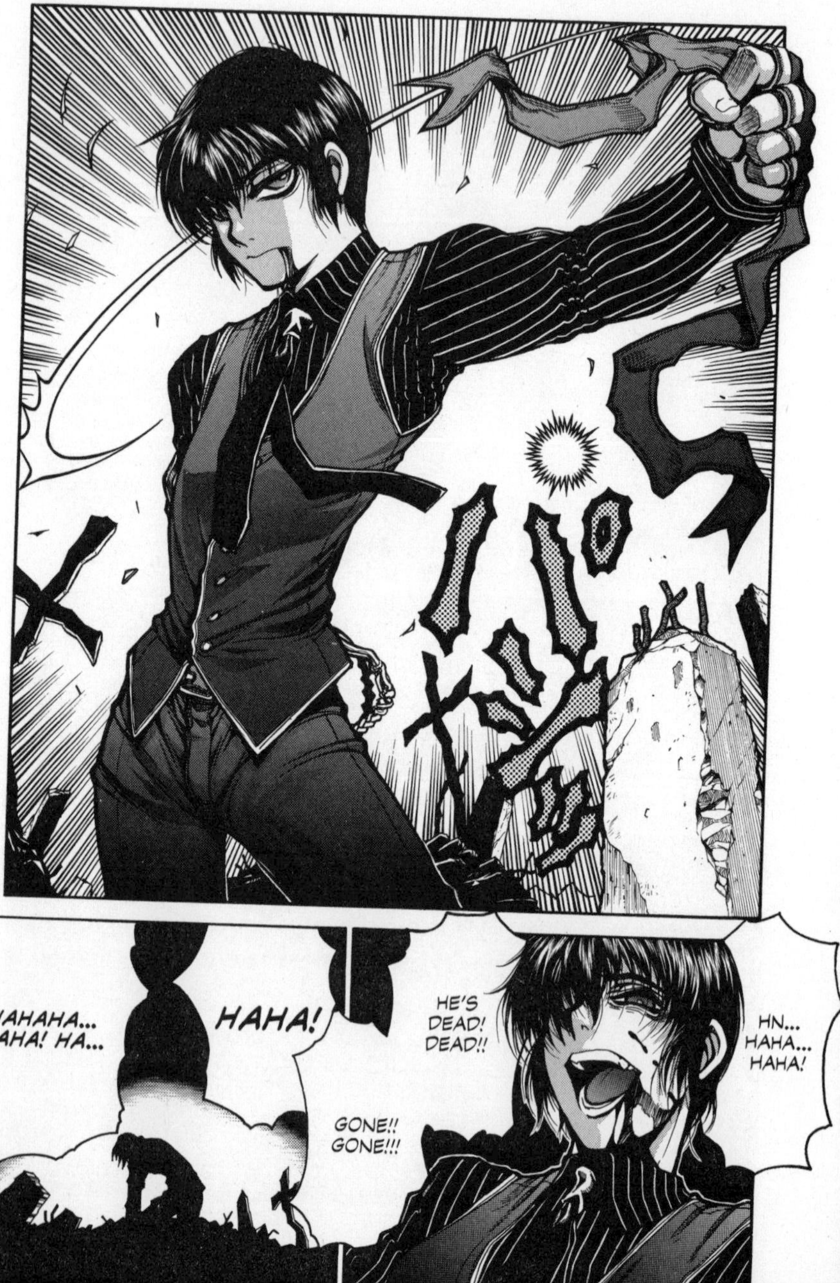
HN... HAHA... HAHA!
HE'S DEAD! DEAD!!
GONE!! GONE!!!
HAHA!
HAHAHA... HAHA! HA...

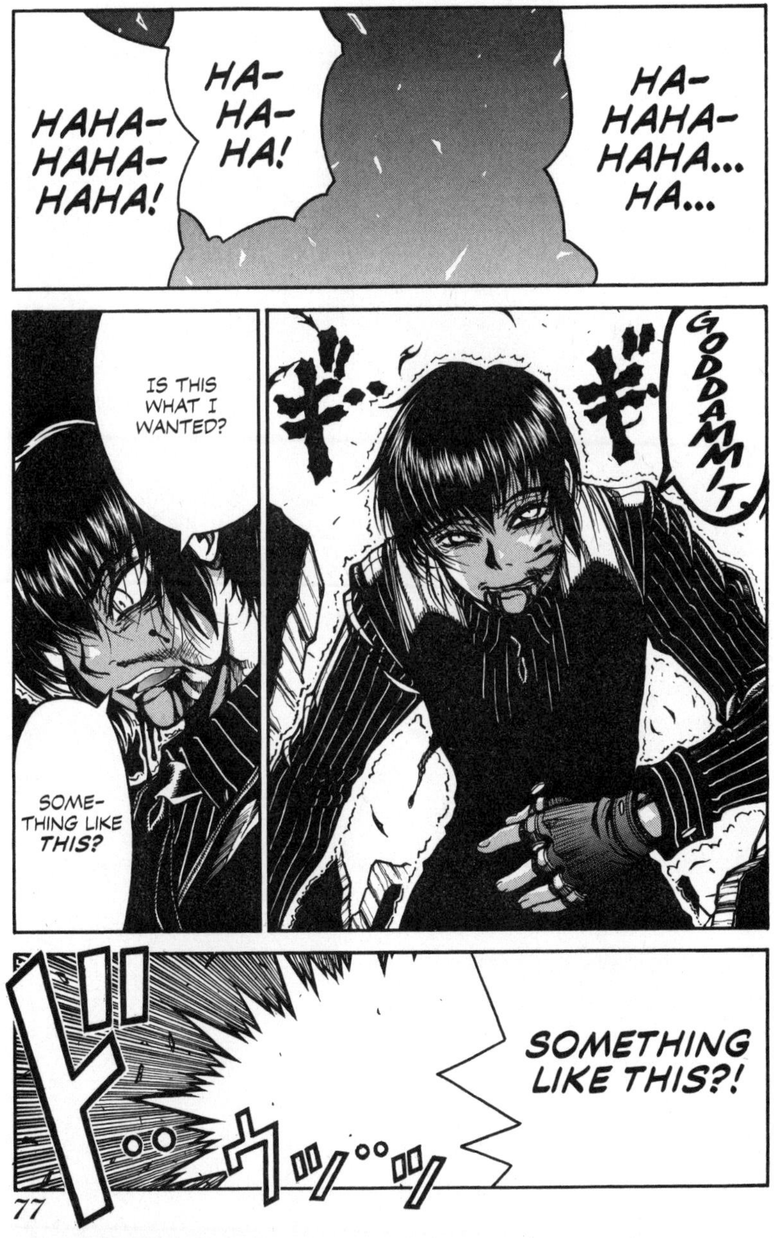
HA-HAHA-HAHA... HA...
HA-HA-HA!
HAHA-HAHA-HAHA!
GODDAMMIT.
IS THIS WHAT I WANTED?
SOME-THING LIKE THIS?
SOMETHING LIKE THIS?!

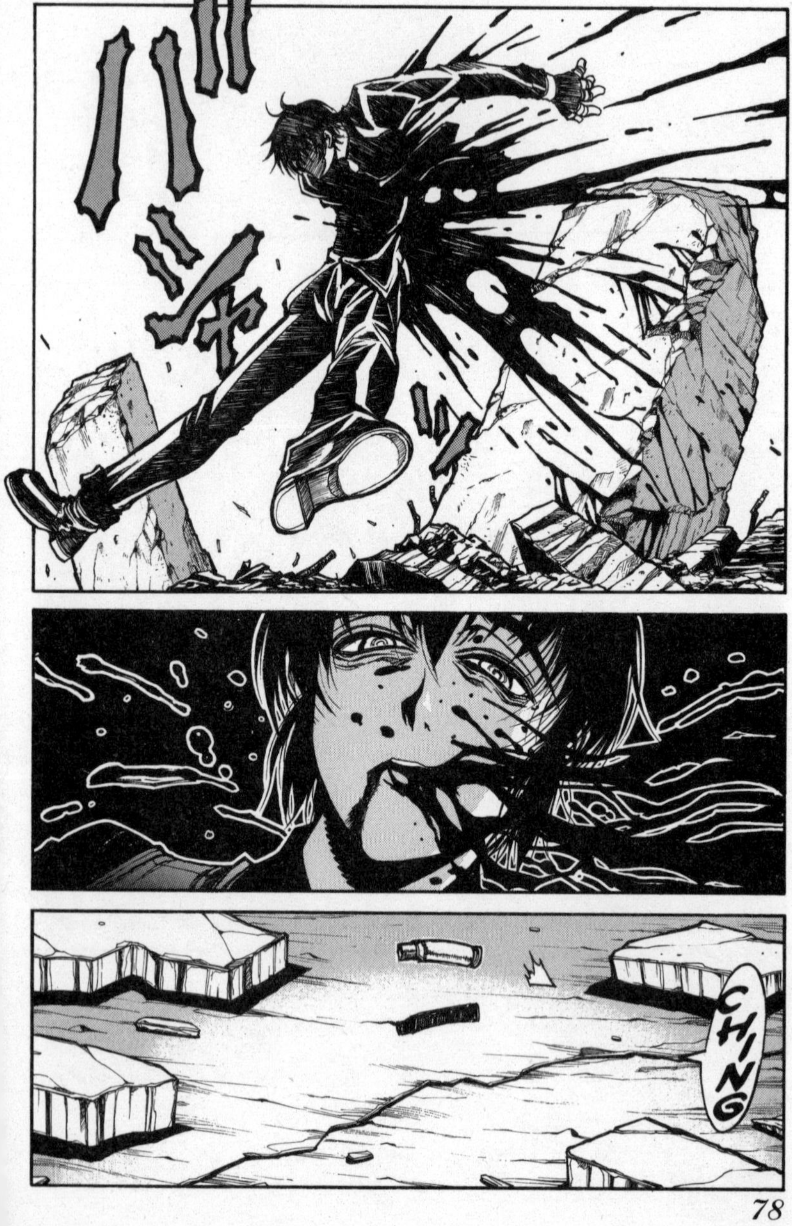
バシャ
CHING

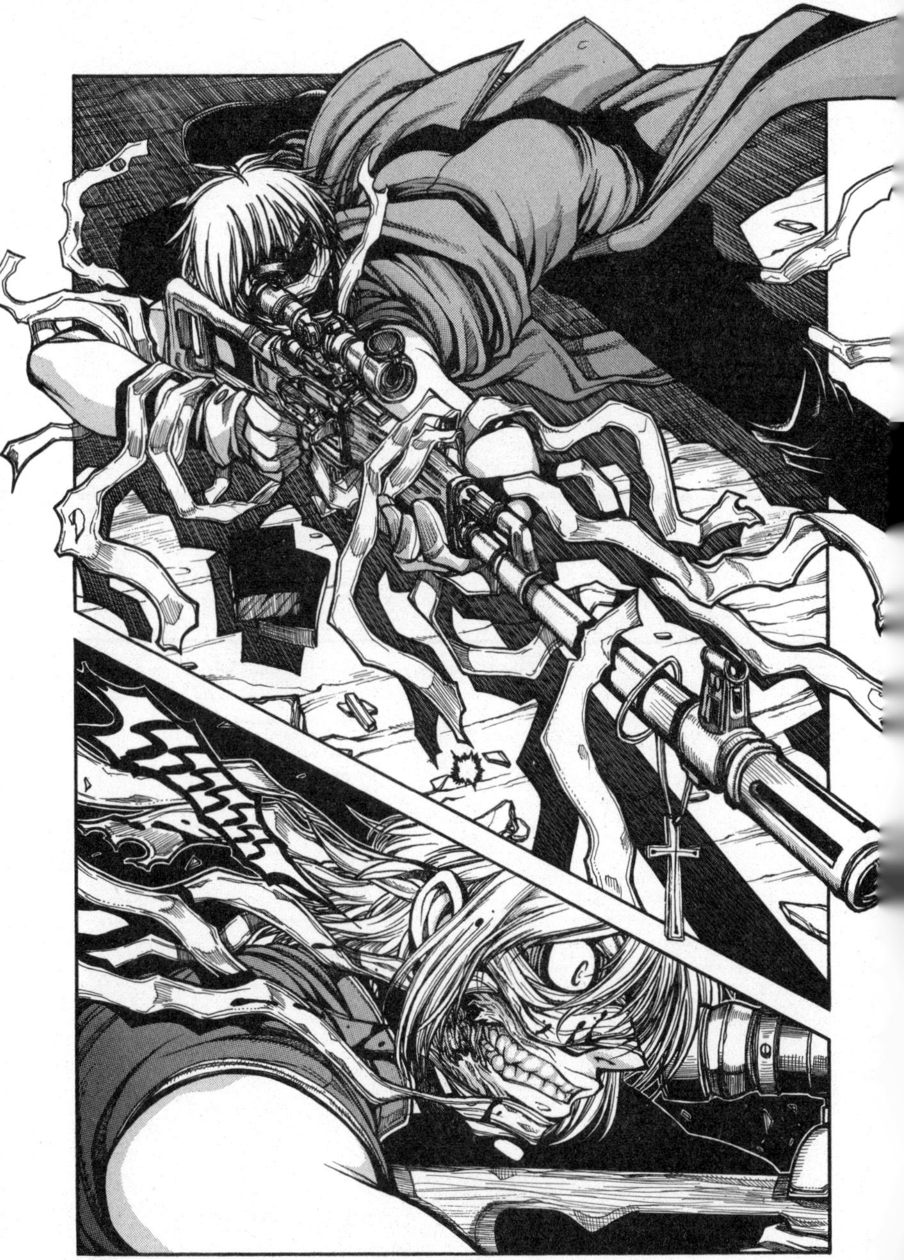

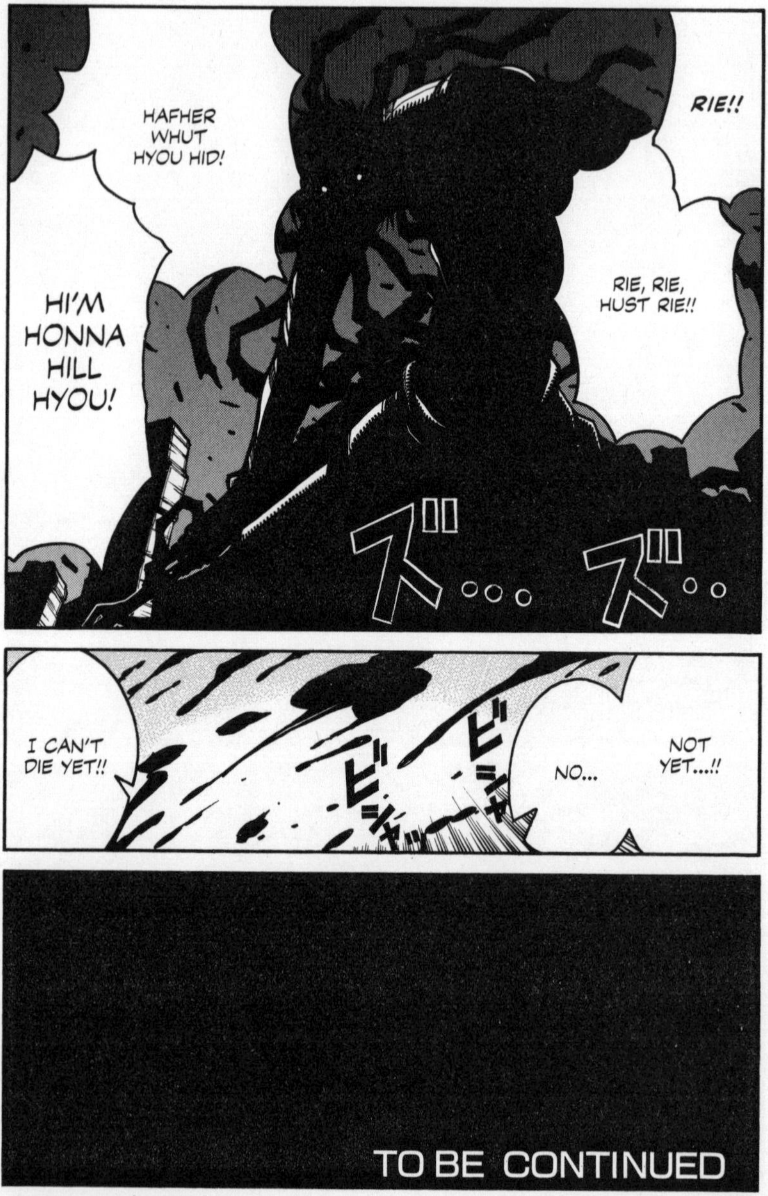
RIE!!
RIE, RIE, HUST RIE!!
HAFHER WHUT HYOU HID!
HI'M HONNA HILL HYOU!
ズ..
ズ...
NOT YET...!!
NO...
I CAN'T DIE YET!!
TO BE CONTINUED

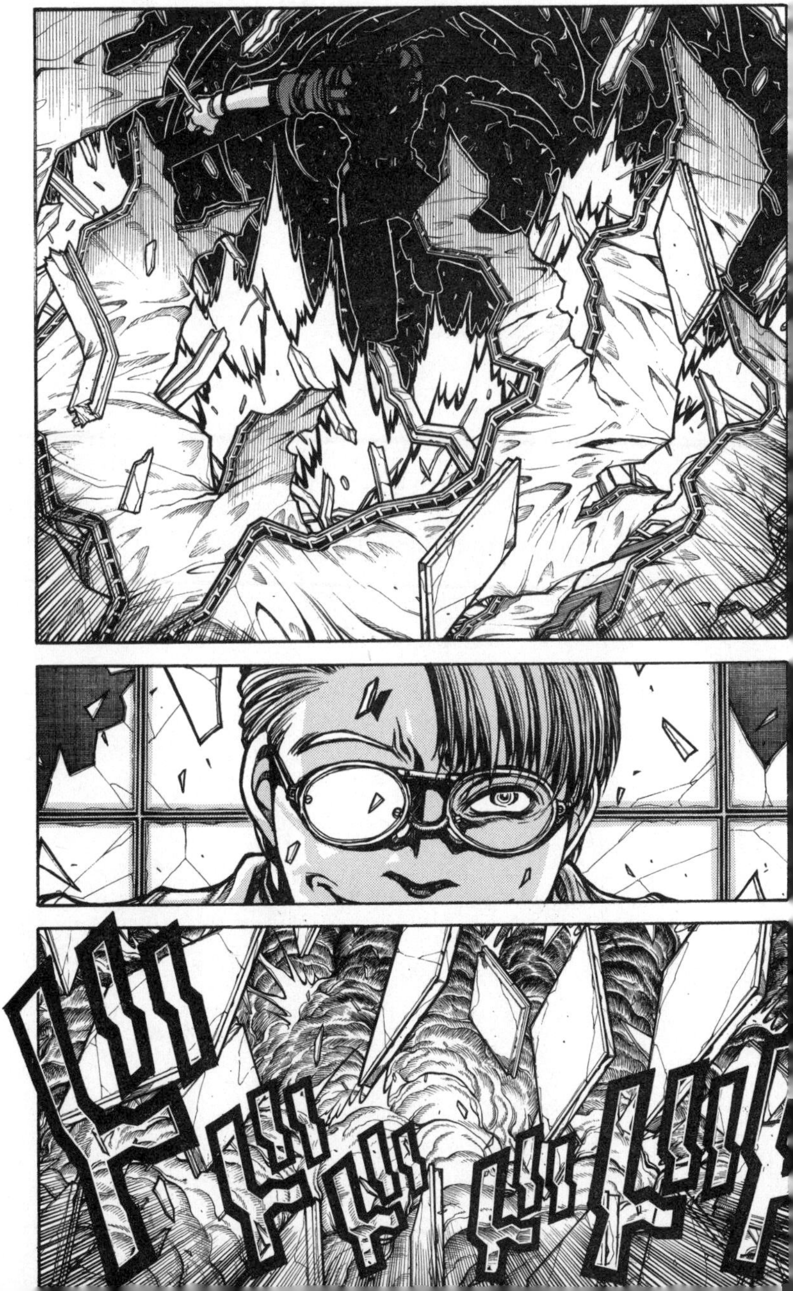

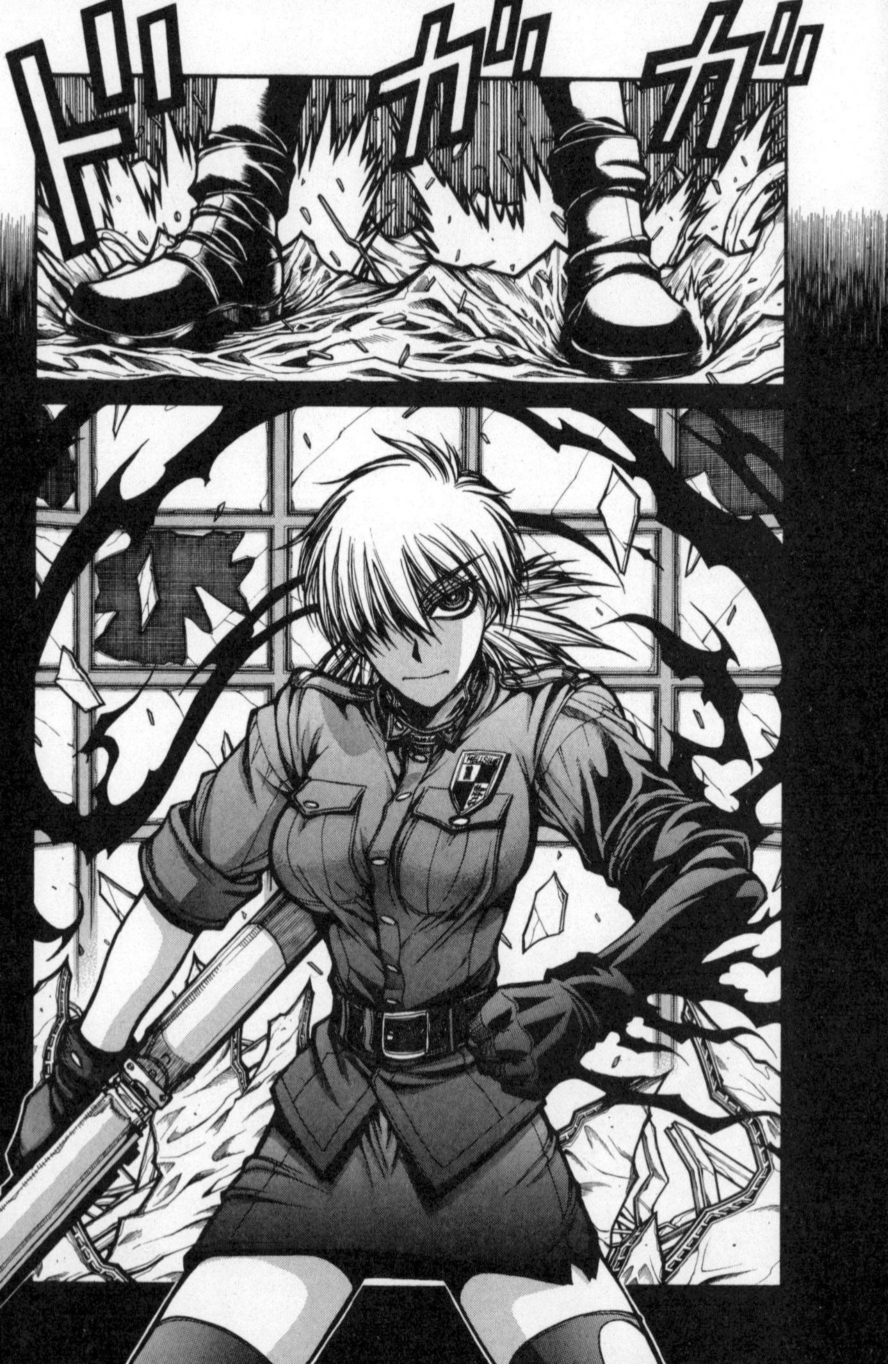
ドガガ

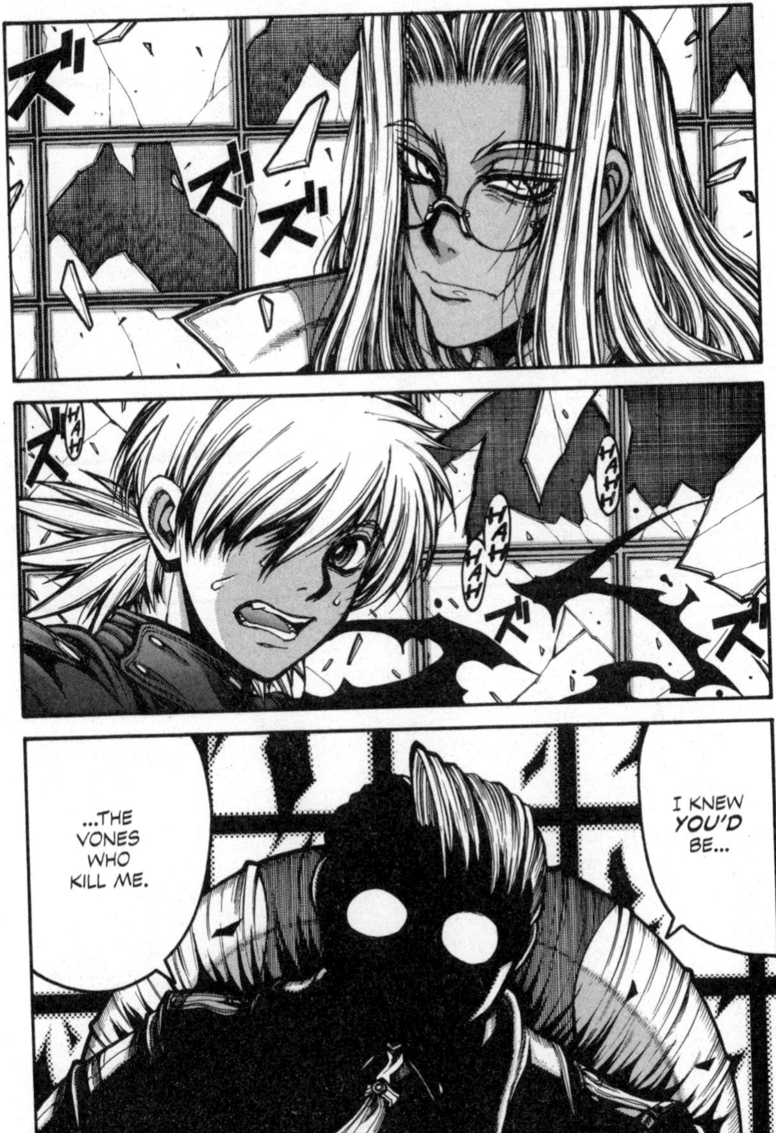
ズ
ズ
ズ
HAH
HAH
HAH
HAH
ズ
ズ
ズ
I KNEW *YOU'D* BE...
...THE VONES WHO KILL ME.

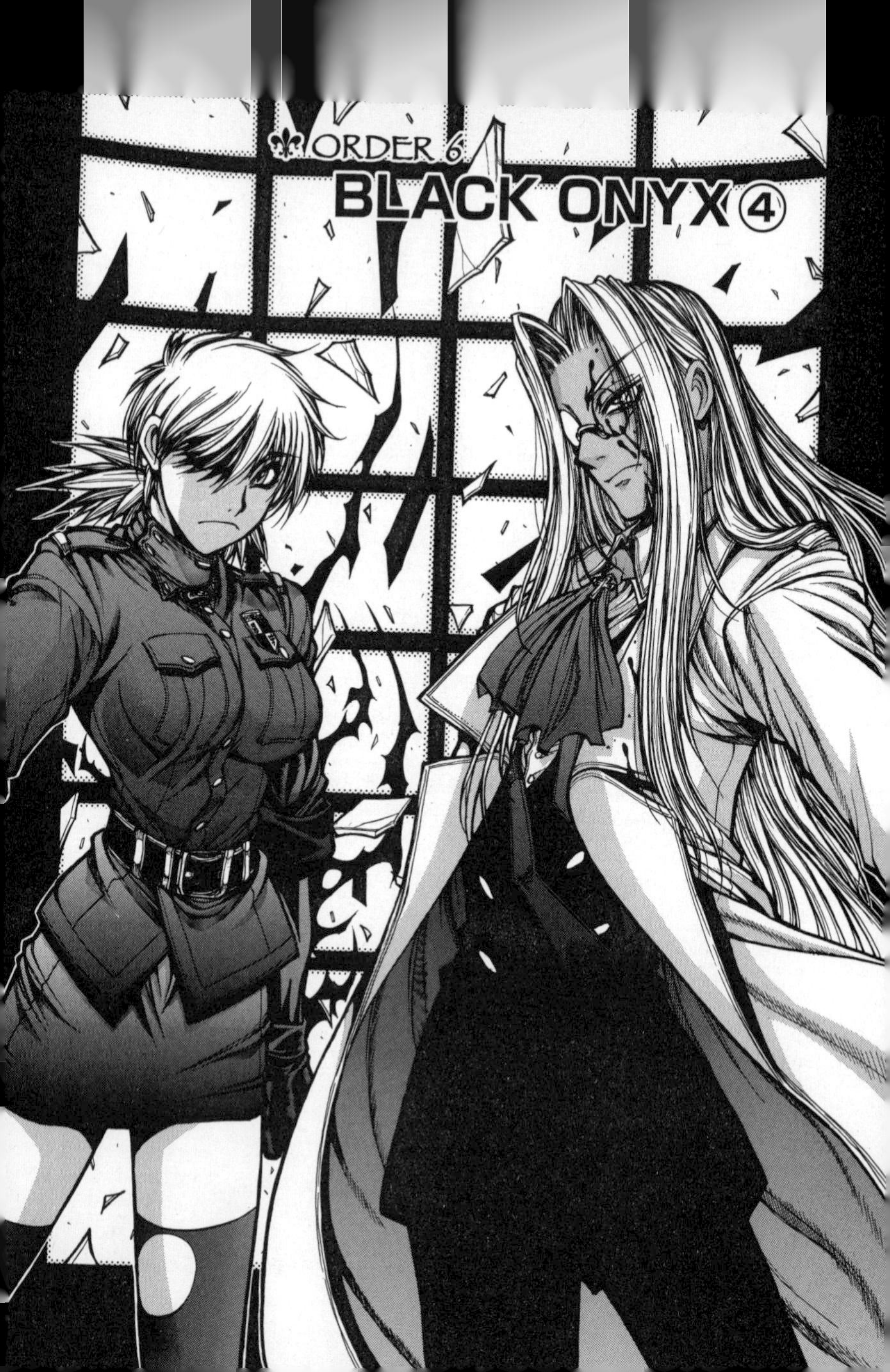
ORDER 6
BLACK ONYX ④

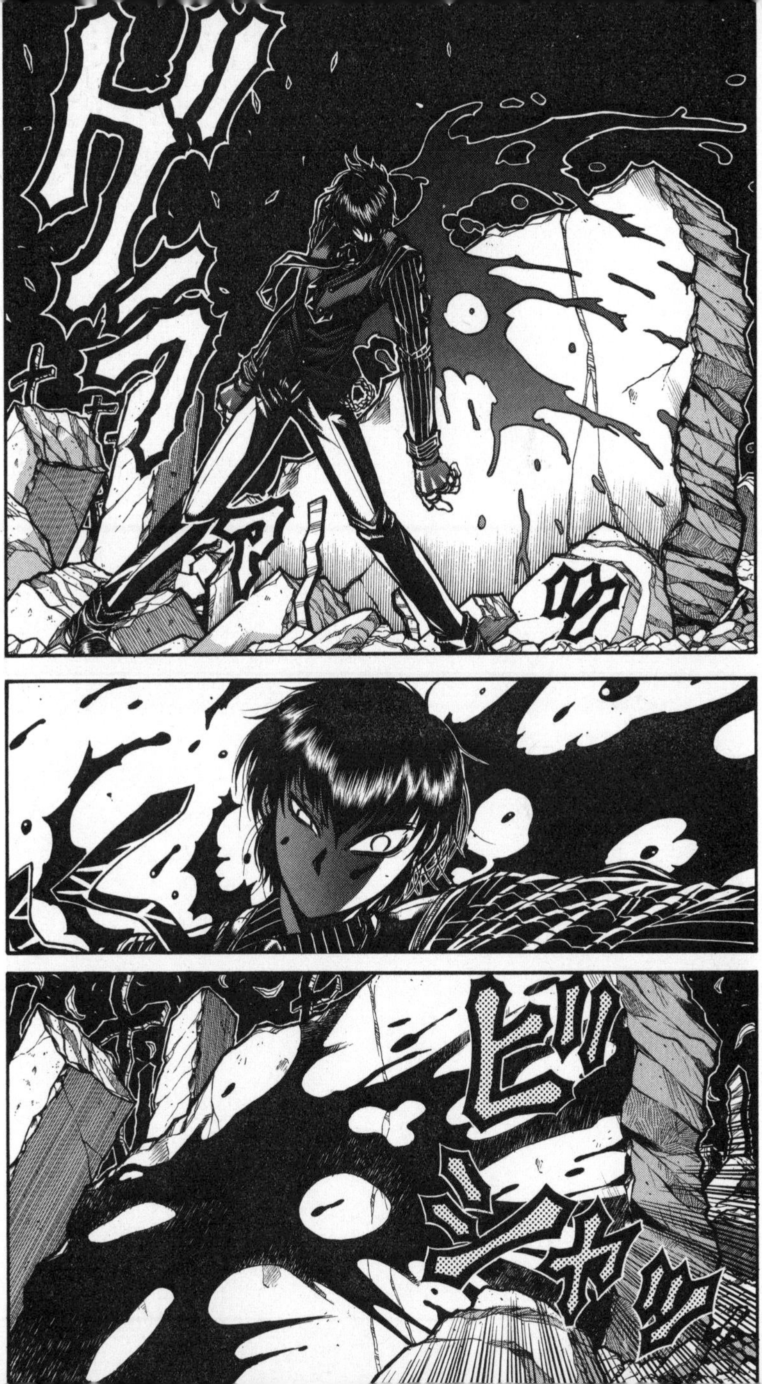

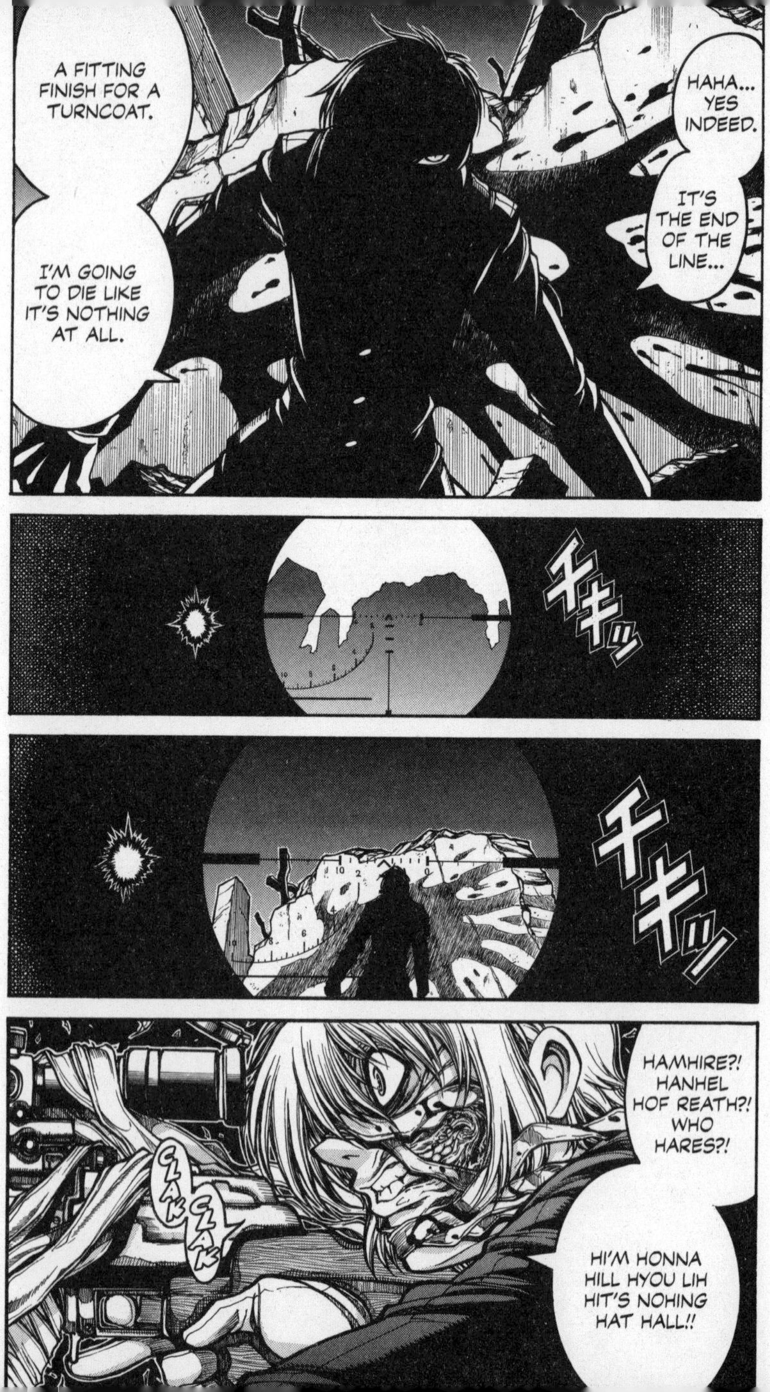
HAHA... YES INDEED.
A FITTING FINISH FOR A TURNCOAT.
IT'S THE END OF THE LINE...
I'M GOING TO DIE LIKE IT'S NOTHING AT ALL.
チキッ
チキッ
HAMHIRE?! HANHEL HOF REATH?! WHO HARES?!
HI'M HONNA HILL HYOU LIH HIT'S NOHING HAT HALL!!
CLAK
CLAK

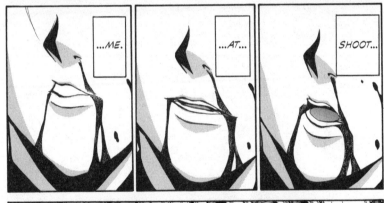

...ME.

...AT...

SHOOT...

GO AHEAD.

SHOOT ME AGAIN.

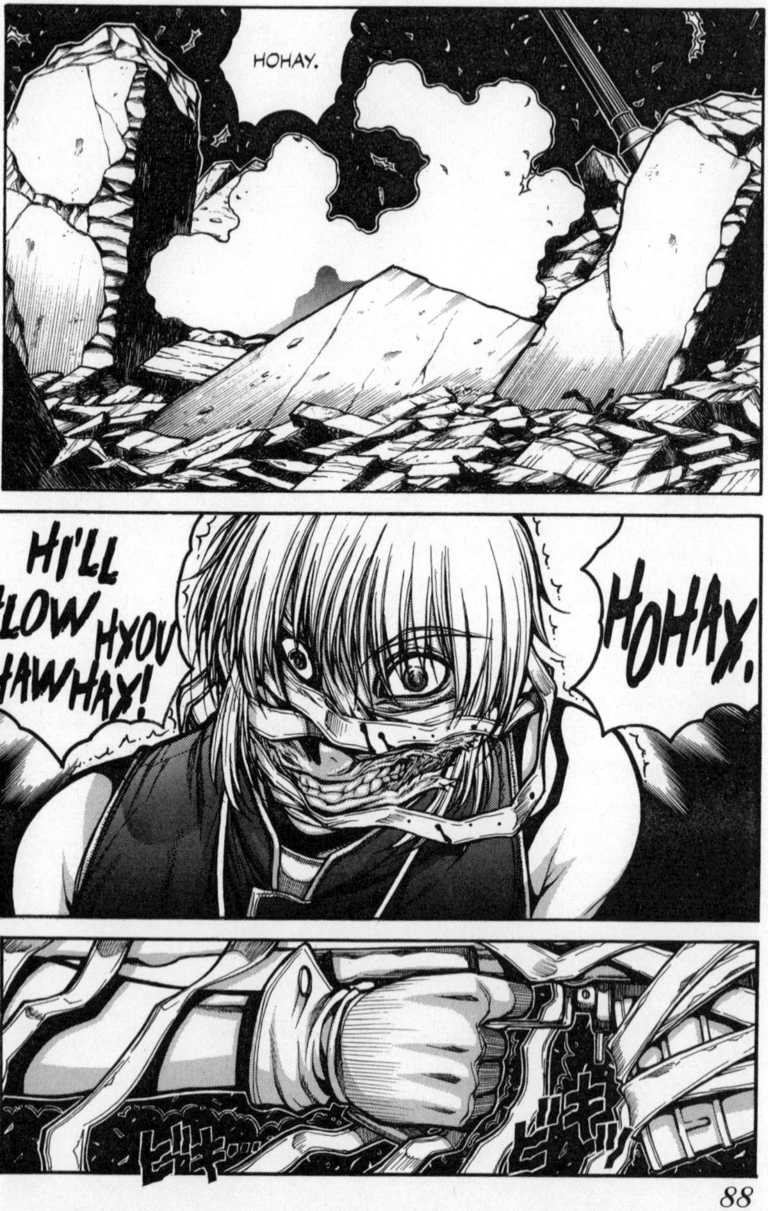
HOHAY.
HOHAY.
HI'LL HLOW HYOU HAWHAY!
ビキッ
ビキ……

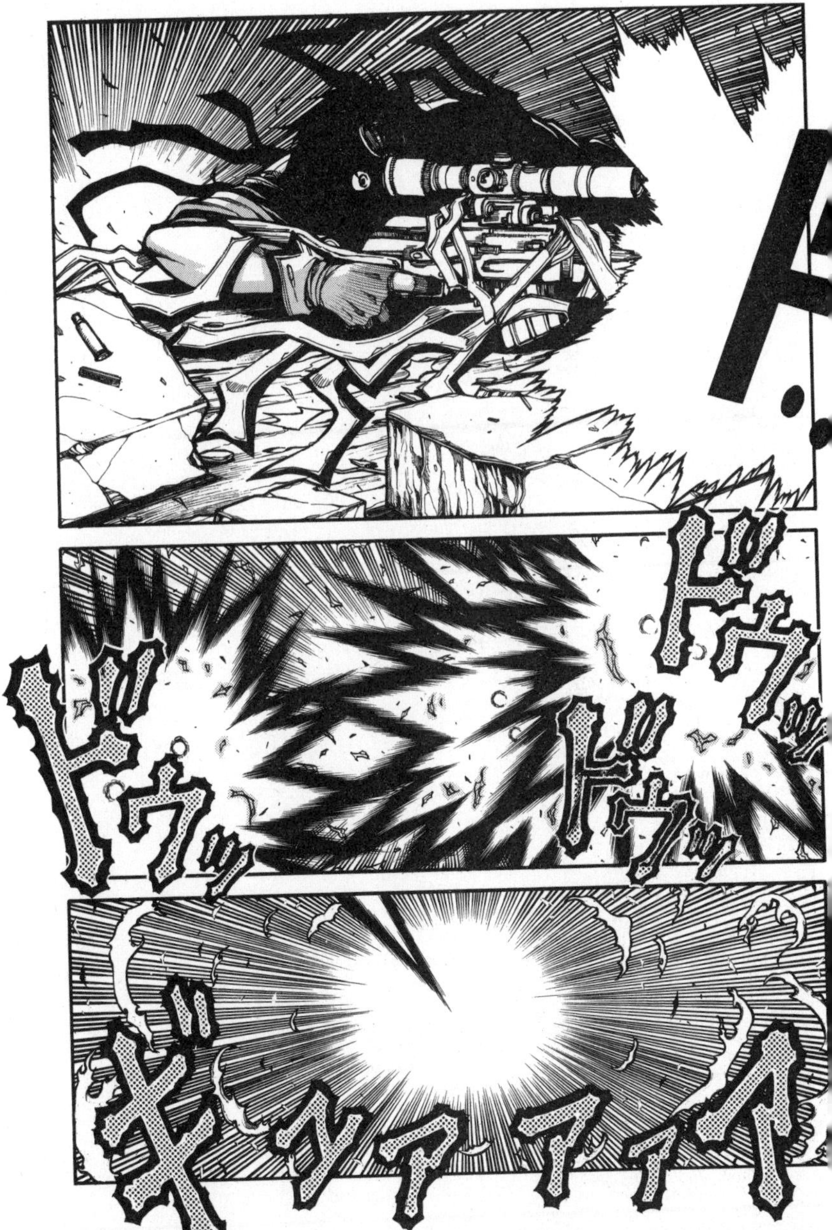
A..
ドウッ
ドウッ
ドウッ
ギッァァィイ

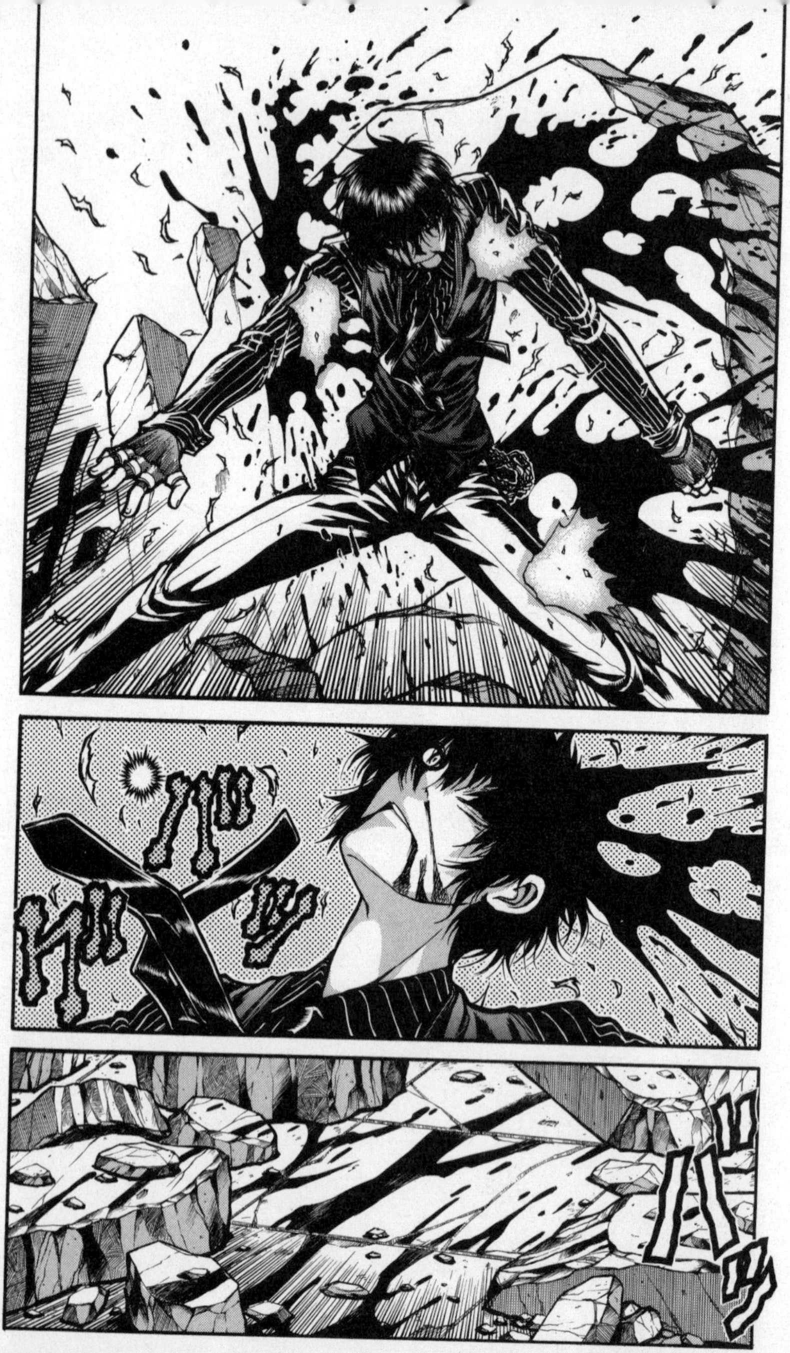
パッ
バッ

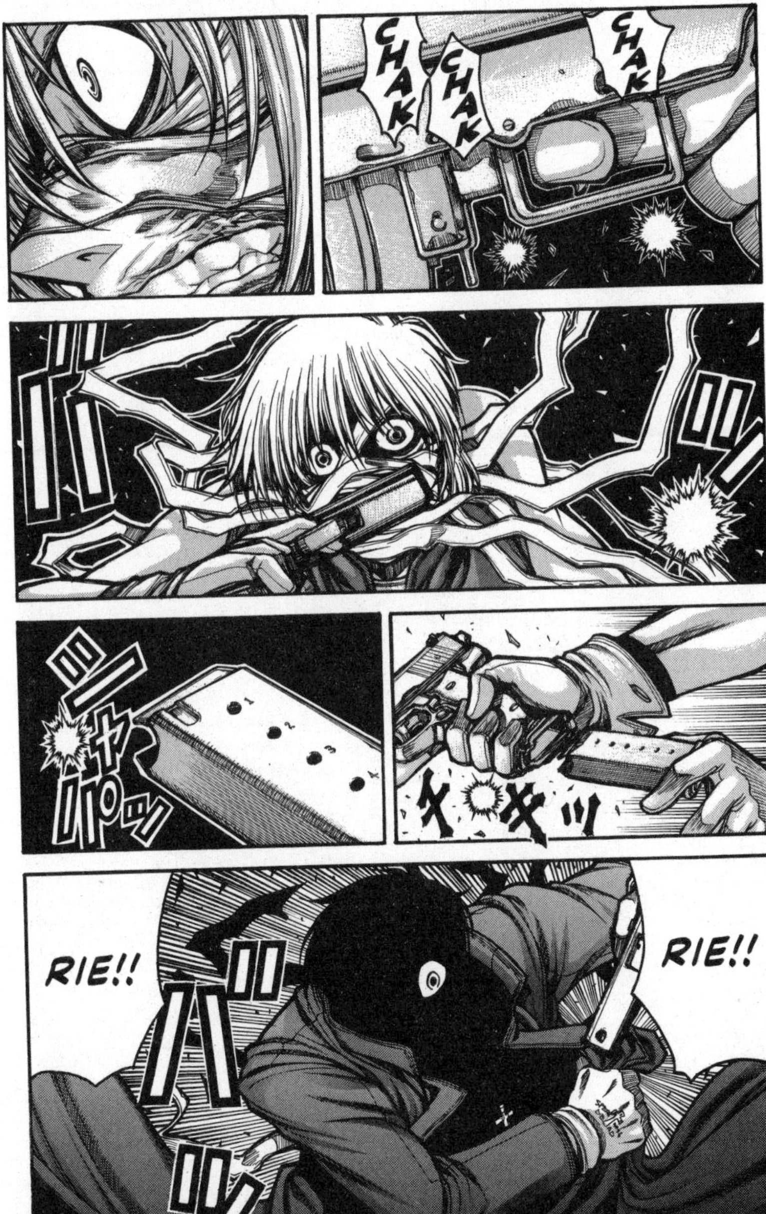
CHAK
CHAK
CHAK
RIE!!
RIE!!

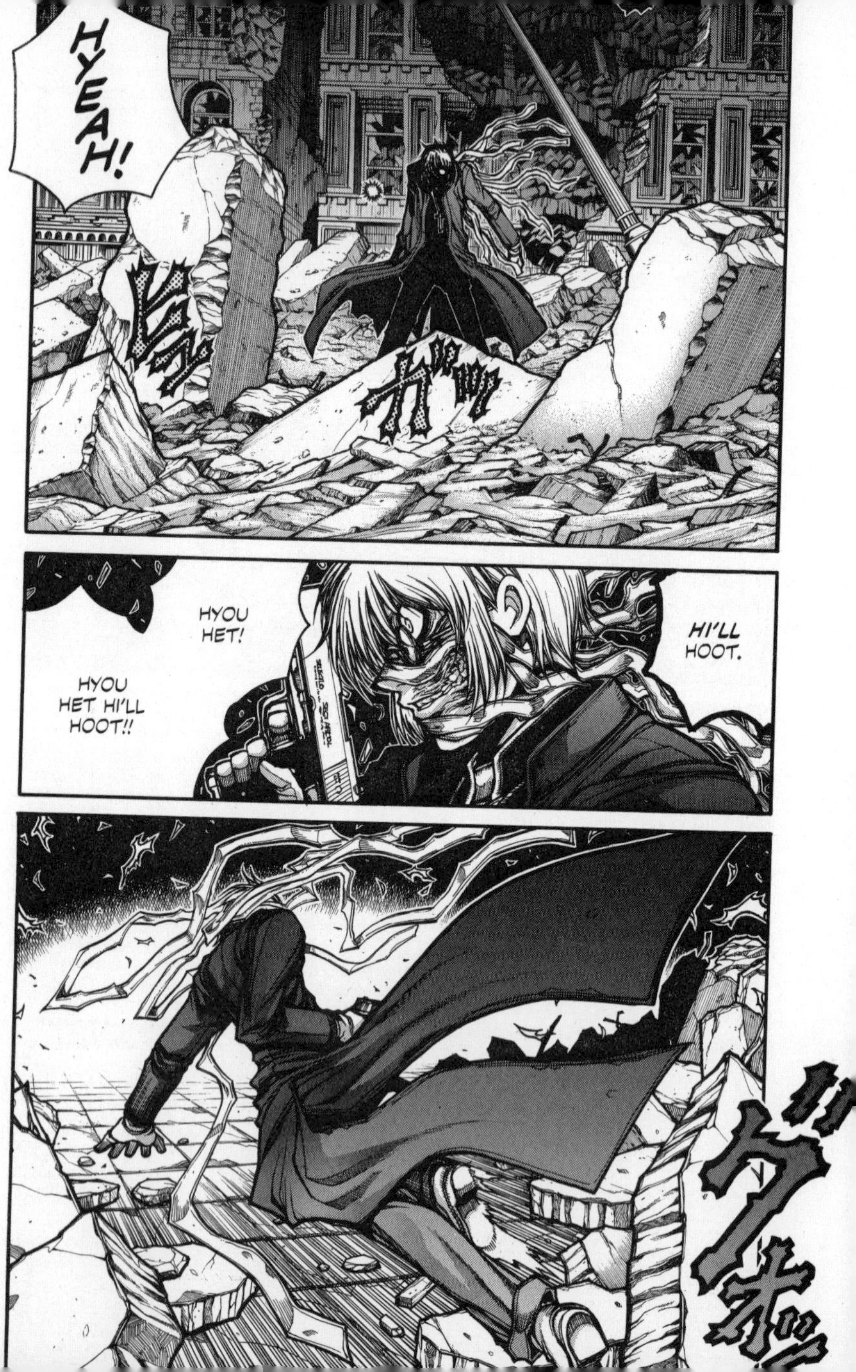
HYEAH!
HI'LL HOOT.
HYOU HET!
HYOU HET HI'LL HOOT!!

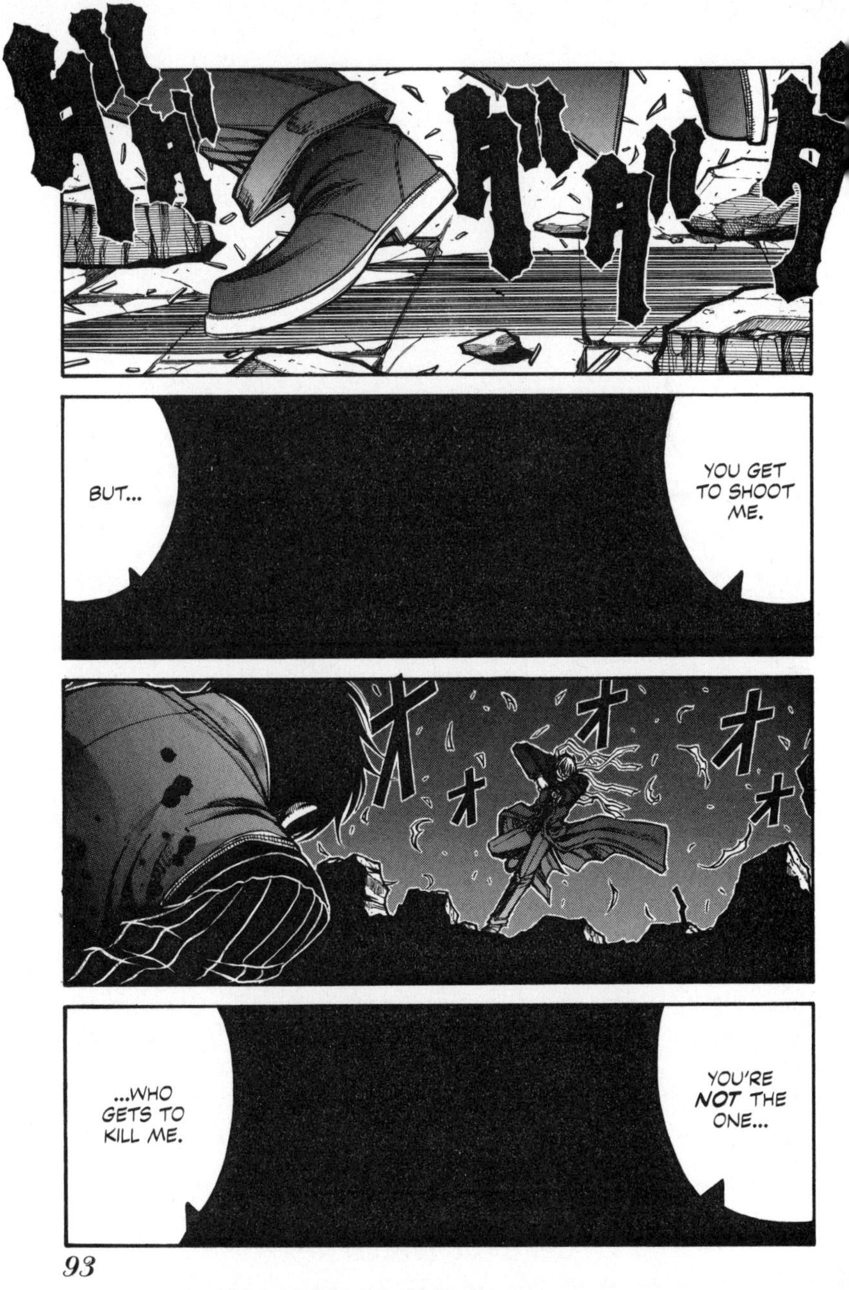
YOU GET TO SHOOT ME.
BUT...
YOU'RE **NOT** THE ONE...
...WHO GETS TO KILL ME.

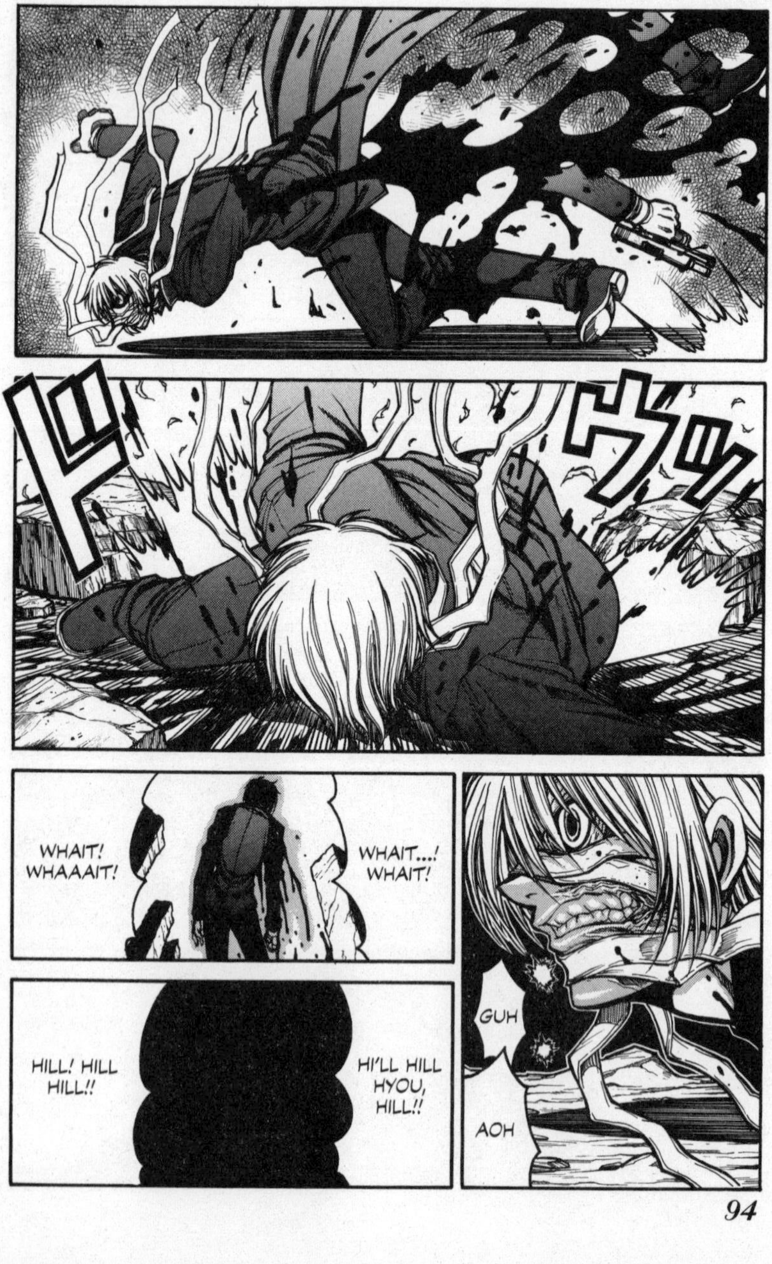
ドヴッ
GUH
AOH
WHAIT...! WHAIT!
WHAIT! WHAAAIT!
HI'LL HILL HYOU, HILL!!
HILL! HILL HILL!!

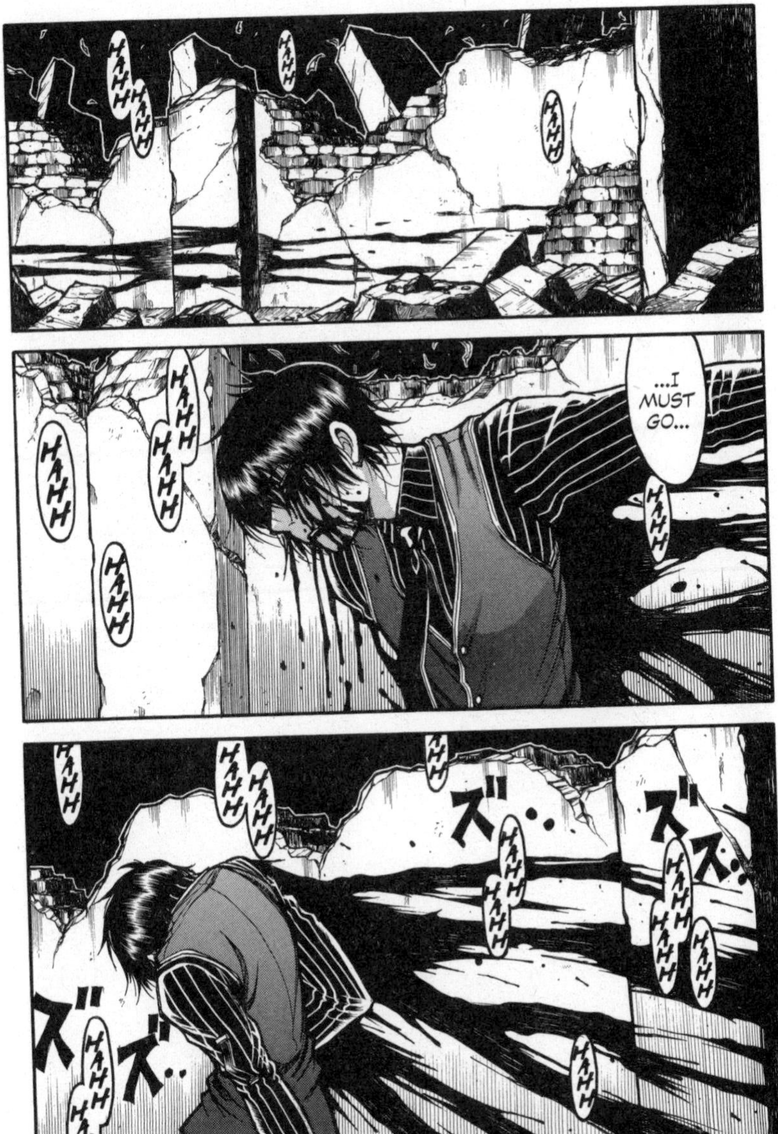
...I MUST GO...
ズズ..
ズ..
ズズ..

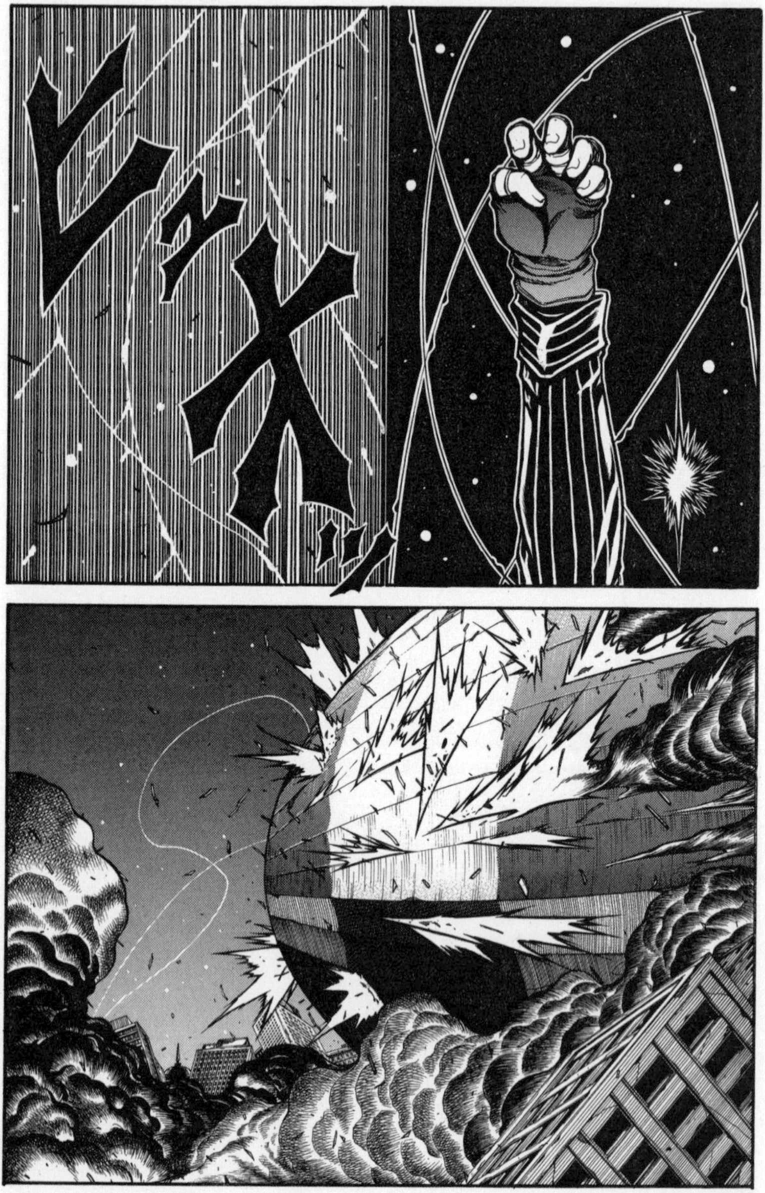

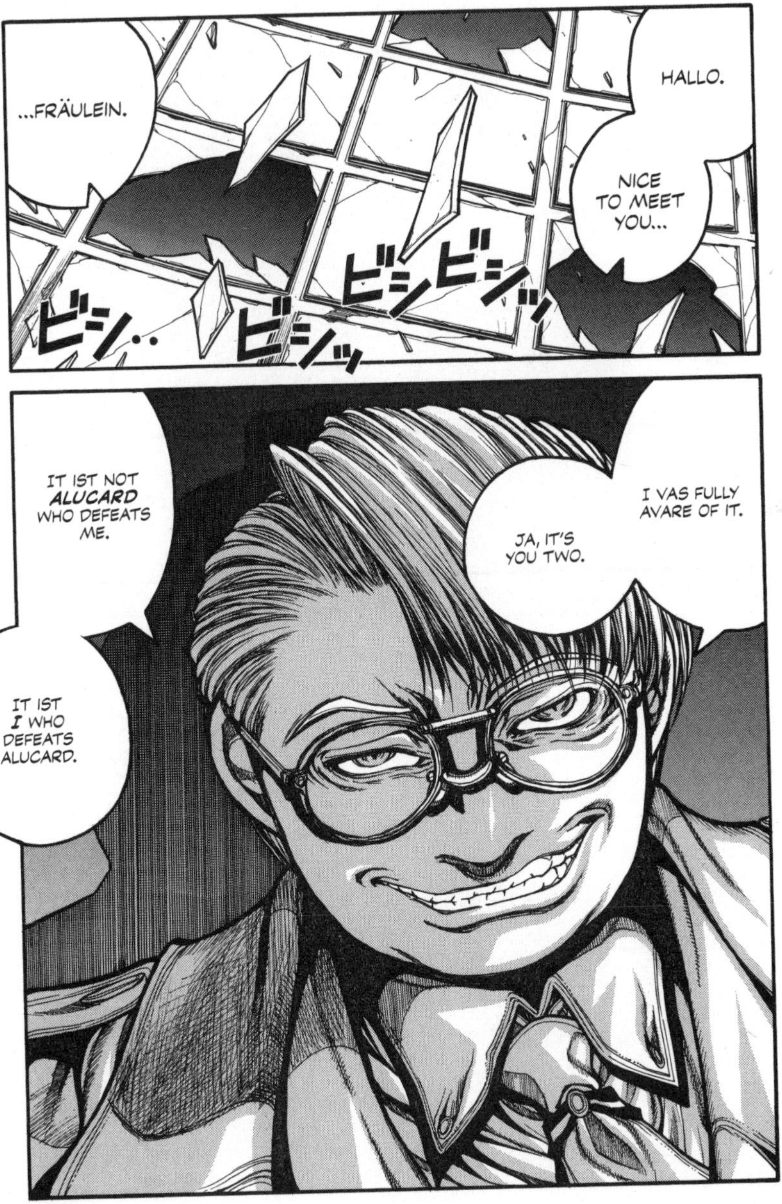

HALLO.
NICE TO MEET YOU...
...FRÄULEIN.
ビシビシッ
ビシッ
ビシ‥
I VAS FULLY AVARE OF IT.
JA, IT'S YOU TWO.
IT IST NOT ALUCARD WHO DEFEATS ME.
IT IST I WHO DEFEATS ALUCARD.

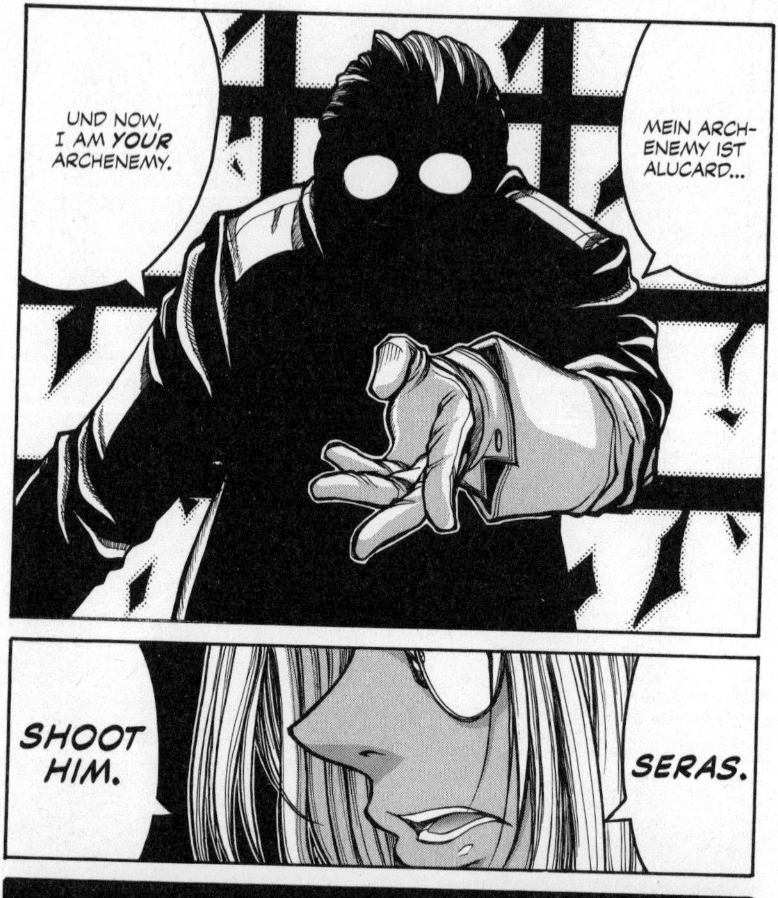
MEIN ARCH-ENEMY IST ALUCARD...
UND NOW, I AM *YOUR* ARCHENEMY.
SERAS.
SHOOT HIM.
TO BE CONTINUED

ORDER 6 / END

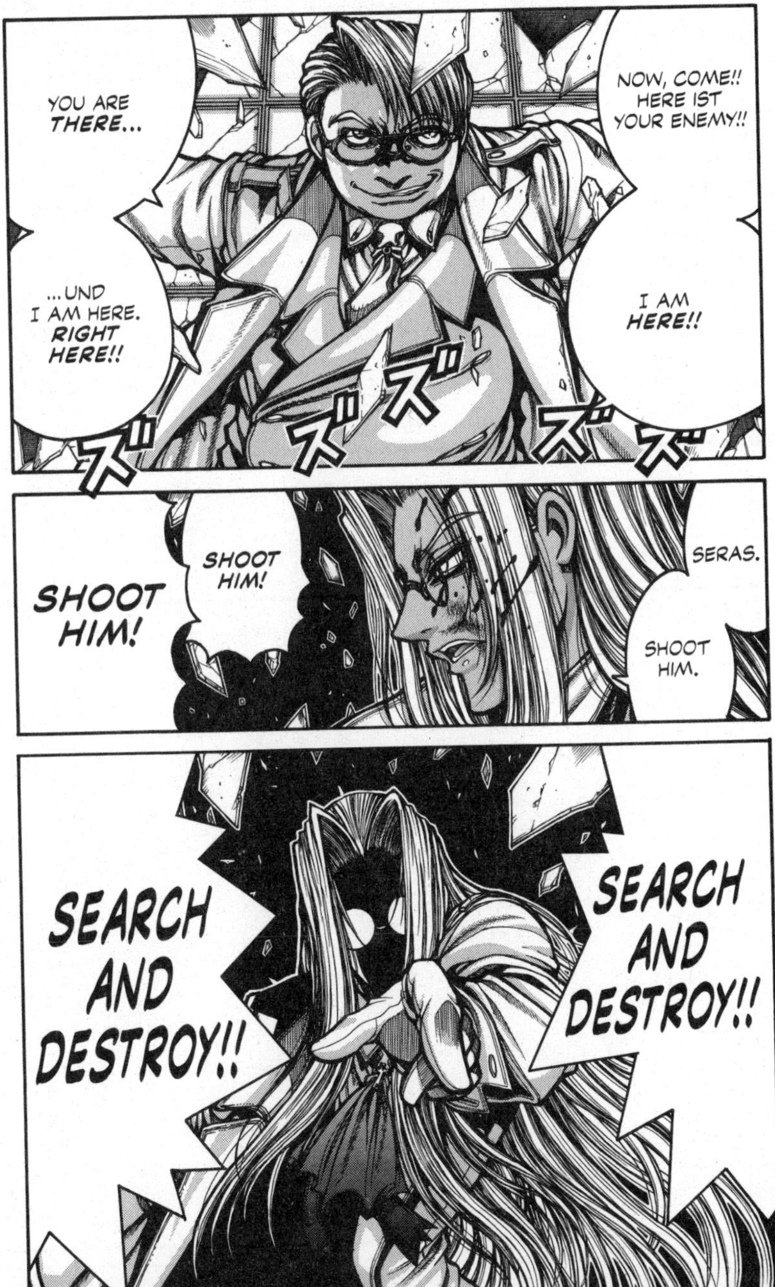
NOW, COME!! HERE IST YOUR ENEMY!!
I AM HERE!!
YOU ARE THERE...
...UND I AM HERE. RIGHT HERE!!
ズズズズズ
SERAS.
SHOOT HIM.
SHOOT HIM!
SHOOT HIM!
SEARCH AND DESTROY!!
SEARCH AND DESTROY!!

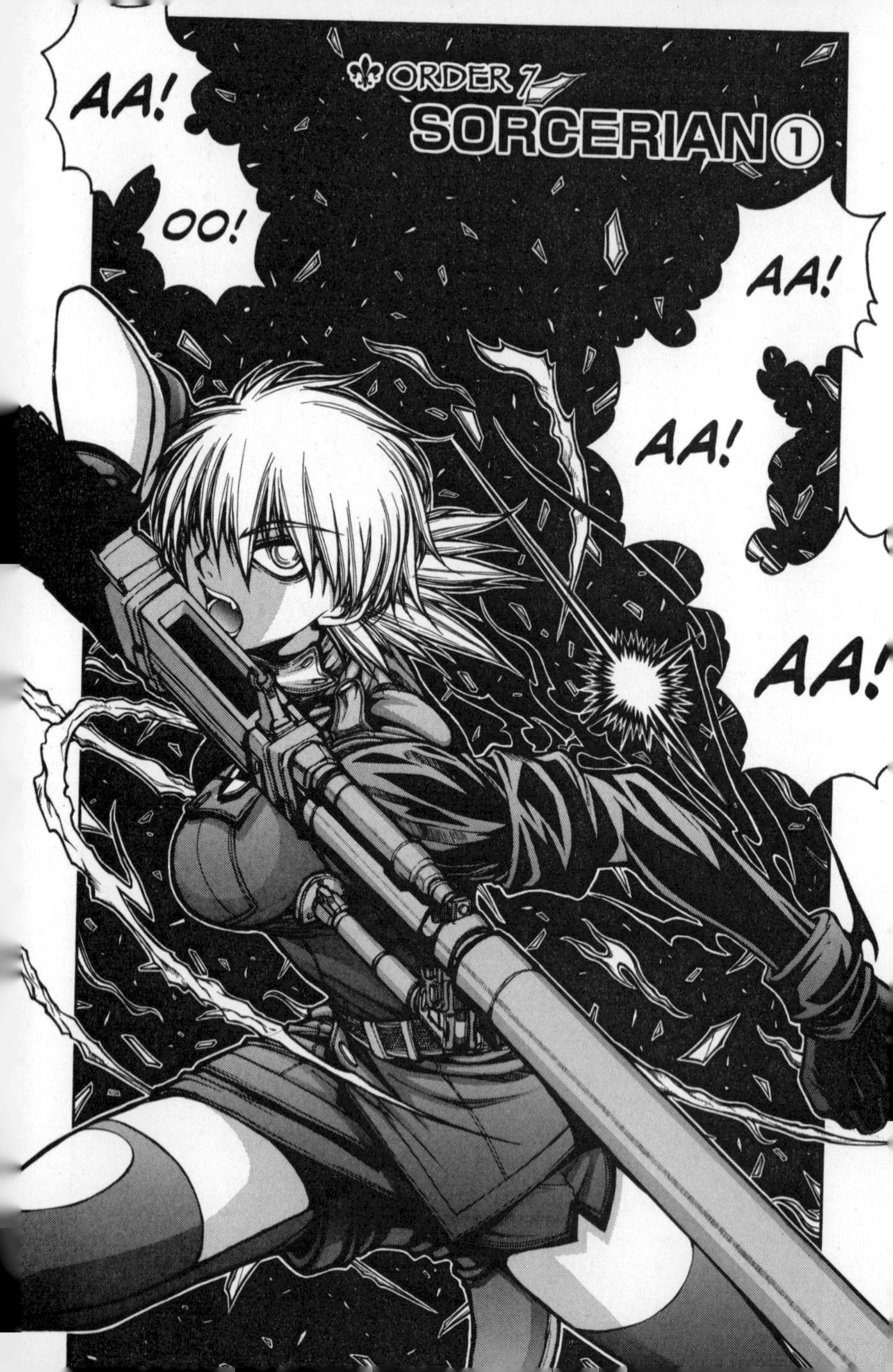
ORDER 7
SORCERIAN ①
AA!
OO!
AA!
AA!
AA!

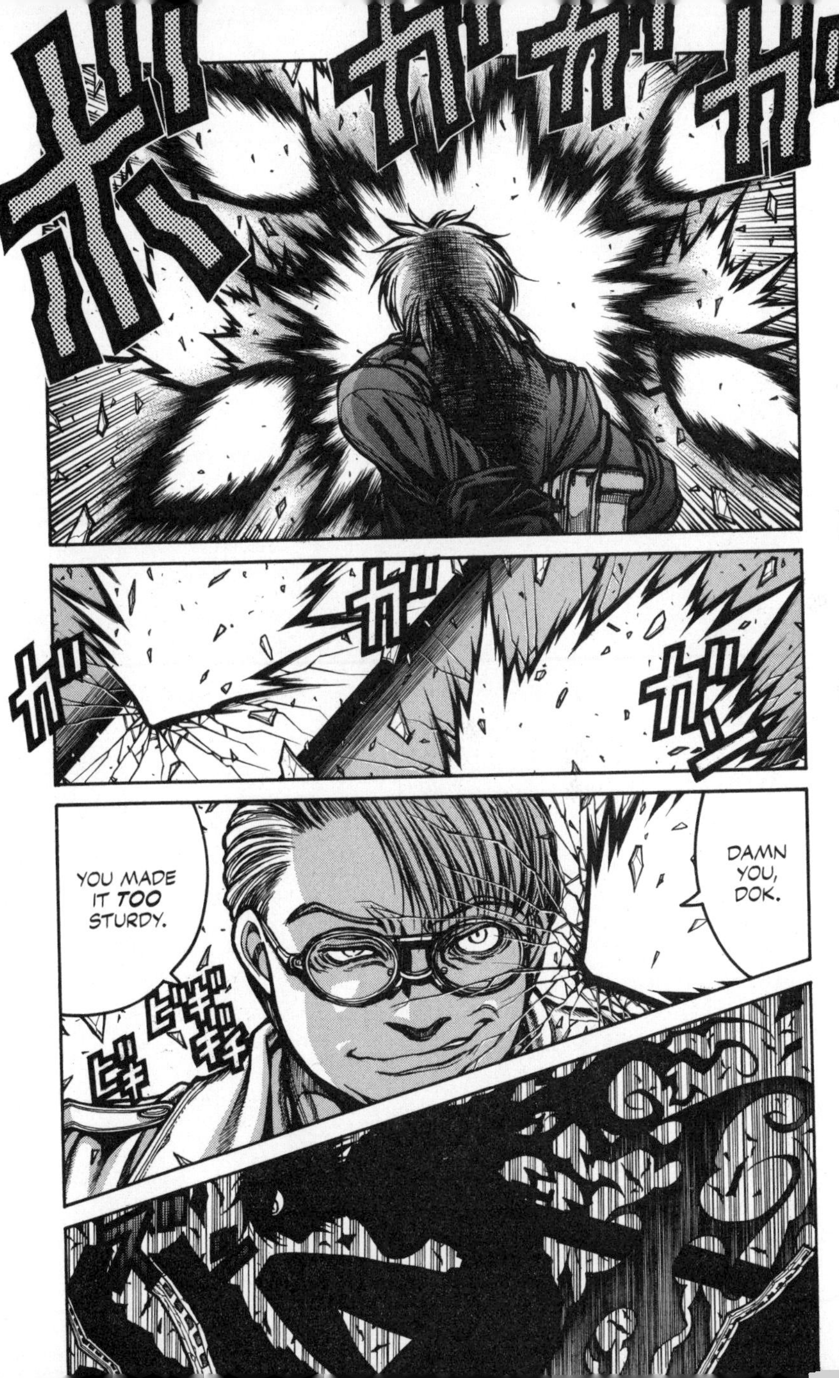
DAMN YOU, DOK.
YOU MADE IT *TOO* STURDY.

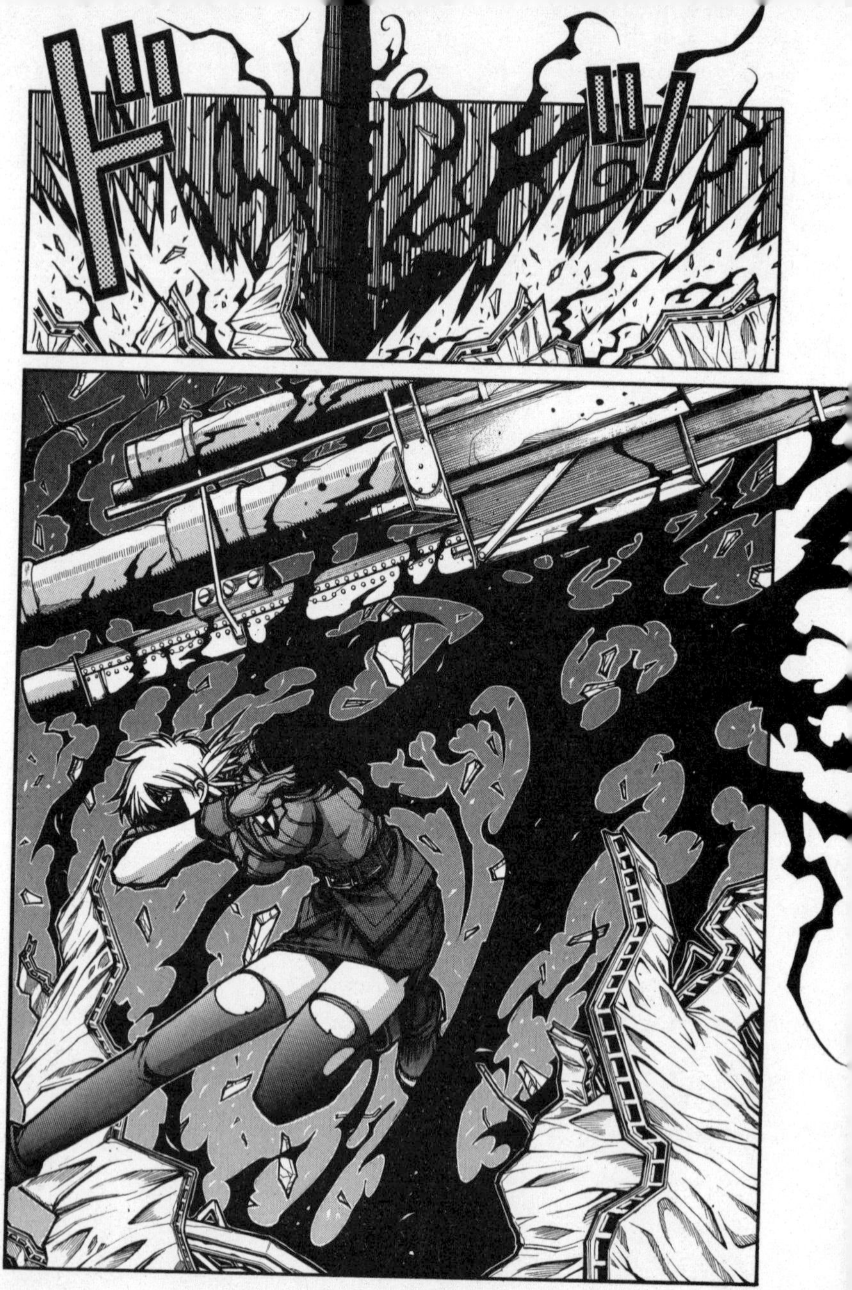

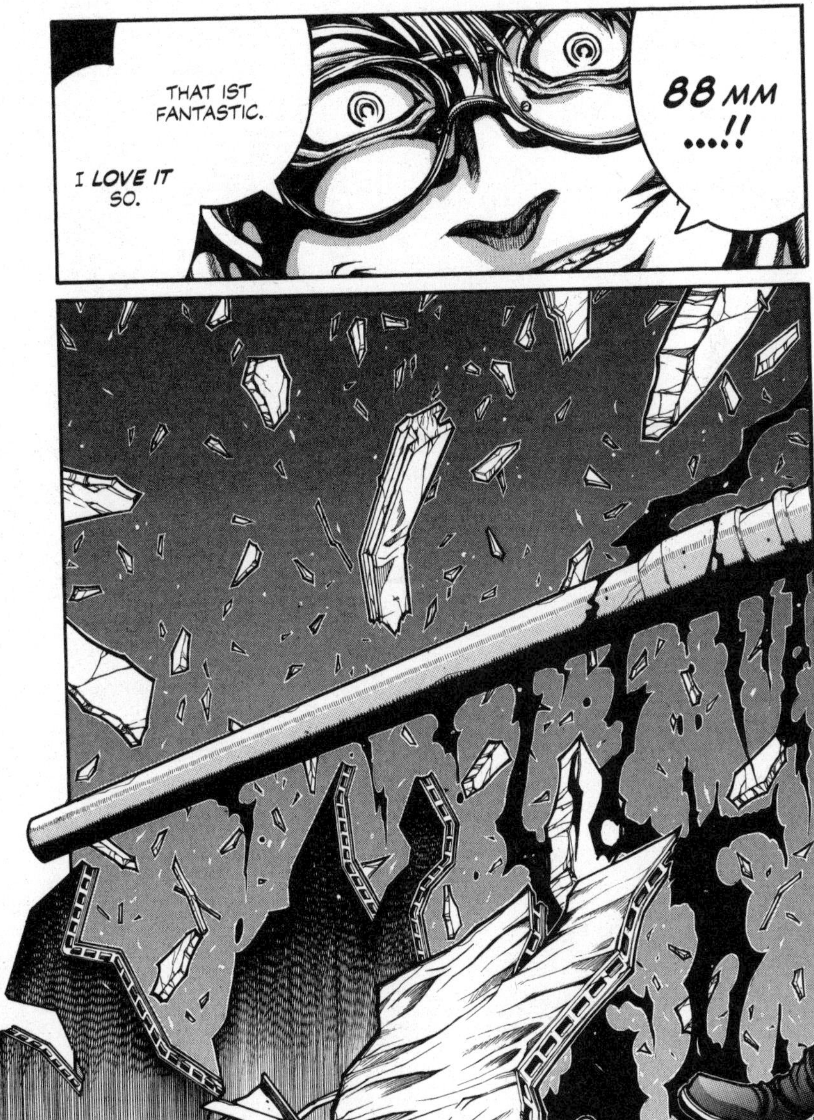
88 MM ....!!
THAT IST FANTASTIC.
I LOVE IT SO.

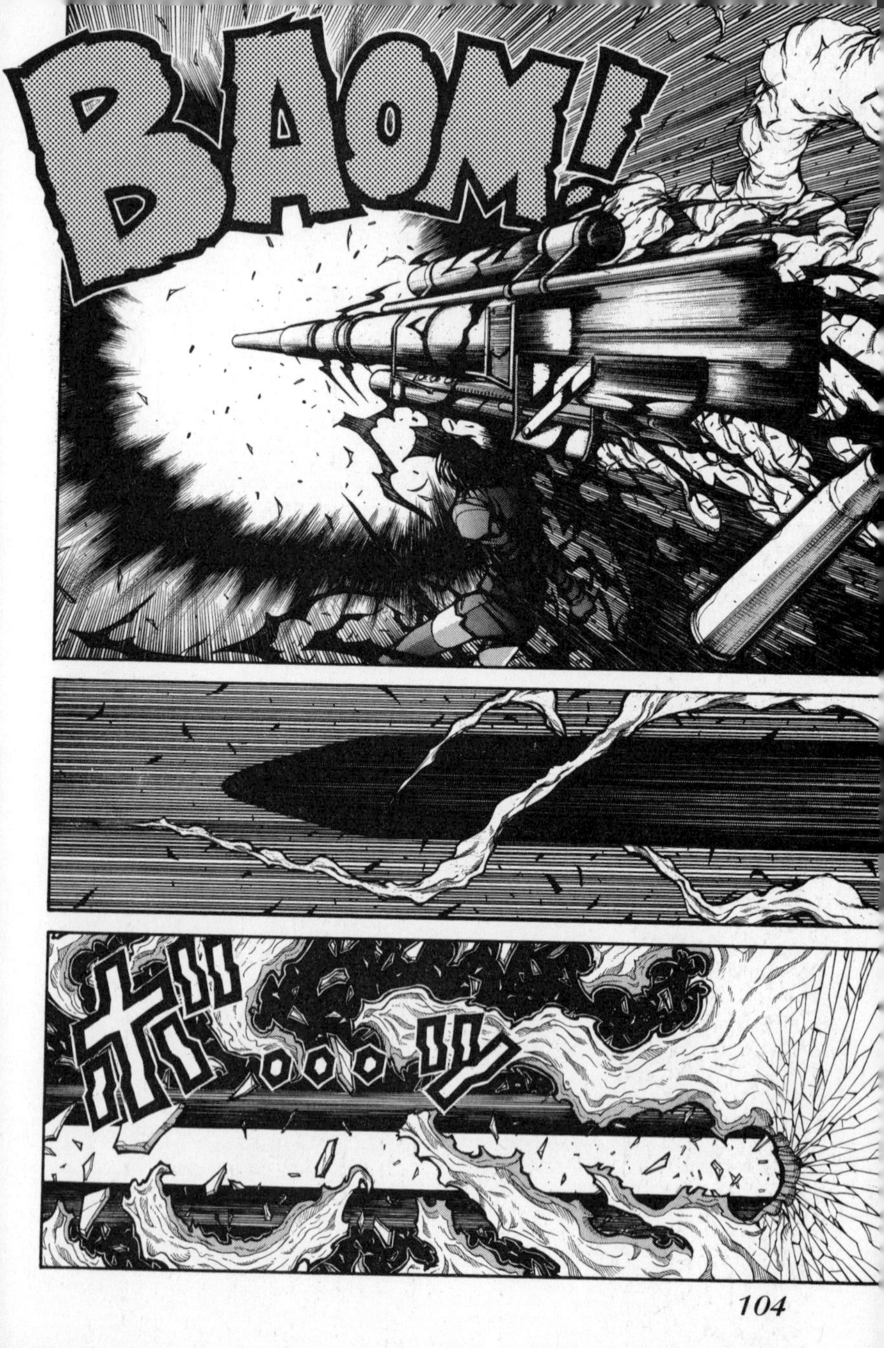
BAOM!
ボ・・・・ッ

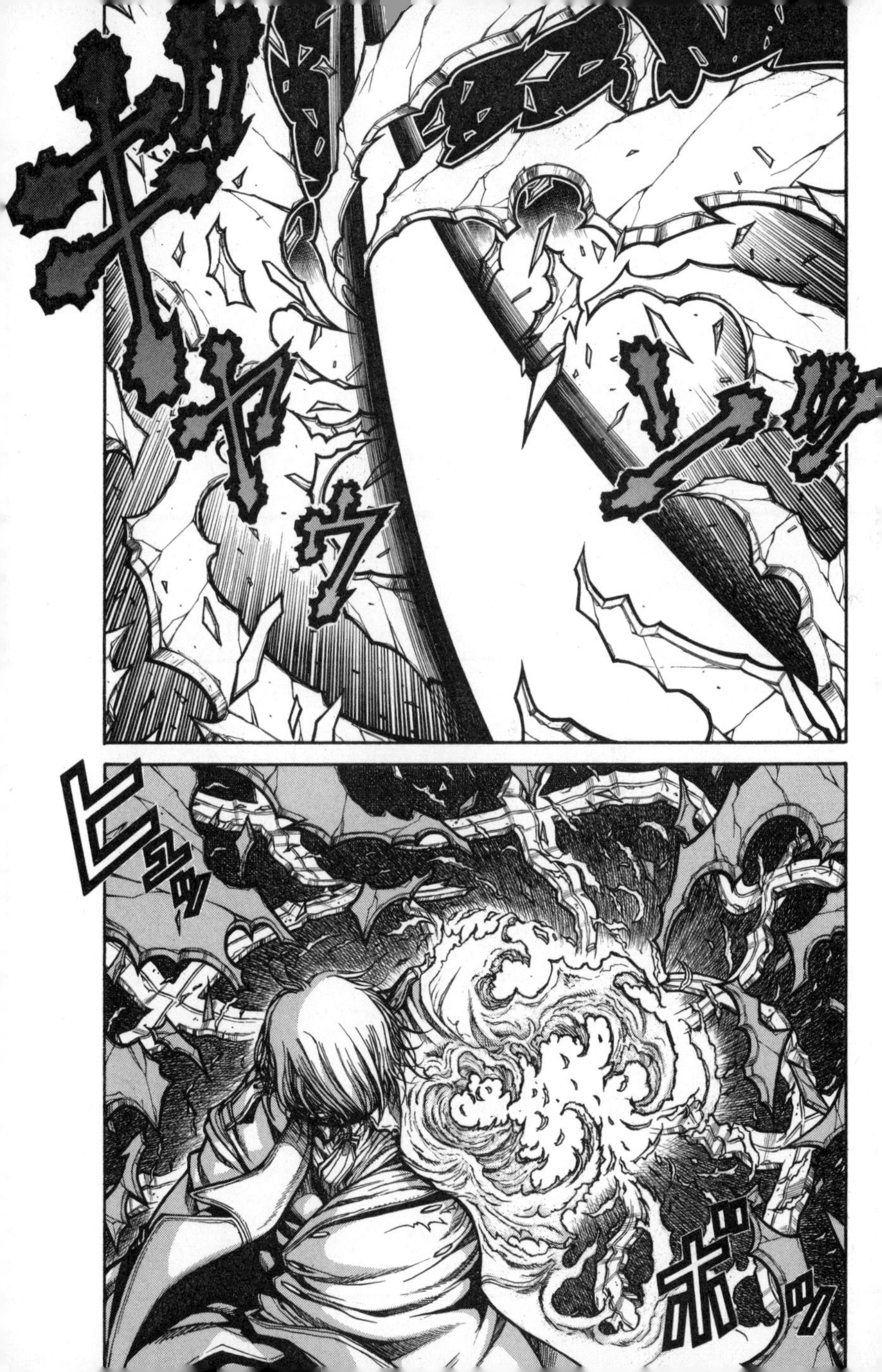
ボッ
ヒュッ

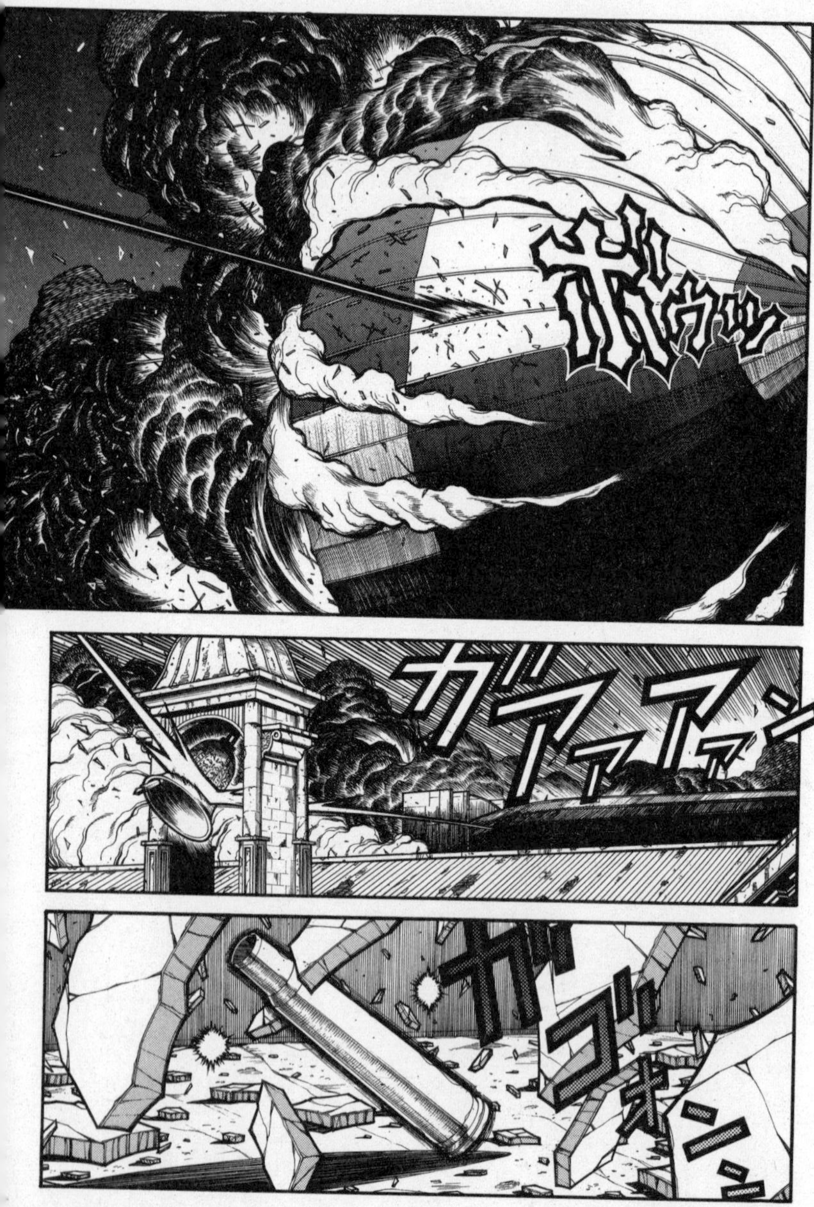
ガアァアァン
ガゴォーン

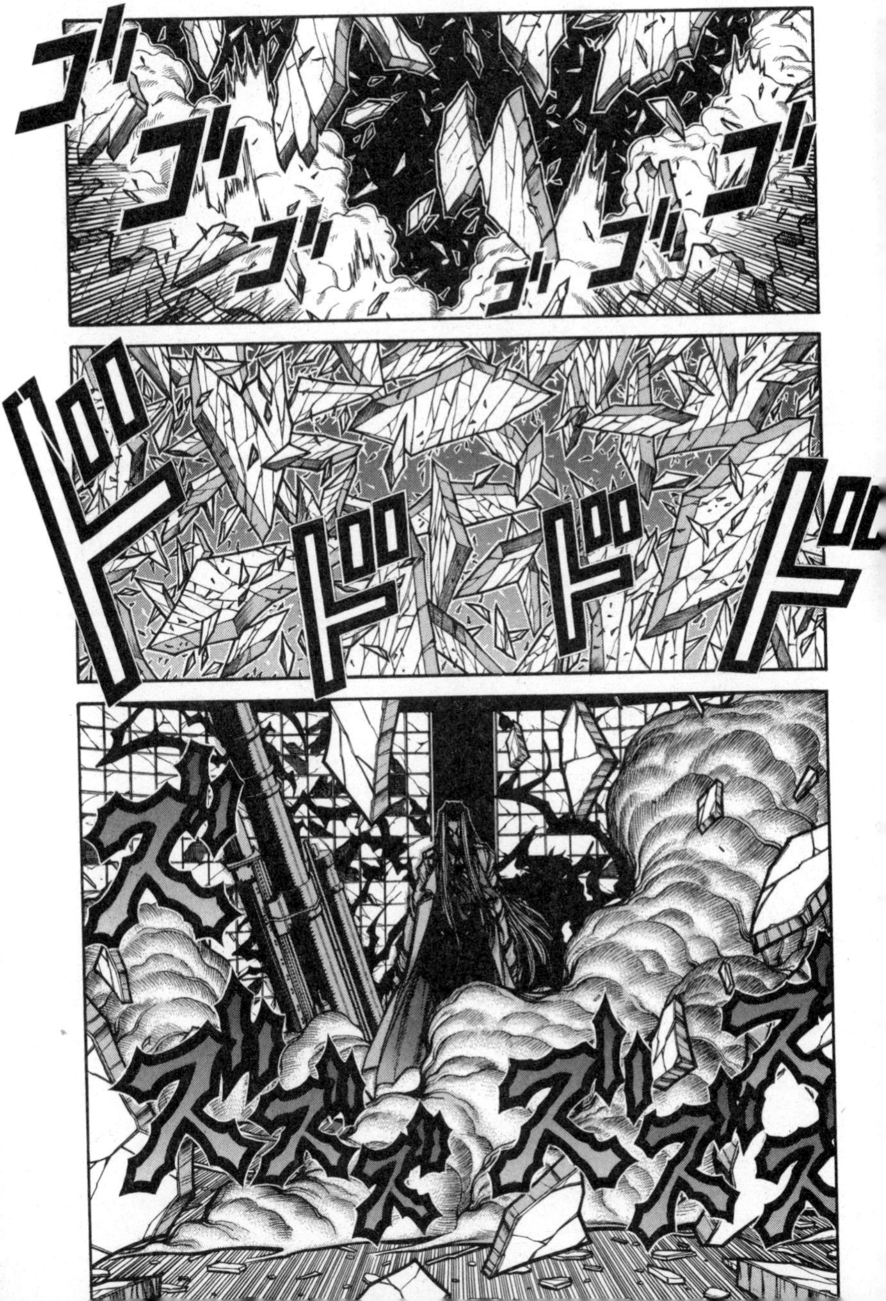
ゴゴゴゴゴゴ
ドドドド
ズズズズズズズ

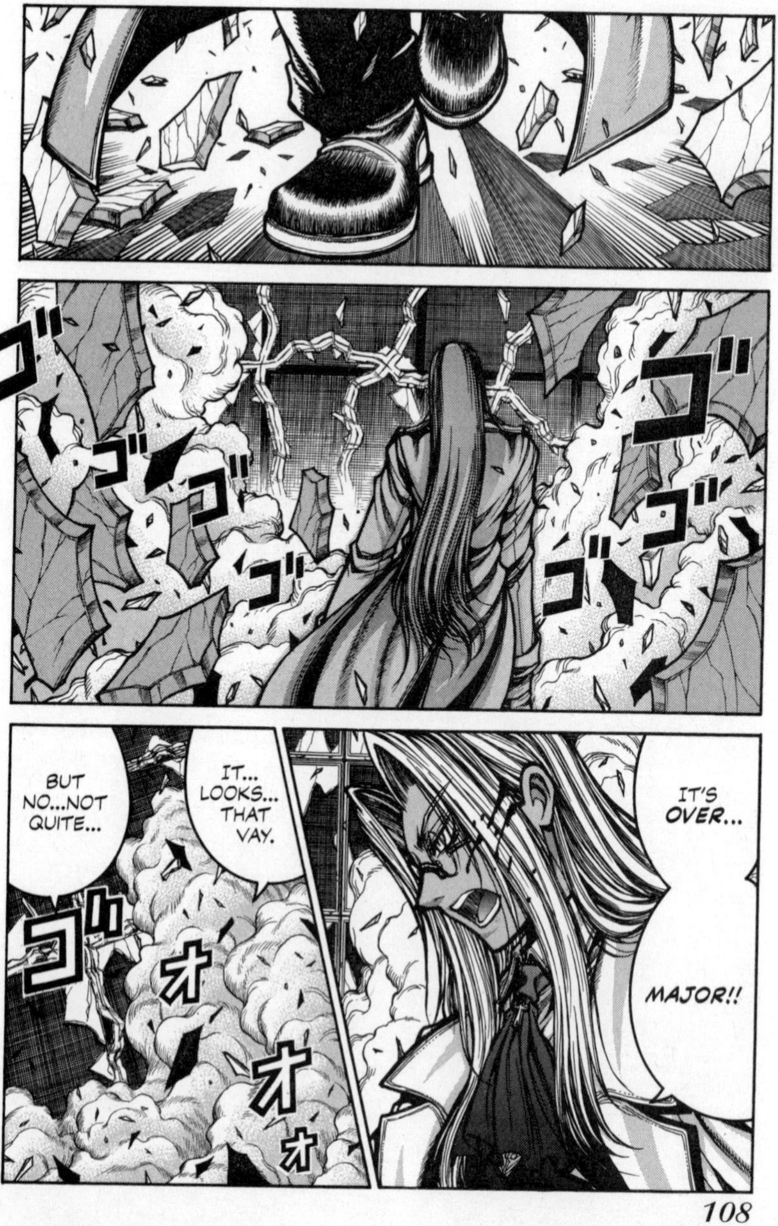

IT'S OVER...
MAJOR!!
IT... LOOKS... THAT VAY.
BUT NO...NOT QUITE...

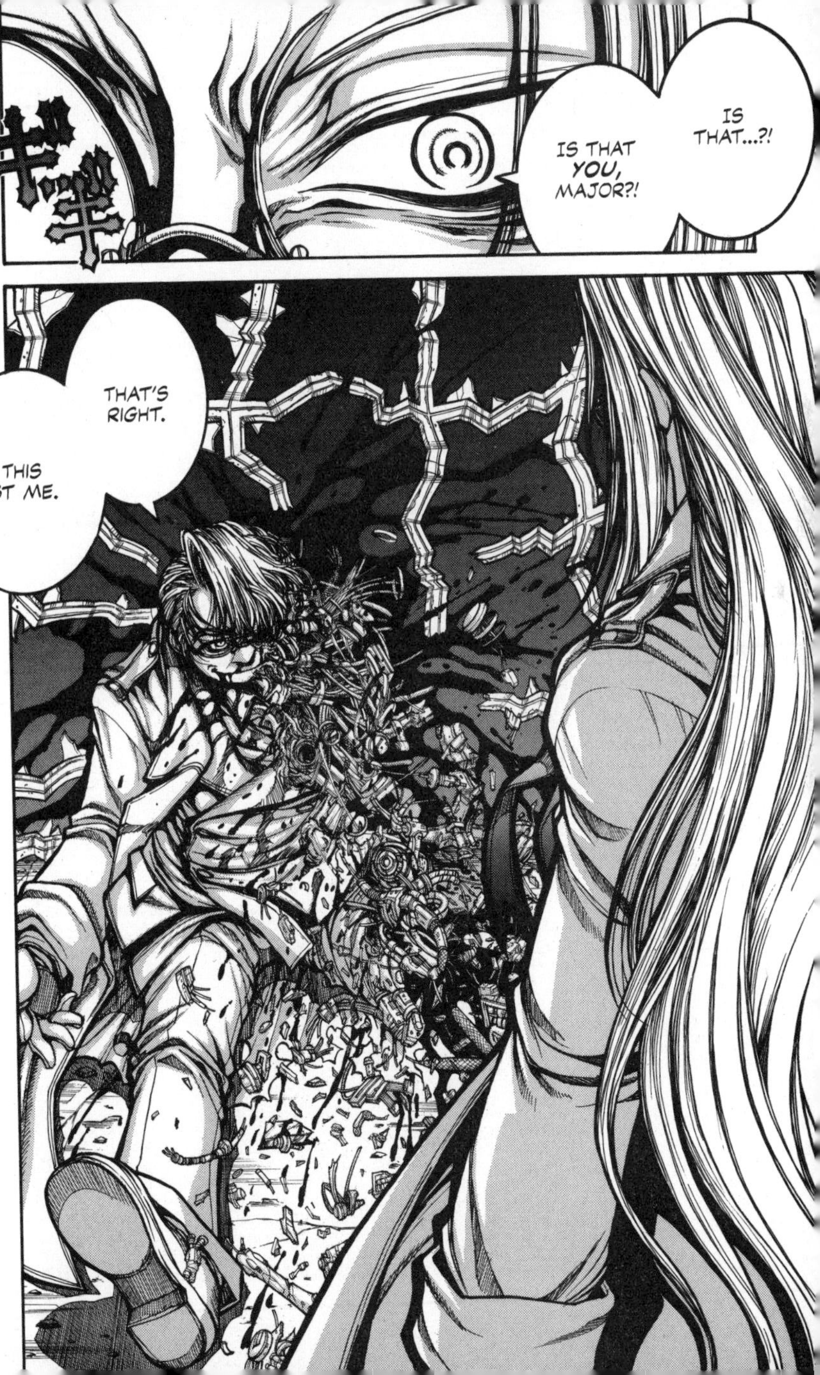
IS THAT...?!
IS THAT YOU, MAJOR?!
THAT'S RIGHT.
THIS IST ME.

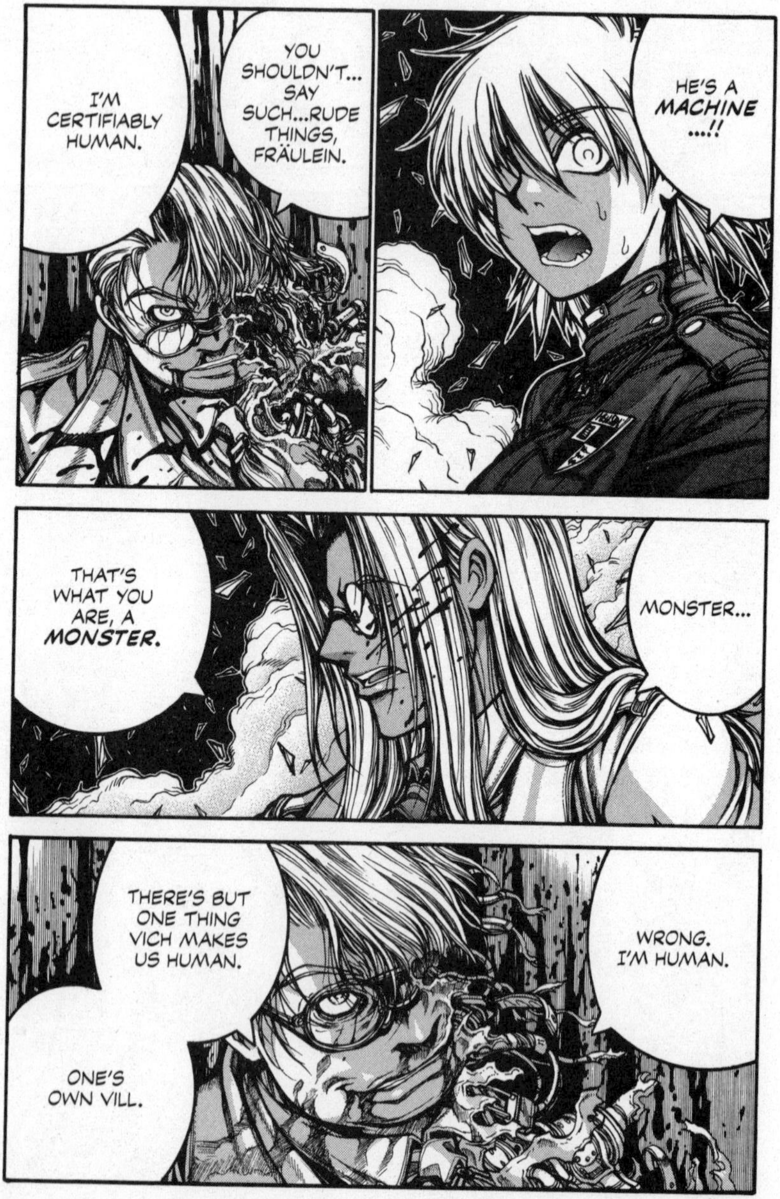
HE'S A *MACHINE* ....!!
YOU SHOULDN'T... SAY SUCH...RUDE THINGS, FRÄULEIN.
I'M CERTIFIABLY HUMAN.
MONSTER...
THAT'S WHAT YOU ARE, A *MONSTER.*
WRONG. I'M HUMAN.
THERE'S BUT ONE THING VICH MAKES US HUMAN.
ONE'S OWN VILL.

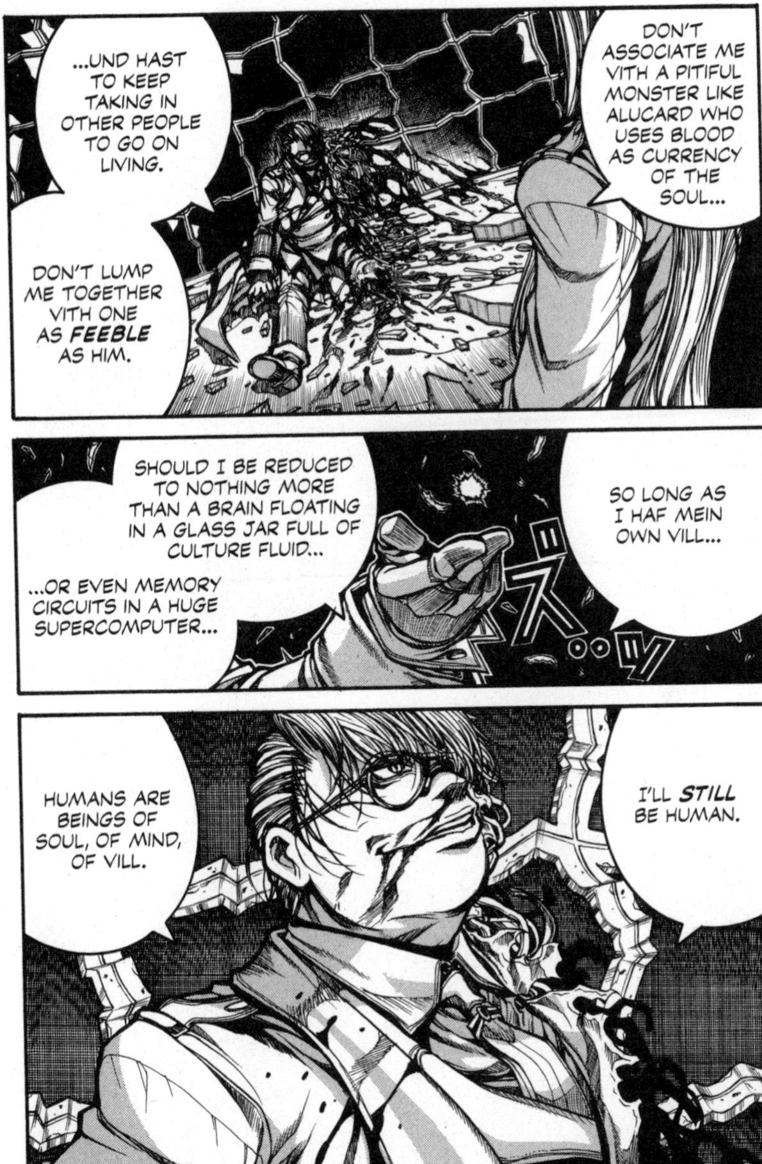
DON'T ASSOCIATE ME VITH A PITIFUL MONSTER LIKE ALUCARD WHO USES BLOOD AS CURRENCY OF THE SOUL...
...UND HAST TO KEEP TAKING IN OTHER PEOPLE TO GO ON LIVING.
DON'T LUMP ME TOGETHER VITH ONE AS ***FEEBLE*** AS HIM.
SO LONG AS I HAF MEIN OWN VILL...
SHOULD I BE REDUCED TO NOTHING MORE THAN A BRAIN FLOATING IN A GLASS JAR FULL OF CULTURE FLUID...
...OR EVEN MEMORY CIRCUITS IN A HUGE SUPERCOMPUTER...
I'LL ***STILL*** BE HUMAN.
HUMANS ARE BEINGS OF SOUL, OF MIND, OF VILL.

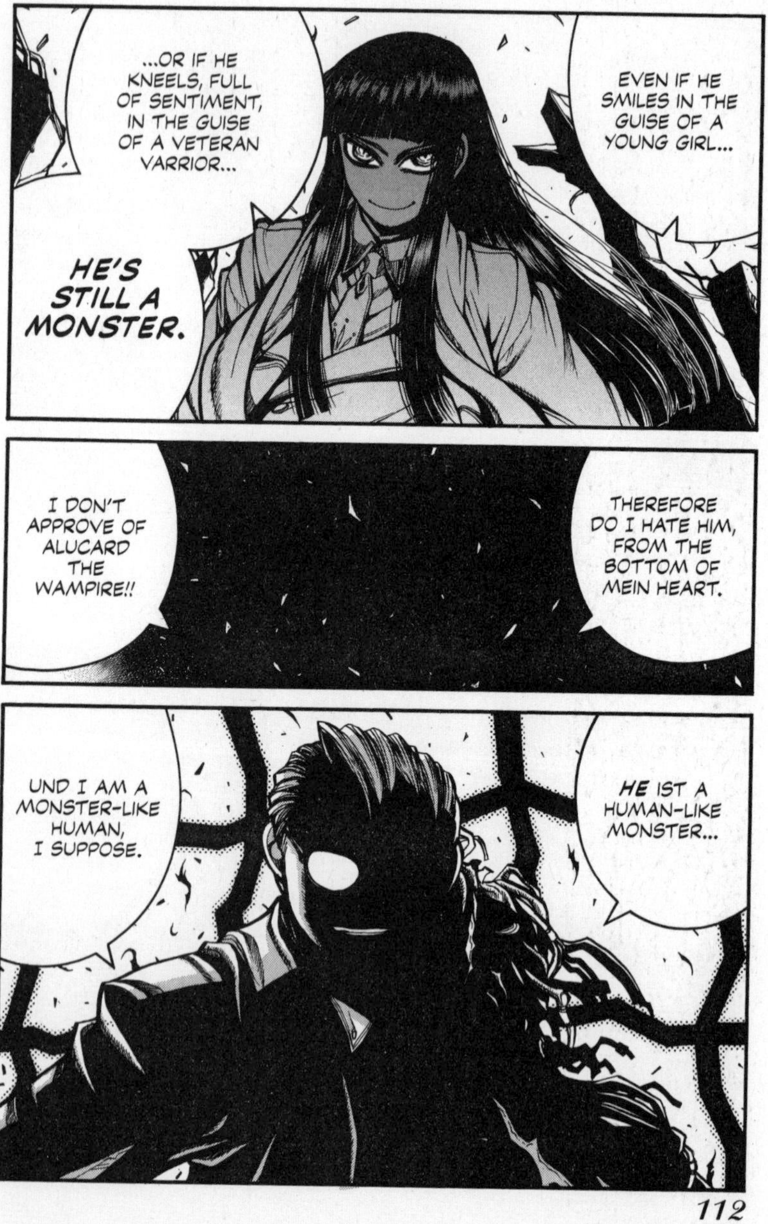

EVEN IF HE SMILES IN THE GUISE OF A YOUNG GIRL...
...OR IF HE KNEELS, FULL OF SENTIMENT, IN THE GUISE OF A VETERAN VARRIOR...
HE'S STILL A MONSTER.
THEREFORE DO I HATE HIM, FROM THE BOTTOM OF MEIN HEART.
I DON'T APPROVE OF ALUCARD THE WAMPIRE!!
HE IST A HUMAN-LIKE MONSTER...
UND I AM A MONSTER-LIKE HUMAN, I SUPPOSE.

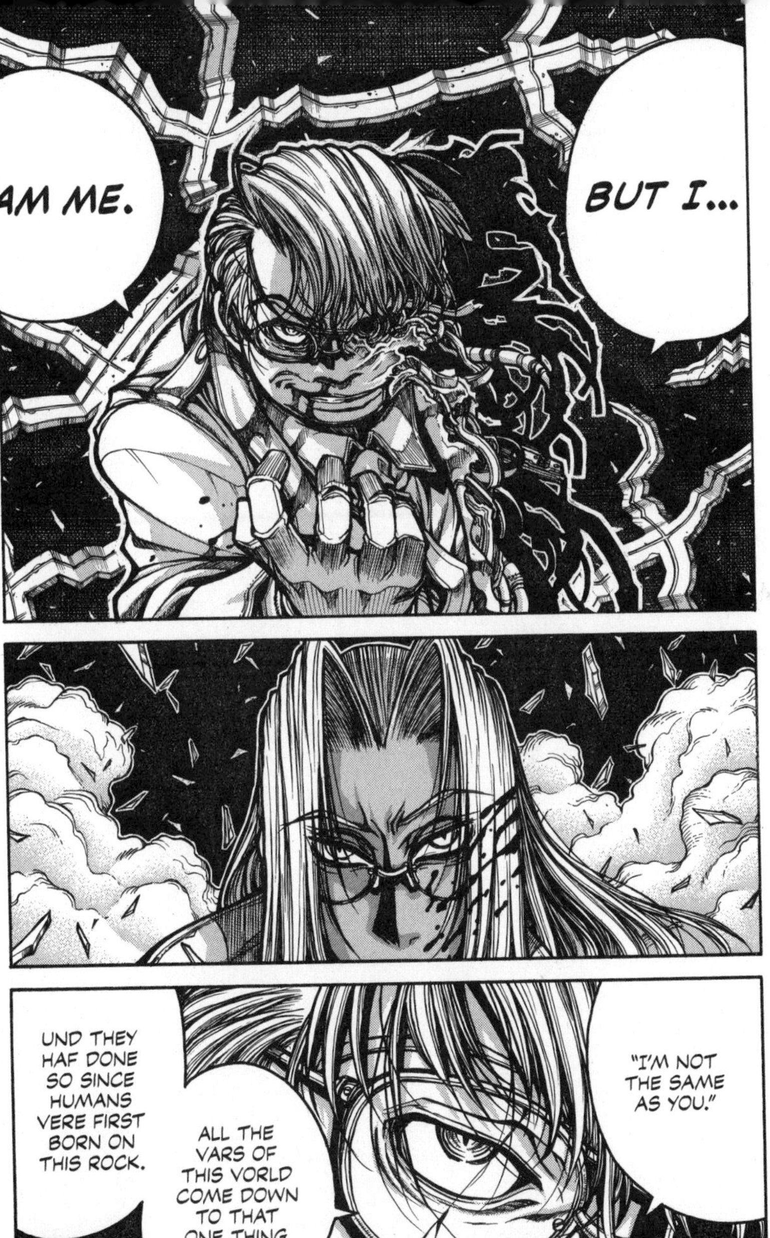
BUT I...
...AM ME.
"I'M NOT THE SAME AS YOU."
ALL THE VARS OF THIS VORLD COME DOWN TO THAT ONE THING.
UND THEY HAF DONE SO SINCE HUMANS VERE FIRST BORN ON THIS ROCK.

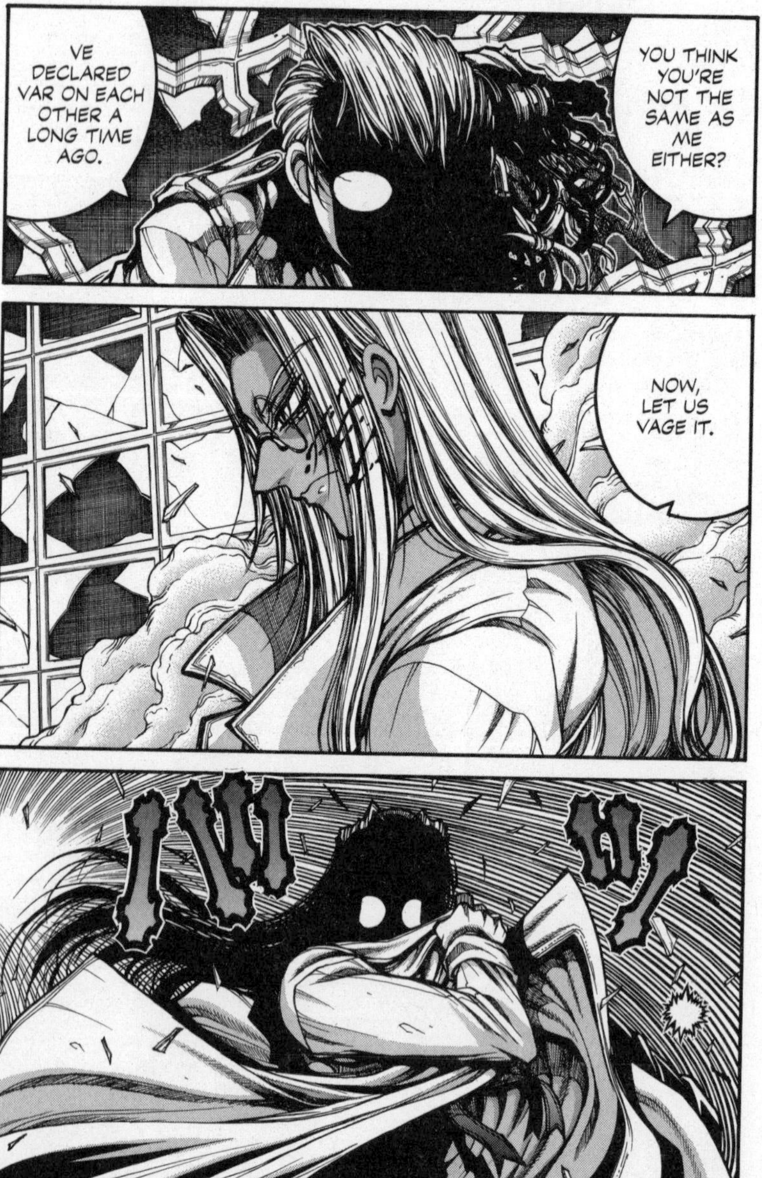
YOU THINK YOU'RE NOT THE SAME AS ME EITHER?
VE DECLARED VAR ON EACH OTHER A LONG TIME AGO.
NOW, LET US VAGE IT.

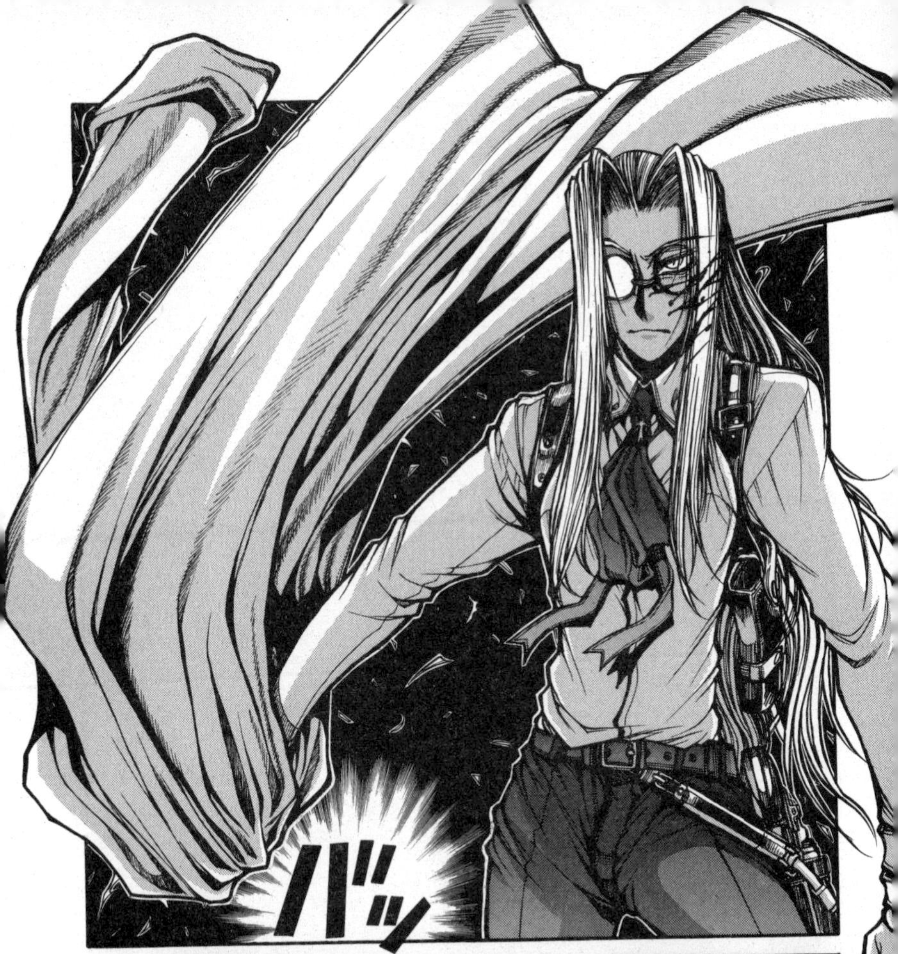
バッ
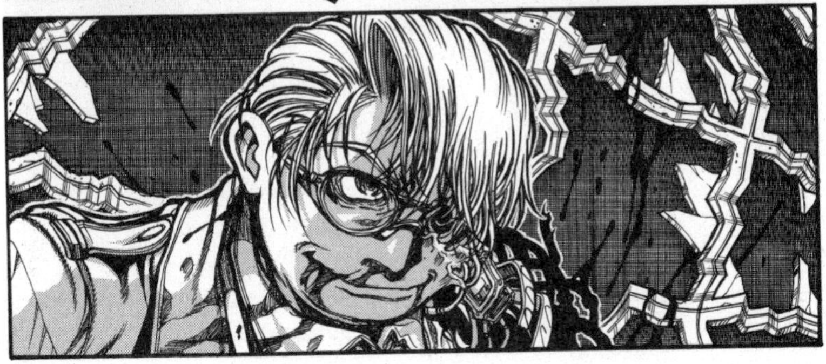

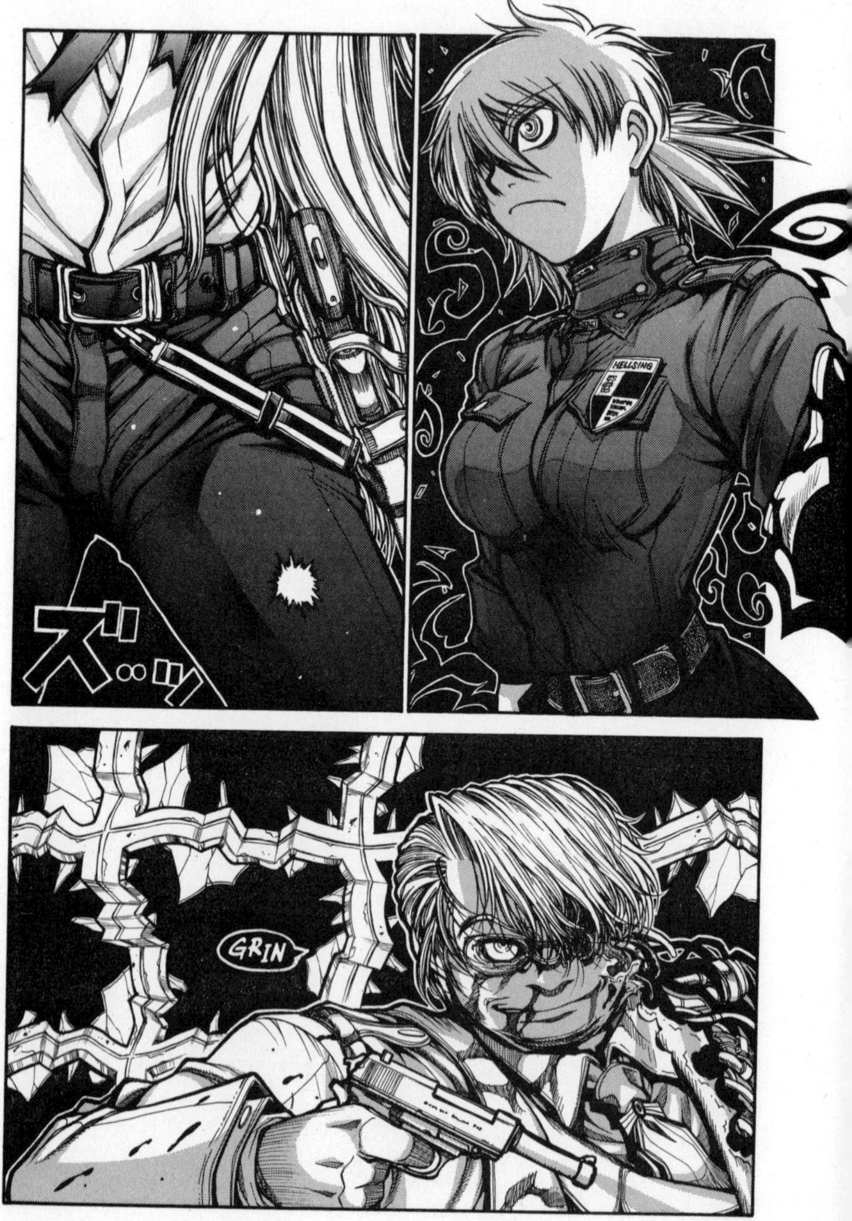
HELLSING
ズッ
GRIN

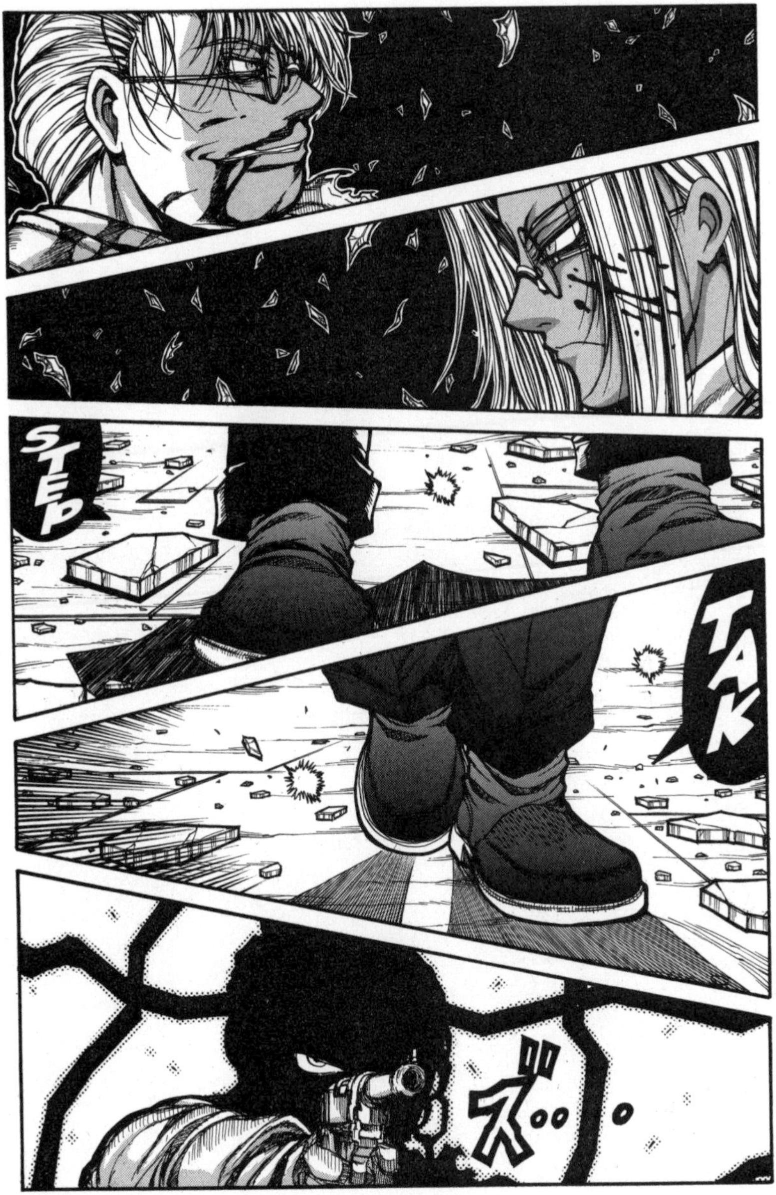
STEP
TAK
ズ・・・

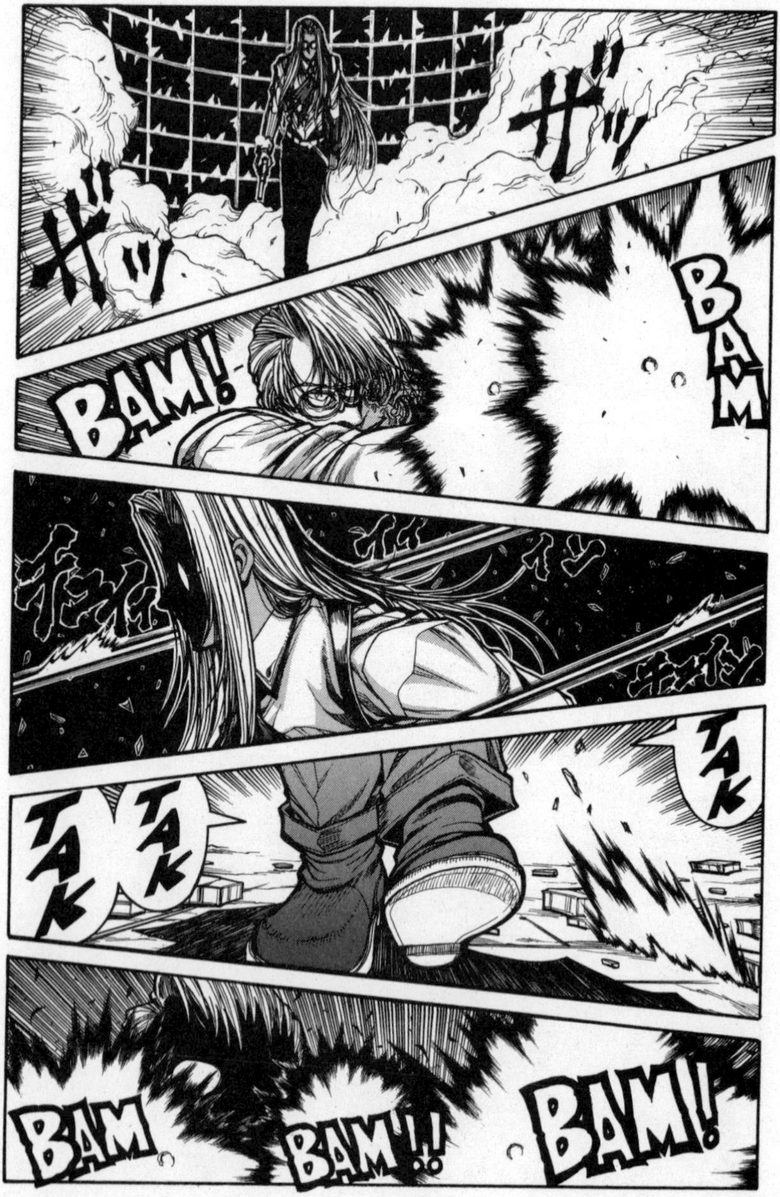
ザッ
ザッ
BAM
BAM!
TAK
TAK
TAK
BAM!
BAM!!
BAM

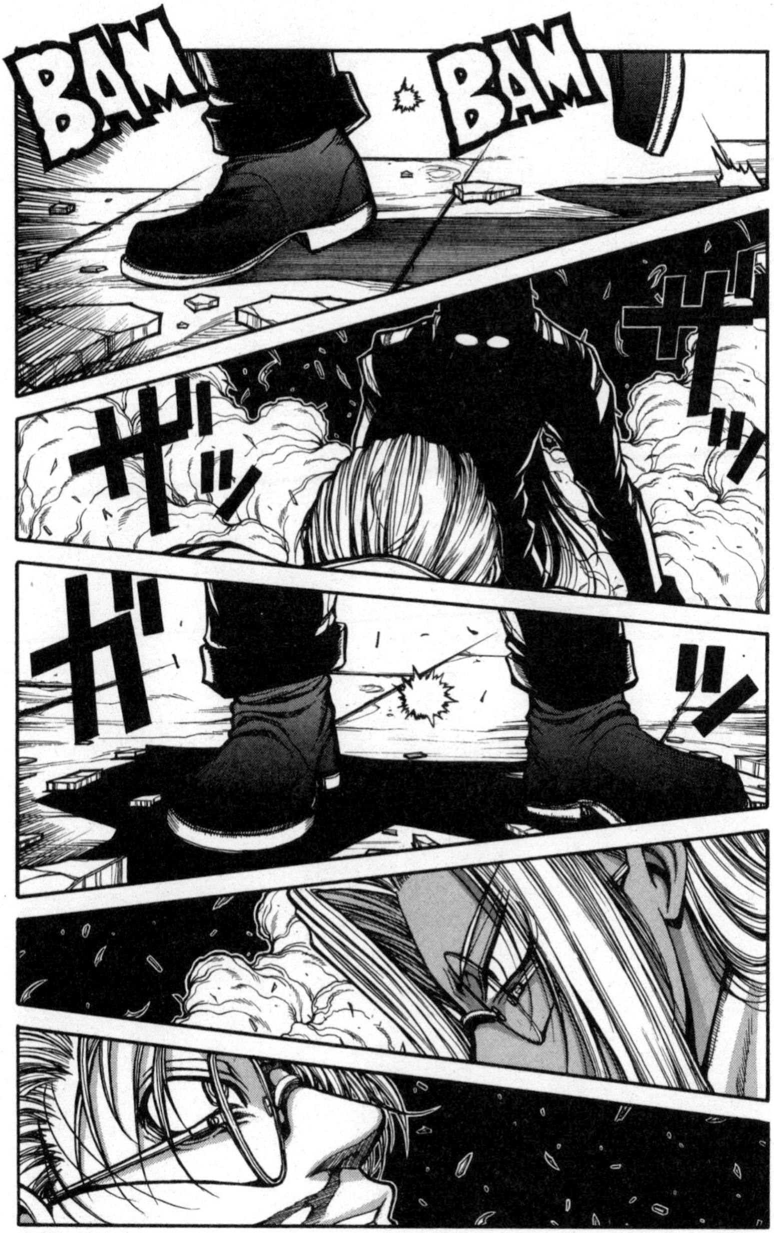
BAM
BAM
ザッ
ザッ
ガッ

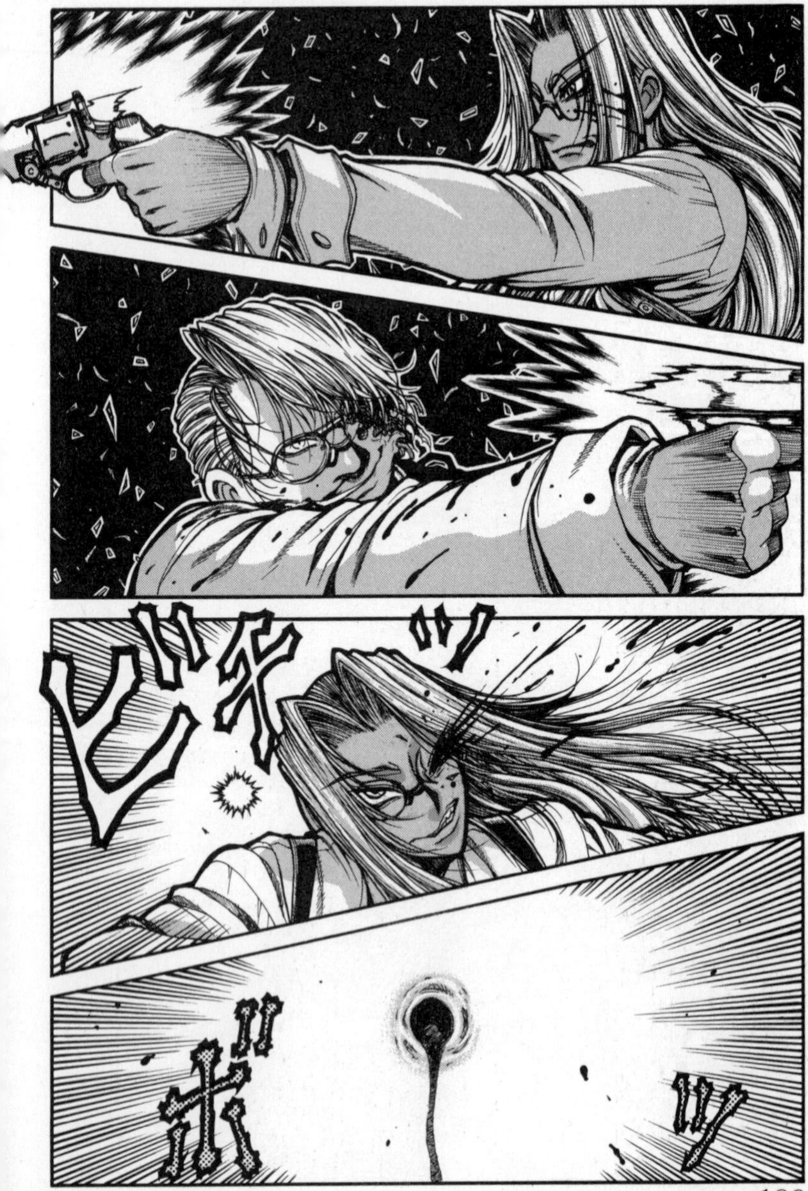
ビスッ
ボッ

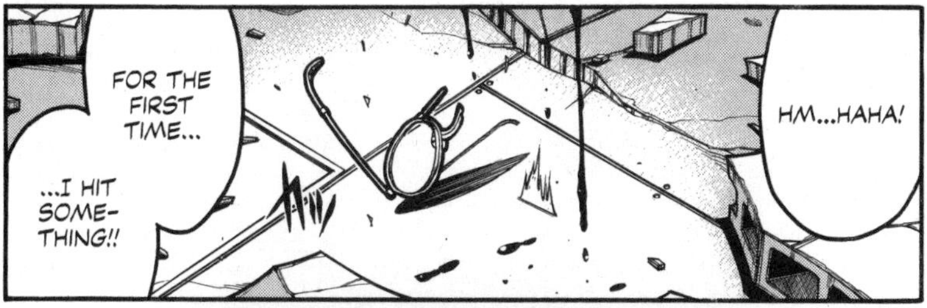
HM...HAHA!
FOR THE FIRST TIME...
...I HIT SOME-THING!!

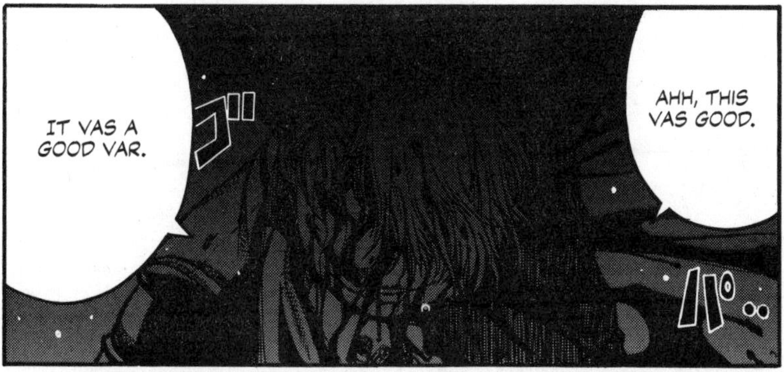
AHH, THIS VAS GOOD.
IT VAS A GOOD VAR.

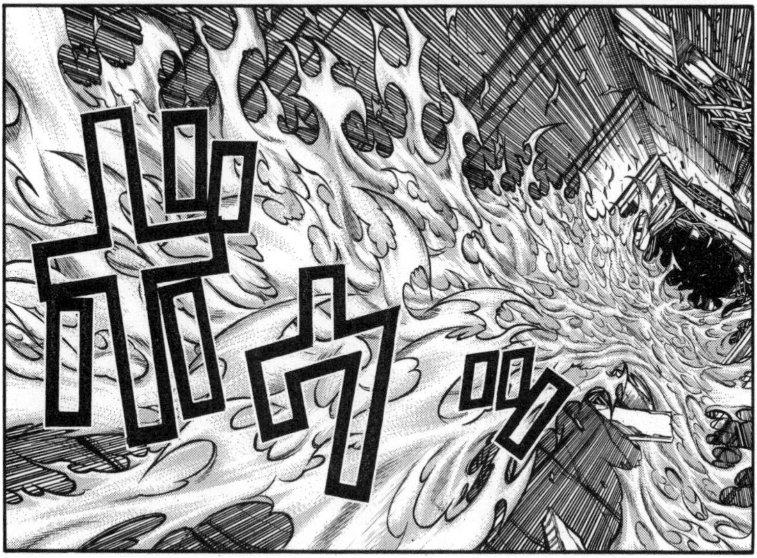

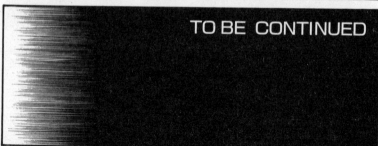

TO BE CONTINUED

ORDER 7 / END

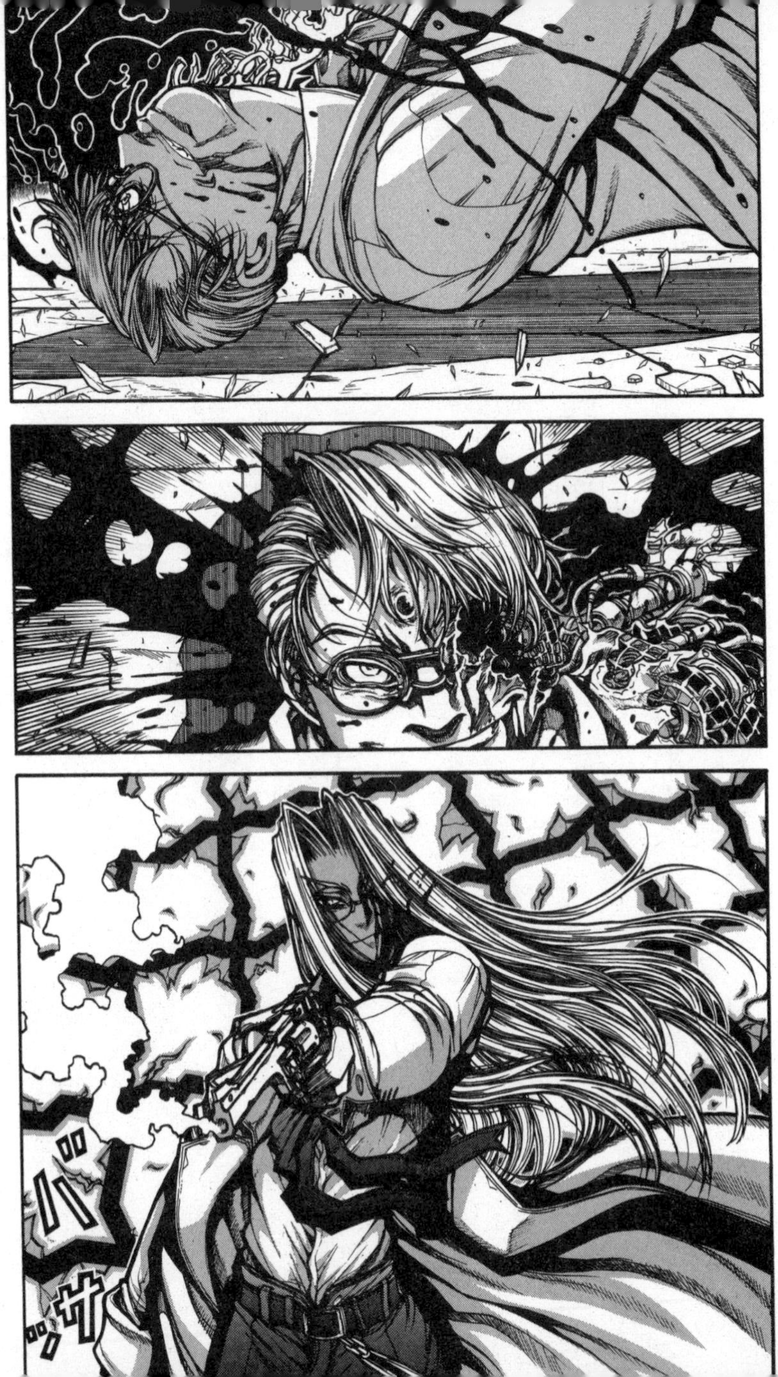
バ
ザ

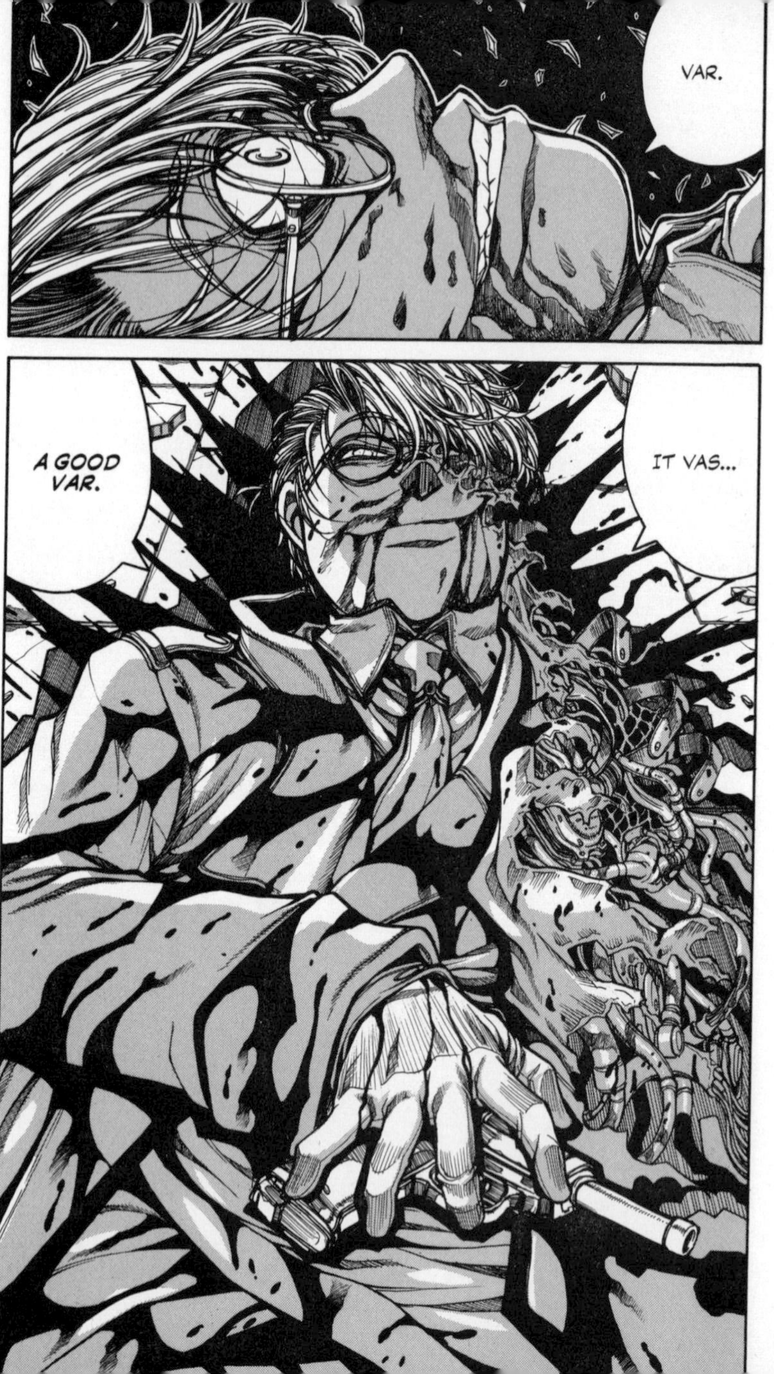
VAR.
IT VAS...
A GOOD VAR.

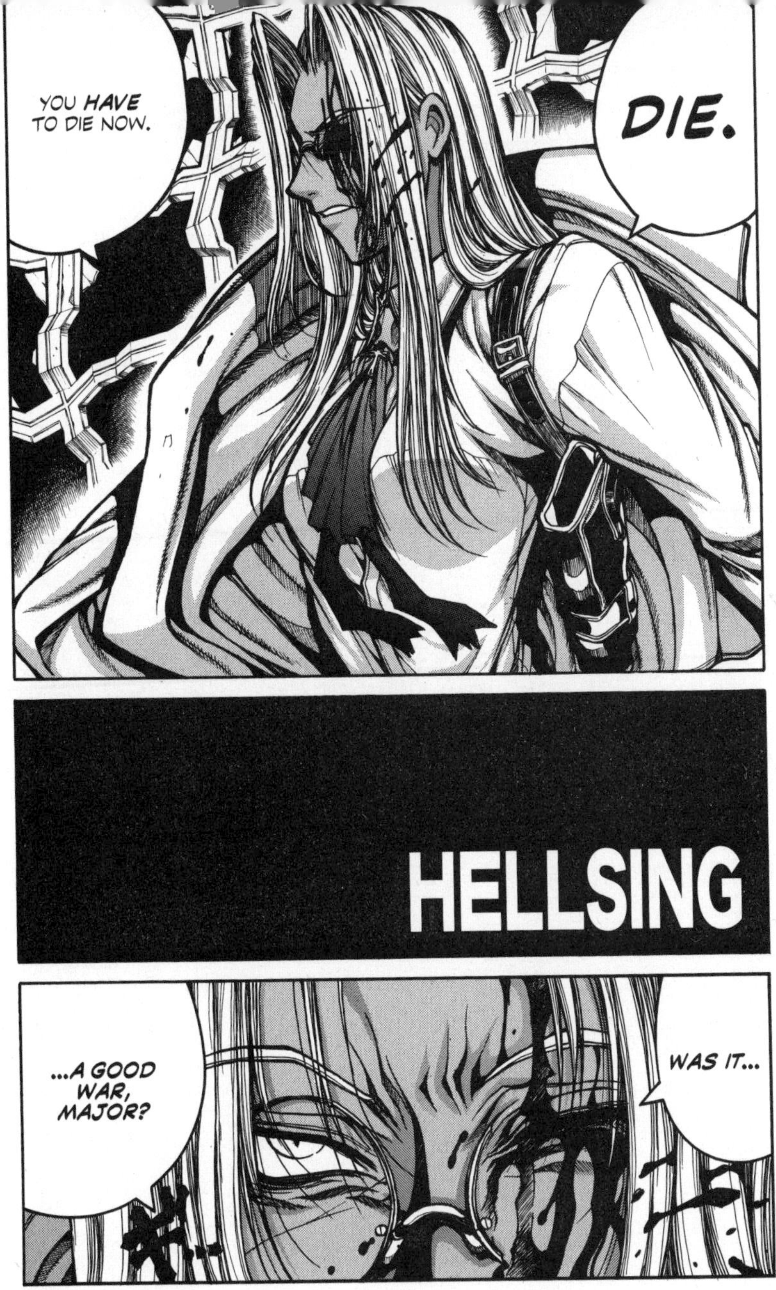
DIE.
YOU HAVE TO DIE NOW.
HELLSING
WAS IT...
...A GOOD WAR, MAJOR?

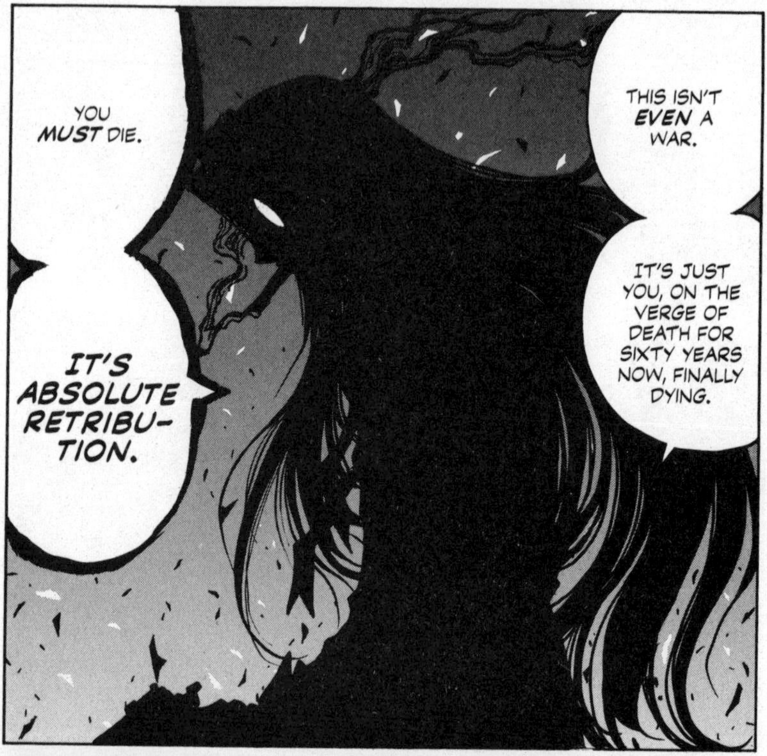
THIS ISN'T EVEN A WAR.
IT'S JUST YOU, ON THE VERGE OF DEATH FOR SIXTY YEARS NOW, FINALLY DYING.
YOU MUST DIE.
IT'S ABSOLUTE RETRIBU-TION.

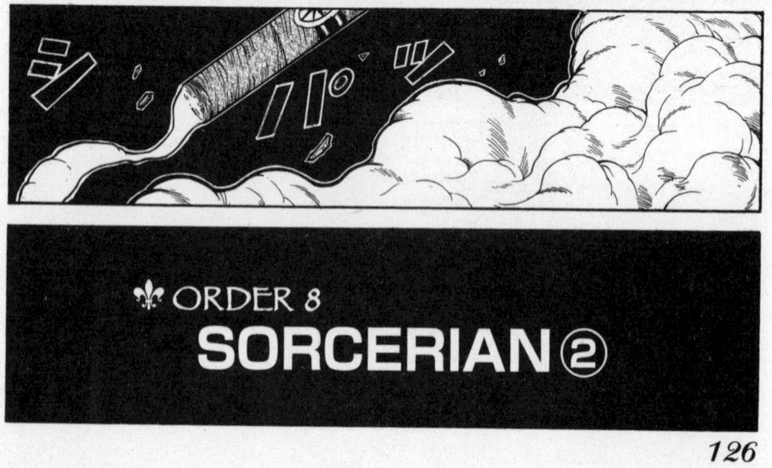
シパッ

ORDER 8

SORCERIAN ②

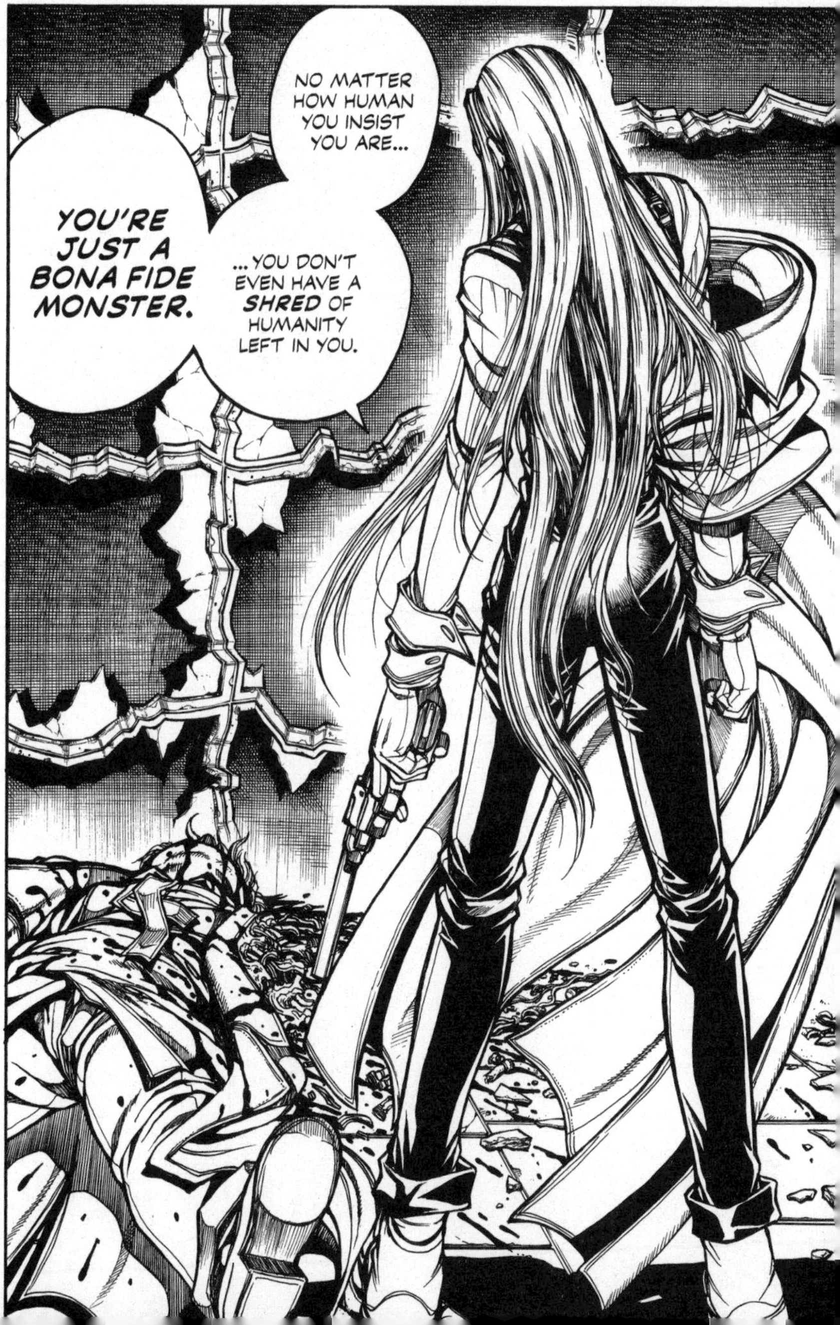
NO MATTER HOW HUMAN YOU INSIST YOU ARE...
...YOU DON'T EVEN HAVE A SHRED OF HUMANITY LEFT IN YOU.
YOU'RE JUST A BONA FIDE MONSTER.

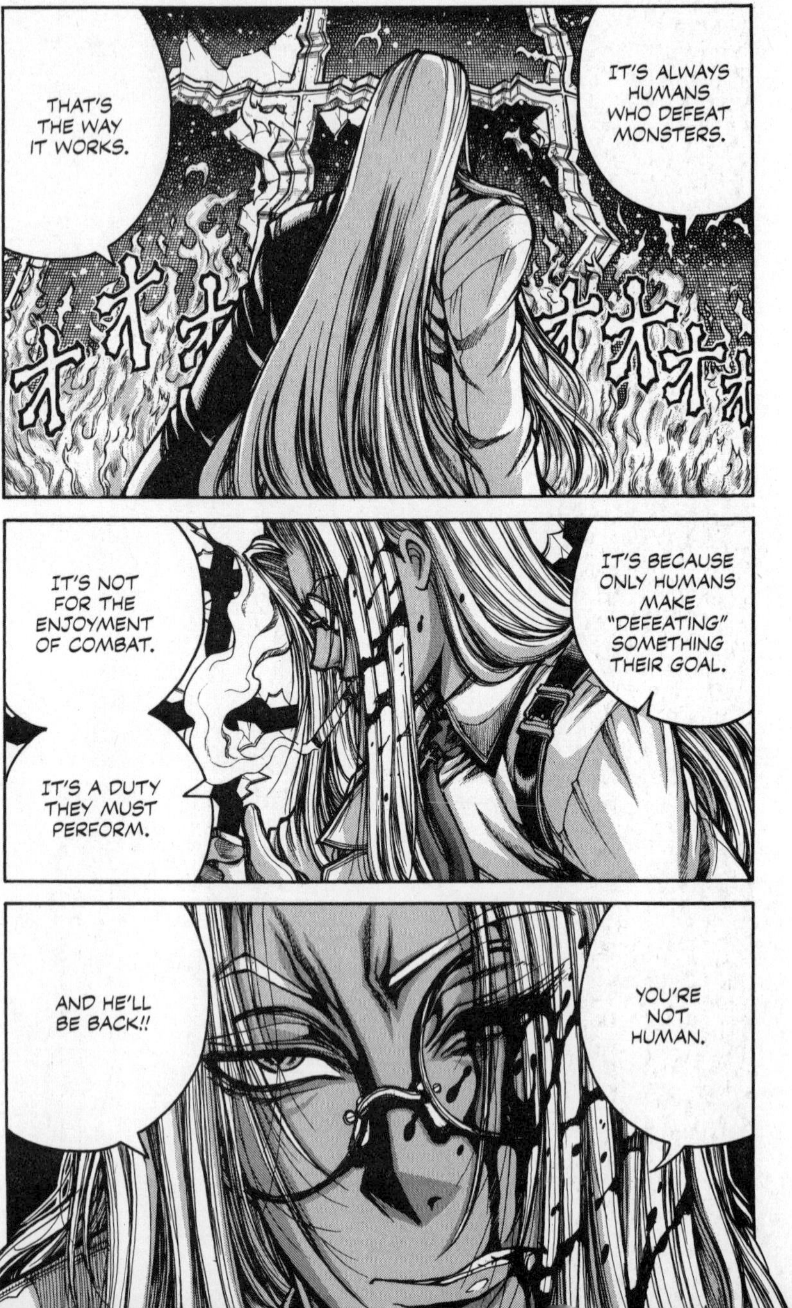
IT'S ALWAYS HUMANS WHO DEFEAT MONSTERS.
THAT'S THE WAY IT WORKS.
オオオ
オオオ
IT'S BECAUSE ONLY HUMANS MAKE "DEFEATING" SOMETHING THEIR GOAL.
IT'S NOT FOR THE ENJOYMENT OF COMBAT.
IT'S A DUTY THEY MUST PERFORM.
YOU'RE NOT HUMAN.
AND HE'LL BE BACK!!

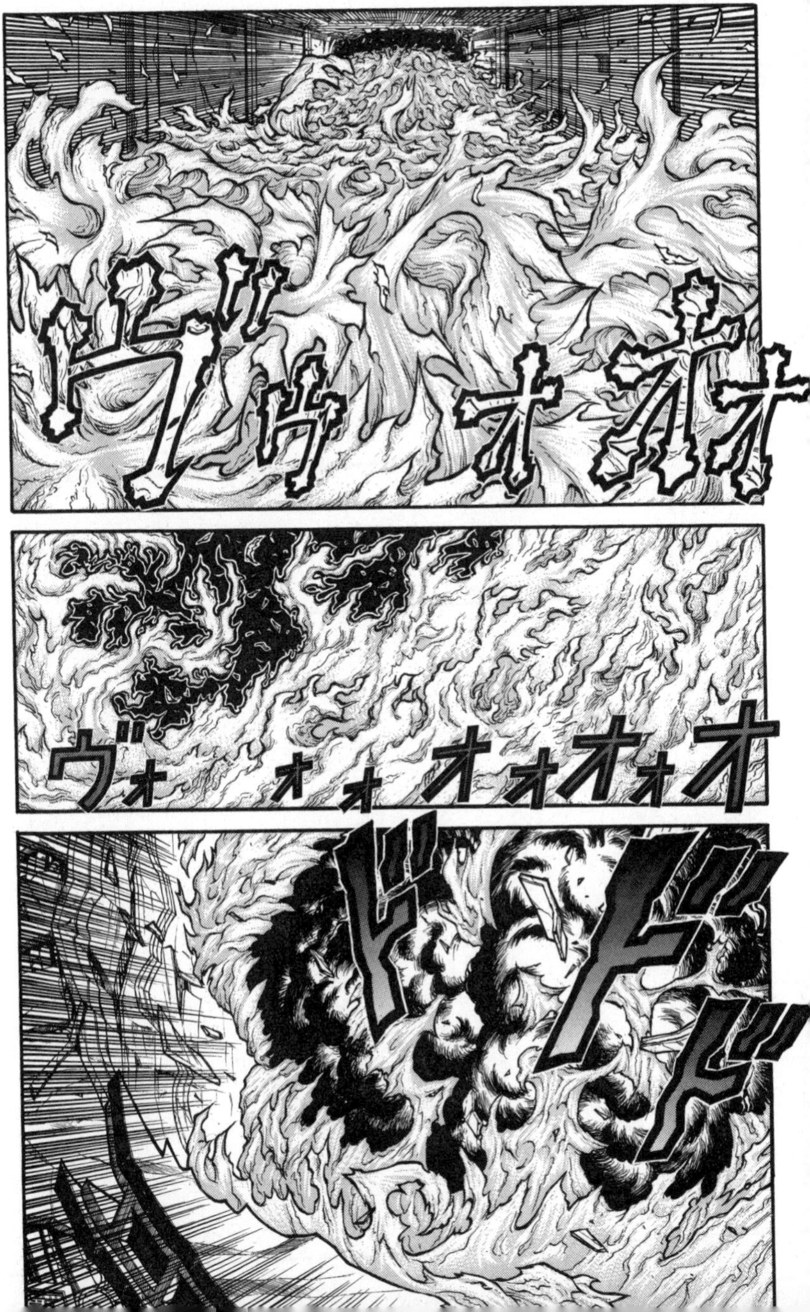
ヴヴオオオ
ヴォォォオォオォオ
ドドド

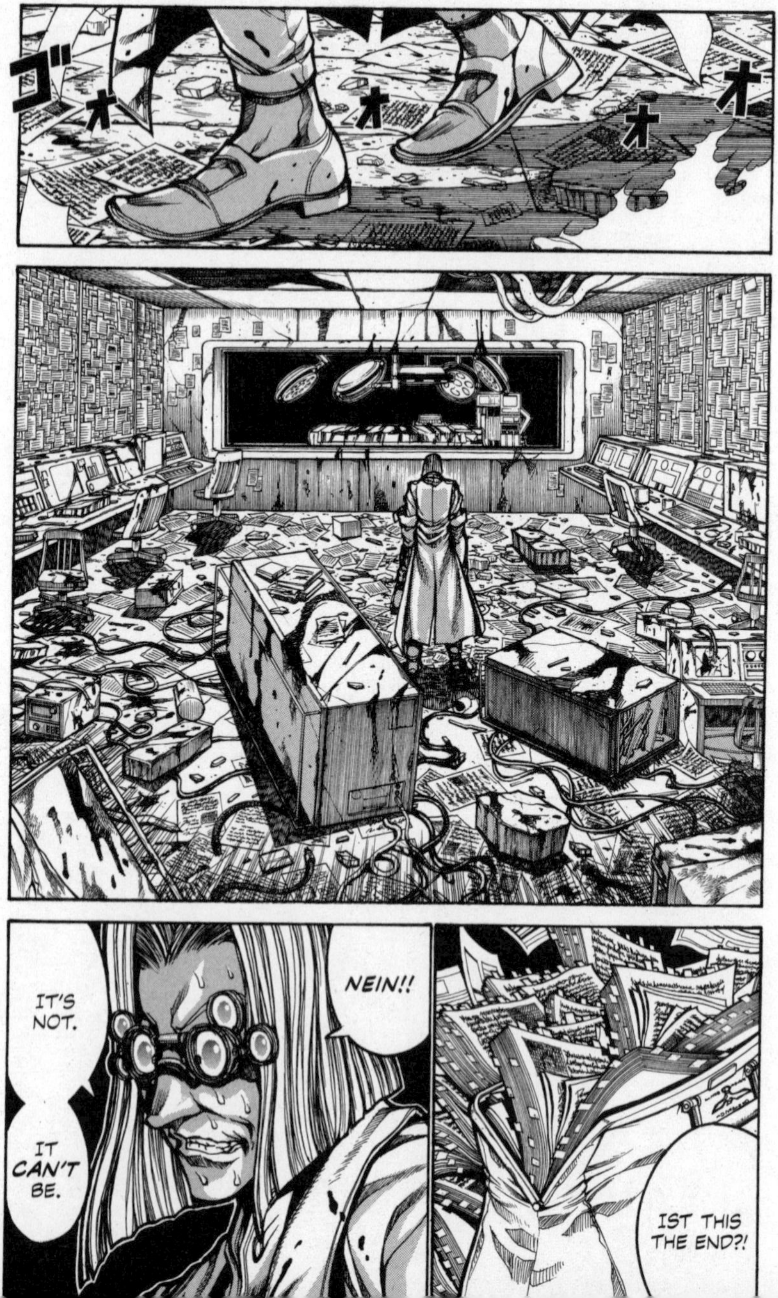
ゴオオオオ
IST THIS THE END?!
NEIN!!
IT'S NOT.
IT CAN'T BE.

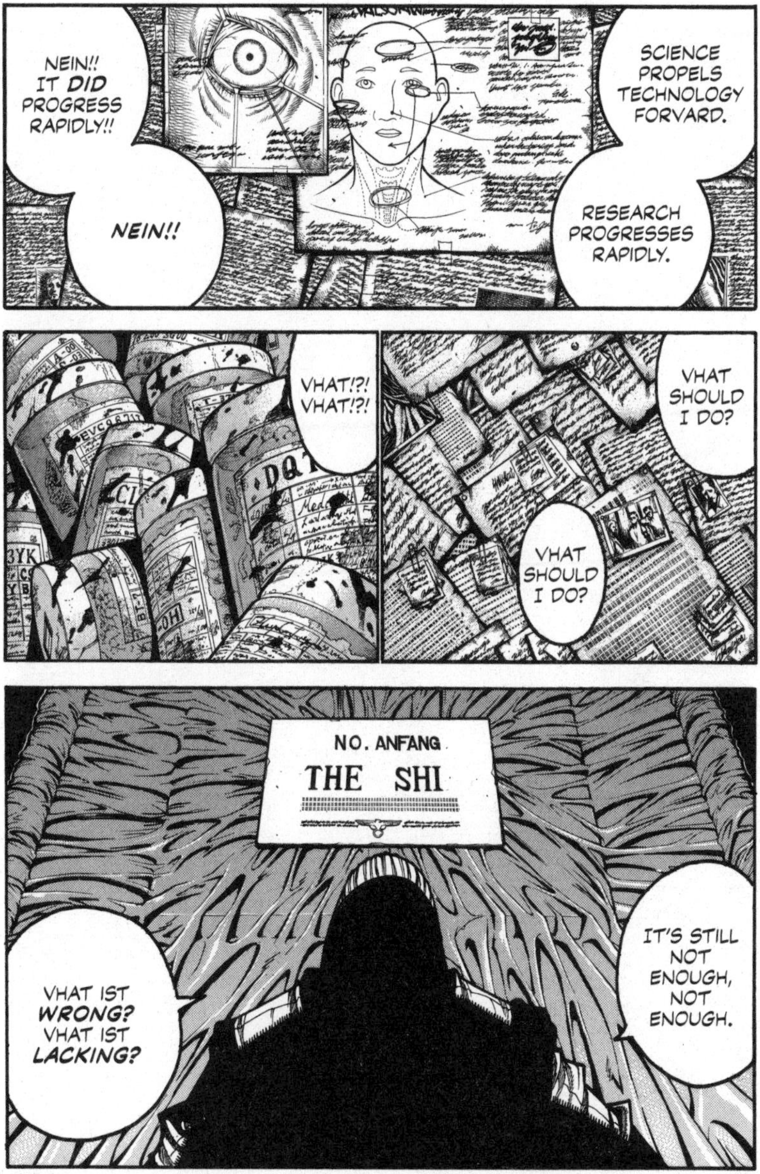
SCIENCE PROPELS TECHNOLOGY FORVARD.
RESEARCH PROGRESSES RAPIDLY.
NEIN!! IT DID PROGRESS RAPIDLY!!
NEIN!!
VHAT SHOULD I DO?
VHAT SHOULD I DO?
VHAT!?! VHAT!?!
NO. ANFANG
THE SHI
IT'S STILL NOT ENOUGH, NOT ENOUGH.
VHAT IST WRONG? VHAT IST LACKING?

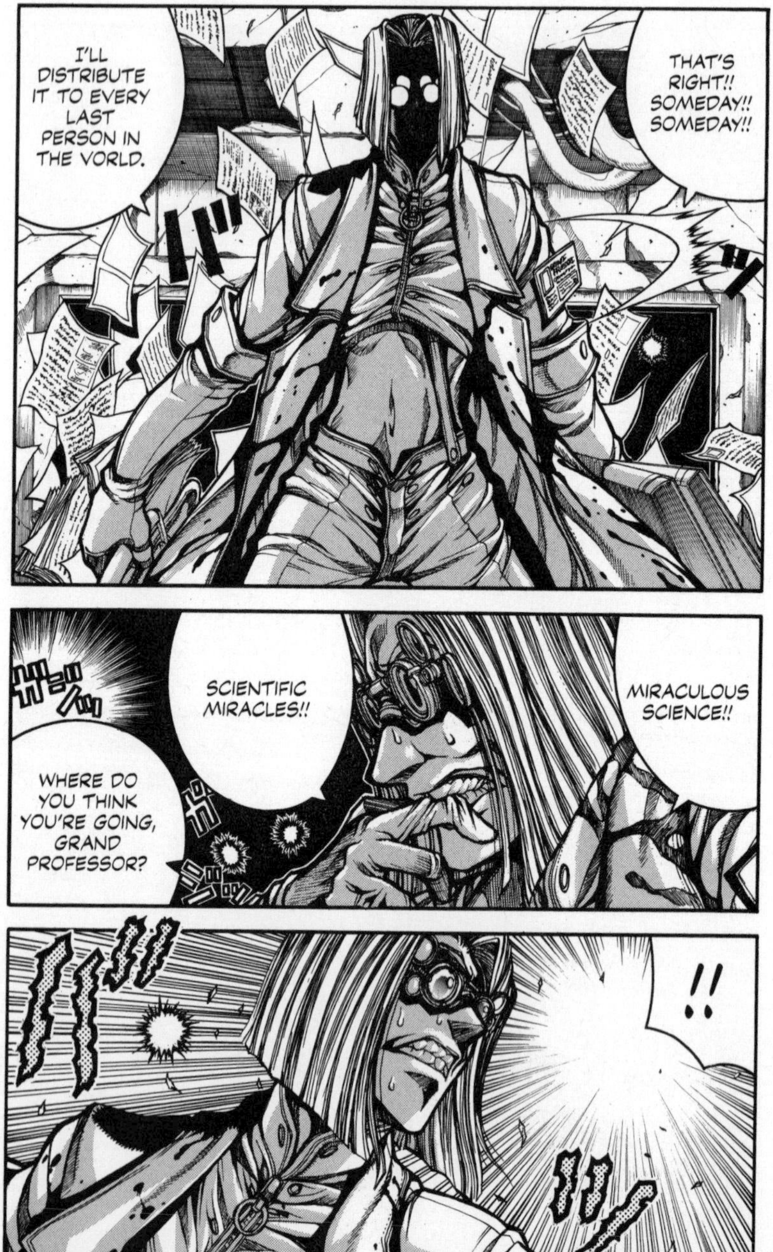
THAT'S RIGHT!! SOMEDAY!! SOMEDAY!!
I'LL DISTRIBUTE IT TO EVERY LAST PERSON IN THE VORLD.
MIRACULOUS SCIENCE!!
SCIENTIFIC MIRACLES!!
WHERE DO YOU THINK YOU'RE GOING, GRAND PROFESSOR?
!!

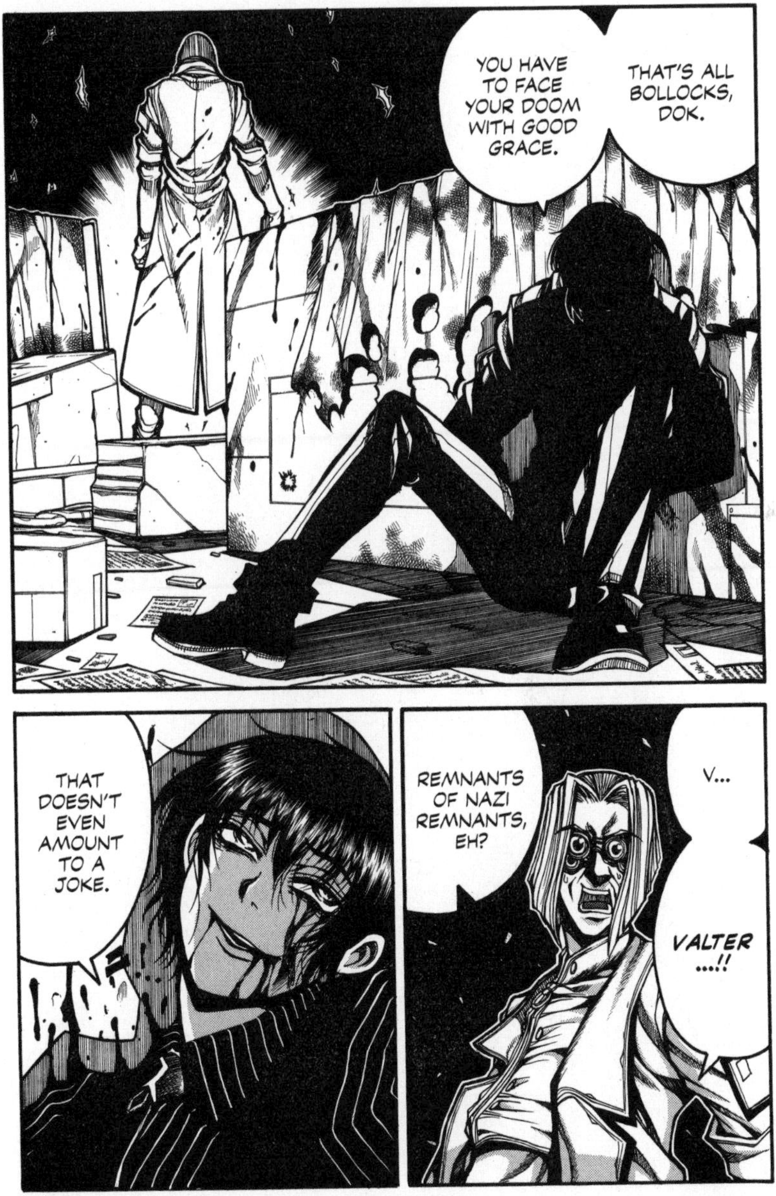
THAT'S ALL BOLLOCKS, DOK.
YOU HAVE TO FACE YOUR DOOM WITH GOOD GRACE.
V...
VALTER ...!!
REMNANTS OF NAZI REMNANTS, EH?
THAT DOESN'T EVEN AMOUNT TO A JOKE.

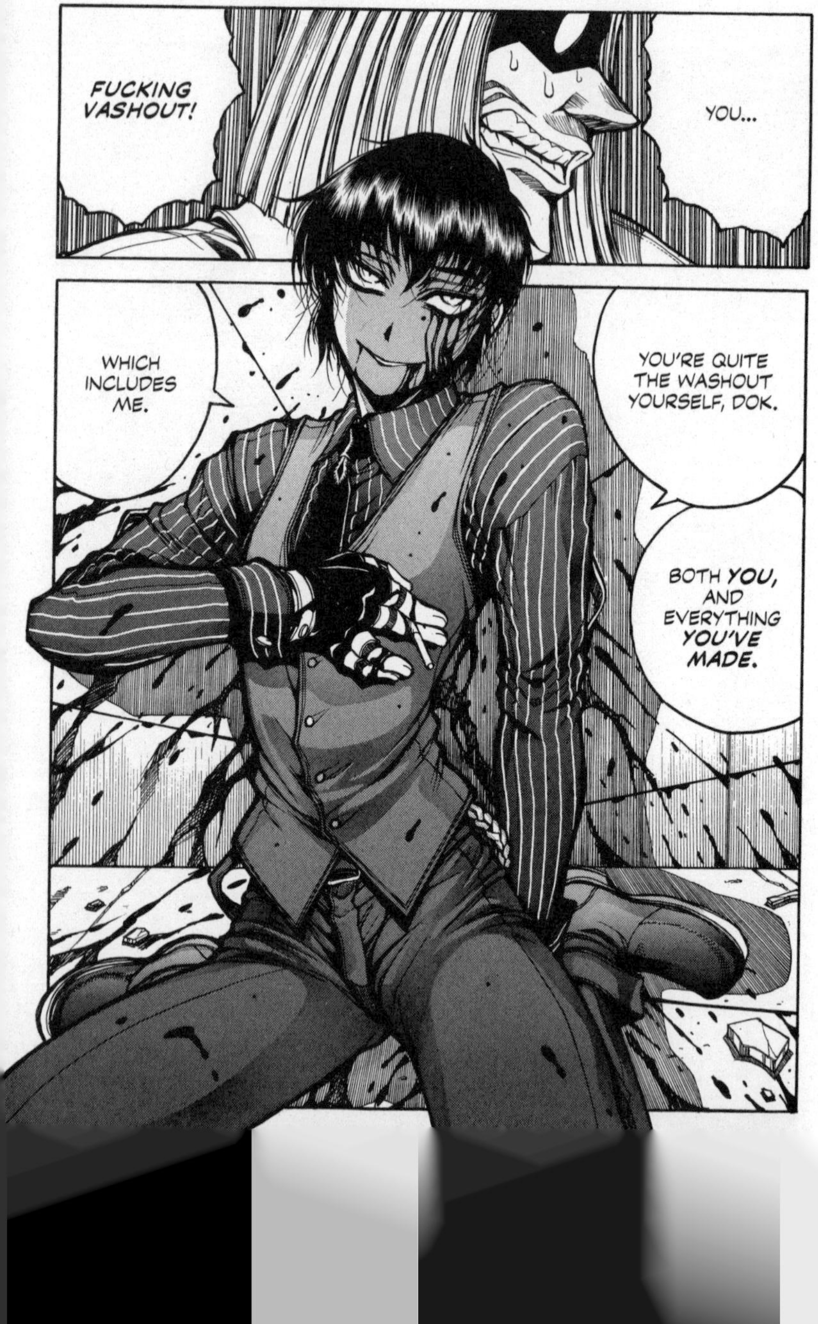
YOU...
FUCKING VASHOUT!
YOU'RE QUITE THE WASHOUT YOURSELF, DOK.
BOTH *YOU*, AND EVERYTHING *YOU'VE MADE*.
WHICH INCLUDES ME.

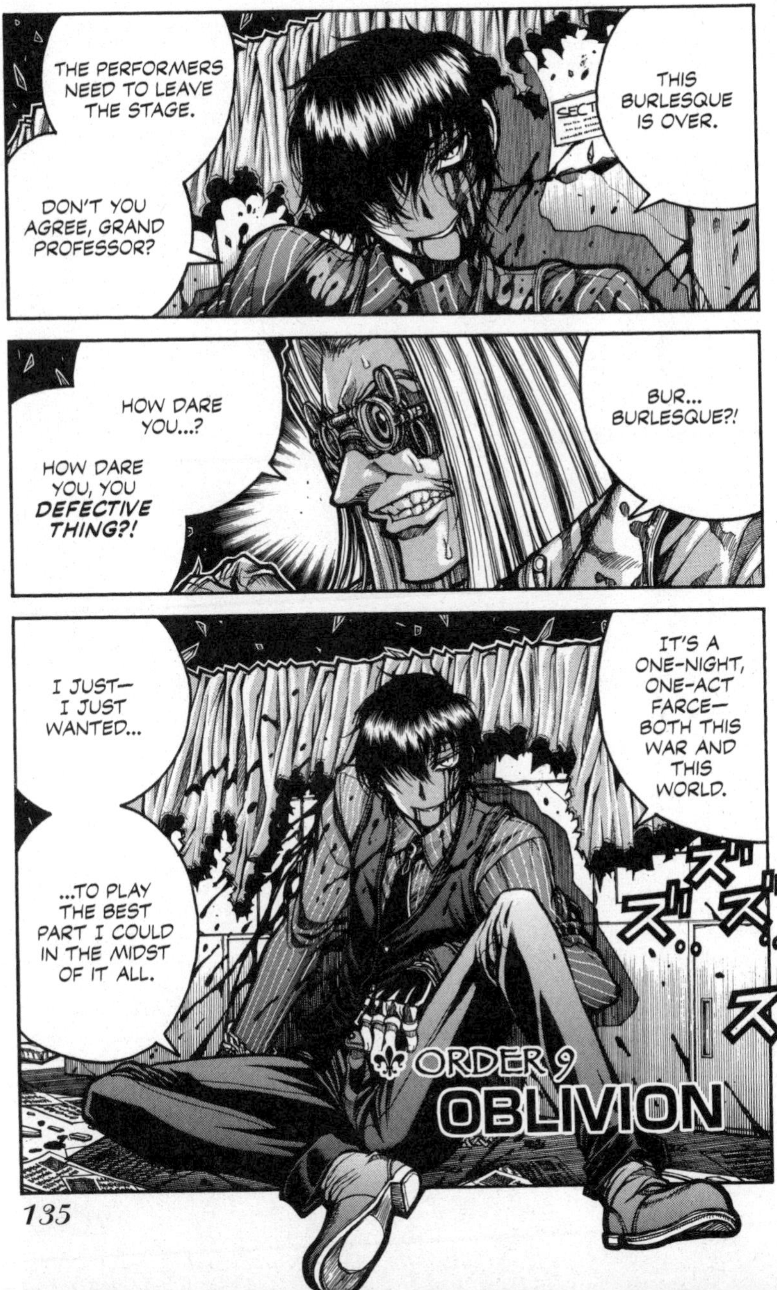
THIS BURLESQUE IS OVER.
THE PERFORMERS NEED TO LEAVE THE STAGE.
DON'T YOU AGREE, GRAND PROFESSOR?
BUR... BURLESQUE?!
HOW DARE YOU...?
HOW DARE YOU, YOU ***DEFECTIVE THING?!***
IT'S A ONE-NIGHT, ONE-ACT FARCE— BOTH THIS WAR AND THIS WORLD.
I JUST— I JUST WANTED...
...TO PLAY THE BEST PART I COULD IN THE MIDST OF IT ALL.
ズズ。ズ。
ズ。
ズ。
ORDER 9
OBLIVION

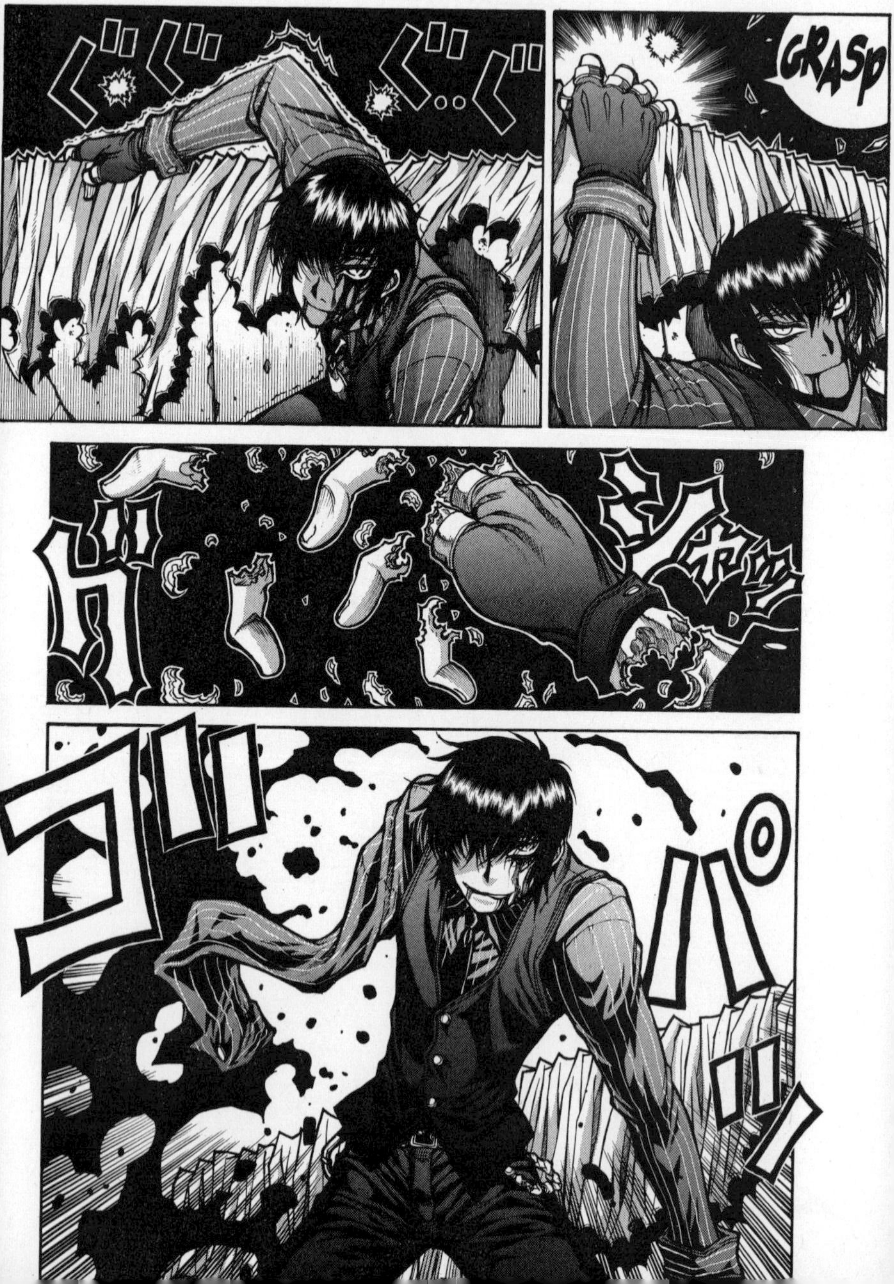
GRASP

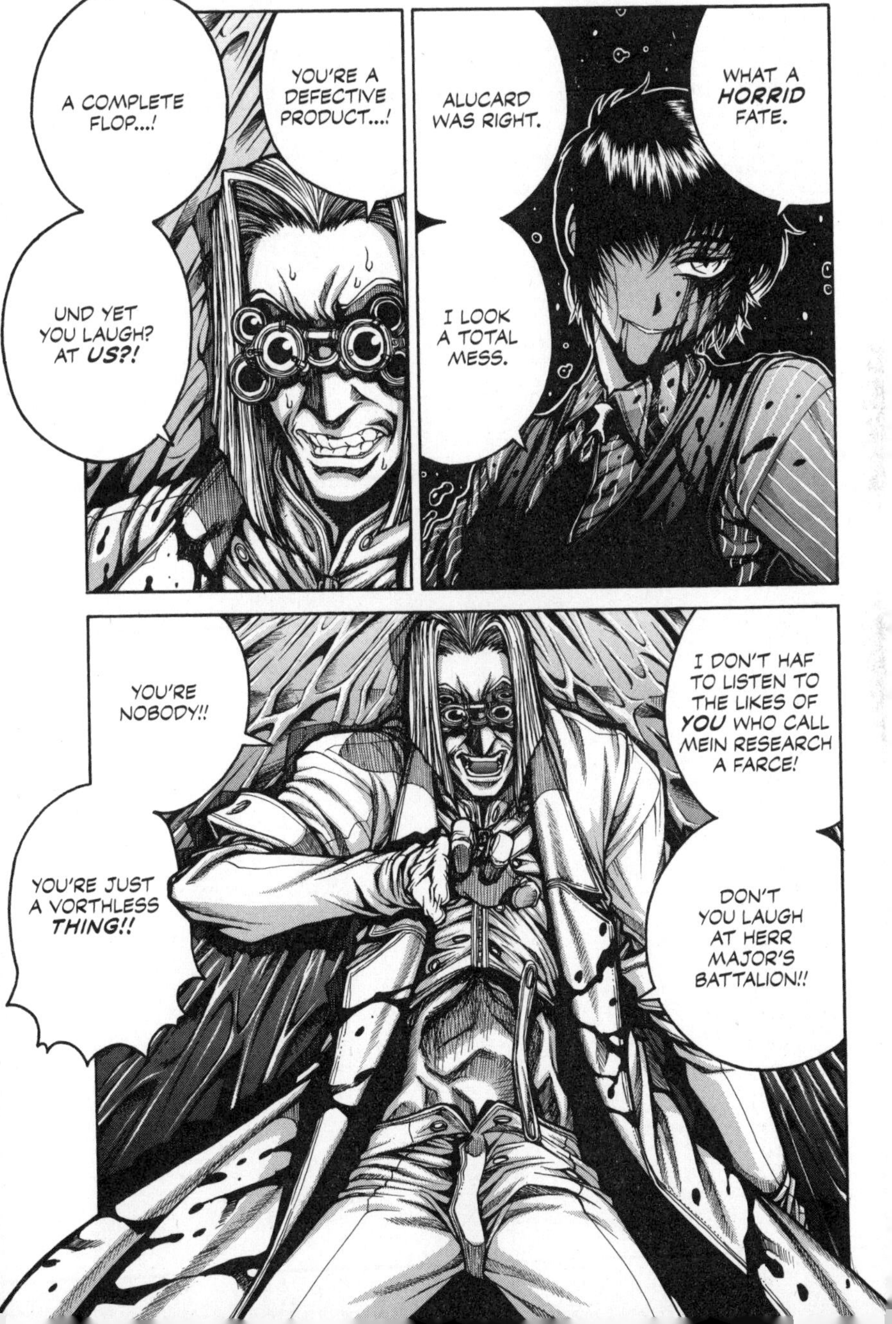
WHAT A **HORRID** FATE.
ALUCARD WAS RIGHT.
I LOOK A TOTAL MESS.
YOU'RE A DEFECTIVE PRODUCT...!
A COMPLETE FLOP...!
UND YET YOU LAUGH? AT **US?!**
I DON'T HAF TO LISTEN TO THE LIKES OF **YOU** WHO CALL MEIN RESEARCH A FARCE!
DON'T YOU LAUGH AT HERR MAJOR'S BATTALION!!
YOU'RE NOBODY!!
YOU'RE JUST A VORTHLESS **THING!!**

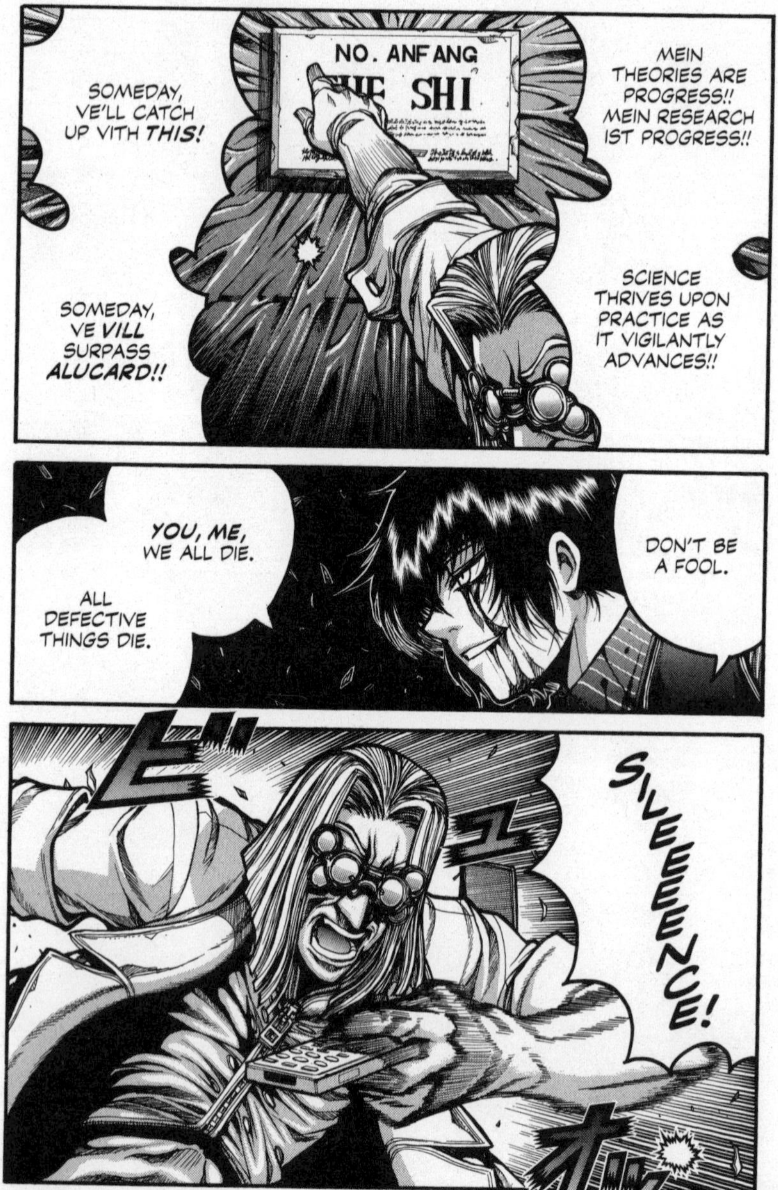
NO. ANFANG
MEIN THEORIES ARE PROGRESS!! MEIN RESEARCH IST PROGRESS!!
SOMEDAY, VE'LL CATCH UP VITH **THIS!**
SCIENCE THRIVES UPON PRACTICE AS IT VIGILANTLY ADVANCES!!
SOMEDAY, VE **VILL** SURPASS **ALUCARD!!**
DON'T BE A FOOL.
YOU, ME, WE ALL DIE.
ALL DEFECTIVE THINGS DIE.
SILEEEENCE!

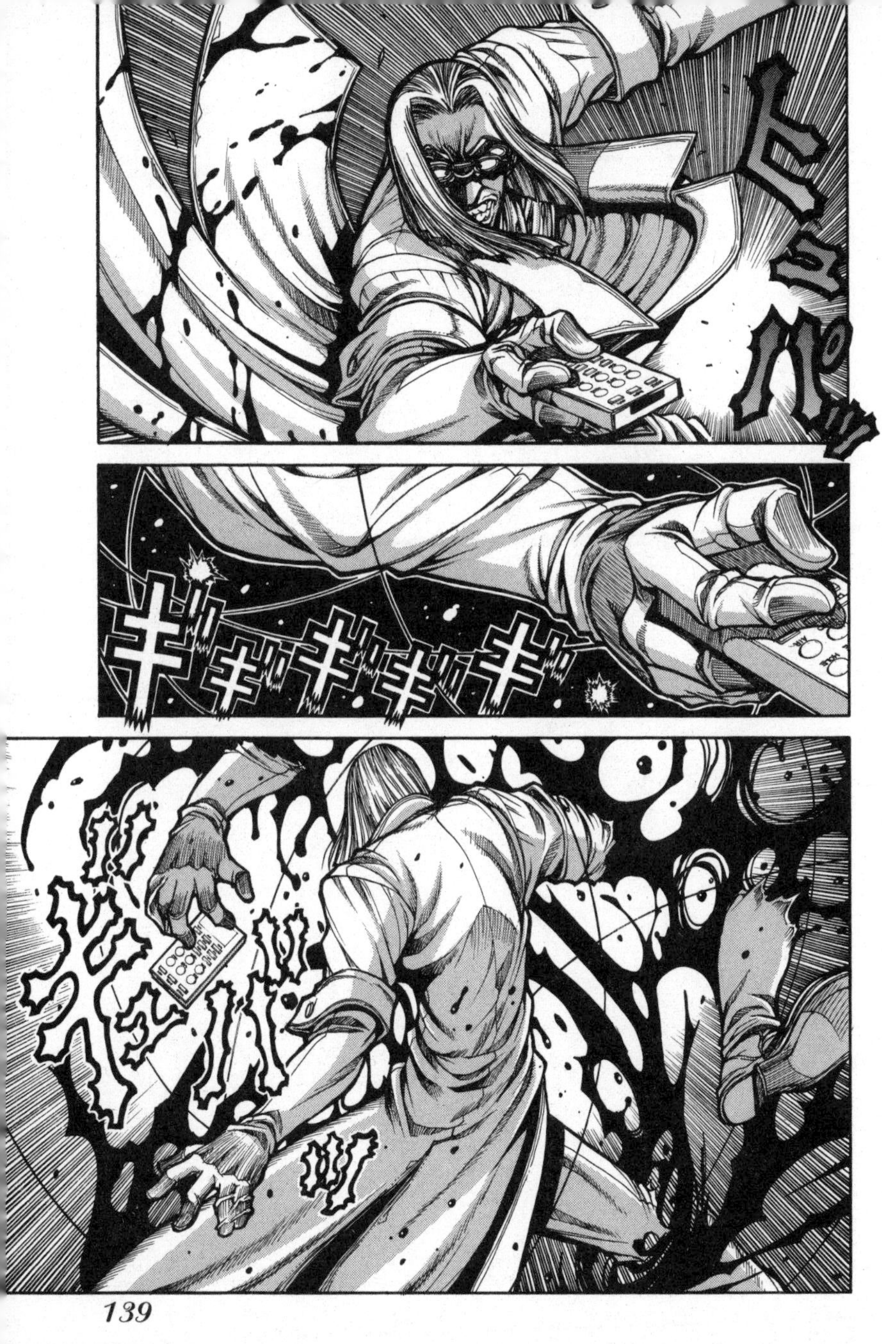
ヒュパッ
ギッギッギッギッギッ

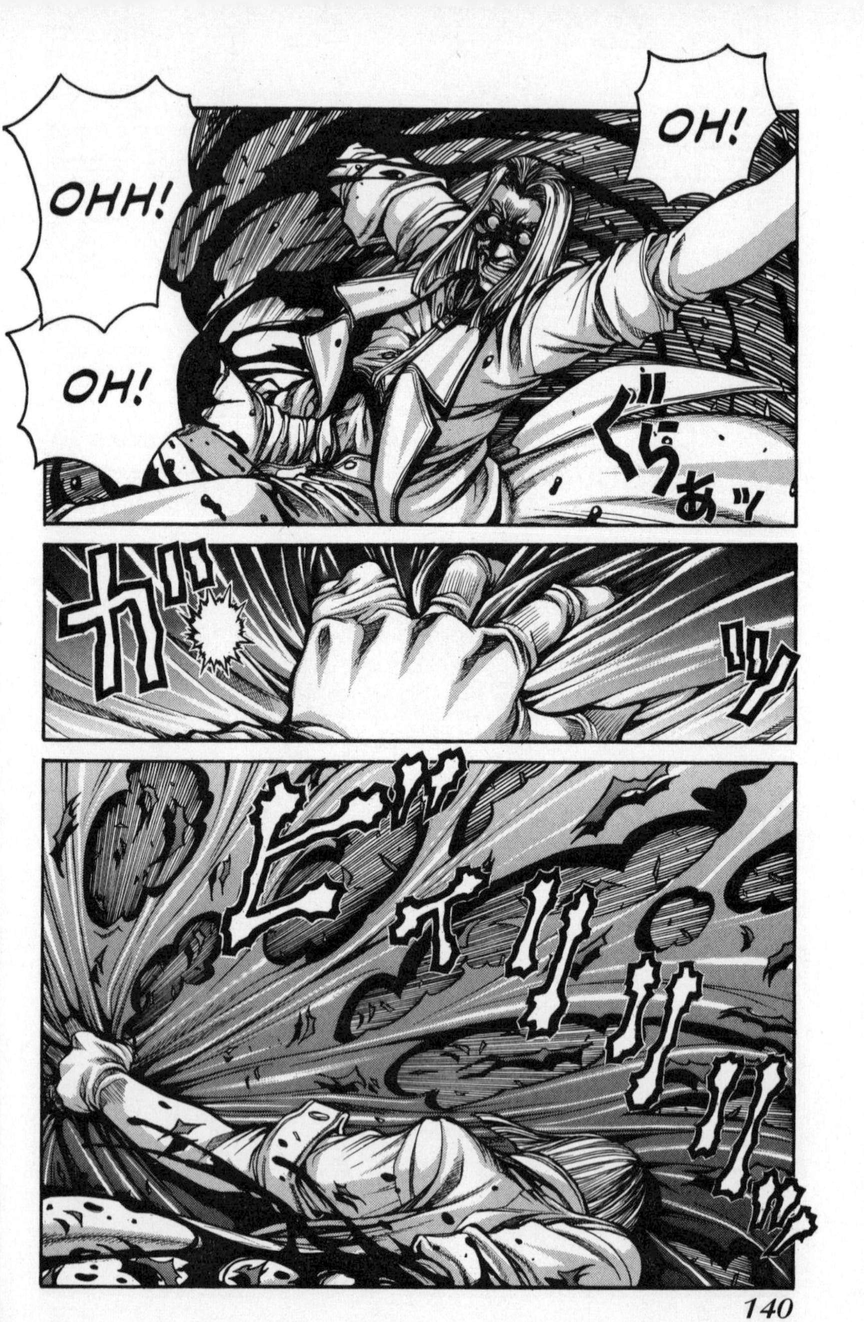
OH!
OHH!
OH!
ぐらあッ
ガッ
ビィリリリリッ

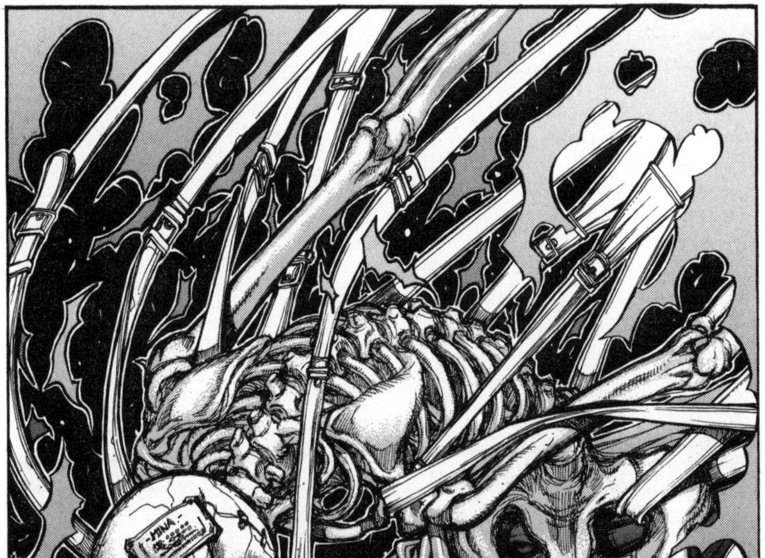
-MINA-
NO.ANFANG
THE SHI
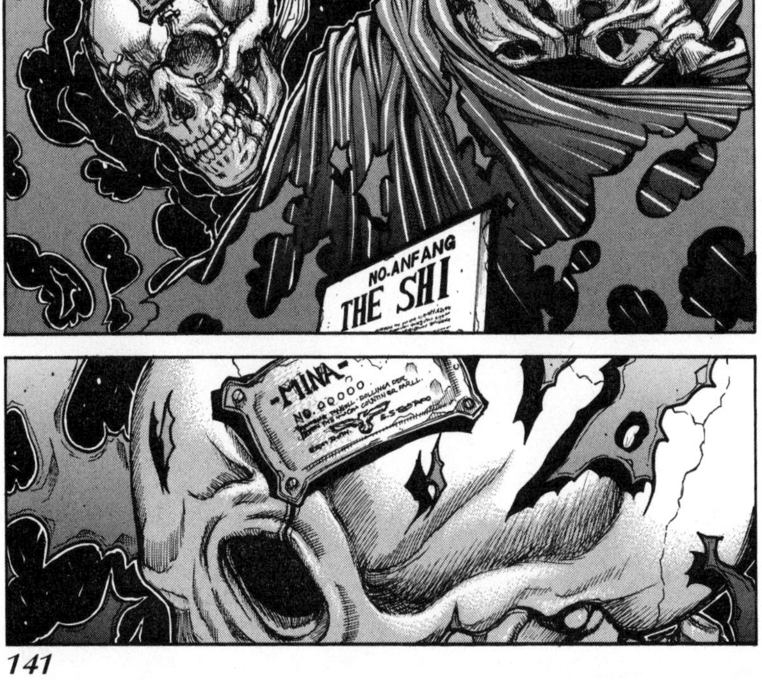
-MINA-
NO. 00000

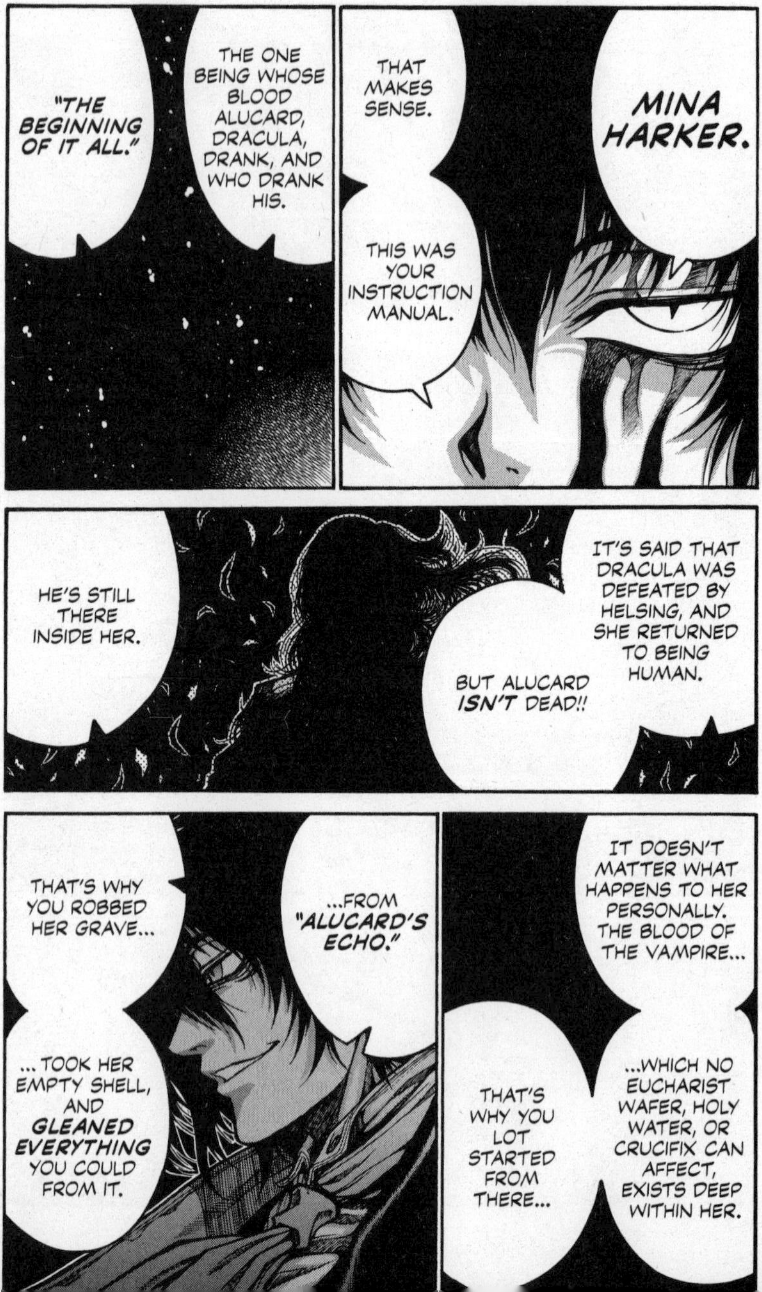
MINA HARKER.
THAT MAKES SENSE.
THIS WAS YOUR INSTRUCTION MANUAL.
THE ONE BEING WHOSE BLOOD ALUCARD, DRACULA, DRANK, AND WHO DRANK HIS.
"THE BEGINNING OF IT ALL."
IT'S SAID THAT DRACULA WAS DEFEATED BY HELSING, AND SHE RETURNED TO BEING HUMAN.
BUT ALUCARD *ISN'T* DEAD!!
HE'S STILL THERE INSIDE HER.
IT DOESN'T MATTER WHAT HAPPENS TO HER PERSONALLY. THE BLOOD OF THE VAMPIRE...
...WHICH NO EUCHARIST WAFER, HOLY WATER, OR CRUCIFIX CAN AFFECT, EXISTS DEEP WITHIN HER.
THAT'S WHY YOU LOT STARTED FROM THERE...
...FROM ***"ALUCARD'S ECHO."***
THAT'S WHY YOU ROBBED HER GRAVE...
...TOOK HER EMPTY SHELL, AND ***GLEANED EVERYTHING*** YOU COULD FROM IT.

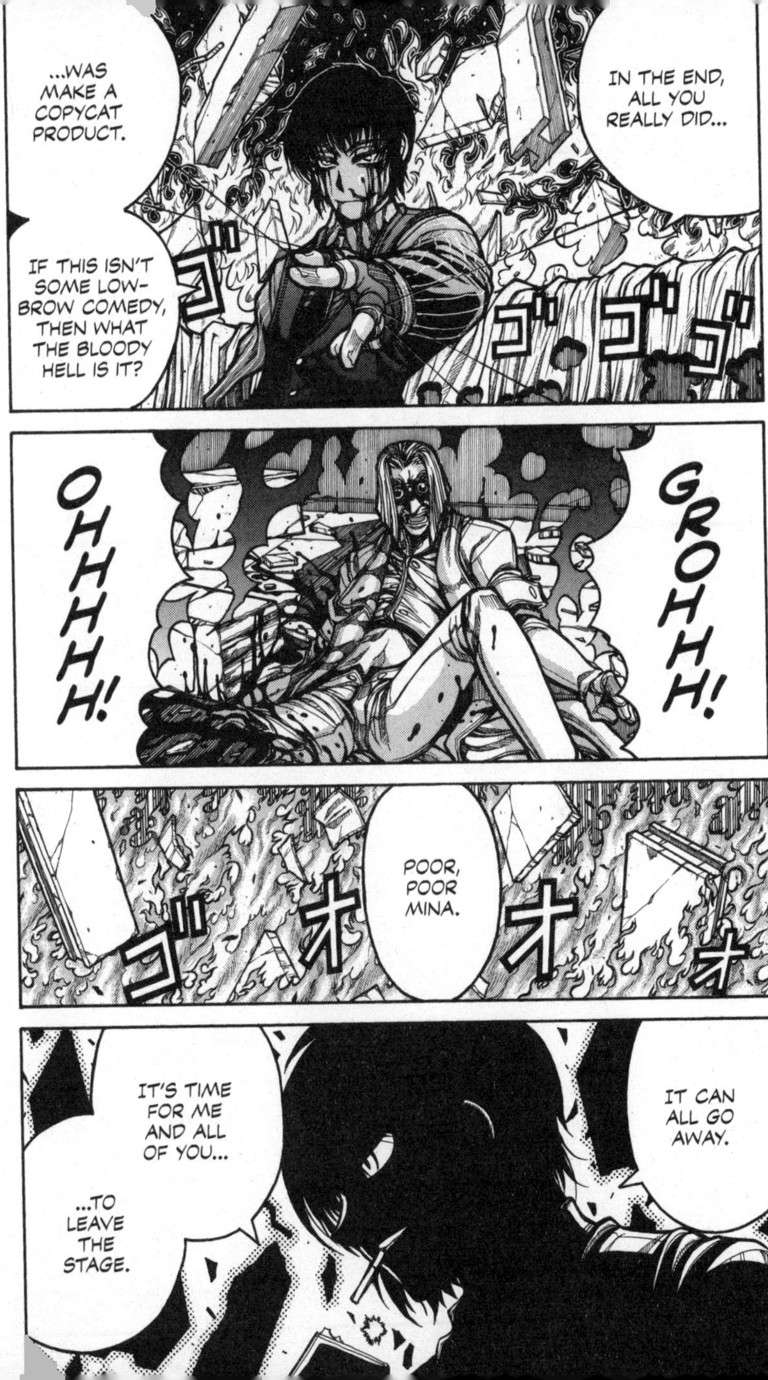
IN THE END, ALL YOU REALLY DID...
...WAS MAKE A COPYCAT PRODUCT.
ゴゴゴ
ゴ
IF THIS ISN'T SOME LOW-BROW COMEDY, THEN WHAT THE BLOODY HELL IS IT?
GROHHHH!
OHHHHH!
ゴオオオ
POOR, POOR MINA.
IT CAN ALL GO AWAY.
IT'S TIME FOR ME AND ALL OF YOU...
...TO LEAVE THE STAGE.

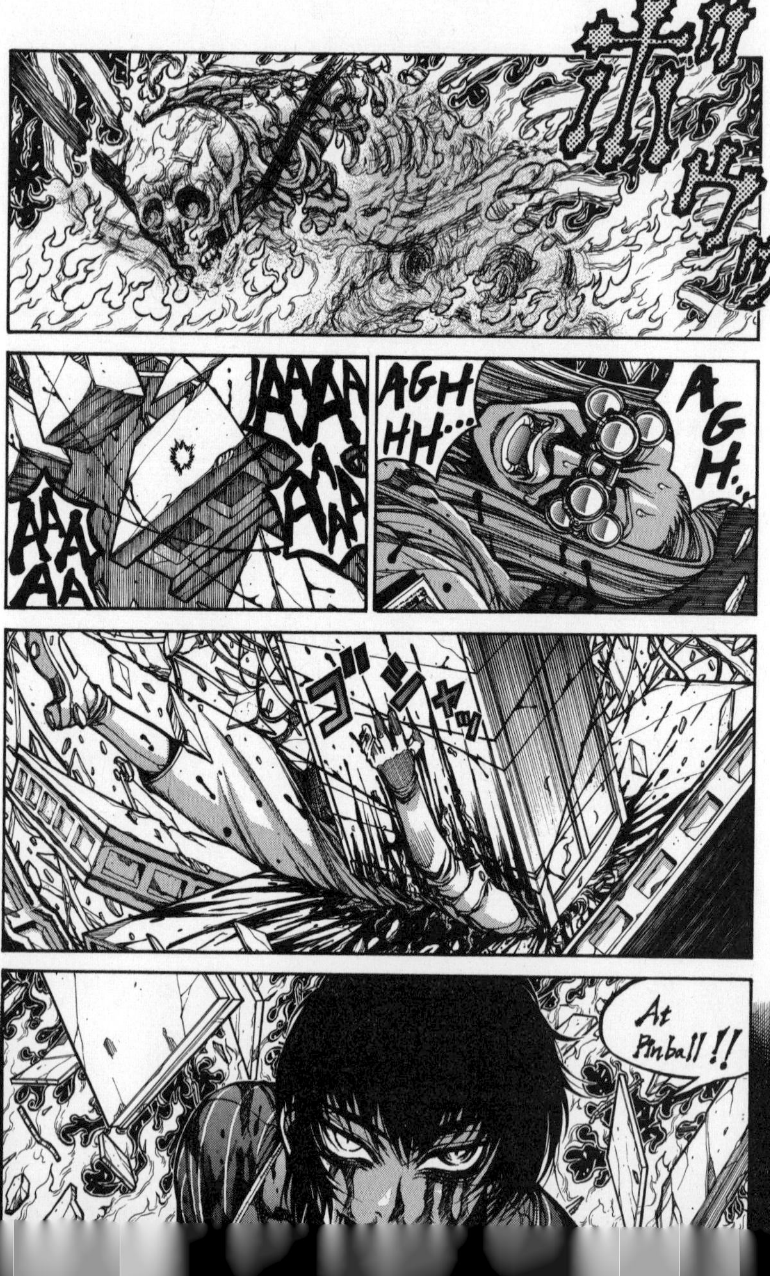
ゴシャッ
AGH...
AGHHH...
AAAAAAAA
AAAAAA
At Pinball!!

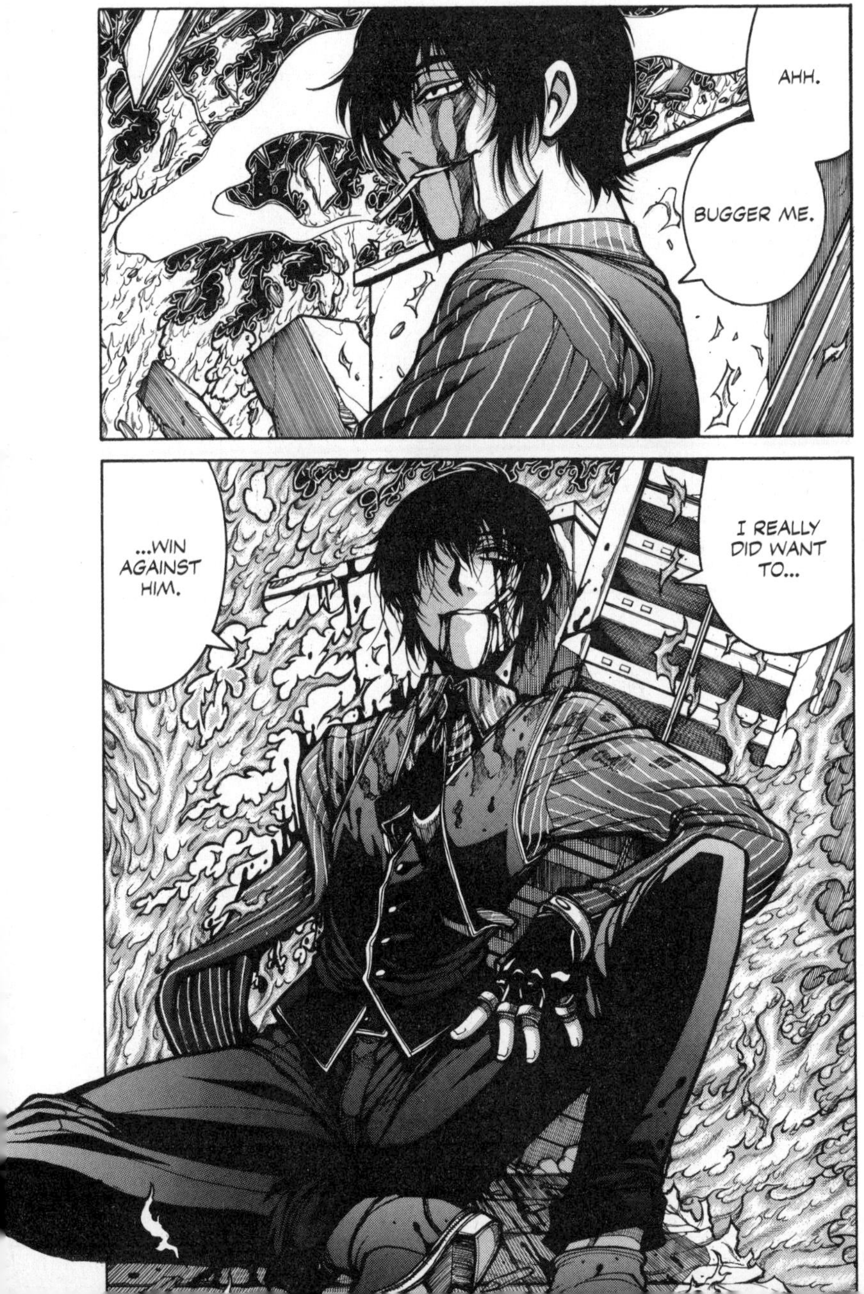
AHH.
BUGGER ME.
I REALLY DID WANT TO...
...WIN AGAINST HIM.

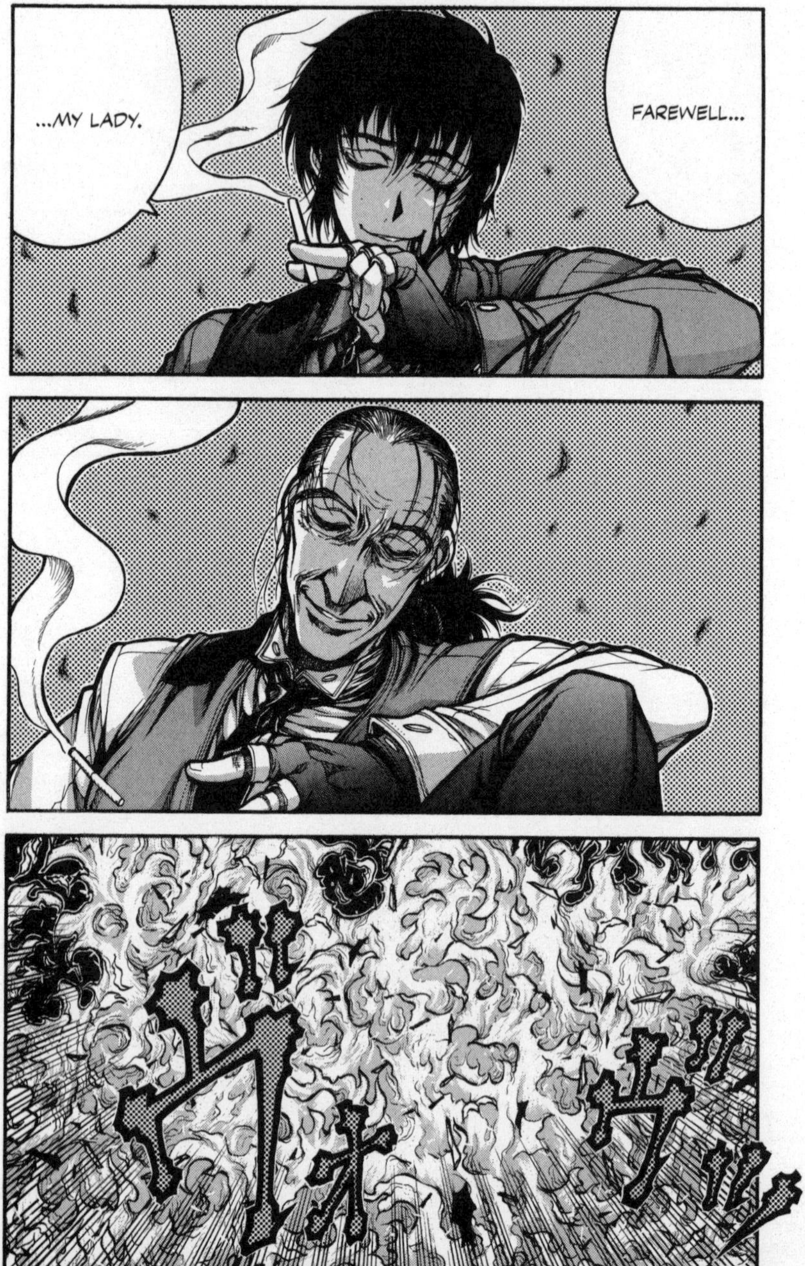
FAREWELL...
...MY LADY.

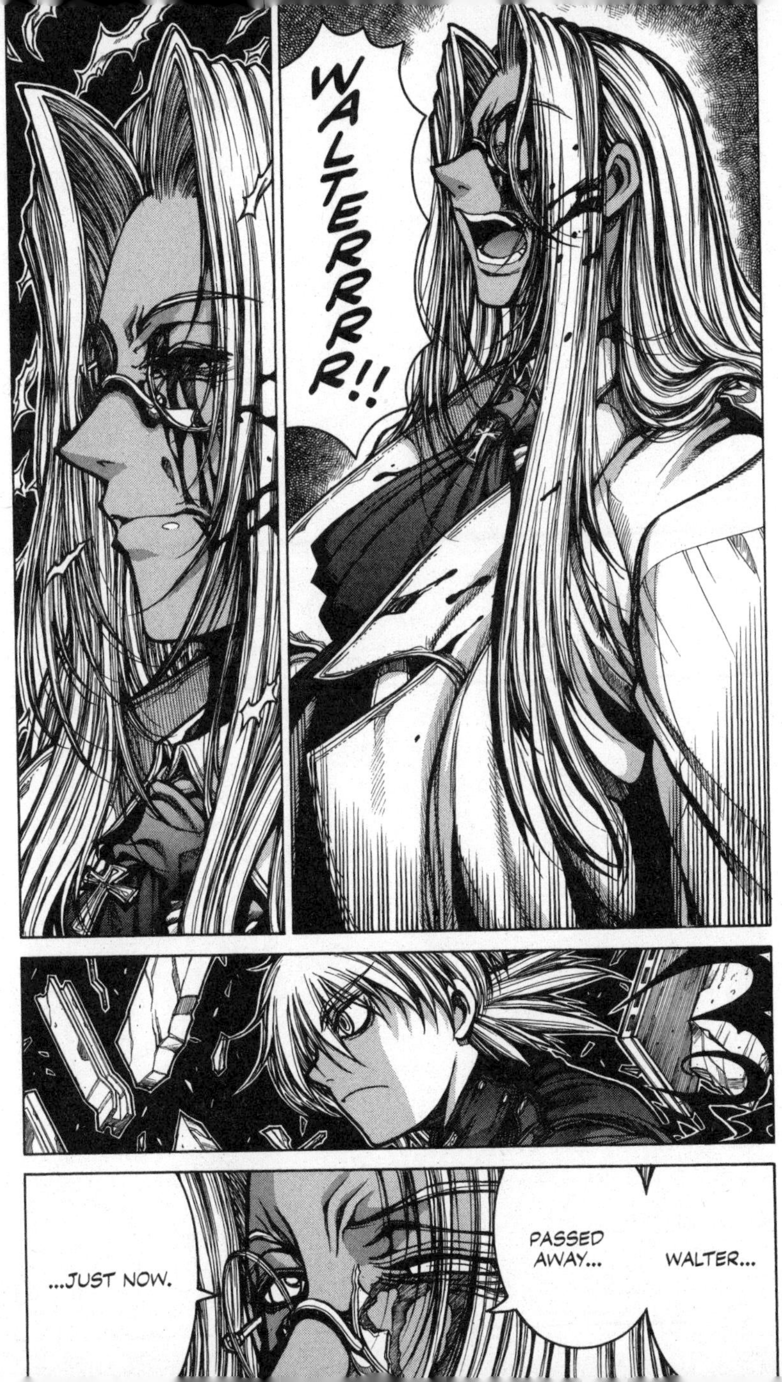
WALTERRRRR!!
WALTER...
PASSED AWAY...
...JUST NOW.

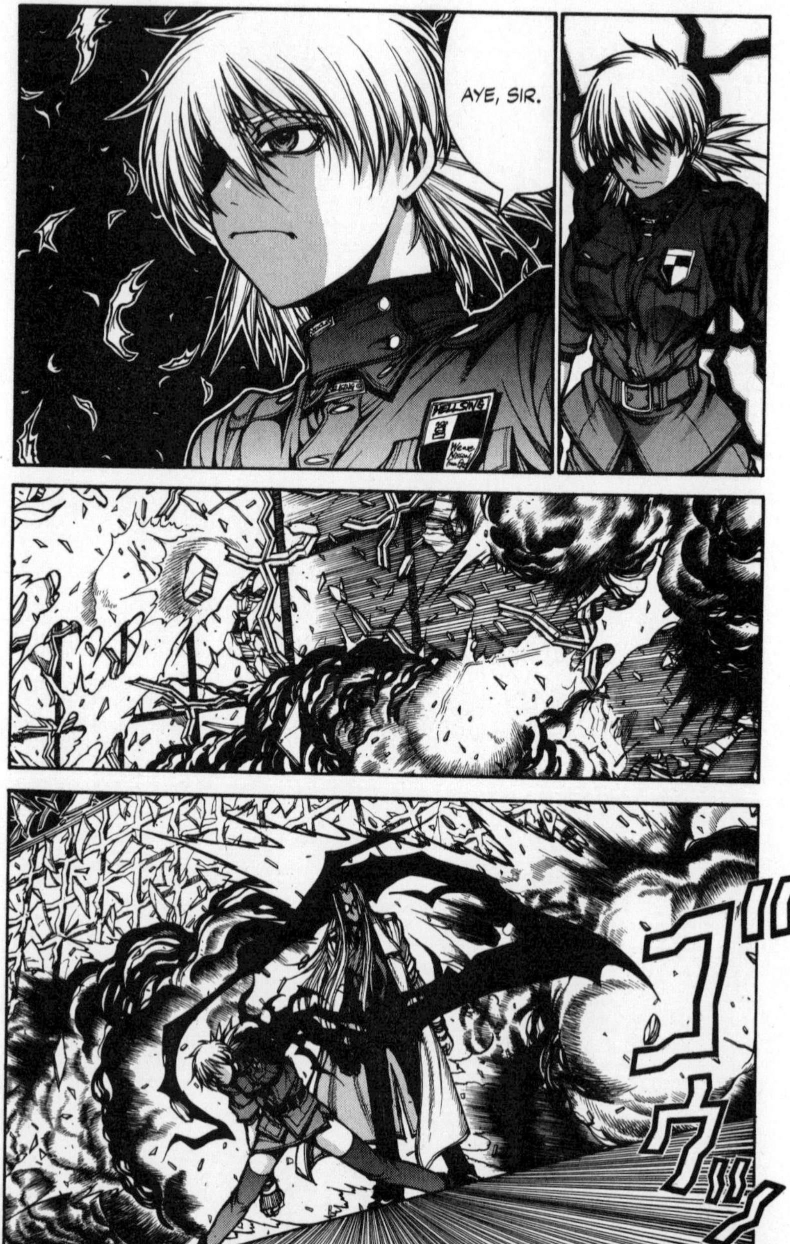
AYE, SIR.
ゴウッ

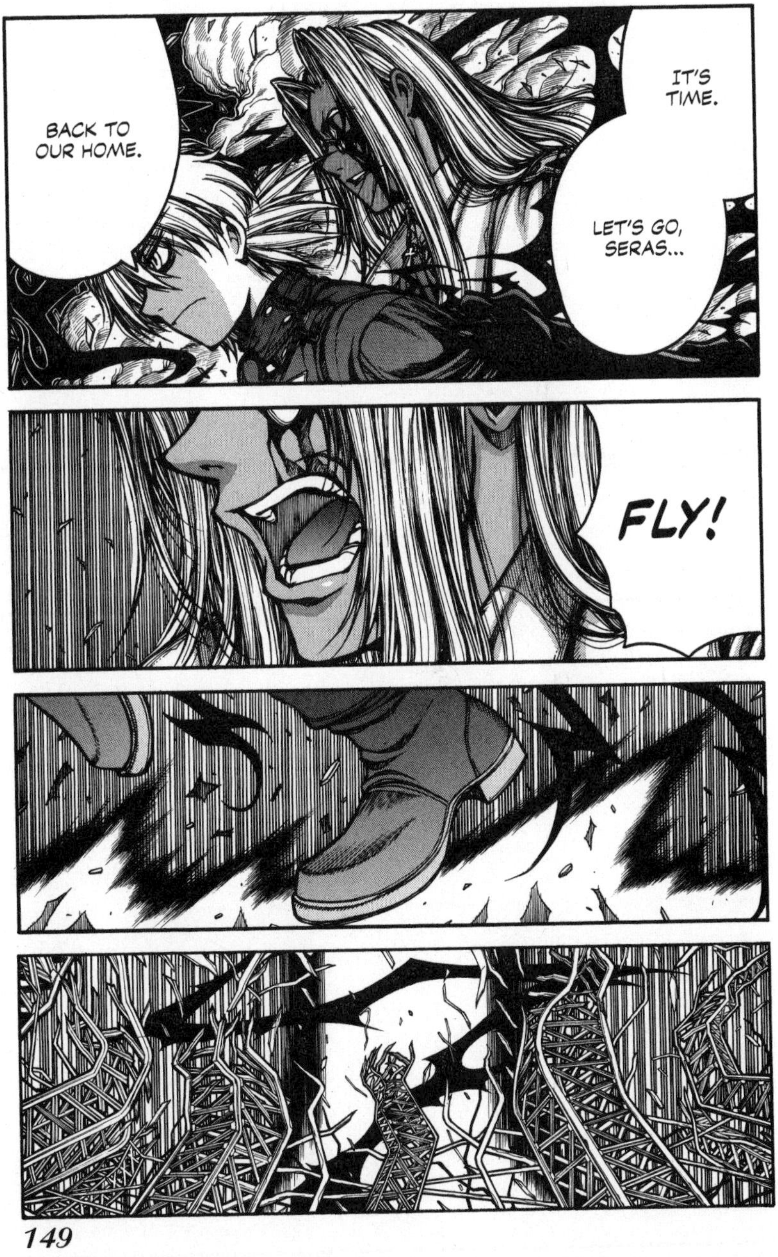
IT'S TIME.
LET'S GO, SERAS...
BACK TO OUR HOME.
FLY!

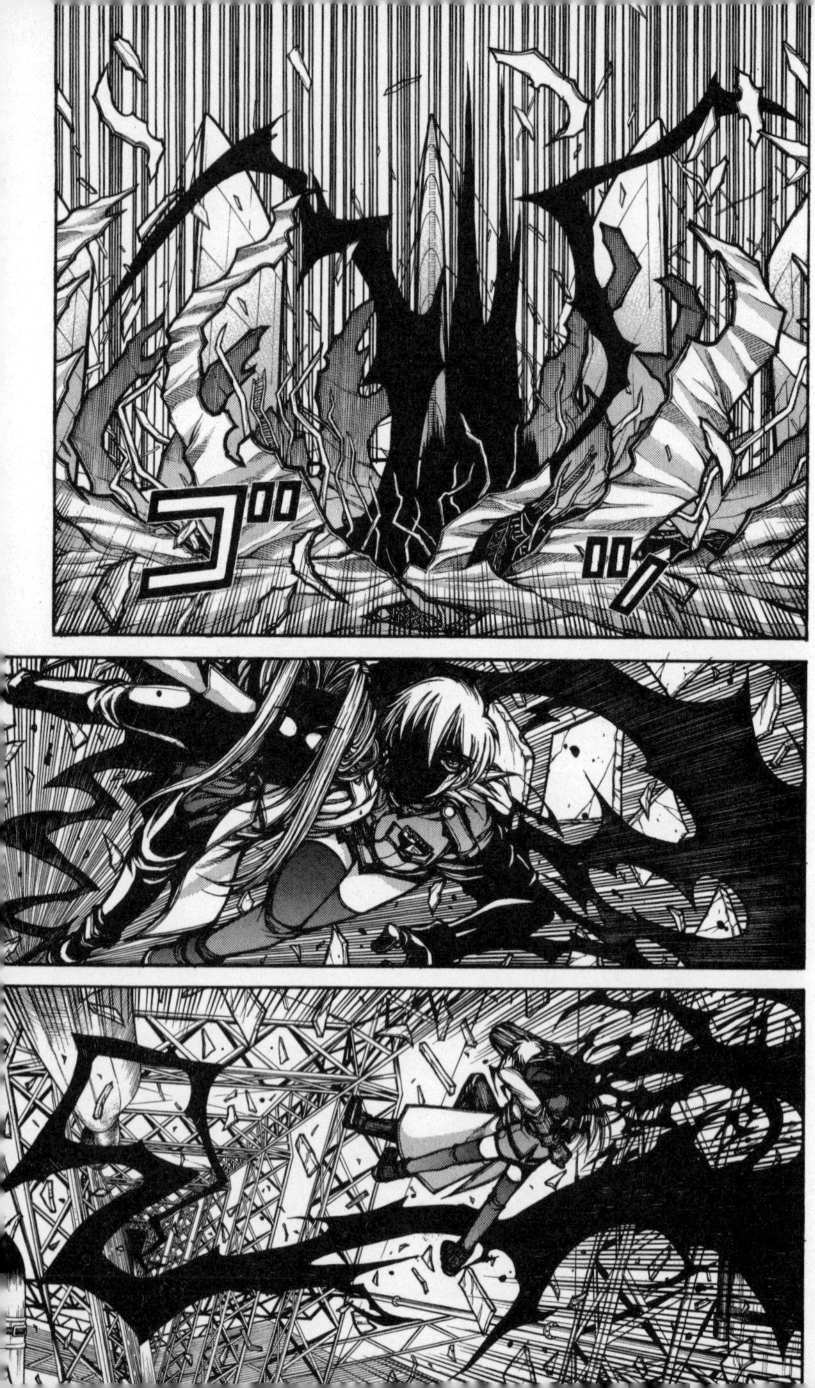
ゴ

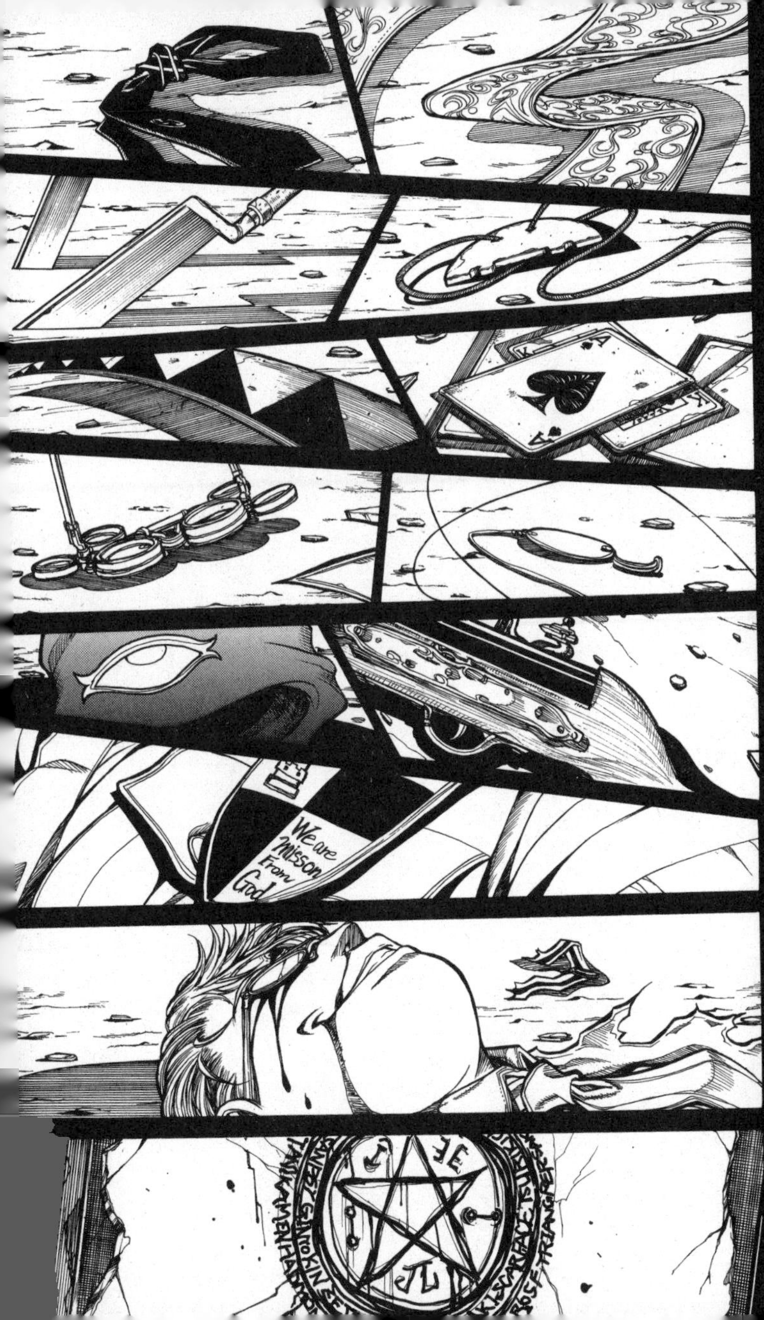
We are misson From God

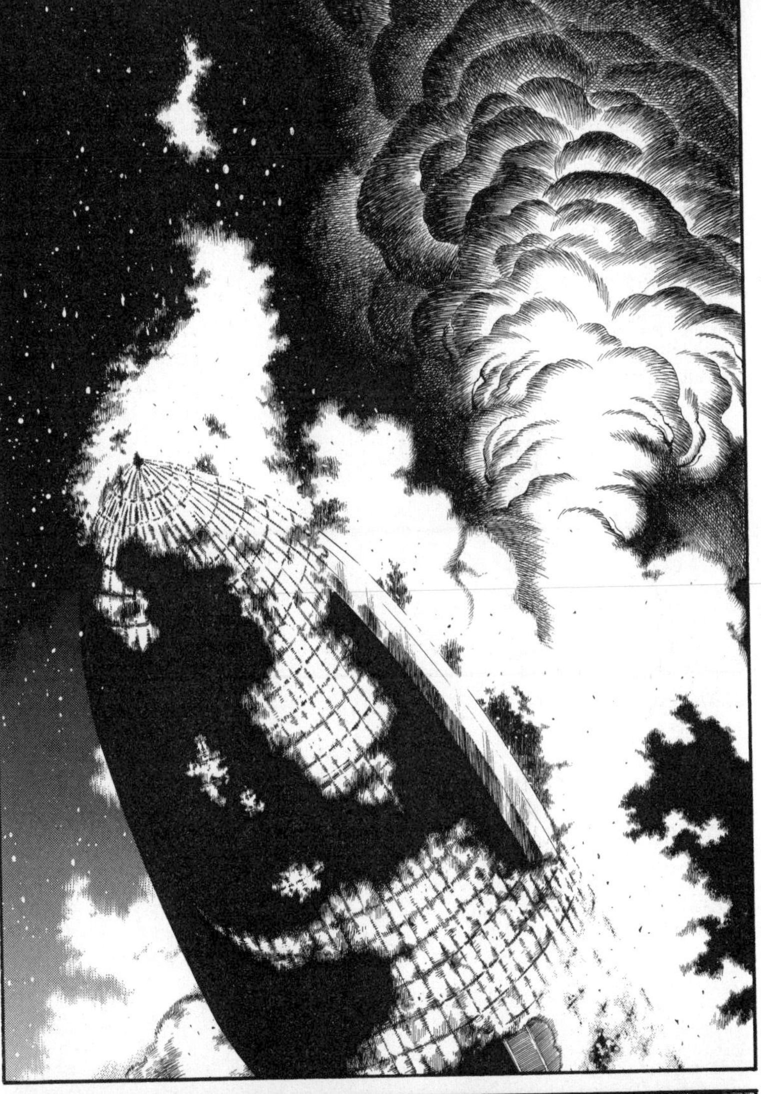

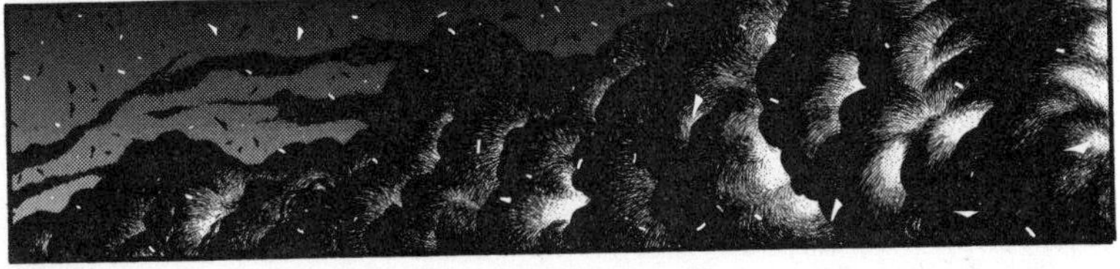

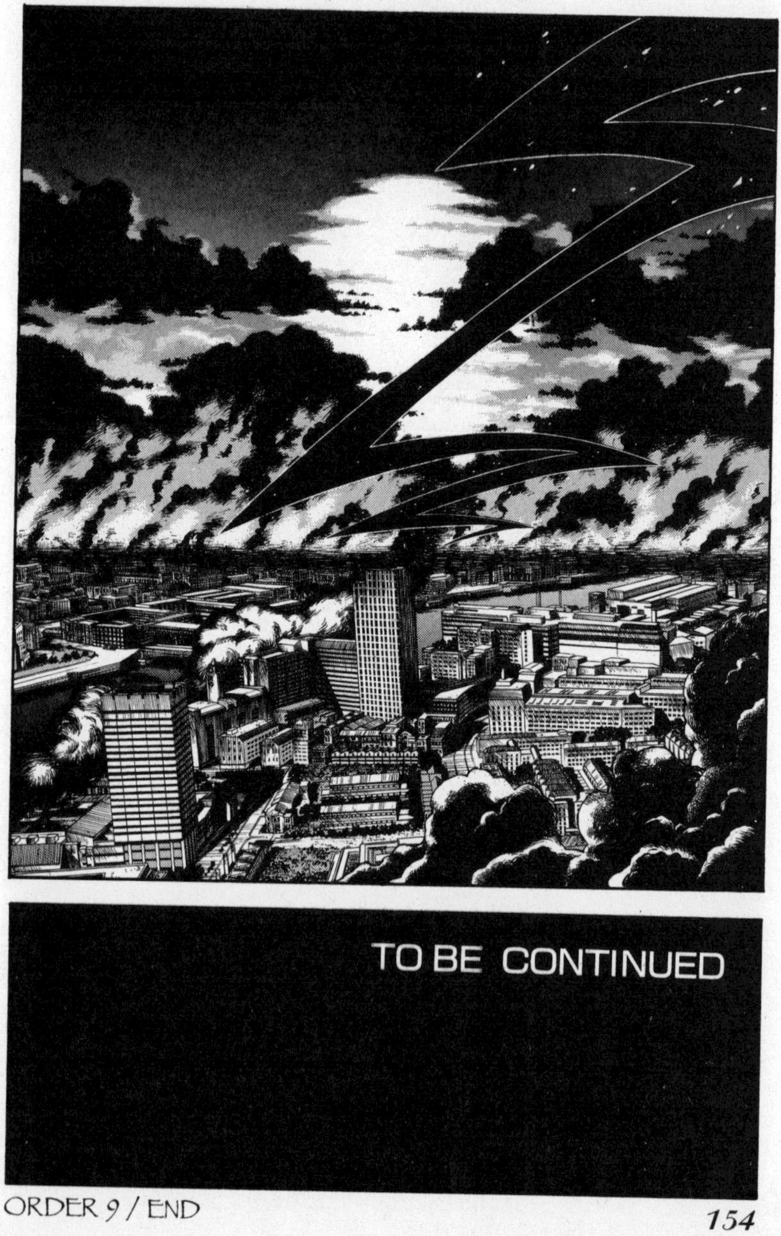

TO BE CONTINUED

ORDER 9 / END

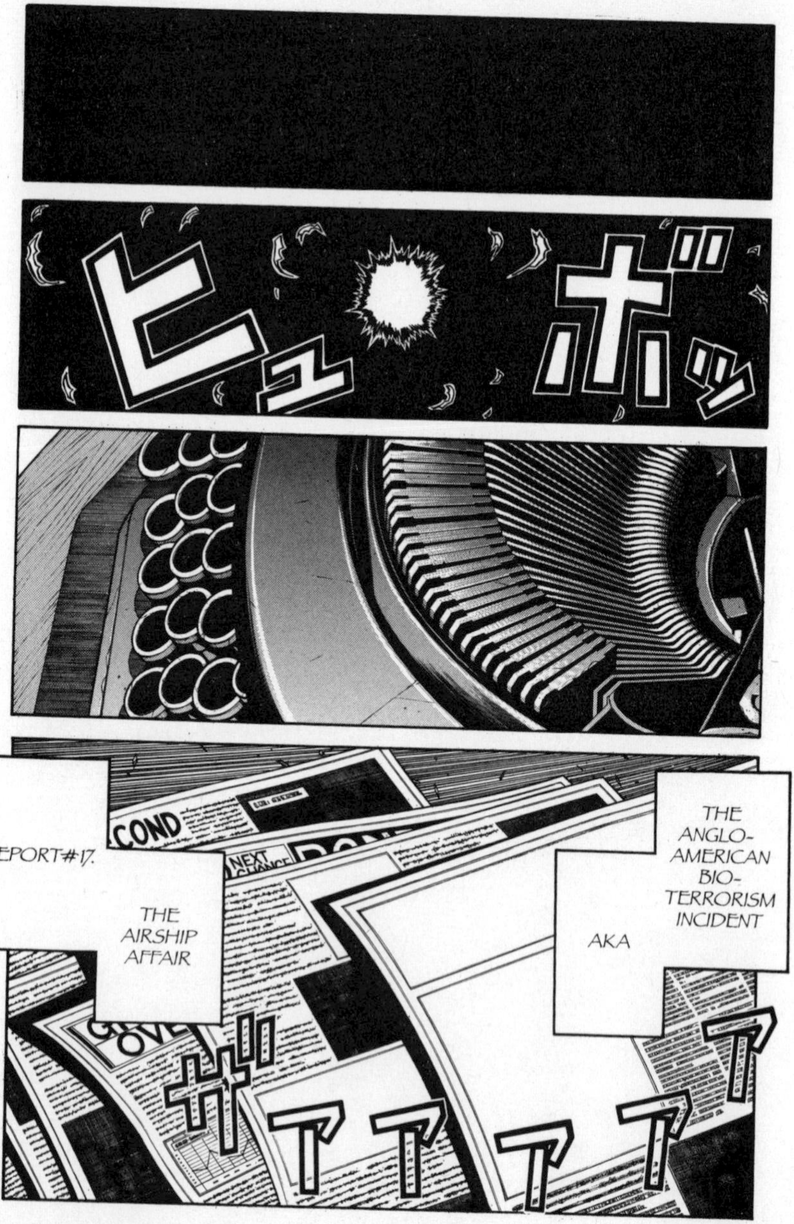
ボッ
ヒュ
THE ANGLO-AMERICAN BIO-TERRORISM INCIDENT
AKA
REPORT #17.
THE AIRSHIP AFFAIR
ザアアアアア

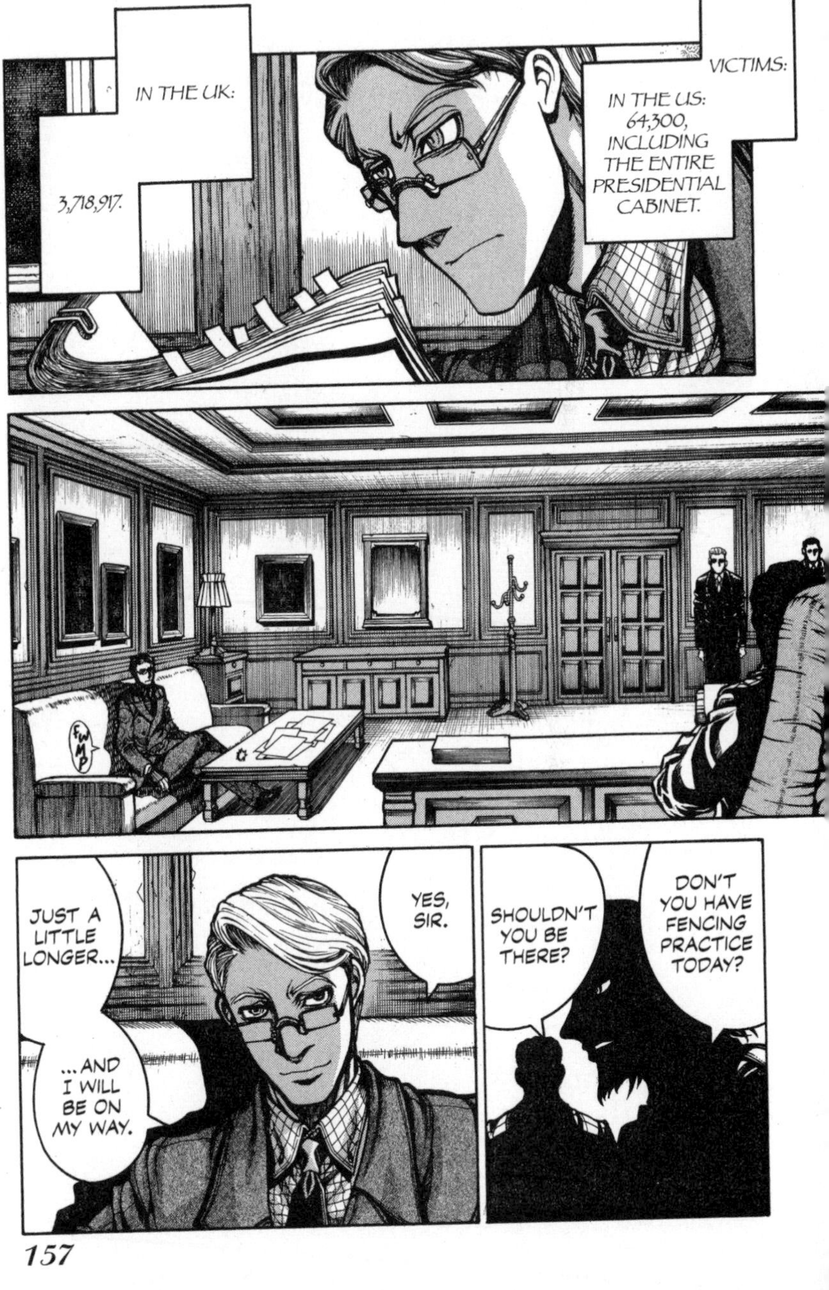
VICTIMS:
IN THE US: 64,300, INCLUDING THE ENTIRE PRESIDENTIAL CABINET.
IN THE UK:
3,718,917.
FWMP
DON'T YOU HAVE FENCING PRACTICE TODAY?
SHOULDN'T YOU BE THERE?
YES, SIR.
JUST A LITTLE LONGER...
...AND I WILL BE ON MY WAY.

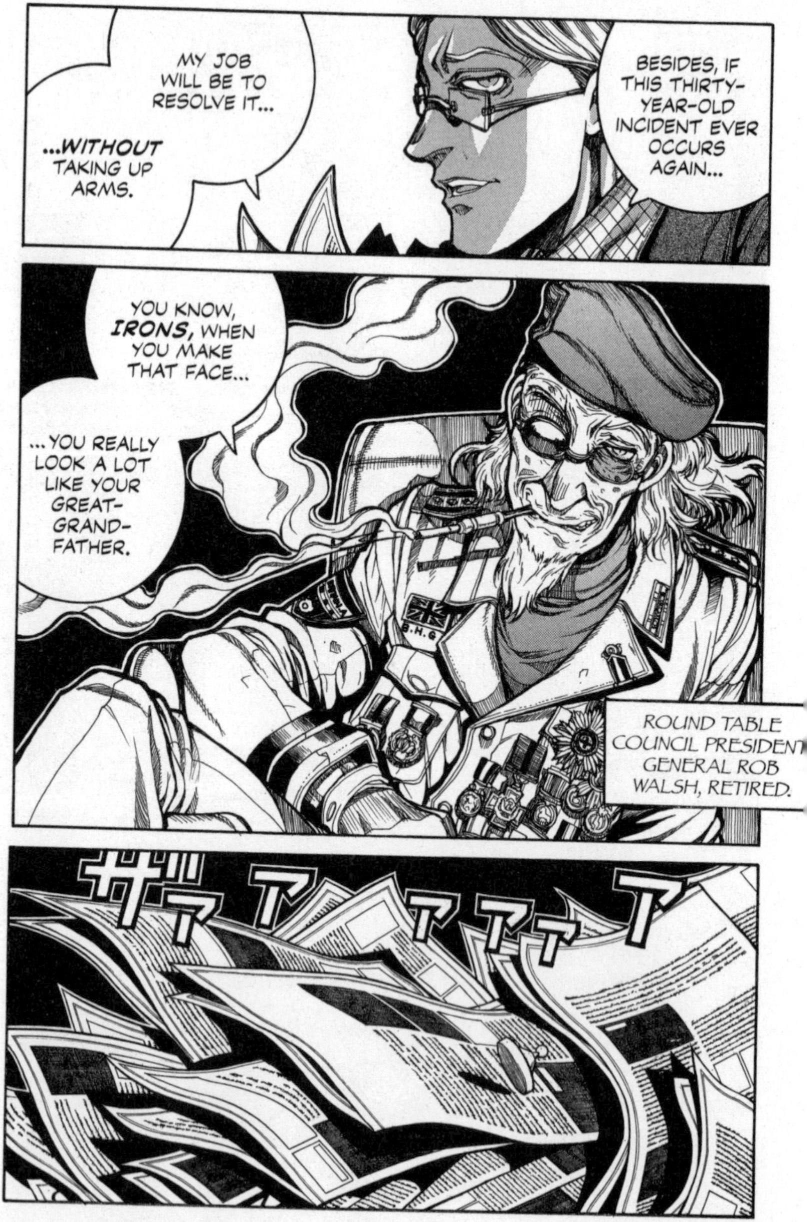
BESIDES, IF THIS THIRTY-YEAR-OLD INCIDENT EVER OCCURS AGAIN...
MY JOB WILL BE TO RESOLVE IT...
...WITHOUT TAKING UP ARMS.
YOU KNOW, IRONS, WHEN YOU MAKE THAT FACE...
...YOU REALLY LOOK A LOT LIKE YOUR GREAT-GRANDFATHER.
ROUND TABLE COUNCIL PRESIDENT GENERAL ROB WALSH, RETIRED.
ザアアアアアア

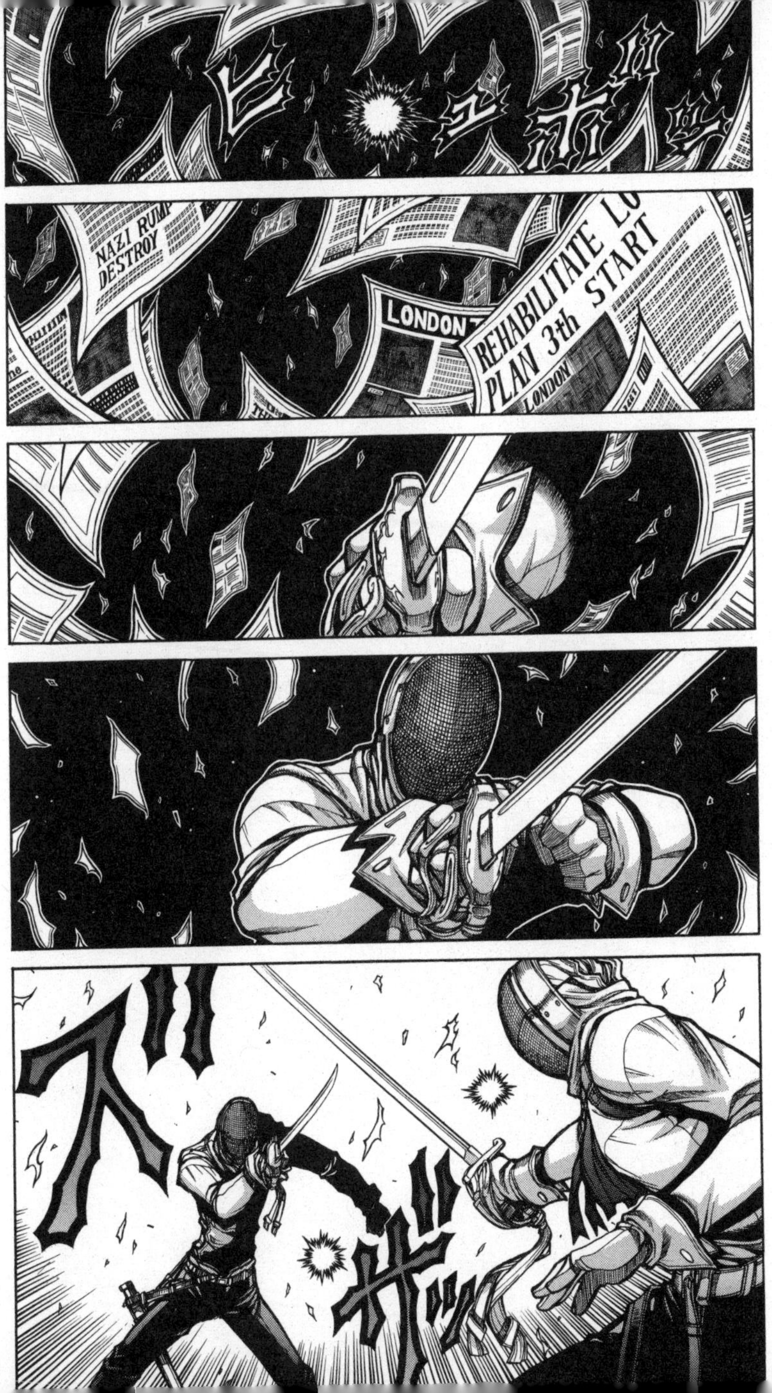
REHABILITATE LO
PLAN 3th START
LONDON
NAZI RUMP
DESTROY
LONDON T

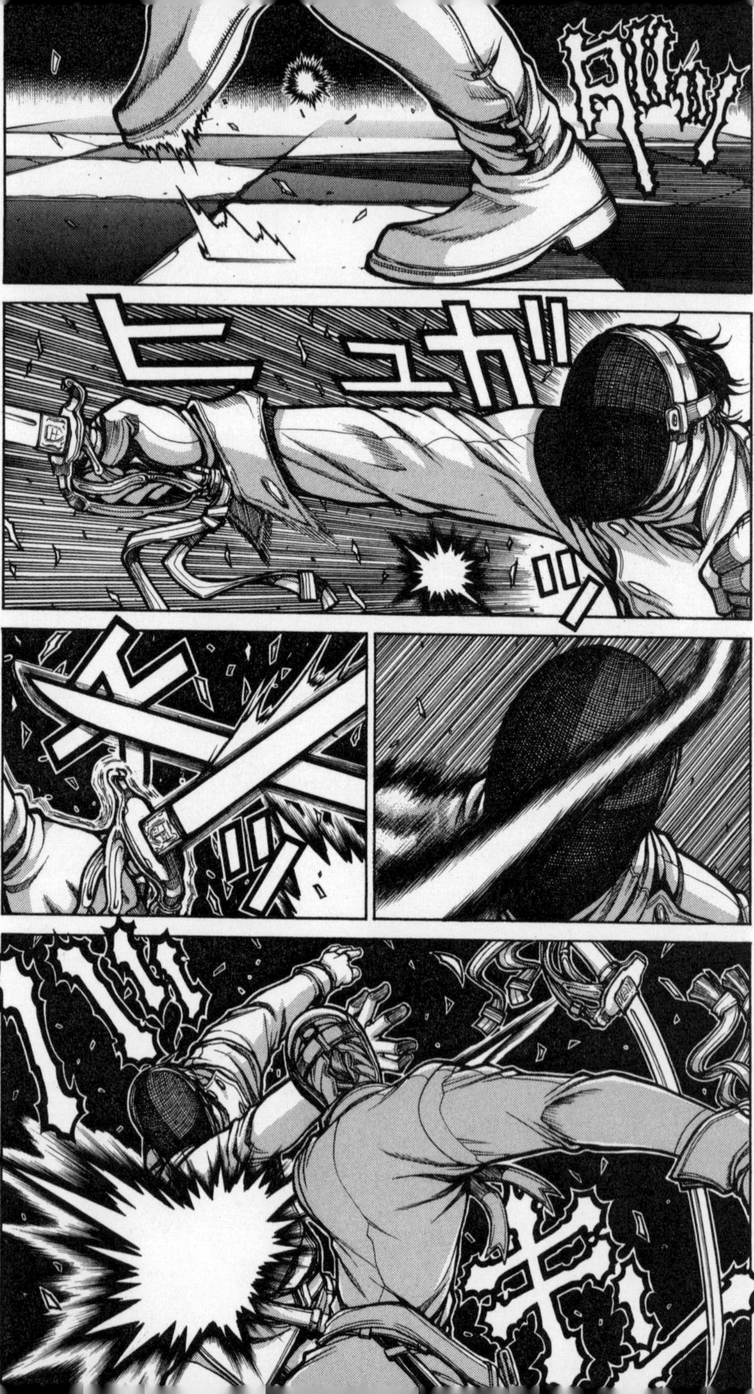
ヒュガ

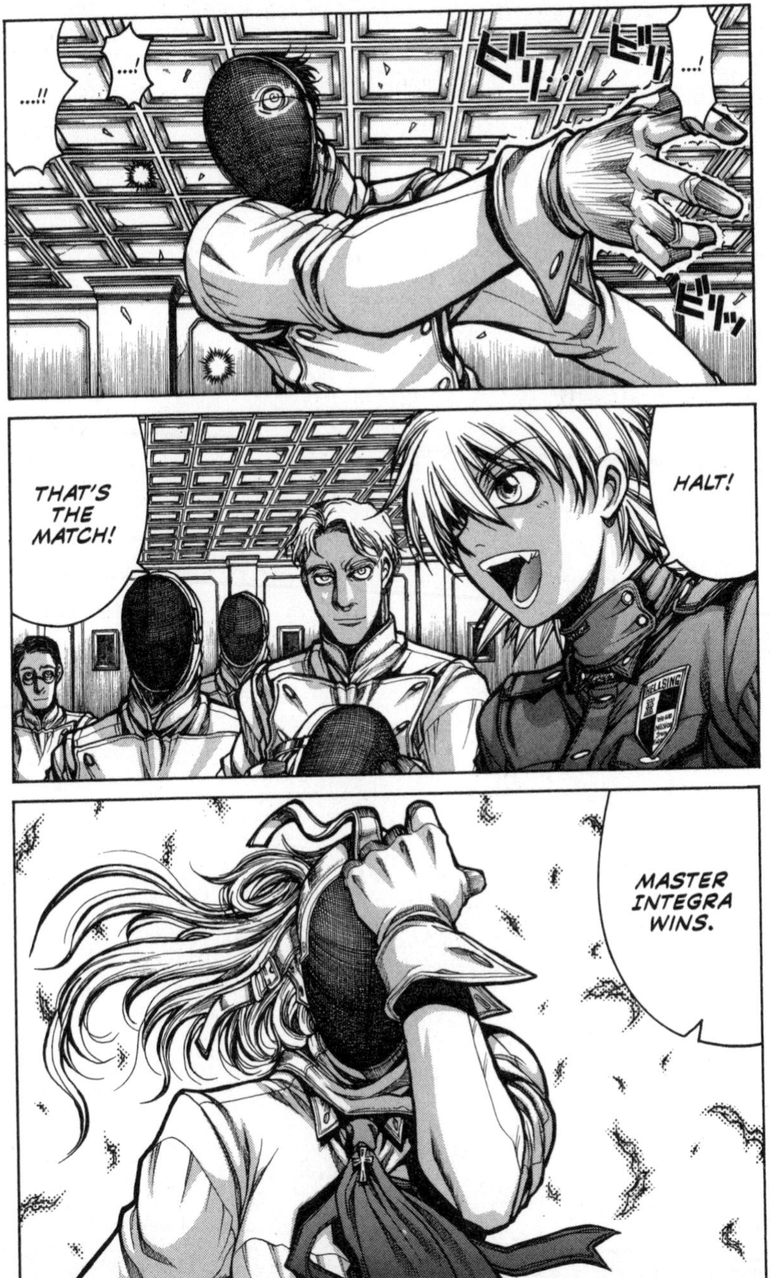
...!
ビリ…ビリ
ビリッ
...!
...!!
HALT!
THAT'S THE MATCH!
MASTER INTEGRA WINS.

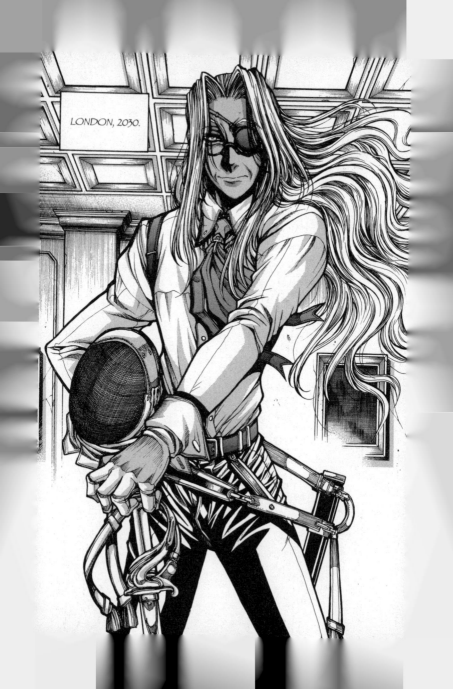

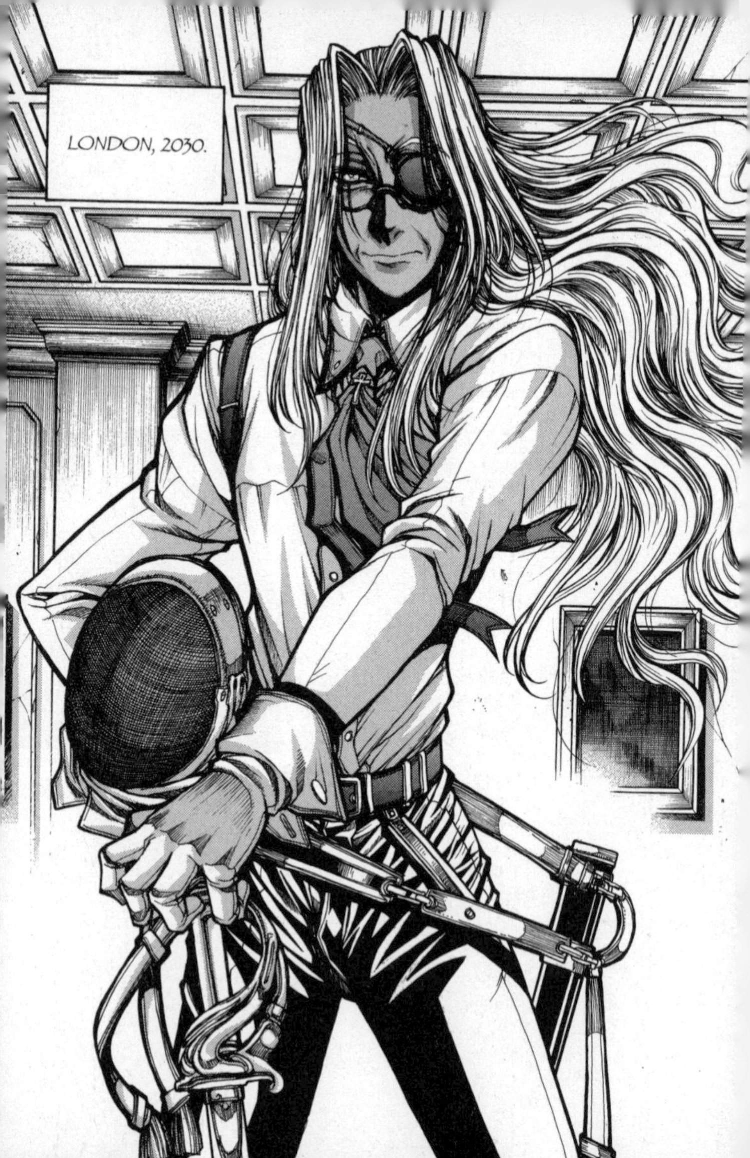
LONDON, 2030.

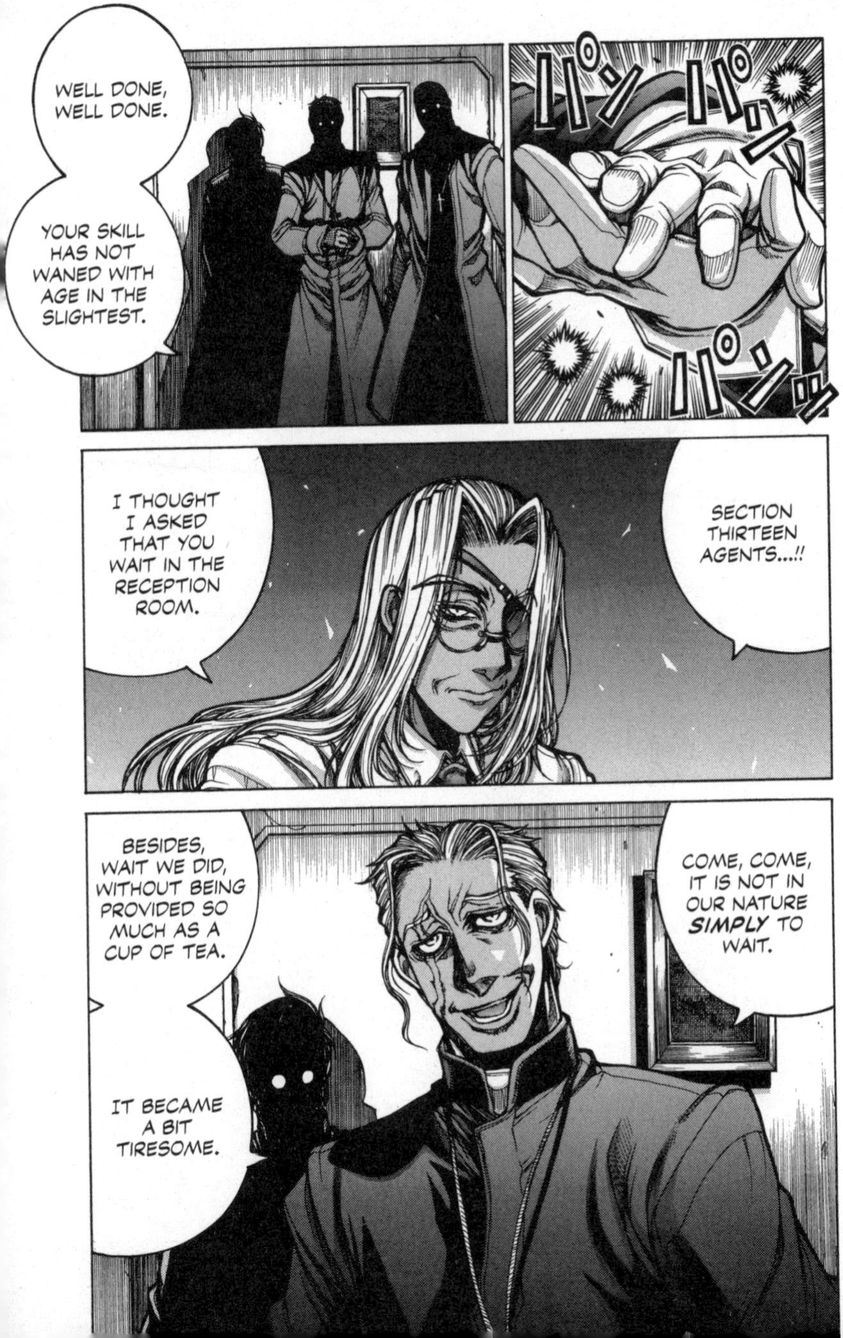
WELL DONE, WELL DONE.
YOUR SKILL HAS NOT WANED WITH AGE IN THE SLIGHTEST.
SECTION THIRTEEN AGENTS...!!
I THOUGHT I ASKED THAT YOU WAIT IN THE RECEPTION ROOM.
COME, COME, IT IS NOT IN OUR NATURE *SIMPLY* TO WAIT.
BESIDES, WAIT WE DID, WITHOUT BEING PROVIDED SO MUCH AS A CUP OF TEA.
IT BECAME A BIT TIRESOME.

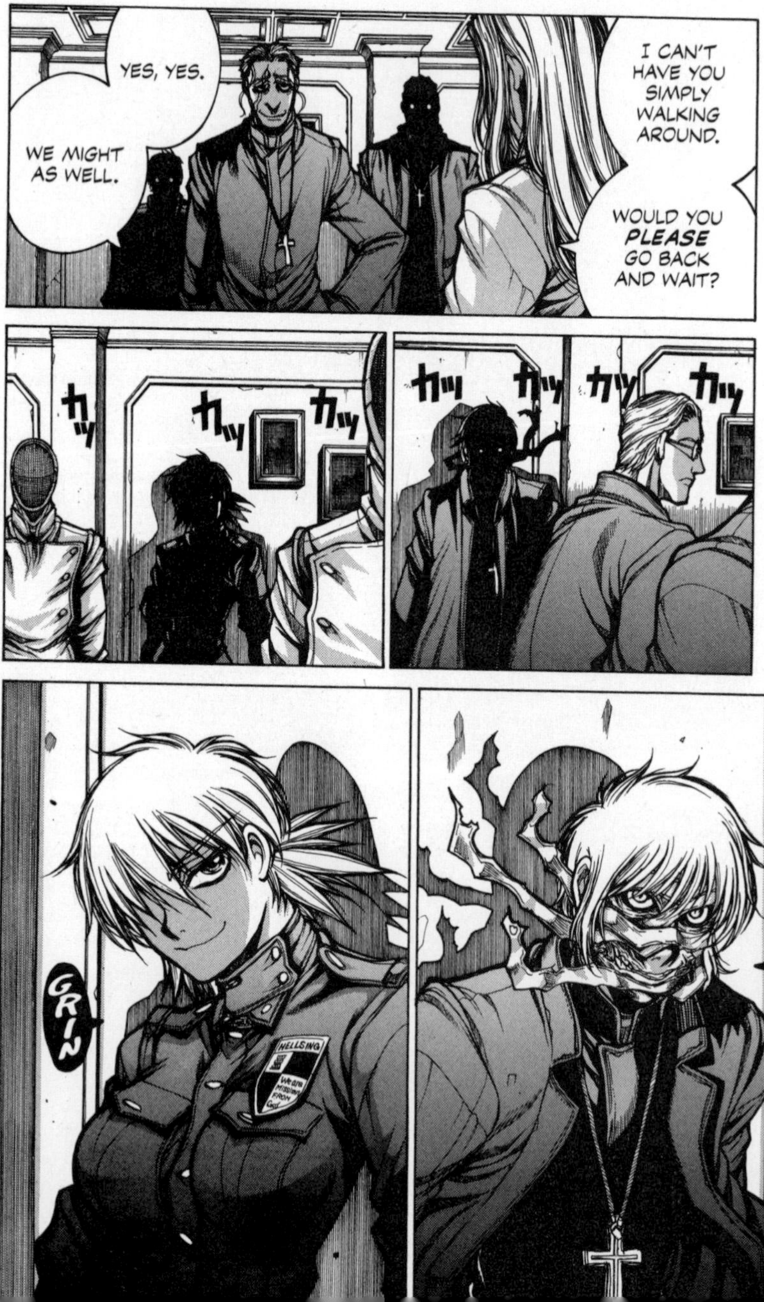
I CAN'T HAVE YOU SIMPLY WALKING AROUND.
WOULD YOU *PLEASE* GO BACK AND WAIT?
YES, YES.
WE MIGHT AS WELL.
カッ
カッ
カッ
カッ
カッ
カッ
カッ
SSS!
GRIN

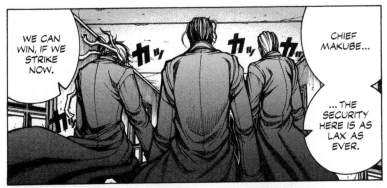

CHIEF MAKUBE...
... THE SECURITY HERE IS AS LAX AS EVER.
カッ
カッ
カッ
WE CAN WIN, IF WE STRIKE NOW.
カッ
HUPID HID.
HYOUR HEYES HARE HLIND.
ゴッ
OW!
グシャッ
?!

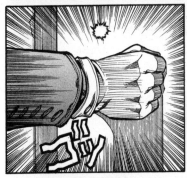

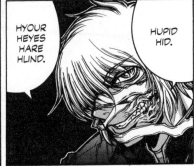

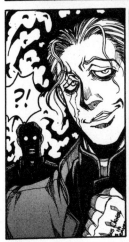

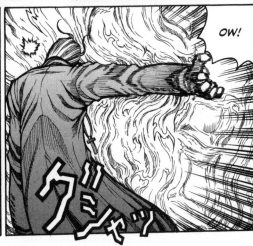

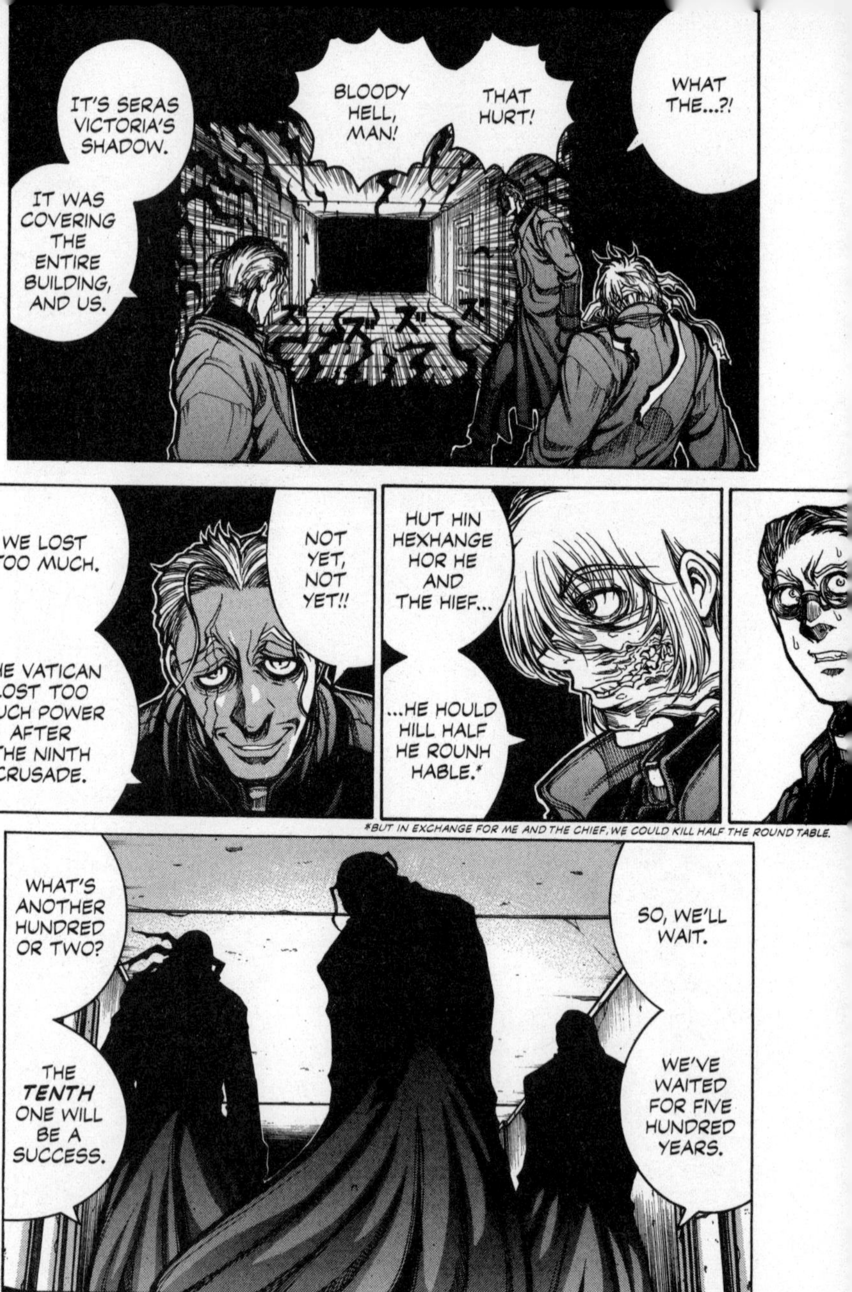
WHAT THE...?!
BLOODY HELL, MAN! THAT HURT!
IT'S SERAS VICTORIA'S SHADOW.
IT WAS COVERING THE ENTIRE BUILDING, AND US.
HUT HIN HEXHANGE HOR HE AND THE HIEF...
...HE HOULD HILL HALF HE ROUNH HABLE.*
NOT YET, NOT YET!!
WE LOST TOO MUCH.
THE VATICAN LOST TOO MUCH POWER AFTER THE NINTH CRUSADE.
SO, WE'LL WAIT.
WE'VE WAITED FOR FIVE HUNDRED YEARS.
WHAT'S ANOTHER HUNDRED OR TWO?
THE *TENTH* ONE WILL BE A SUCCESS.

*BUT IN EXCHANGE FOR ME AND THE CHIEF, WE COULD KILL HALF THE ROUND TABLE.

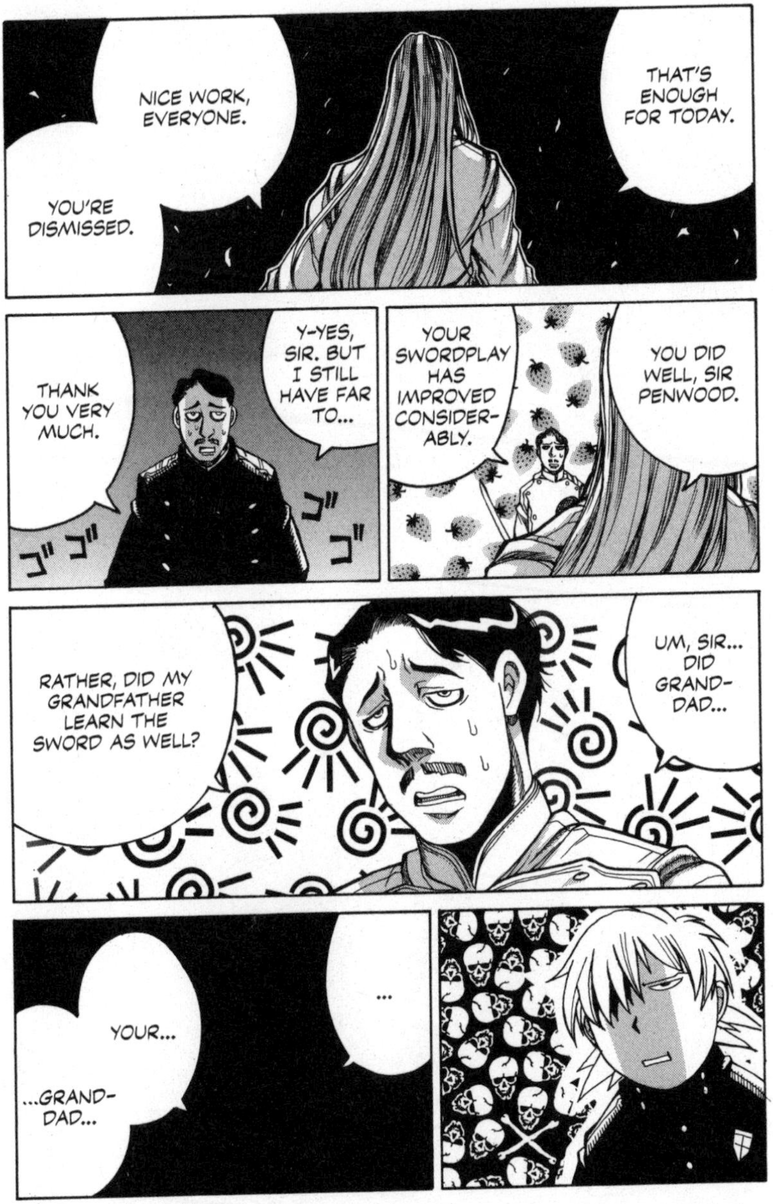
THAT'S ENOUGH FOR TODAY.
NICE WORK, EVERYONE.
YOU'RE DISMISSED.
YOU DID WELL, SIR PENWOOD.
YOUR SWORDPLAY HAS IMPROVED CONSIDER-ABLY.
Y-YES, SIR. BUT I STILL HAVE FAR TO...
THANK YOU VERY MUCH.
ゴゴゴゴ
UM, SIR... DID GRAND-DAD...
RATHER, DID MY GRANDFATHER LEARN THE SWORD AS WELL?
...
YOUR...
...GRAND-DAD...

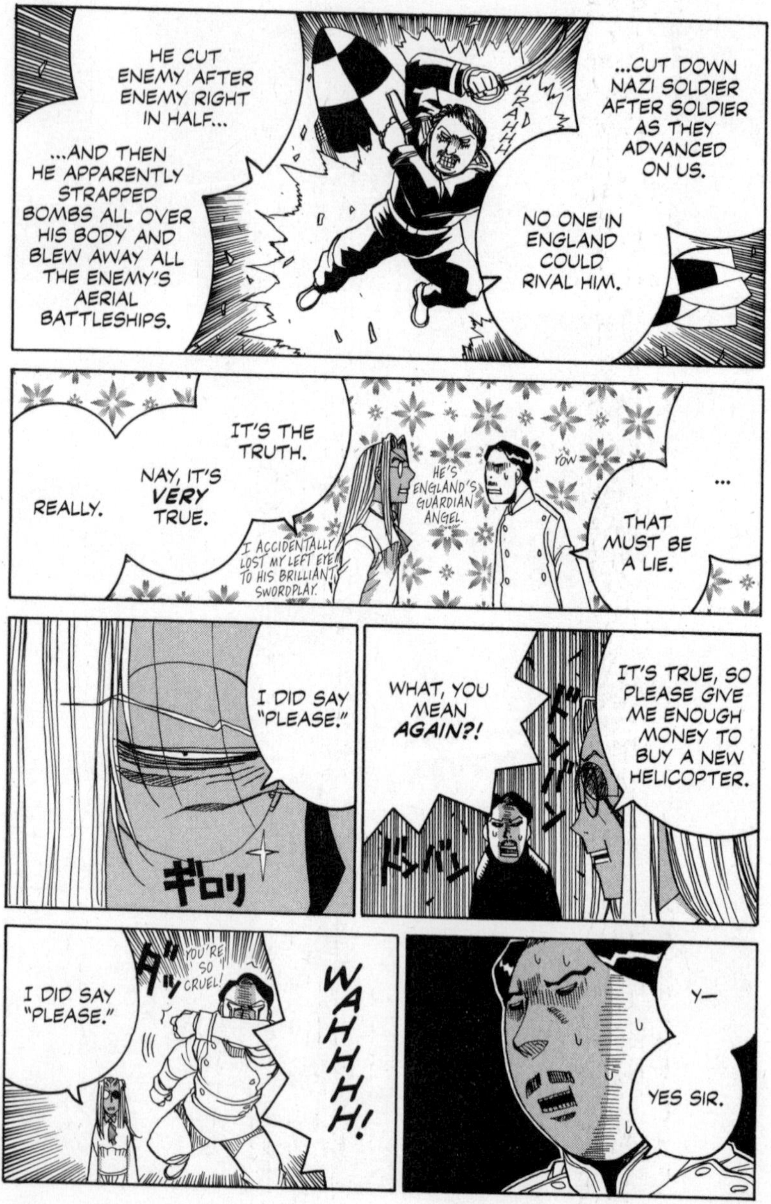
...CUT DOWN NAZI SOLDIER AFTER SOLDIER AS THEY ADVANCED ON US.
NO ONE IN ENGLAND COULD RIVAL HIM.
HRAHHH
HE CUT ENEMY AFTER ENEMY RIGHT IN HALF...
...AND THEN HE APPARENTLY STRAPPED BOMBS ALL OVER HIS BODY AND BLEW AWAY ALL THE ENEMY'S AERIAL BATTLESHIPS.
...
THAT MUST BE A LIE.
YOW
HE'S ENGLAND'S GUARDIAN ANGEL.
I ACCIDENTALLY LOST MY LEFT EYE TO HIS BRILLIANT SWORDPLAY.
IT'S THE TRUTH.
NAY, IT'S ***VERY*** TRUE.
REALLY.
IT'S TRUE, SO PLEASE GIVE ME ENOUGH MONEY TO BUY A NEW HELICOPTER.
WHAT, YOU MEAN ***AGAIN?!***
I DID SAY "PLEASE."
ギロリ
Y—
YES SIR.
WAHHHH!
YOU'RE SO CRUEL!
ダッ
I DID SAY "PLEASE."

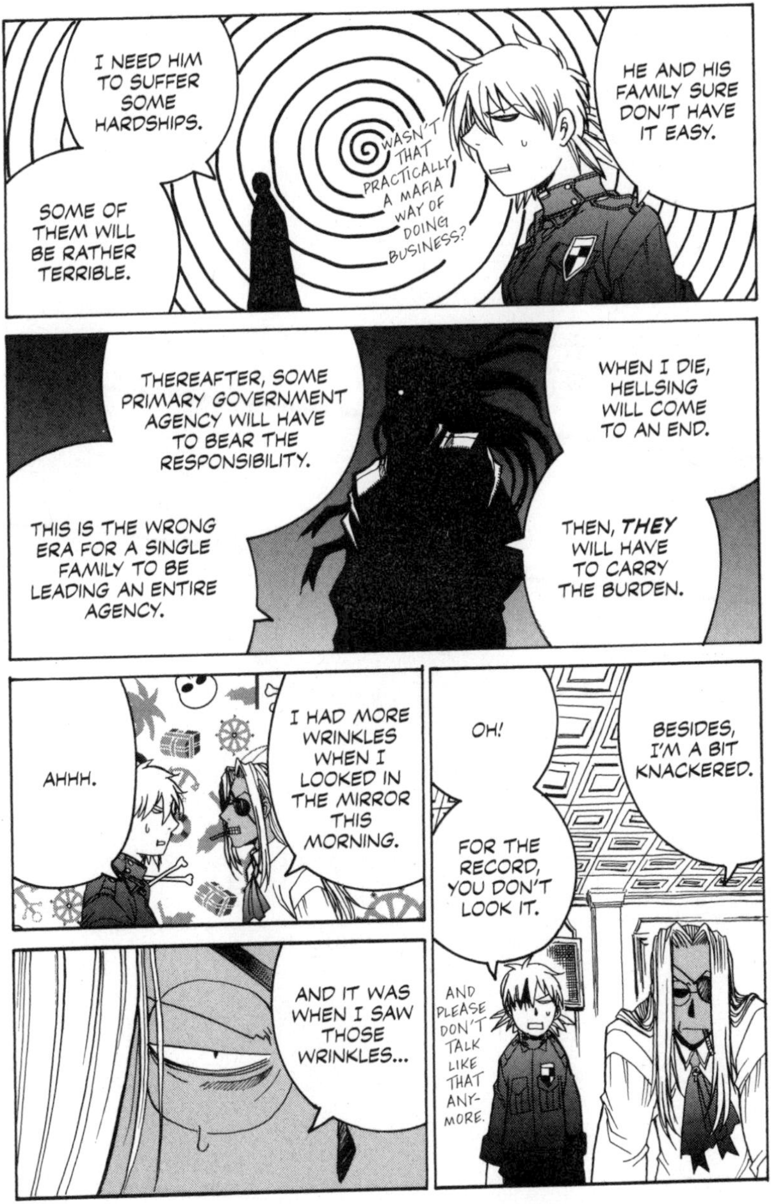
HE AND HIS FAMILY SURE DON'T HAVE IT EASY.
WASN'T THAT PRACTICALLY A MAFIA WAY OF DOING BUSINESS?
I NEED HIM TO SUFFER SOME HARDSHIPS.
SOME OF THEM WILL BE RATHER TERRIBLE.
WHEN I DIE, HELLSING WILL COME TO AN END.
THEREAFTER, SOME PRIMARY GOVERNMENT AGENCY WILL HAVE TO BEAR THE RESPONSIBILITY.
THEN, *THEY* WILL HAVE TO CARRY THE BURDEN.
THIS IS THE WRONG ERA FOR A SINGLE FAMILY TO BE LEADING AN ENTIRE AGENCY.
BESIDES, I'M A BIT KNACKERED.
OH!
FOR THE RECORD, YOU DON'T LOOK IT.
AND PLEASE DON'T TALK LIKE THAT ANYMORE.
I HAD MORE WRINKLES WHEN I LOOKED IN THE MIRROR THIS MORNING.
AHHH.
AND IT WAS WHEN I SAW THOSE WRINKLES...

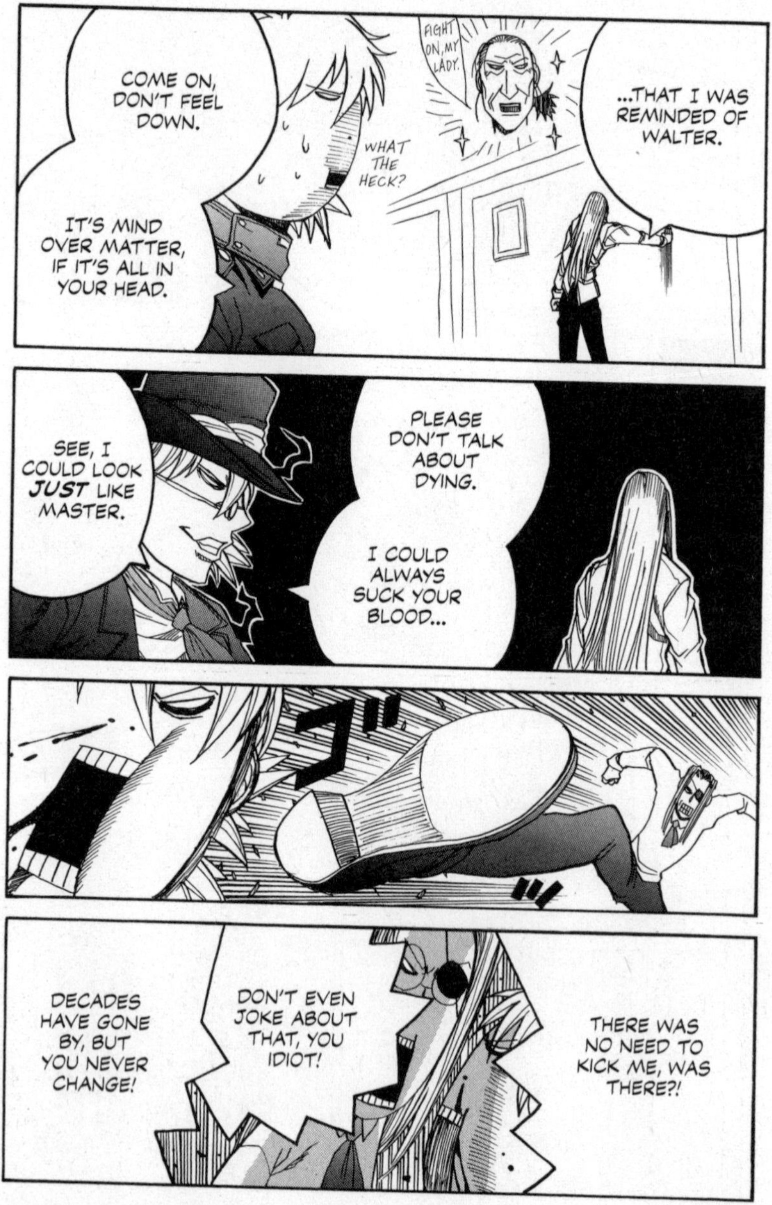
...THAT I WAS REMINDED OF WALTER.
FIGHT ON, MY LADY.
WHAT THE HECK?
COME ON, DON'T FEEL DOWN.
IT'S MIND OVER MATTER, IF IT'S ALL IN YOUR HEAD.
PLEASE DON'T TALK ABOUT DYING.
I COULD ALWAYS SUCK YOUR BLOOD...
SEE, I COULD LOOK **JUST** LIKE MASTER.
THERE WAS NO NEED TO KICK ME, WAS THERE?!
DON'T EVEN JOKE ABOUT THAT, YOU IDIOT!
DECADES HAVE GONE BY, BUT YOU NEVER CHANGE!

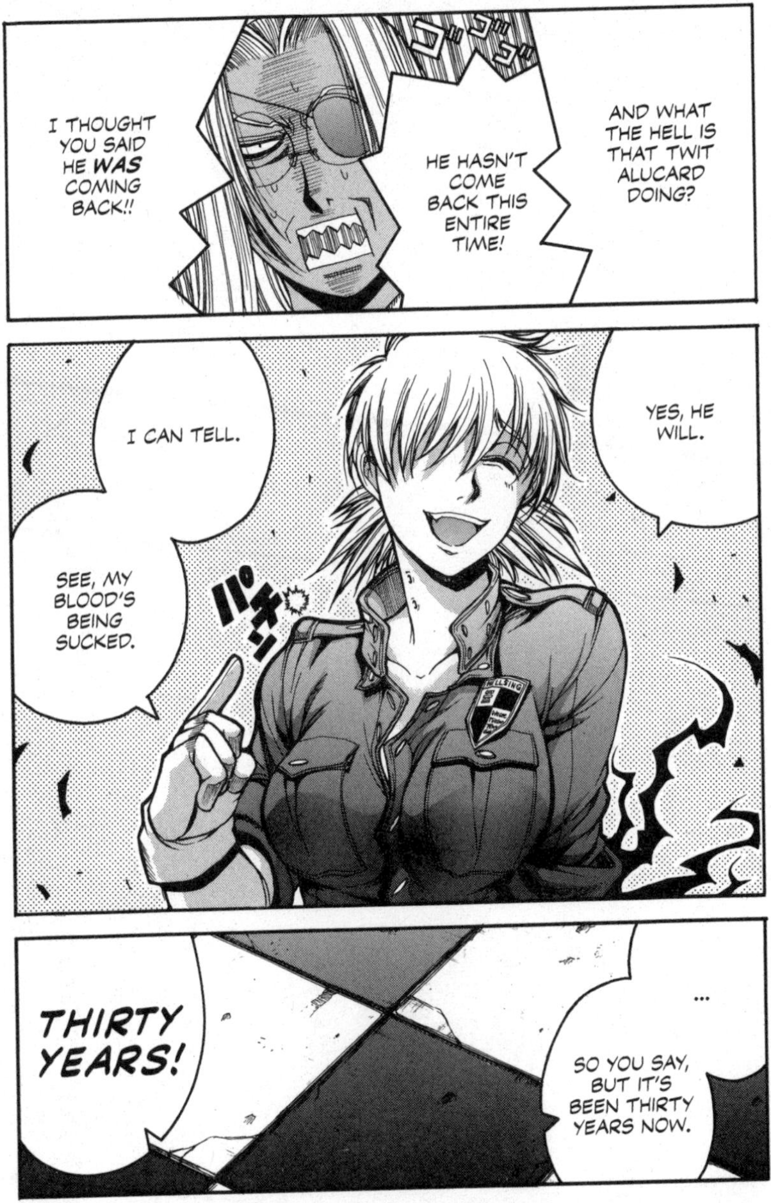
AND WHAT THE HELL IS THAT TWIT ALUCARD DOING?
HE HASN'T COME BACK THIS ENTIRE TIME!
I THOUGHT YOU SAID HE **WAS** COMING BACK!!
YES, HE WILL.
I CAN TELL.
SEE, MY BLOOD'S BEING SUCKED.
...
SO YOU SAY, BUT IT'S BEEN THIRTY YEARS NOW.
THIRTY YEARS!

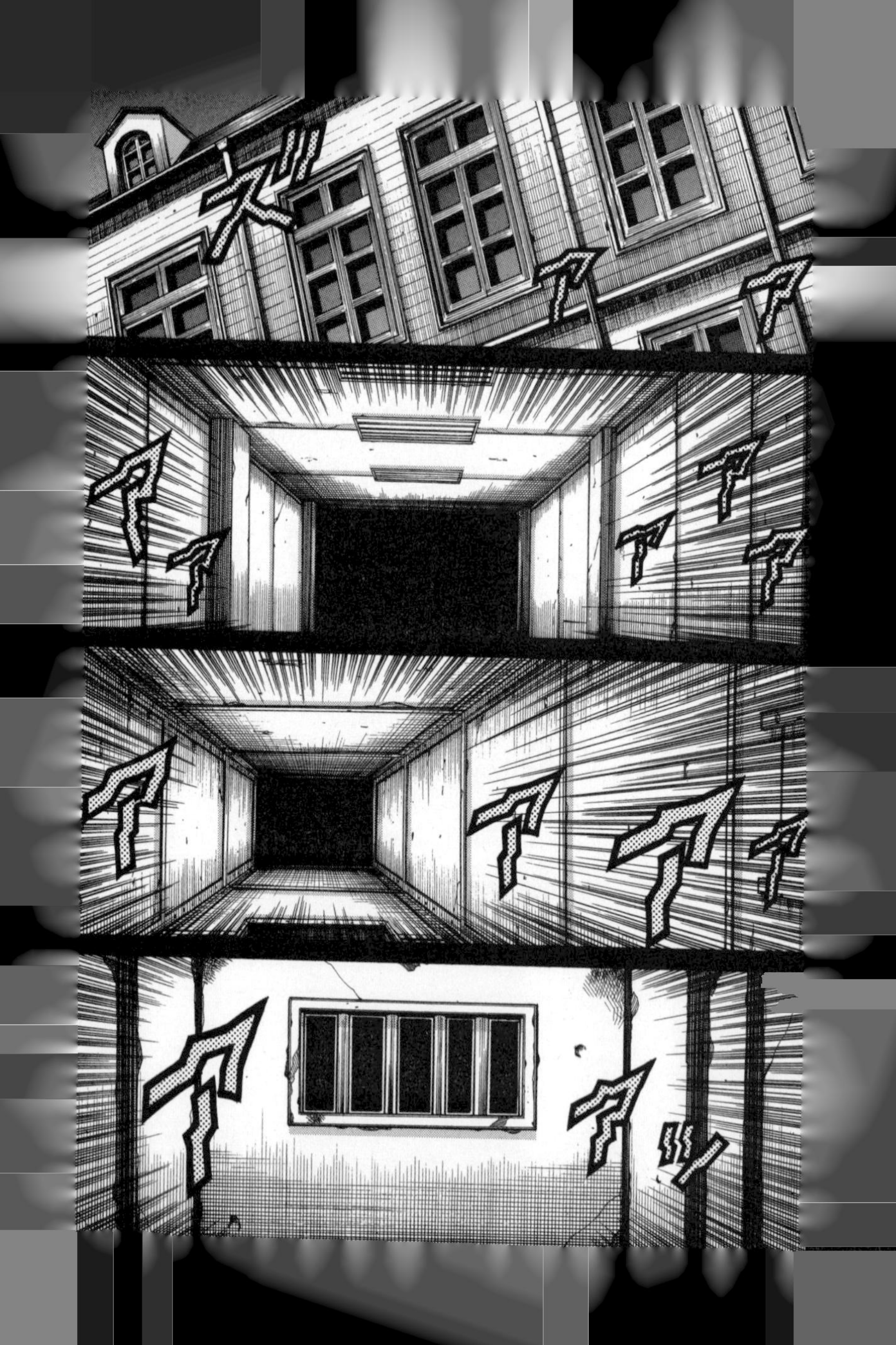
ズァア
アアアアアア
アアアア
アアッ

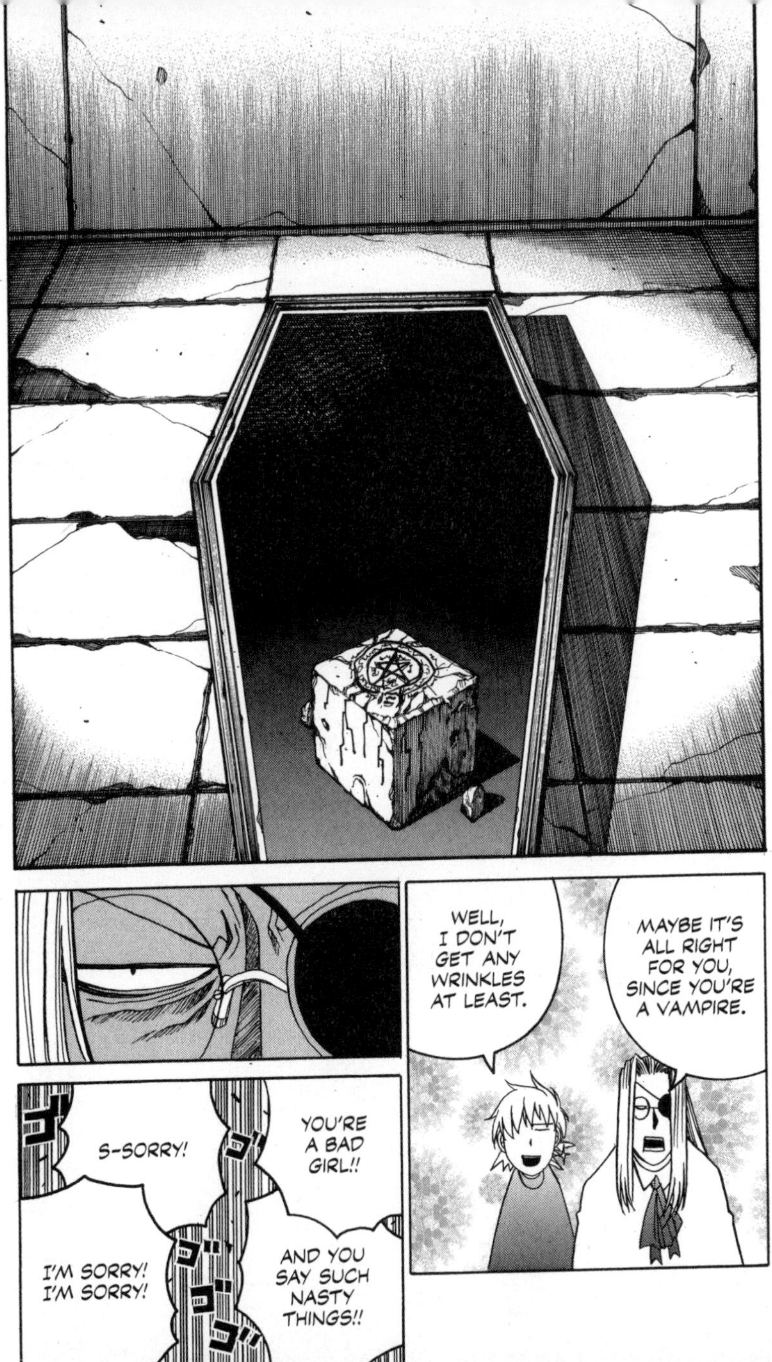
MAYBE IT'S ALL RIGHT FOR YOU, SINCE YOU'RE A VAMPIRE.
WELL, I DON'T GET ANY WRINKLES AT LEAST.
YOU'RE A BAD GIRL!!
S-SORRY!
AND YOU SAY SUCH NASTY THINGS!!
I'M SORRY! I'M SORRY!

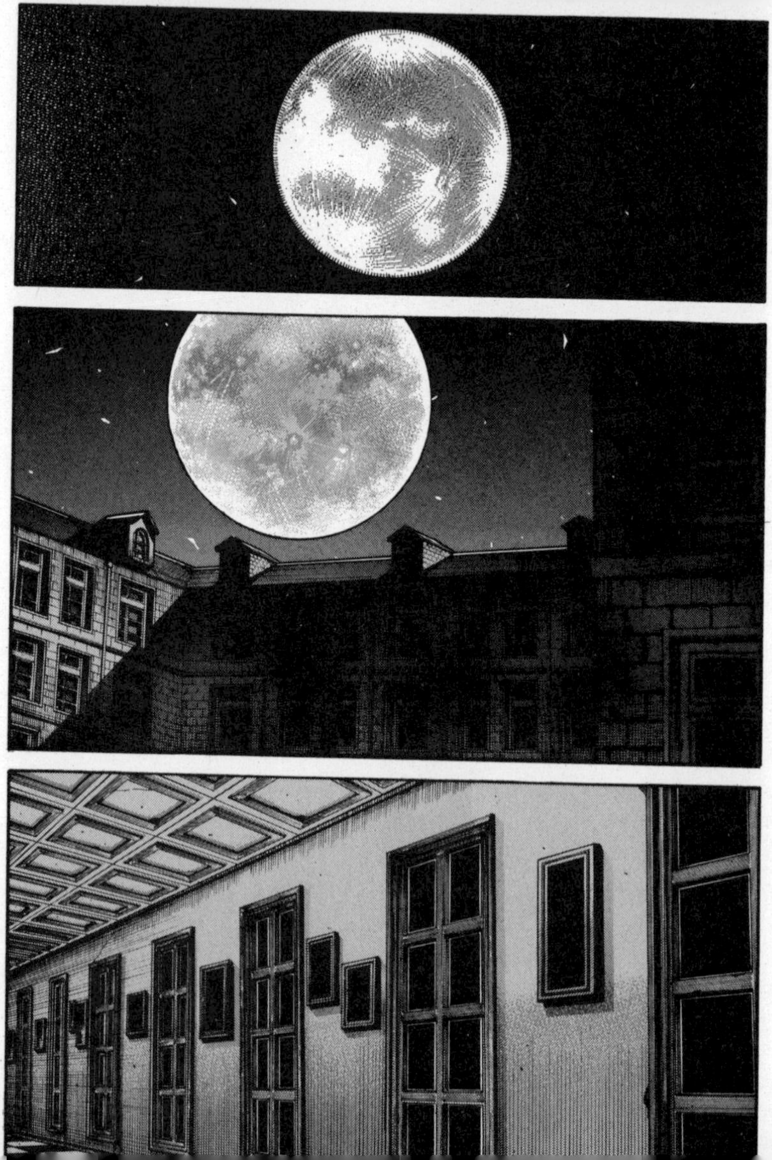

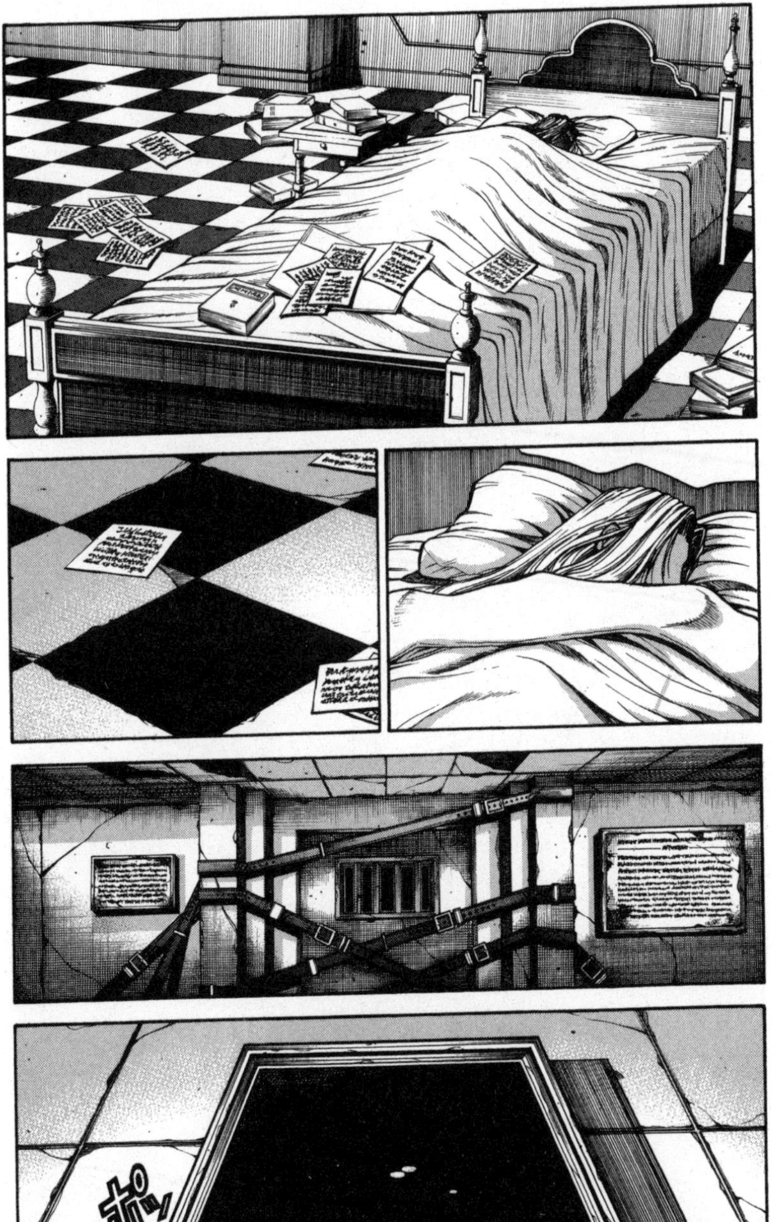
ポッ

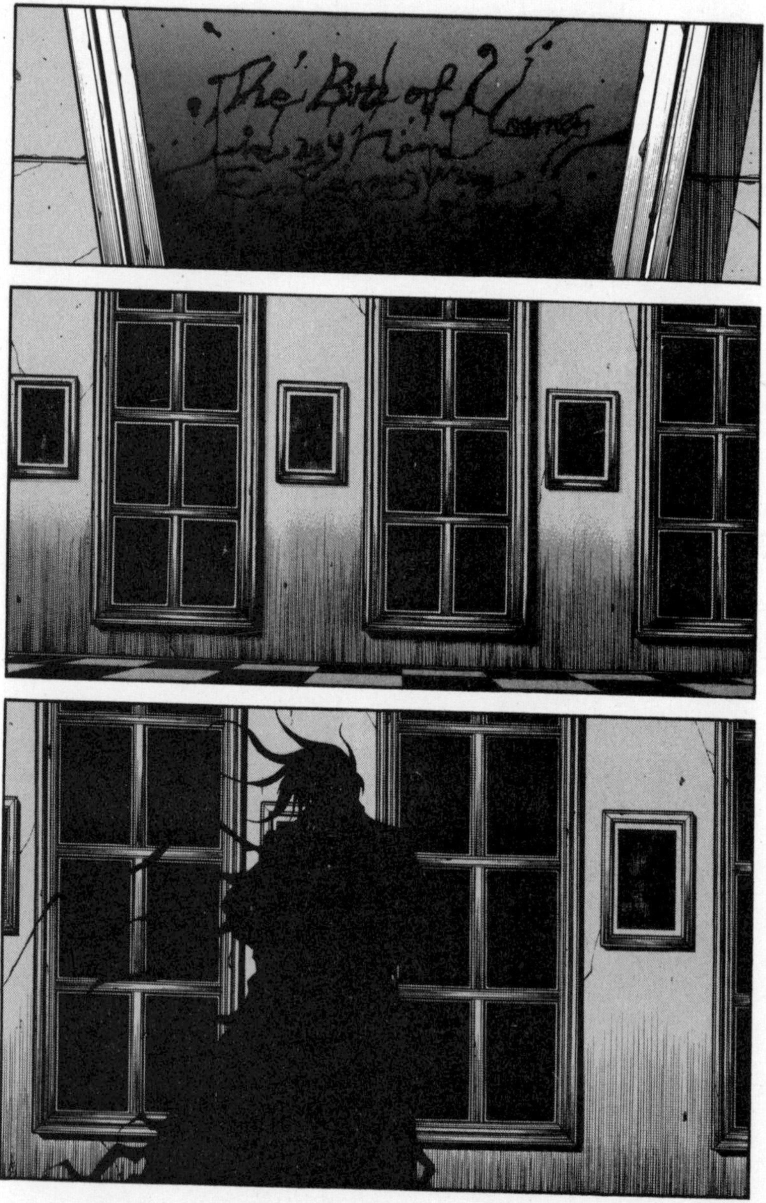

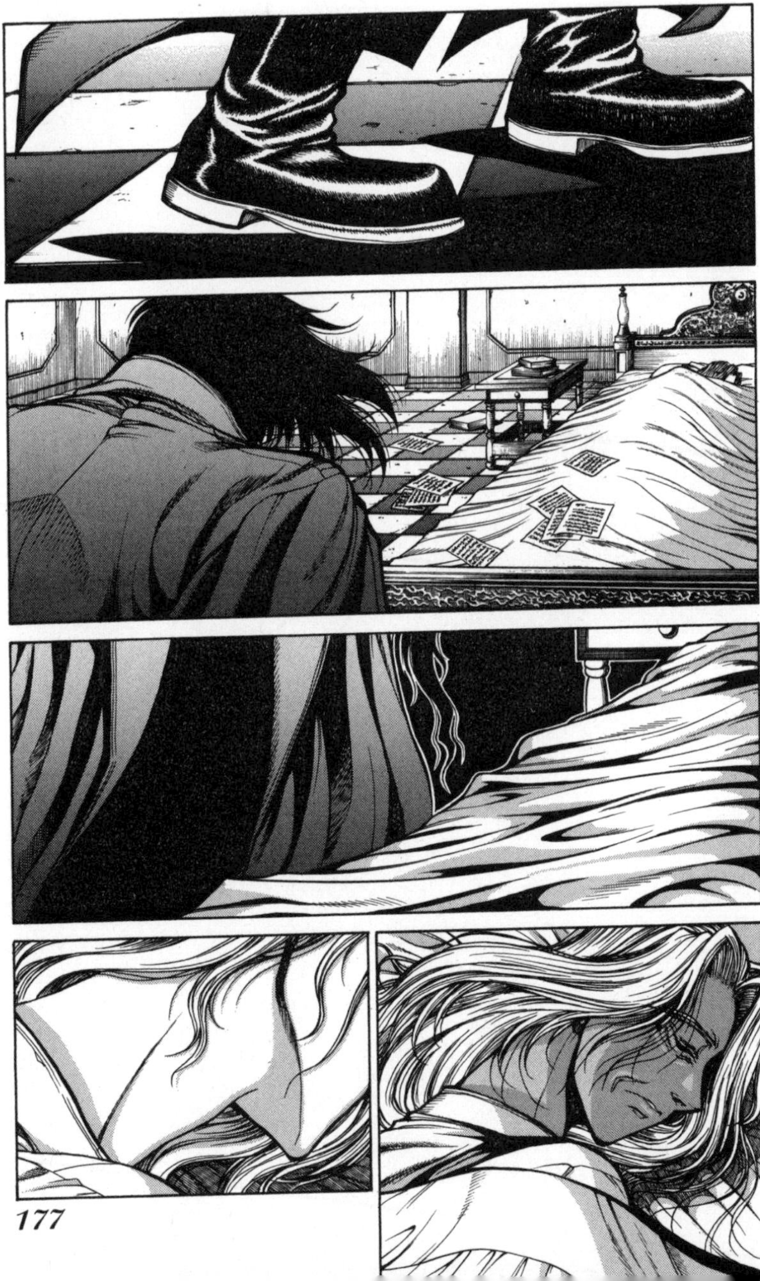

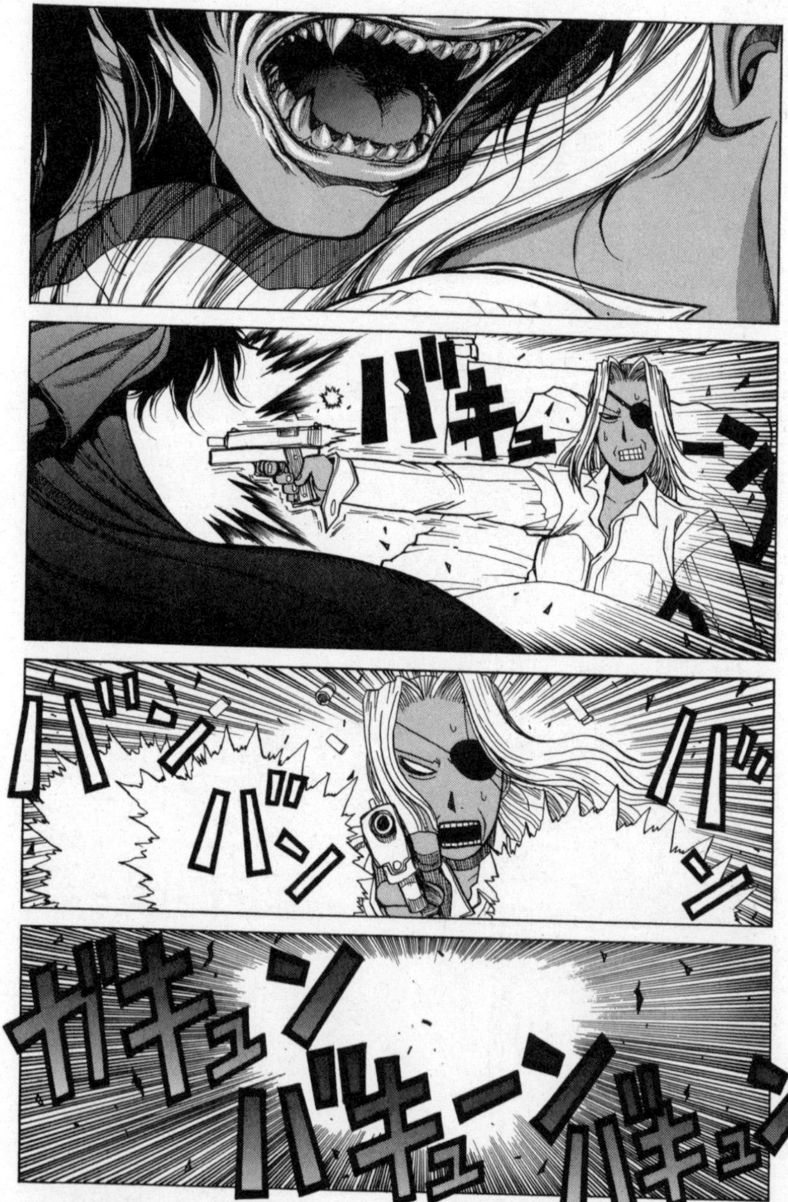
バキューン
バン
バン
バッ
ガキュン
バキューン
バキュン

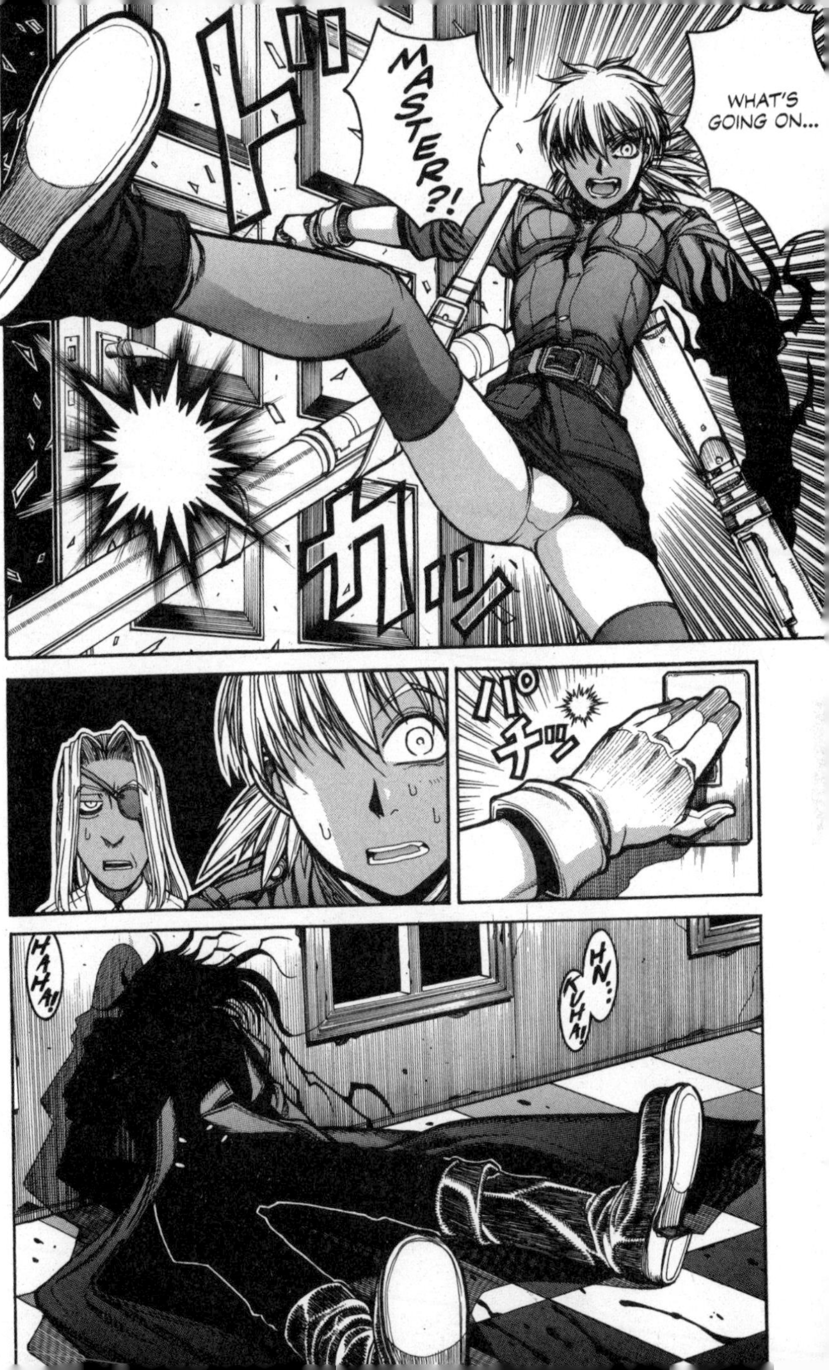
WHAT'S GOING ON...
MASTER?!
ドッ
カッ
パチッ
HN... KUHA!
HAHAHA!

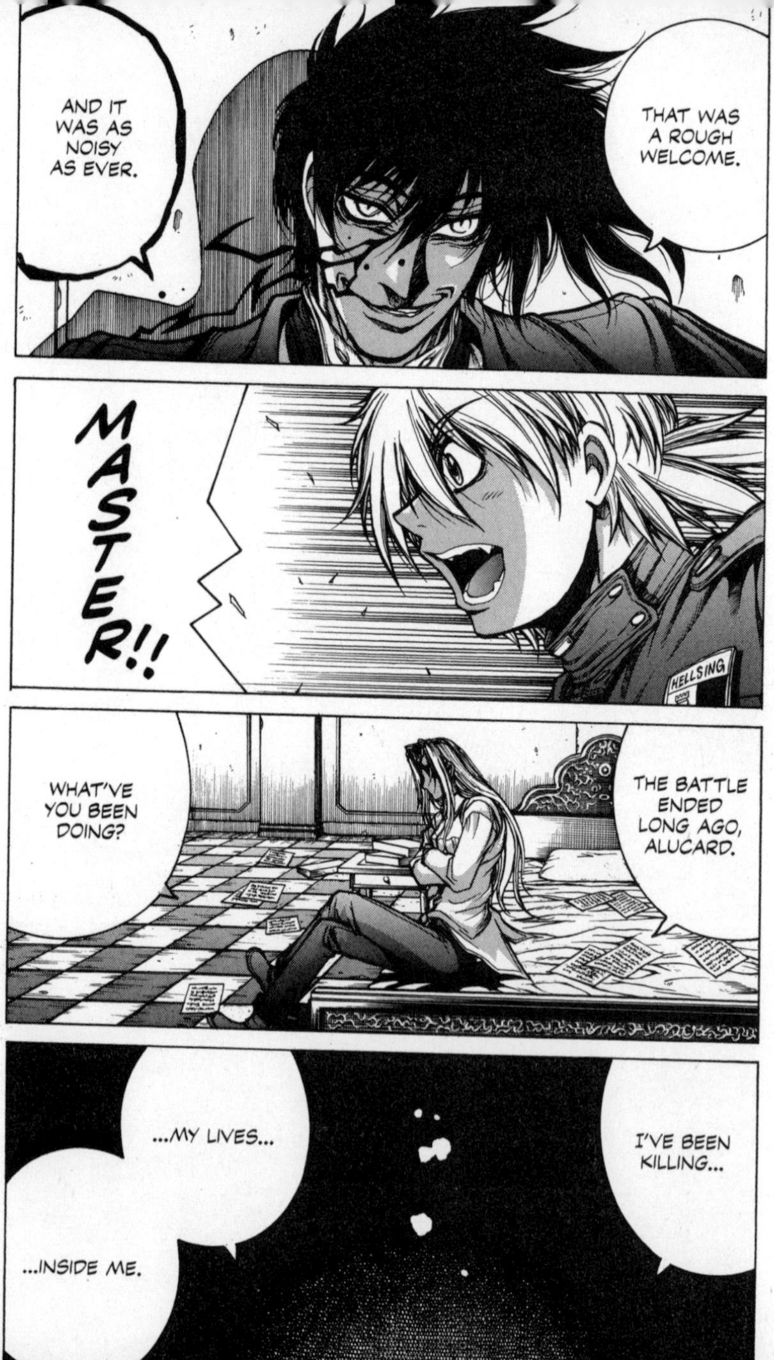
THAT WAS A ROUGH WELCOME.
AND IT WAS AS NOISY AS EVER.
MASTER!!
HELLSING
THE BATTLE ENDED LONG AGO, ALUCARD.
WHAT'VE YOU BEEN DOING?
I'VE BEEN KILLING...
...MY LIVES...
...INSIDE ME.

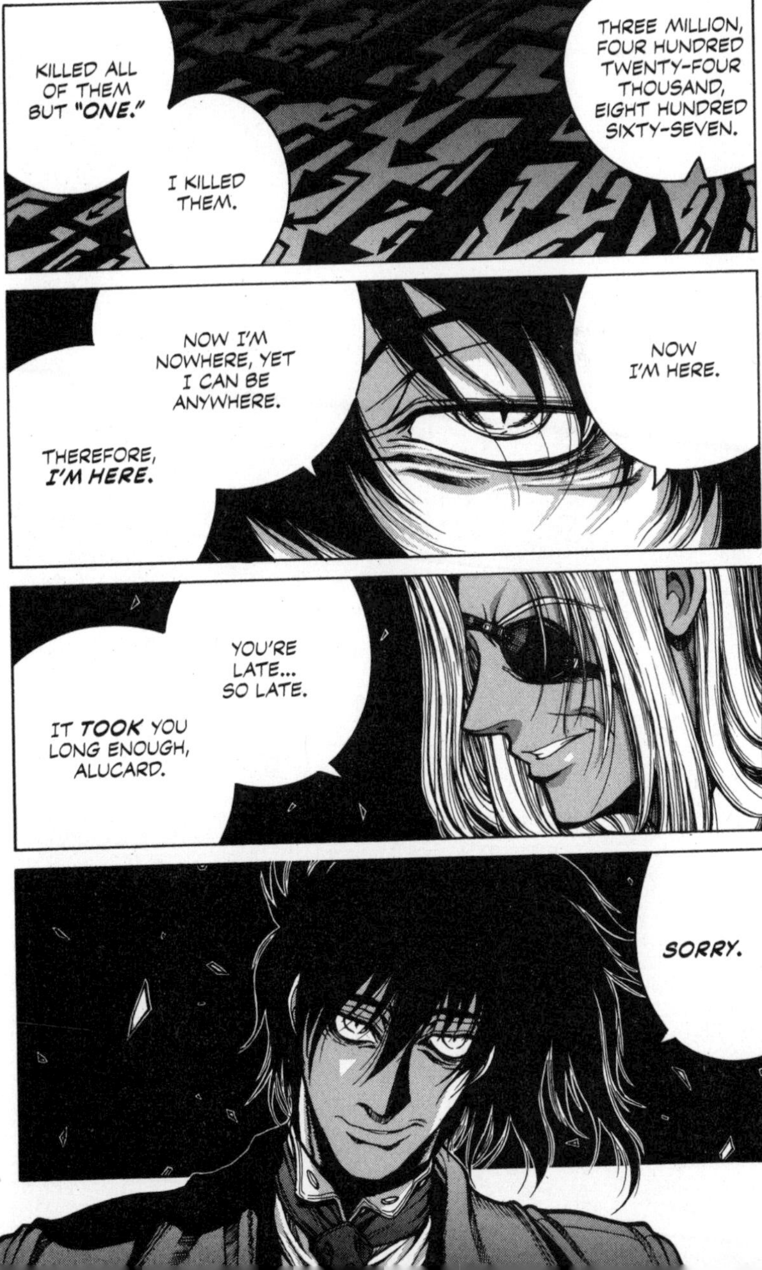
THREE MILLION, FOUR HUNDRED TWENTY-FOUR THOUSAND, EIGHT HUNDRED SIXTY-SEVEN.
I KILLED THEM.
KILLED ALL OF THEM BUT "ONE."
NOW I'M HERE.
NOW I'M NOWHERE, YET I CAN BE ANYWHERE.
THEREFORE, I'M HERE.
YOU'RE LATE... SO LATE.
IT TOOK YOU LONG ENOUGH, ALUCARD.
SORRY.

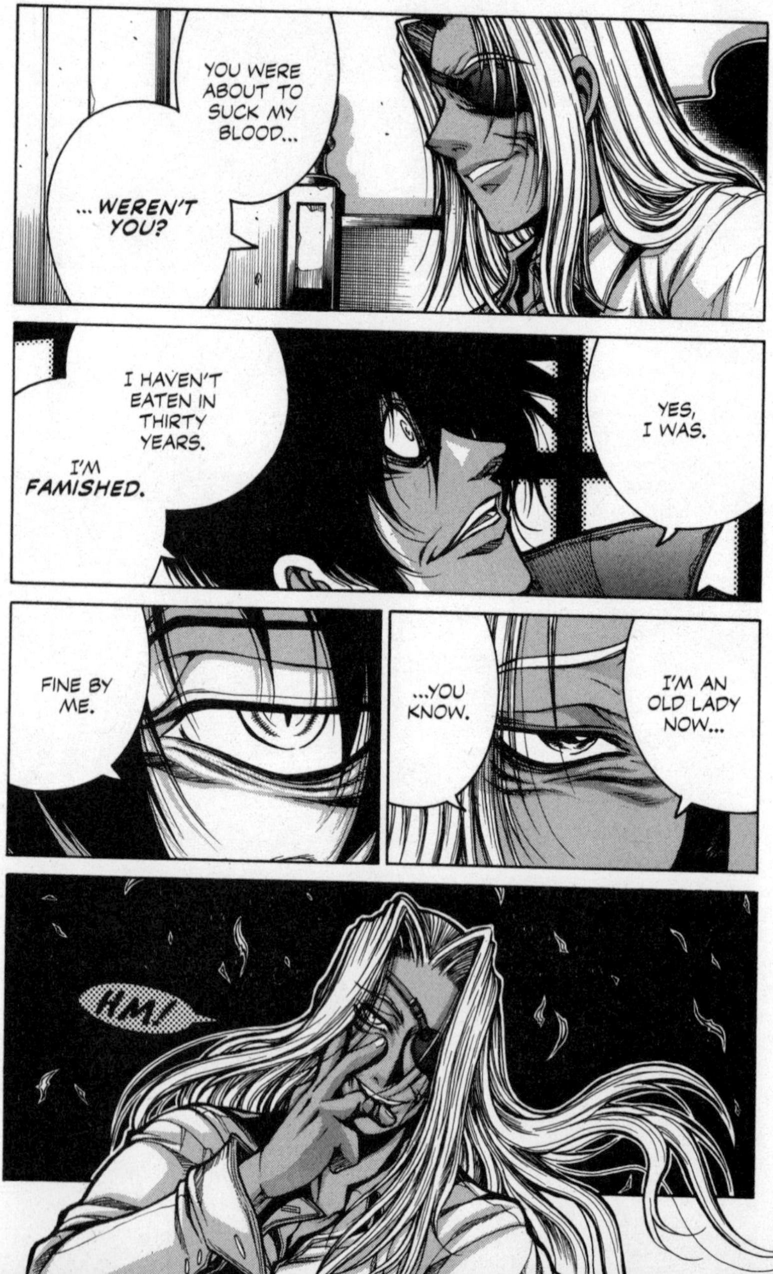
YOU WERE ABOUT TO SUCK MY BLOOD...
... WEREN'T YOU?
YES, I WAS.
I HAVEN'T EATEN IN THIRTY YEARS.
I'M FAMISHED.
I'M AN OLD LADY NOW...
...YOU KNOW.
FINE BY ME.
HM!

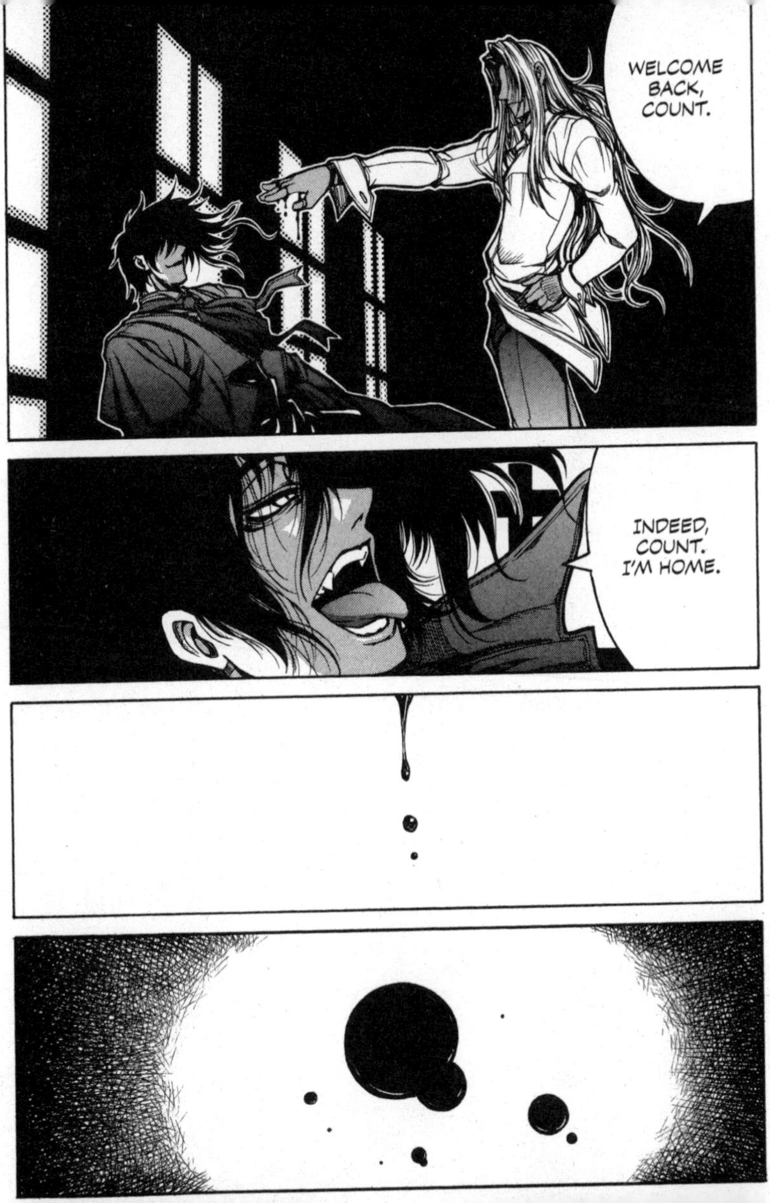
WELCOME BACK, COUNT.
INDEED, COUNT. I'M HOME.

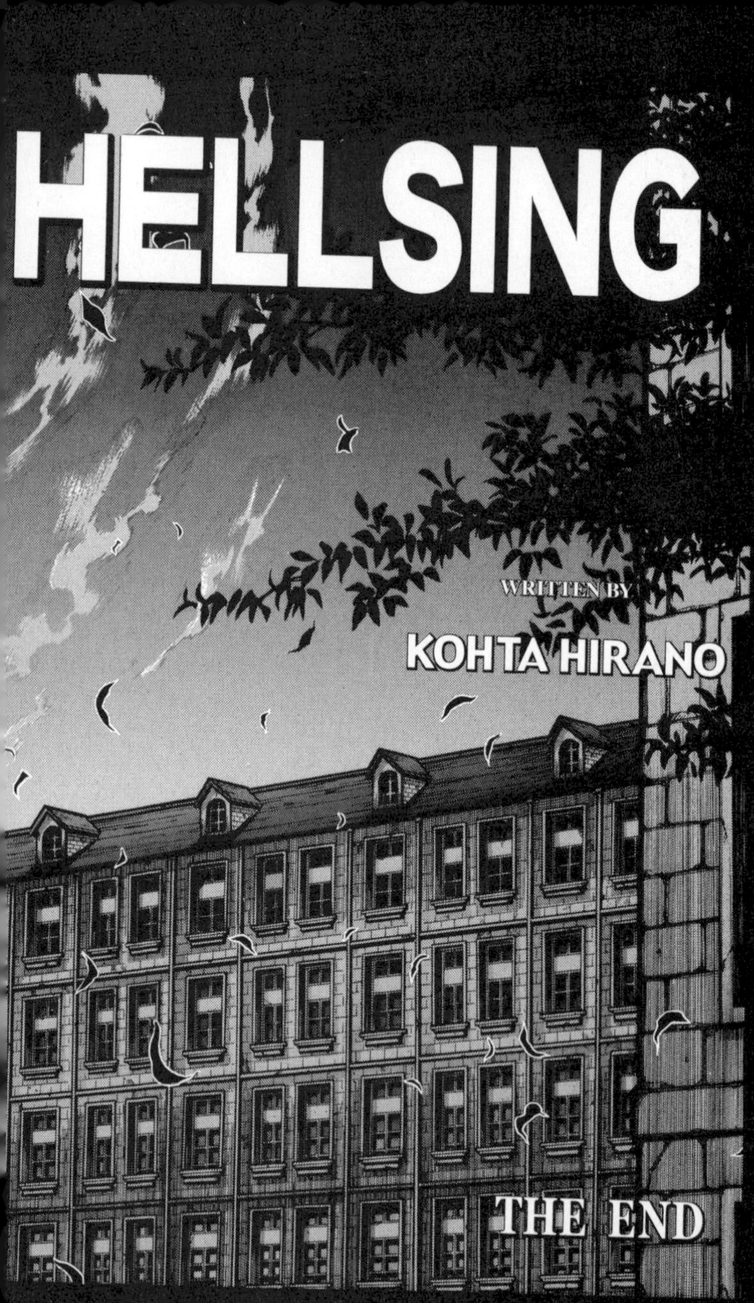
HELLSING
WRITTEN BY
KOHTA HIRANO
THE END

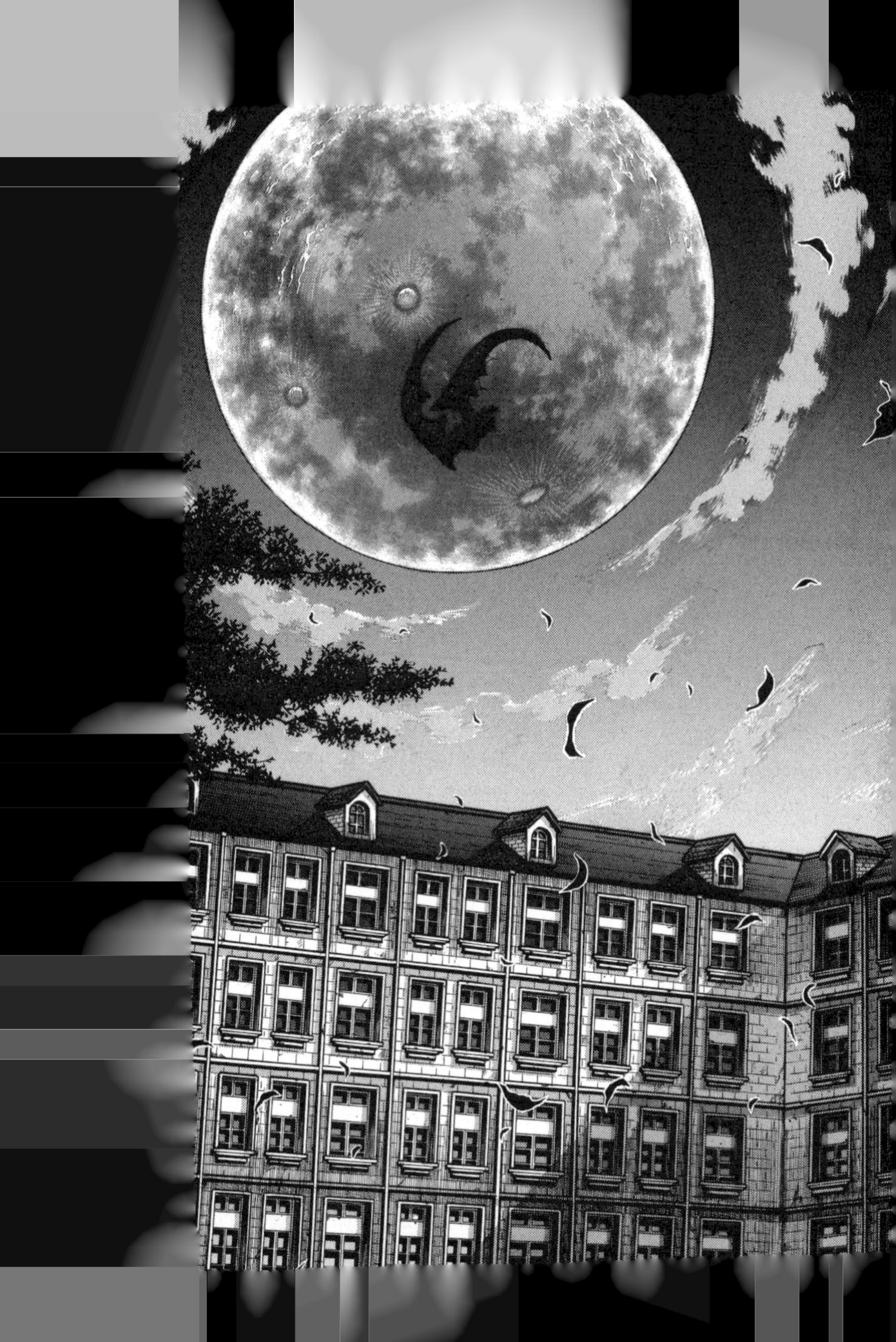

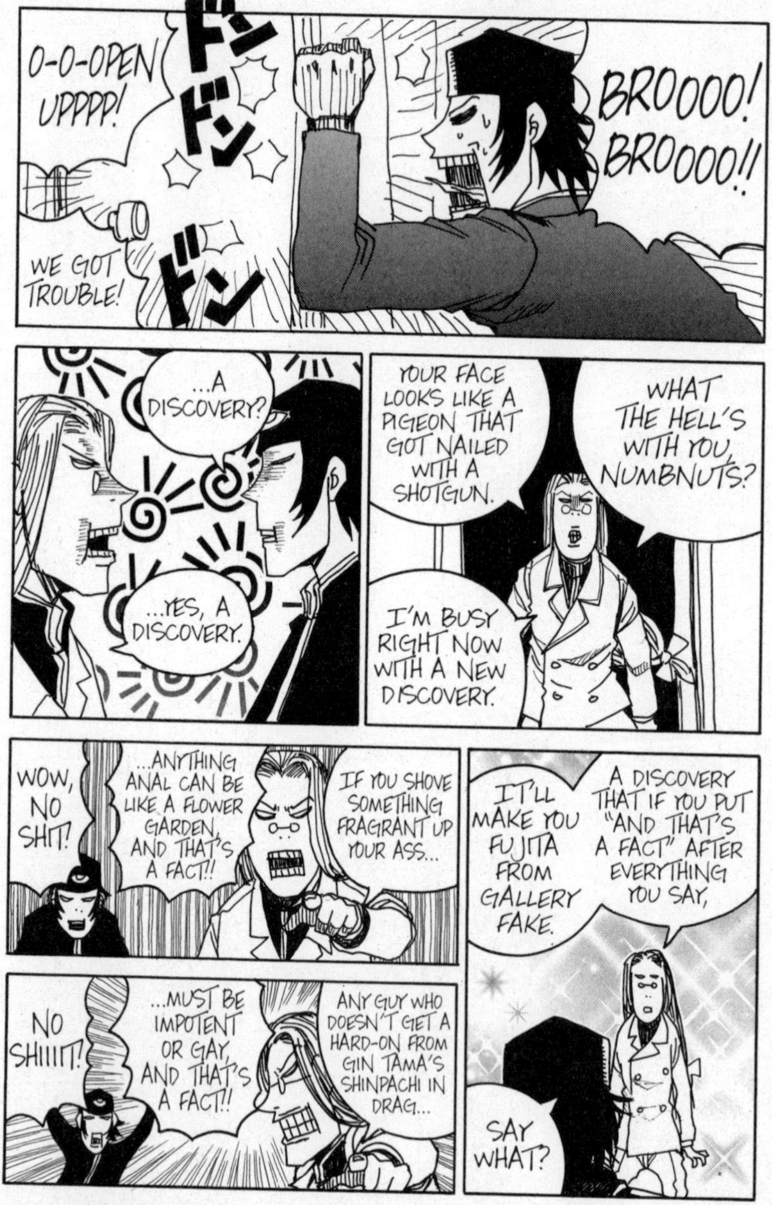
BROOOO! BROOOO!!
ドン
ドン
O-O-OPEN UPPPP!
WE GOT TROUBLE!
ドン
WHAT THE HELL'S WITH YOU, NUMBNUTS?
YOUR FACE LOOKS LIKE A PIGEON THAT GOT NAILED WITH A SHOTGUN.
I'M BUSY RIGHT NOW WITH A NEW DISCOVERY.
...A DISCOVERY?
...YES, A DISCOVERY.
A DISCOVERY THAT IF YOU PUT "AND THAT'S A FACT" AFTER EVERYTHING YOU SAY,
IT'LL MAKE YOU FUJITA FROM GALLERY FAKE.
SAY WHAT?
IF YOU SHOVE SOMETHING FRAGRANT UP YOUR ASS...
...ANYTHING ANAL CAN BE LIKE A FLOWER GARDEN, AND THAT'S A FACT!!
WOW, NO SHIT!
ANY GUY WHO DOESN'T GET A HARD-ON FROM GIN TAMA'S SHINPACHI IN DRAG...
...MUST BE IMPOTENT OR GAY, AND THAT'S A FACT!!
NO SHIIIIT!

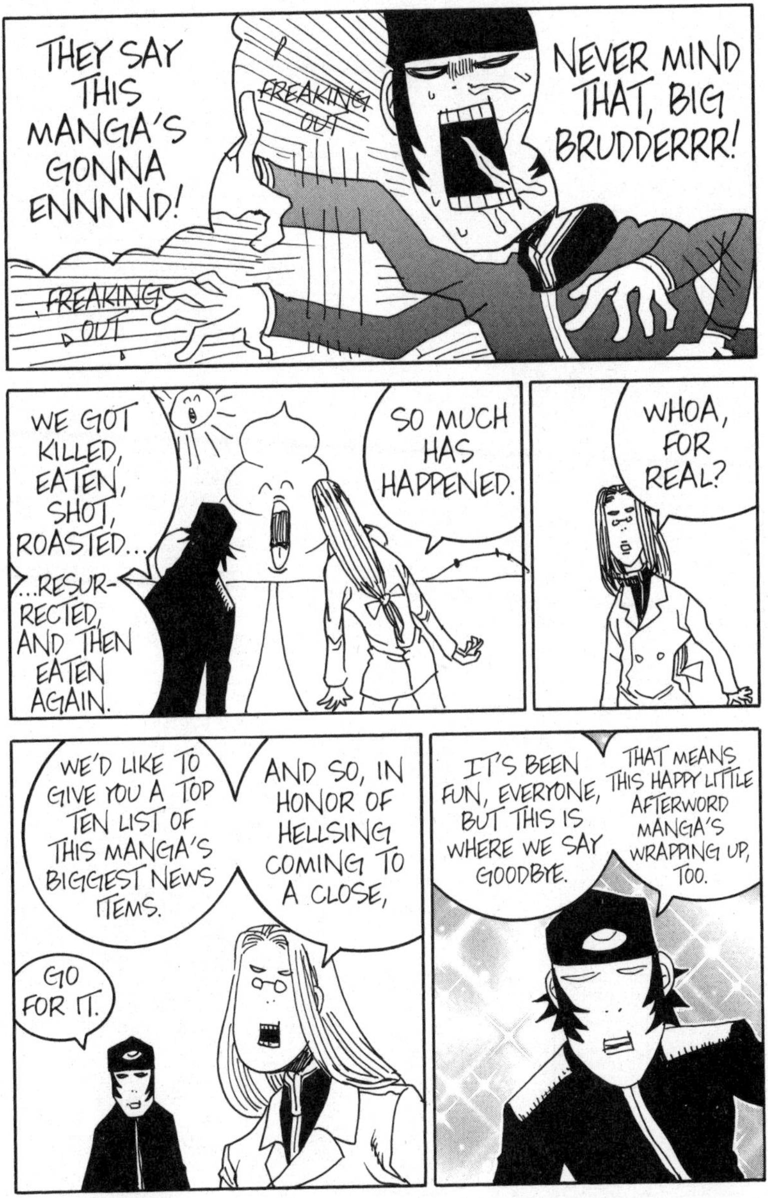
NEVER MIND THAT, BIG BRUDDERRR!
THEY SAY THIS MANGA'S GONNA ENNNND!
FREAKING OUT
FREAKING OUT
WHOA, FOR REAL?
SO MUCH HAS HAPPENED.
WE GOT KILLED, EATEN, SHOT, ROASTED...
...RESURRECTED, AND THEN EATEN AGAIN.
THAT MEANS THIS HAPPY LITTLE AFTERWORD MANGA'S WRAPPING UP, TOO.
IT'S BEEN FUN, EVERYONE, BUT THIS IS WHERE WE SAY GOODBYE.
AND SO, IN HONOR OF HELLSING COMING TO A CLOSE,
WE'D LIKE TO GIVE YOU A TOP TEN LIST OF THIS MANGA'S BIGGEST NEWS ITEMS.
GO FOR IT.

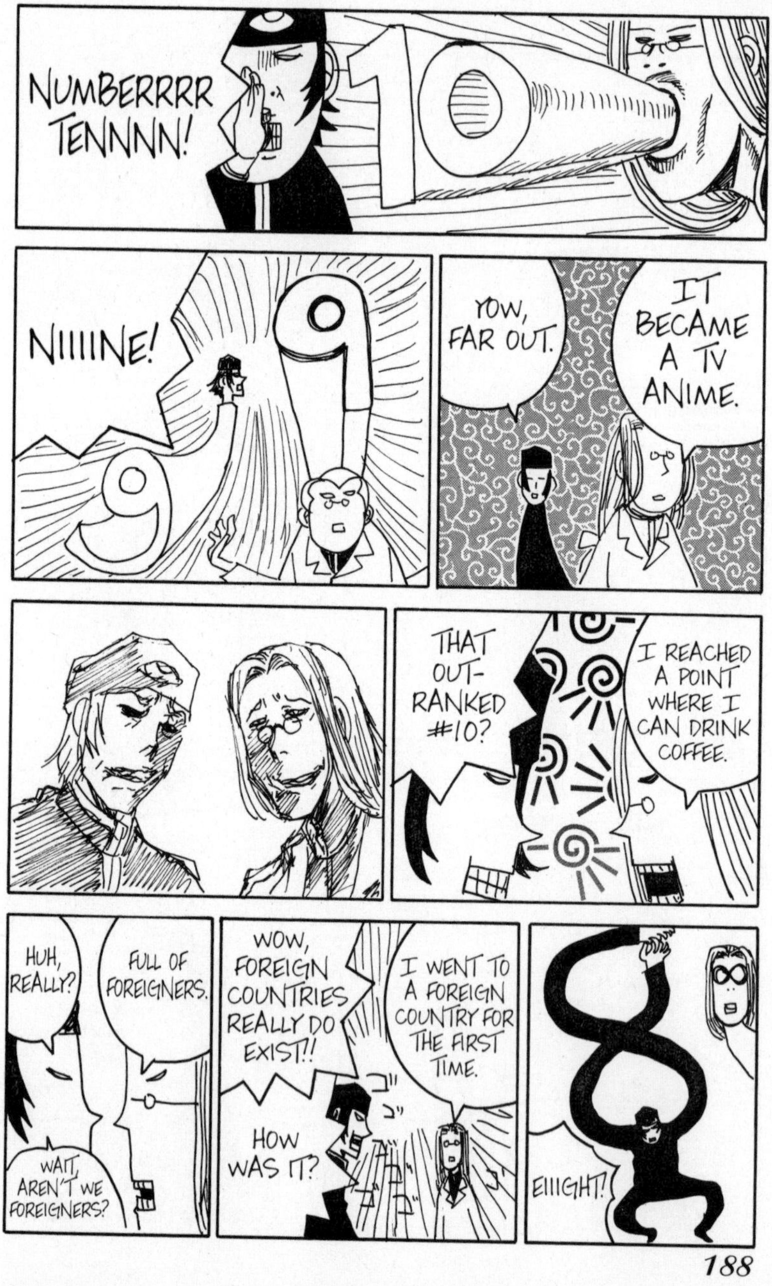
NUMBERRRR TENNNN!
IT BECAME A TV ANIME.
YOW, FAR OUT.
NIIIINE!
I REACHED A POINT WHERE I CAN DRINK COFFEE.
THAT OUT-RANKED #10?
EIIIGHT!
I WENT TO A FOREIGN COUNTRY FOR THE FIRST TIME.
WOW, FOREIGN COUNTRIES REALLY DO EXIST?!
HOW WAS IT?
FULL OF FOREIGNERS.
HUH, REALLY?
WAIT, AREN'T WE FOREIGNERS?

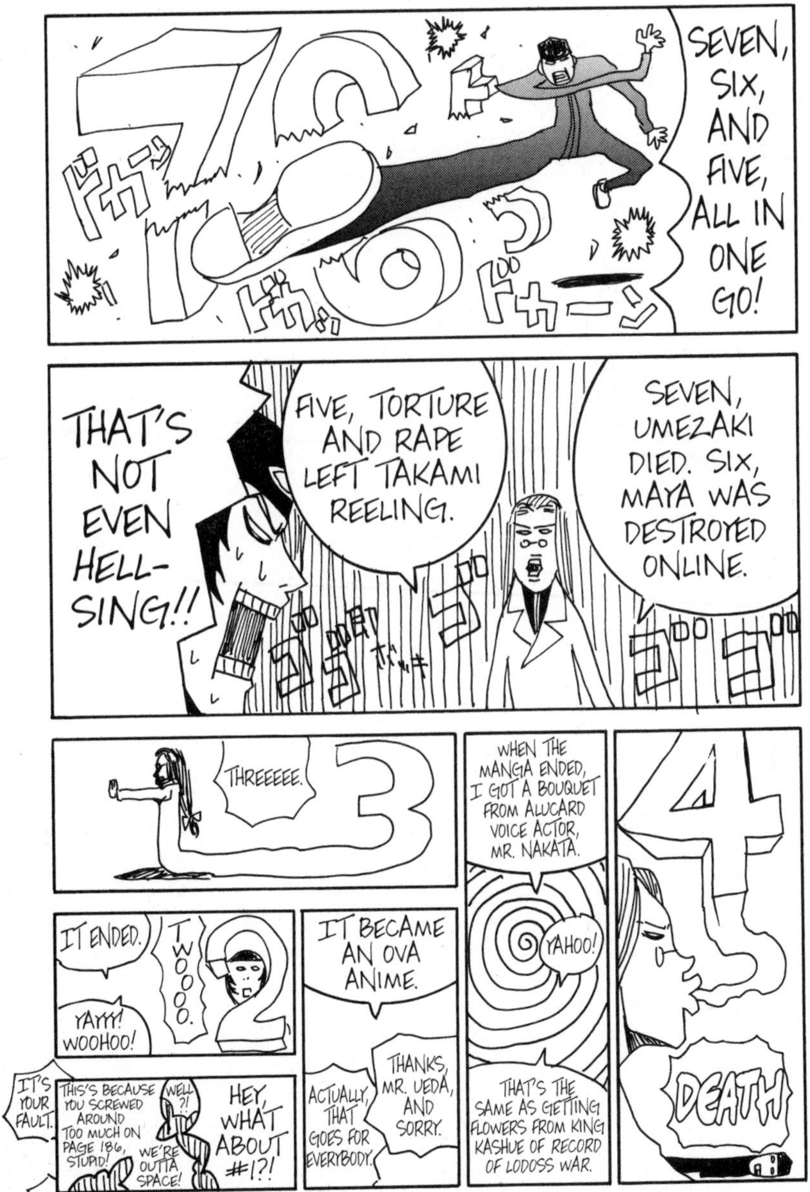

SEVEN, SIX, AND FIVE, ALL IN ONE GO!
SEVEN, UMEZAKI DIED. SIX, MAYA WAS DESTROYED ONLINE.
FIVE, TORTURE AND RAPE LEFT TAKAMI REELING.
THAT'S NOT EVEN HELL-SING!!
4
DEATH
WHEN THE MANGA ENDED, I GOT A BOUQUET FROM ALUCARD VOICE ACTOR, MR. NAKATA.
YAHOO!
THAT'S THE SAME AS GETTING FLOWERS FROM KING KASHUE OF RECORD OF LODOSS WAR.
THREEEEE.
3
IT BECAME AN OVA ANIME.
THANKS, MR. UEDA, AND SORRY.
ACTUALLY, THAT GOES FOR EVERYBODY.
TWOOOOO.
2
IT ENDED.
YAYYY! WOOHOO!
HEY, WHAT ABOUT #1?!
WELL ?!
THIS'S BECAUSE YOU SCREWED AROUND TOO MUCH ON PAGE 186, STUPID!
WE'RE OUTTA SPACE!
IT'S YOUR FAULT.
YOU CAN KISS MY ASS!
#1 IS...NONE OTHER THAN THESE TWO GUYS, THEMSELVES.

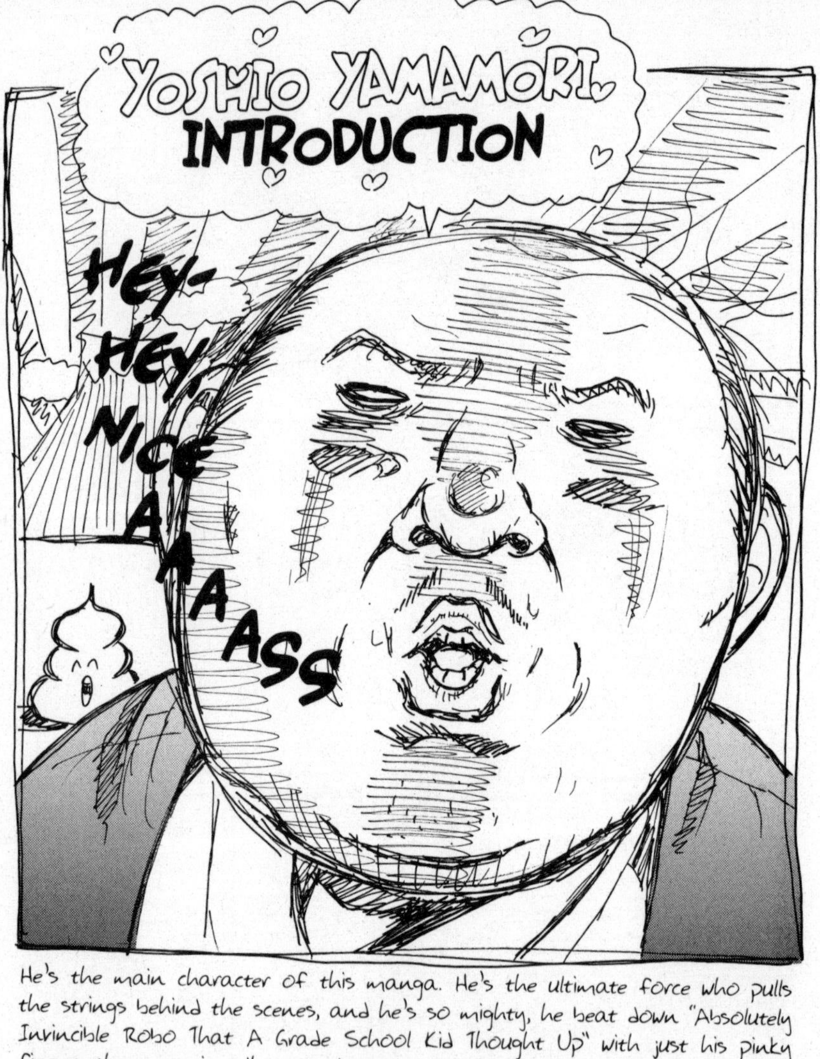
YOSHIO YAMAMORI
INTRODUCTION
HEY-HEY, NICE AAAAASS

He's the main character of this manga. He's the ultimate force who pulls the strings behind the scenes, and he's so mighty, he beat down "Absolutely Invincible Robo That A Grade School Kid Thought Up" with just his pinky finger, then ate it. What a pinnacle of atrocity he is. By the way, the Yakuza in the Yamamori gang, even the punks at the bottom, pack Storm-bringer swords and Angel Arm guns. The energy bullets he spits out of his mouth separate Gurren Lagann, rendering it never able to combine again. He's a feared Yakuza. He loves okonomiyaki. He mainly eats those, and maple manjuu.

Character Introductions

Integra Old Bag - nuff said 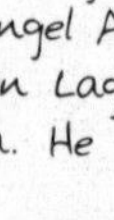

Alucard Gramps - nuff said 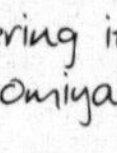

Seras Huge Tits - nuff said 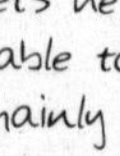

Walter Shota - nuff said 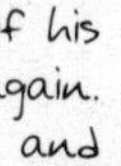

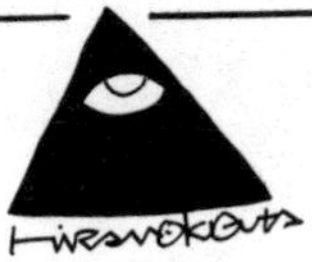

- "Long time no see! It's me!! Hirano!! Huh?! By a gorilla...?! ...D...Dead? Is that true?" (That's an Adachi dialect abbreviation for "good job, man.")
  So here we are at the last volume, and look at the state it's been in this whole time.
  Still, ten years have gone by. A whole decade. I can't believe I've been drawing this that long...
  In Nico Robin terms, that's long enough for a loli to become a professional killer.
  In Gundam terms, that's long enough for a Zaku II to evolve into a Hamma-Hamma... Scary.

- A lot of things happened these ten years.
  ¥1000 heads of broccoli dropped to ¥20.
  Not a single thing happened, besides that.

- Now about the manga. I went overboard in a lot of ways.
  But my dream is, as long as I get to draw tits and ass, murder is meaningless.
  I'm satisfied in many ways. Manzoku. Porn mag.

- We've got page space left over, and as this is the end, I will sing a song.

  ♪ The Hellsing Song -British Dimwit Marching Song-

  Ahhhh, we're out of tea, out of smokes.
  Milady's going through withdrawal again today.
  (Ahhh, Britain, Britain)
  Boobs, blonde hair, love birds.
  War, madness, fanatics.
  (Ahhh, warmongers, warmongers)
  "Today London is again at peace, miss." "No way." "Gyahhh!"
  "Murder means nothing if I get to drink some tea." "Diiiie!"
  The Aura road has been opened.
  (Heavy Metal)
  "No way."

See yaaa! Bye byyye!
Alright everybody, take care.

STOP

This is the back of the book!

This manga collection is translated into English but oriented in right-to-left reading format at the creator's request, maintaining the artwork's visual orientation as originally published in Japan. If you've never read manga in this way before, take a look at the diagram below to give yourself an idea of how to go about it. Basically, you'll be starting in the upper right corner and will read each balloon and panel moving right to left. It may take some getting used to, but you should get the hang of it very quickly. Have fun!

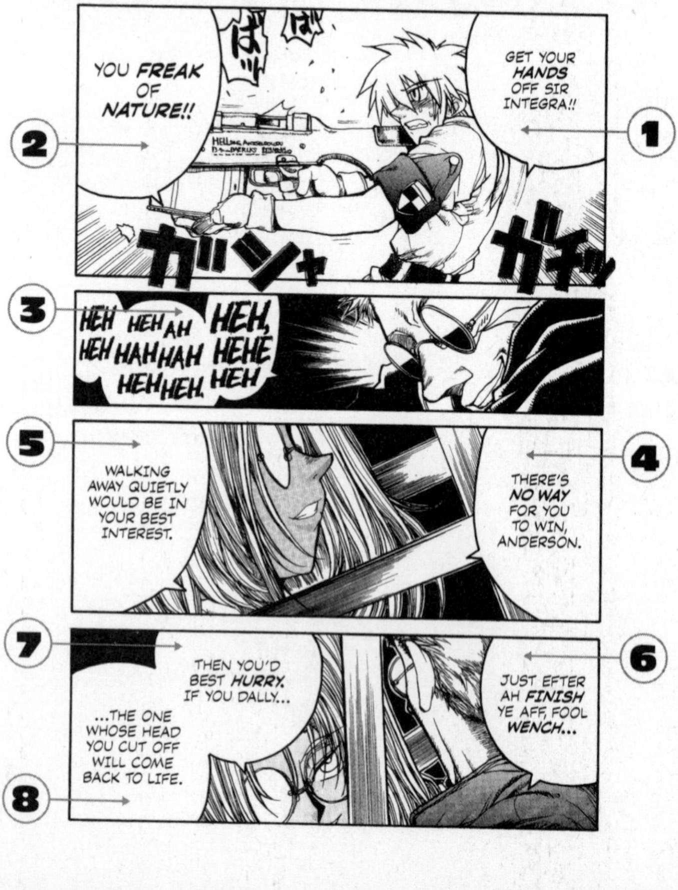

1
GET YOUR HANDS OFF SIR INTEGRA!!
2
YOU FREAK OF NATURE!!
3
HEH, HEHE HEH
HEH AH HAH HAH HEH HEH.
HEH HEH
4
THERE'S NO WAY FOR YOU TO WIN, ANDERSON.
5
WALKING AWAY QUIETLY WOULD BE IN YOUR BEST INTEREST.
6
JUST EFTER AH FINISH YE AFF, FOOL WENCH...
7
THEN YOU'D BEST HURRY. IF YOU DALLY...
8
...THE ONE WHOSE HEAD YOU CUT OFF WILL COME BACK TO LIFE.